Runic Revelation

Books by Clayton Taylor Wood:

The Runic Series

Runic Awakening
Runic Revelation
Runic Vengeance
Runic Revolt

The Fate of Legends Series

Hunter of Legends
Seeker of Legends
Destroyer of Legends

Runic Revelation

Book II of the Runic Series

Clayton Taylor Wood

Special thanks to my brothers, my father, and my wife for their invaluable advice. And to my son, for whom this book was written.

Table of Contents

Runic Revelation

Prologue

Ampir stands in a huge underground chamber beneath the city of Stridon, his wife Vera propped up against the large circular dais in the center of the room, their son Junior at her side. Four huge stone pillars at the corners of the room rise upward to the majestic domed ceiling some forty feet above. Swirls of dust glimmer like fireflies in the soft light cast by the lanterns hanging on the walls around him, a shower of dust and small stones raining down from the ceiling onto the floor.

Boom.

The entire chamber trembles, more cracks appearing on the ceiling.

"What's that, Daddy?" Junior asks.

Ampir turns to his son. Barely four years old, the boy has already seen too much. Ampir can only hope that Junior is too young to remember his grandpa's throat being sliced open, blood pouring down the old man's neck and chest. And Vera being brutally stabbed in the back.

"I don't know," Ampir lies.

Boom.

More dust falls from the ceiling, and Ampir gazes upward again, knowing all-too-well that it is the Behemoth standing above them, an enormous machine over ten stories tall standing in the middle of the city above ground. Created by a man Ampir once knew, a man he'd trusted.

Sabin.

1

"Ampir," Vera calls out.

He turns to her, his breath catching in his throat. She is as lovely as the day they'd met, tall and slender, with auburn hair cascading in gentle waves to her lower back. Her white nightgown clings to her, soaked with her sweat...and blood. The crimson stain on her lower back has barely grown, but the internal bleeding...

"Hold me," Vera murmurs.

Ampir reaches for her, scooping her up in his arms and staring down at her.

"Hold on baby," he urges, leaning over to kiss her on the forehead. "Just a little while longer."

He focuses on the gray stone dais in the center of the chamber. A brilliant red crystal is embedded in its center, refracting and reflecting the light from the lanterns above. Three feet in diameter, the crystal has innumerable tiny runes etched on its surface...and countless more deeper within. It is Renval's greatest invention, a teleportation device. But it is much more advanced than his earlier prototypes.

Ampir studies its runes, tracing the faint blue glow identifying each of them. Then he frowns; there's something very odd about the destination coordinates. They're unlike anything he's ever seen...and he helped build the original prototype. He focuses on the crystal's activation runes, sending a stream of magic to it, and the teleporter pulses, its runes glowing the faintest blue.

But nothing else happens.

Ampir stares at the crystal, his brow furrowing. The runes are supposed to be bright blue, but they're barely glowing...its magic supply must have been damaged.

"Shit," he swears under his breath.

"What baby?" Vera asks.

"There isn't enough magic," he answers. "Shit!"

"Your armor," Vera suggests. "Use it."

Ampir nods, realizing that she's right. The black metallic armor he wears is filled with an enormous amount of magic, powering the countless runes inscribed upon its surface. Runes that, combined, make him nearly invincible...a god among men. But in draining them of their magic, he would make himself vulnerable.

Boom.

2

He focuses on his armor, pulling magic out of its runes and redirecting it to the crystal on the dais. The teleporter's runes glow a little brighter, then fade.

"It needs a lot," he states. "Way more than it should." Even teleporting a hundred miles away shouldn't have required this much magic. But Vera doesn't respond; her eyes are closed, her breathing coming in shorter gasps now. Sweat beads up on her pale forehead.

"Stay with me baby," he urges.

He drains more of his armor, emptying parts of it completely, pouring the magic into the red crystal. Its runes grow a little brighter, but nothing happens.

Maybe it's broken, Ampir thinks, terror seizing him. He glances at his son, standing there helplessly, dust from the crumbling ceiling above coating him. He grits his teeth, fighting through the fear. The runes in the crystal glow brighter as he empties his armor; the air in the chamber begins to stir, a faint blue light appearing in the air above the dais.

Come on...

Another deafening *boom* echoes through the chamber, parts of the ceiling breaking away. Huge slabs of stone fall toward them, shattering on the floor less than a dozen feet from where they stand. Ampir weaves magic rapidly, creating a large domed gravity shield above their heads; falling dust and rubble bounce off of it, landing harmlessly around them.

Far above, beyond the widening holes in the ceiling, Ampir sees a massive black metallic foot...and beyond that, a huge, green, diamond-shaped eye staring down at them.

The Behemoth!

He resists the urge to grab Junior and flee, knowing that Vera's only chance at surviving lay in teleporting to safety. With the Tower destroyed, the nearest trauma center is hours away...and her time is quickly running out. He draws the last of the magic from his armor, shoving it toward the crystal. Its runes flash a bright blue, and suddenly the air ten feet above the dais *tears* open, forming a black circular portal.

Yes!

3

Ampir stares at the portal, realizing that it's only a foot in diameter...far too small for Vera or himself to fit through. He struggles to stream more magic to the teleporter, but he barely has any left.

"What's wrong?" Vera asks. Ampir shakes his head.

"It's too small," he replies, staring at the portal in disbelief. He'd put an enormous amount of magic into the teleporter...the portal shouldn't be that small!

"We'll go one at a time," she offers weakly.

"It's too damn *small*," he retorts angrily. "We can't fit through it." He grits his teeth. "*Shit!*"

Vera stares up at the rift, then looks at Junior.

"He can," she counters.

Ampir looks down at Junior. She's right, of course. As small as he is, the rift is just large enough for him to fit through.

The Behemoth's massive foot rises, then slams down on the fractured ceiling. The dome sinks inward, huge fragments of stone breaking away and falling toward them. The pieces strike the shield above their heads, barely deflected by the magical barrier. Ampir struggles to maintain the shield, the magic reserves in his mind all but exhausted. He feels Vera's hand on his cheek.

"Send him," Vera urges. "Save him."

"I need to save *you*," he protests. But Vera shakes her head.

"Do it," she orders, her tone harsh. He swallows in a dry throat, looking up at the rift. It's starting to shrink, he realizes. The magic powering the teleporter is running out. He turns to Junior.

"Get up on that," he commands, gesturing at the dais. Junior hesitates, staring at his father, then his mother. "Do it!" Ampir shouts. Junior flinches, but obeys, climbing up onto the dais beside the huge red crystal. Ampir hesitates, then leans forward, kissing his son on the forehead.

I'll come for you, he vows silently.

He reaches for the ring hanging on the necklace around his own neck...the engagement ring Vera had proposed to him with. He tears it from the necklace, staring at it intently. The band is silver, the large yellow gemstone on top glittering in the faint light. Tiny words had been etched into the band.

To my husband, for eternity.

4

He closes his eyes, pulling cords of power into his mind's eye, twisting them around each other to form a throbbing knot in the center. He throws it outward, rapidly etching tiny runes into the ring's gemstone, almost too small for the eye to see. Dozens of interconnected runes, working together for a single purpose.

This way, I'll never lose you.

He gives the ring to Junior, holding Vera in his other arm. He strains to carry her now, his armor no longer giving him near-unlimited strength. He puts a hand on Junior's cheek, giving him a weak smile.

"I love you, son."

He weaves magic in his mind's eye one last time, throwing it outward at Junior. The boy levitates upward in the air, flying toward the steadily shrinking portal above. Ampir thrusts as much magic as he can at his son, lifting him up through the rift. Junior's head passes through, followed by his shoulders. Then his waist passes through.

The portal closes more rapidly now, threatening to slice Junior in half.

Ampir grimaces, *ripping* magic from his mind's eye and shoving it at the boy. Junior bursts upward, his legs passing through...just as the portal snaps shut. Something small falls from where the rift had been, bouncing off of the dais and falling onto the floor. Ampir stares at it, taking a moment to realize what it is.

A toe.

He looks back up to the space where his son had just been, feeling a terrible emptiness come over him. Whatever destination Renval had set the teleporter to, it was far away...so far that he had the sinking feeling that he would never see Junior again. At least he knew that wherever Renval had set the teleporter to transport his son to, it would be safe. Renval would never leave the coordinates in a dangerous location. He feels eyes upon him, and looks down at Vera. She smiles, gazing back at him with her painfully beautiful eyes.

"See something you like?" she inquired.

He smiles back at her, swallowing past a sudden lump in his throat.

"I do now," he replies.

She closes her eyes then, resting her head against his armored shoulder. Her breaths come more slowly now, her skin terribly pale.

"Kiss me," she murmurs.

5

He leans down, pressing his lips against hers. He can smell her perfume, the same intoxicating scent she'd worn the day they'd met. Tears spill down his cheeks, and he chokes back a sob, pulling his head away. He looks down at her, taking a deep, shuddering breath in, then letting it out.

It takes him a moment to realize she isn't breathing.

"Baby," he calls out, shaking her a little. She doesn't move.

Oh god no. Please, no!

An ear-splitting *boom* echoes through the chamber. Ampir looks up seeing the ceiling above them disintegrating, the Behemoth's huge, metallic foot – nearly half the size of the massive chamber itself – falling toward them, bringing the shattered ceiling down with it in a deadly free-fall.

He looks down at his wife, her pale skin seeming to glow the faintest of blues. He runs his hand through her hair.

"I love you baby," he whispers.

Then he looks upward, just before the massive metallic foot slams into them from above.

Chapter 1

Kyle yelled out, bolting upright, his heart pounding in his chest. He jerked his head upward, half-expecting to see a massive foot falling toward him, but found a dull white ceiling there instead. He relaxed, realizing he was in a modestly-sized bedroom. Sunlight shone through the large window beside his bed, casting brilliant rays of light across his bedsheets. Everything in the room – the bed, the sheets, the bureau, the gilded mirror atop the bureau – was tastefully ornate, unlike his bedroom back on Earth. It was the kind of room one would expect a very rich man to own – and indeed, the owner was possessed of enormous wealth and power. For he was Grand Weaver Kalibar, co-leader of the most powerful empire in the known world. And he just so happened to be Kyle's legal guardian, mentor, and – despite their vast difference in age – his best friend.

Kyle took a deep breath in, exhaling slowly. He felt his pulse slowing, the nightmare losing its power over him. He hadn't had a nightmare like that for over a week now. He used to get them every night – extraordinarily vivid dreams, memories transmitted to him from a mysterious man who died – or rather, *should* have died – over two thousand years ago.

He happened to glance downward, and groaned. His sheets were completely soaked – and not just with sweat. A quick sniff test confirmed his worst fears...once again, he'd wet the bed. It'd been over a week since he'd done that, too...he'd rather hoped he'd finally out-grown the problem.

Suddenly he heard muffled voices coming from just beyond his bedroom door. He felt terror grip him, and he leaped off of the bed, making a mad dash for the door. Had he locked it? If anyone caught him like this...! But as he reached for the doorknob, he realized there wasn't one. It took him a moment to remember that most doors here opened and closed magically, not mechanically. They were also locked magically, and to his relief, a small blue light in the center of the door indicated that the locking mechanism had been engaged.

He fought down the wave of panic, rushing back to his bed and peeling off the wet bedsheets, trying to avoid touching the soaked parts. He threw these to the floor, then glanced at the bare mattress. Luckily it was waterproof. With only the sheets soaked, he still had a chance to get rid of the evidence before Jenkins, Kalibar's head butler, came in to tidy up his room. No one here knew about his little problem, and he had no intention of them ever finding out.

Kyle bent down to gather up the damp bedding into one enormous ball, picking it up and lugging it into the bathroom. Luckily, every guest room in Kalibar's suite had its own full bath; Kyle brought the sheets to the luxurious tub therein, dropped the bedding into it, then stepping back to consider his options. If he rinsed off the urine, then dried the sheets, Jenkins would never be the wiser. But the faucet for the tub was far too low to do the job...there wasn't a shower head. Luckily, he had magic on his side!

He closed his eyes, feeling a pulsing thread of power in the middle of his skull, and grabbed it with his will, weaving it into a tight knot. He thrust it outward toward the air right above the tub. Almost in-stantly, a strong, cold wind whipped through his hair, and at the same time, a veritable waterfall appeared above the tub. Water splashed over the soiled bedding until it was completely soaked, the urine seeping from the fabric and spilling down the drain. In less than a minute, no pee-smell remained, and he stopped the magical stream. He shivered then; the air in the bathroom was suddenly much colder than it had been seconds ago. Water creation magic required a great deal of heat, and it stole that heat from everything around it, cooling the surround-ings significantly.

Kyle put his hands on his hips, surveying his work. Now what? He couldn't just leave the bedding in the tub...someone was bound to find it and start asking questions. He needed to get the sheets dry, so no one would be the wiser. What if he used the fire pattern? With a thought, he could create a flame that would hover in the air wherever he wanted. If he used the tiniest bit of magic, he might be able to warm up the sheets a bit, evaporating the water. Yes, it had to work! He stood back, weaving the tiniest bit of magic into the fire pattern, then throwing it out at the bedding.

The fabric hissed and sputtered, then burst promptly into flames.

He recoiled in horror, instantly severing the stream of magic. But the bedding continued to burn, the flames growing taller by the second. Black smoke rose from the tub, making Kyle cough, his eyes stinging sharply. He stifled the urge to bolt from the room screaming for help, and instead wove magic rapidly, creating another waterfall atop the burning bedding. The cool water doused the flames with an angry hiss, steam billowing up to the ceiling.

Kyle stood there, gawking at the blackened mountain of fabric, suddenly wishing that Xanos had killed him when he'd had the chance. What the heck was he going to do now? Kalibar was going to have him hanged!

Just then, he heard a knock on his bedroom door.

Kyle nearly leaped out of his skin, sprinting out of the bathroom. Then he skid to a halt, turning around and slamming the bathroom door shut to hide the evidence. He turned about again, peering through the smoky haze that had filled his bedroom, holding back another coughing fit. He needed to get rid of this smoke...and fast!

"One minute!" he yelled.

He rushed to the window by his bed, pulling it open. A slight breeze wafted in...not good enough. What he needed was a fan to blow the smoke out...but fans didn't exist here. He stared out of the window, then he had a sudden burst of inspiration. He wove some more magic, throwing it a few feet beyond his window, and a stream of water appeared there. Air was sucked toward the stream – a consequence of a gas being fused together to make a liquid – pulling the smoky air in the bedroom outside. Within moments, the entire room had been cleared. Kyle crossed his arms in front of him, rather pleased at his handiwork.

Then he heard some shouting from down below, and stuck his head out of the window, looking down. Forty stories below, a group of men in black robes were looking upward at him, gesticulating furiously, their hair and fine clothing completely soaked. Kyle recoiled in horror, slamming the window shut and backpedaling quickly. Had the men seen his face? No, they couldn't have...his room was over eight hundred feet up...

He heard more knocking at the door.

Kyle spun around, running to answer the door. He felt something wet on his belly as he ran, and stopped right before the door, glancing down at himself. The entire front of his pajamas was soaked with urine! He turned to his bureau, on top of which a neatly folded stack of black clothing lay. Jenkins must have left the new set for him, bless the butler's heart! Kyle scrambled out of his clothes, throwing them in the tub with the burnt bedding. Then he changed rapidly, having just managed to pull on his pants when the blue light in the center of the door went dark, signaling that it had been unlocked from the outside. The door opened, a man's head peering in from behind it.

"You okay in there?" the man asked. It was one of Kalibar's elite guards, powerful armored Battle-Weavers that acted as the personal bodyguards of the Empire's rulers – and by extension, Kyle. Kyle nodded sheepishly, hoping he didn't look as guilty as he felt. The guard frowned. "I smelled smoke coming from your room," he added suspiciously.

"Smoke, sir?" Kyle asked, trying his best to look innocent. The guard sniffed the air.

"Guess not," he muttered. Then he opened the door all the way. He was clad in black metal armor, but wore no helmet. Helmets had lost their appeal in Stridon of late. "Come with me," he ordered. "Master Owens is expecting you."

Kyle nodded, walking out of his room and following the guard into the main living room of Kalibar's magnificent suite. The guard stopped suddenly, turning about and facing Kyle.

"The Aegis," he reminded. Kyle nearly slapped his own forehead; he'd forgotten to wear his protective chest-piece. He ran back into his

10

room, grabbing it from his dresser and putting it on. The magical armor had been given to him by Kalibar as a gift during his coronation ceremony a few days ago; it was over two thousand years old, and extraordinarily powerful, able to protect Kyle from just about any attack. Kalibar had insisted that Kyle wear the armor every day, only taking it off before he went to bed. Kalibar's enemies would stop at nothing to defeat him, even if that meant attacking his new family. Kyle always felt safer with it on.

That done, Kyle and his chaperone walked back into the main room of the suite. The Grand Weaver had two suites in the Great Tower; this one, which he had acquired after his first term as Grand Weaver six years ago, and an even larger suite one floor above. Kyle trailed behind the guard, exiting Kalibar's suite and taking the magical elevator – a riser, they called it – all the way down to the first floor. The two made their way down the long hallway from the riser to the main lobby, which was already bustling with students rushing to get to their classes. The crowd gave Kyle and his elite guard wide berth, parting before them. Kyle ignored the stares of the students; as the newly adopted son of the most powerful Weaver in the land, Kyle had become a bit of a celebrity. He'd enjoyed the attention for the first day or two, but now he wished people would just get over it already.

He followed his guard through the lobby past the gawking students, stepping through massive double doors to go outside. The Great Tower was surrounded on all sides by a large campus, with dormitories and other buildings scattered across miles of verdant fields. The campus in turn was encircled by a huge circular fence three stories tall, a fence that created a massive domed gravity shield protecting the entire campus. It was called the Gate Shield, and it had protected the Tower for over two hundred years. Together, the Tower and the campus were known as the Secula Magna, the school of magic. The Great Tower was also the political center of the Empire, home to its highest-ranking government officials.

Kyle and his guard stepped out into the morning sunlight, pushing past the steady stream of students pouring into the Tower. The Gate Shield shimmered hundreds of feet above their heads, barely visible against the cloudless blue sky beyond.

Master Owens was the Weaver Kalibar had chosen to teach Kyle magic. Kyle had only learned three magic patterns during his harrowing imprisonment at the hands of the Dead Man – how to make light, fire, and water – and there were dozens more he needed to commit to memory before he could ever call himself a true Weaver. Master Owens had apparently been quite the Battle-Weaver in his day. The old man had been teaching Kyle in one of the courtyards just outside of the Tower for almost a week now. He was kind and patient, but not quite the teacher the Dead Man had proven to be. As manipulative and sadistic as the Dead Man had been, he'd also had the benefit of over a century and a half of experience, something Master Owens had no hope of ever obtaining.

The guard escorted Kyle about a half-mile from the Tower, veering from one of the countless cobblestone pathways and striding across the lawn toward a short man clad in long black robes. Kyle immediately recognized him as Master Owens. Master Owens smiled as Kyle approached.

"Good morning Kyle," he greeted amiably, his brown eyes darting to the elite guardsman at Kyle's side. The guard bowed, then turned and left the way he'd come. Master Owens cleared his throat, returning his gaze to Kyle. "Had a bit of trouble getting up this morning?" he inquired. Kyle blushed.

"Yes sir," he replied. "Sorry sir," he added sheepishly. Master Owens smiled. He must have been sixty or so, but he had a cherub face that hid his years, with short gray hair springing messily from his head. He was clean-shaven, and almost always smiling. It was, consequently, impossible to dislike the man.

"Quite all right," Master Owens replied good-naturedly. "Of course, I expect you to be as early tomorrow as you were late today," he added. Kyle sighed, nodding obediently. That was Master Owens' way...if you made him wait, he'd make you wait. Despite his affable nature, the man was a strict disciplinarian.

"Now," Mr. Owens stated, "...do you remember yesterday's lesson?" Kyle nodded again. Master Owens had taught him two new patterns in the last few days: one that allowed him to manipulate gravity, the other creating a gooey, sticky substance out of thin air. Kyle wasn't

12

quite sure what the substance was for, but he'd found the gravity pattern to be enormously useful. With it, he could easily create a sphere of gravitational energy in mid-air, one that would suck objects into itself until they floated in its center. Of course, he'd fallen into his own sphere the first time he'd woven it. Apparently everyone did; the gravity field sucked in quite a bit of air when first created, making a vacuum that was all too easy for the uninitiated to get pulled into. The other type of gravity field – the opposite of the pulling-in kind – was the reverse-gravity field. It pushed everything outward. Gravity fields could be created in all sorts of shapes and sizes, and had an enormous number of applications.

Perhaps the most important use of gravity fields was also the predominant method of magical protection in the Empire: gravity *shields*. Constructed of two thin gravity spheres, the outer shell pushing outward, the inner one pushing inward to prevent air from being sucked out of the sphere, a gravity shield could deflect a sword, a crossbow bolt...just about anything thrown at it. Gravity shields were actually enormously complicated, and had taken Kyle quite a while to master. Creating an impermeable sphere around yourself meant preventing any air from getting in or out...meaning you'd suffocate if you didn't find a way to let air in. This was accomplished by creating a semi-circular gravity shield, closed at the head but open at the feet. The lower part of the gravity shield couldn't touch the ground, otherwise it would push against it and make you levitate. That's why it had to be open at the bottom...which left the feet potentially vulnerable.

"Create a gravity field in front of you," Master Owens ordered, stepping backward. Kyle complied, grabbing a thread of magic within his mind and weaving it into the gravity pattern. The pattern was more complicated than the water or fire pattern had been, but Kyle had a knack for remembering patterns, and within a few seconds a gravity-sphere was floating in front of him.

"Now, keep the gravity field there, and make some *punk* in the center of the field," his teacher continued. *Punk* was the name of the tar-black, sticky substance Master Owens had taught him how to create out of thin air yesterday. Kyle complied, and soon a ball of the goop was floating in front of him, suspended in the center of his gravity sphere.

"Now," Master Owens instructed, walking to stand at Kyle's side. "Use the fire pattern to set the *punk* on fire within the gravity field."

Kyle nodded, concentrating harder. Making a gravity field – or any other magical construct – required him to both generate a knot of magical energy – the pattern – and to attach a continuous stream of magic to the pattern to keep it running. Without the magic stream, the pattern would work for a moment, then unravel. He'd already made one magic stream; making two at once still required a bit of concentration. But he did so, weaving the fire pattern, then throwing it out to the *punk*, attaching a magic stream to keep the flames burning.

The *punk* burst into flames, forming a fiery ball in the center of the gravity field. Because the gravity of the field pulled inward quite strongly, the flames weren't very tall.

"You don't need the magic stream for the fire pattern," Master Owens noted. "*Punk* is quite flammable itself. It makes for a dangerous projectile weapon," he added. "If thrown, it will stick to just about any surface, and it will burn until consumed."

Kyle nodded, stopping the magic stream to the fire pattern. Sure enough, the *punk* continued to burn slowly, hovering within the confines of the gravity field. He felt beads of sweat forming on his forehead; if he accidentally dropped the *punk*, it'd light the grass below on fire. How was he going to extinguish those flames?

"Now, use the water pattern to snuff out the *punk*," Master Owens instructed. Kyle nearly slapped himself in the forehead; of course! He threw out the water pattern, and a stream of water fell into the center of the sphere, covering the *punk* and dousing the flames. A small hunk of blackened *punk*, surrounded by a rippling sphere of water, hovered in mid-air in front of him. It reminded him suddenly of Earth...of home.

"Very good," Master Owens stated. "You may release the gravity pattern," he added. Kyle did so, watching as the sphere of water fell to the grass with a plop. Then he hopped backward, realizing too late that he'd just soaked his feet. Master Owens laughed good-naturedly. "I provide the patterns," he said with a wink. "Life teaches the rest." Kyle blushed, shaking a few droplets off of his sodden shoes. He was always doing stuff like that; getting all the details right, then missing

14

the practical stuff. Still, he couldn't help but be proud that he'd managed to complete the lesson the first time through.

"Good morning, Master Owens," a light, feminine voice said from behind Kyle. Kyle spun around, seeing a taller, slender girl standing behind him. She had long brown hair tied into a ponytail, with large, almond-shaped brown eyes, and was dressed in a simple black shirt and pants. Her skin was still a little pale from over a year spent underground. She looked quite fetching, as always.

"Oh, good morning, Ariana," Master Owens replied, turning to regard the girl. "You're quite late this morning."

"I was at a Council meeting," Ariana explained. That, Kyle knew, was true; the Council was a group of twelve men who were second only to the Grand Weaver and Grand Runic in governing Stridon, and by extension, the Empire. The meeting had been about the Death Weaver base at Crescent Lake. Kalibar had already sent his Battle-Weavers there to destroy the base, but the Council wanted as much information about the Death Weavers – and the Dead Man – as they could get. Ariana had lived among the enemy for over a year, and was therefore the foremost expert on the issue.

"Ah, of course," Master Owens replied. "I had forgotten," he added. "You're not one to be late." He glanced at Kyle then, and Kyle blushed at the unspoken truth; *he* had a bad habit of showing up late, for a variety of reasons that always seemed out of his control. Ariana was, as always, much better at following directions.

"What lesson are we learning today, Master Owens?" Ariana inquired.

"Ah, yes," the old Weaver replied. "Both of you, stand a bit apart...I don't want anyone getting hurt." The two did so, standing a few feet from each other, facing Mr. Owens. "Now," he continued, "...create a gravity field in front of you..."

Master Owens lead them both through the series of patterns he'd showed Kyle earlier, and soon a levitating hunk of burning *punk* was floating in front of Kyle. Ariana, on the other hand, was still struggling to create the *punk* inside of her own gravity sphere. She was much better than him at thinking on his feet, especially during a crisis, but he when it came to memorizing patterns, he was the quicker study. They'd been taught the *punk* pattern yesterday, and Kyle had rapidly

15

memorized it...much to Ariana's dismay. He paused for a moment, watching as Ariana continued to struggle, then dropped his gravity sphere, pretending to screw up his magic stream.

"Oops," he said, then did a double-take; the *punk* was still burning, and now it was setting the grass in front of him on fire! "Oh!" he exclaimed, stomping on the burning grass. The gooey *punk* stuck to the bottom of his shoe, and started burning that, too. He yelped, sliding his foot across the grass, trying to scrape the burning goo off. Mr. Owens just stood there, watching silently as Kyle finally extinguished the flames. When Kyle looked up, Ariana was staring at him, her expression unreadable. Kyle glanced down; there were a few scorch marks on the otherwise immaculate lawn. The blood drained from his face.

"Kyle, why don't you take a break for today," Master Owens said, patting Ariana on the shoulder. "I'll meet you back in the Tower lobby in a bit." Kyle nodded, bowing at Master Owens, and giving Ariana a weak smile. She just stared back at him silently...which meant that she was mad.

Kyle felt the blood rush back to his cheeks with a vengeance, and turned about, walking back to the main entrance of the Tower. Despite the warmth of the morning sun beating on his back, and the brilliant blue of the cloudless sky, his disposition was far from sunny. All he'd wanted to do was make sure Ariana wouldn't look bad in front of Master Owens. Why couldn't she understand that? She was hardly being appreciative...and after everything he'd done for her! After all, if it weren't for him, she'd still be stuck in the Dead Man's underground lair.

Kyle sighed, kicking a pebble across the path. His dad had always maintained that he didn't understand women, despite having tricked one into marrying him. Kyle had apparently inherited that deficiency.

It wasn't long before Kyle reached the massive double-doors of the Great Tower, which were perpetually open. Streams of people walked in and out of those doors on a near-constant basis. Many wore either all-white or all-black uniforms; Runic students wore white, Weavers black. There was a rather lively rivalry between the Runic and Weaver students. As in politics, each thought their art to be vastly and obviously superior to the other, and despite centuries of argument, neither side had become convinced of the others' worth. The younger Runics and Weavers poked fun of each other constantly. Kyle had found himself immune to these debates; having an emperor for a guardian – the most powerful Battle-Weaver in the Empire – might have had something to do with it.

Kyle strolled through the double-doors, nodding politely at people who greeted him as he passed. He walked to one of the many plush couches in the Tower lobby, his black boots clip-clopping on the polished granite floor, then plopped himself down on an empty seat, staring up idly at the ceiling. Crowds of people milled about upside-down a few stories up, held in place by powerful gravitational fields generated by runes embedded into the ceiling. Upside-down fountains spewed water downward, the water arcing back upward to land in upside-down pools. No matter how much time Kyle had spent staring up at that ceiling, he still marveled at the sight. Nothing on Earth rivaled it.

Earth, he thought, picturing his mother's house perched on its hill, his mom waving to him as he ran up the driveway from the bus stop. It'd been weeks since he'd seen his mom and dad, and he missed them terribly. The homesickness had become almost unbearable of late. He'd spent the last few nights imagining his parents searching frantically for him, losing hope as the days and weeks passed. He'd pictured them standing over his casket at his funeral, weeping over their lost son. What he wouldn't give to be with them again...to hug his mom and dad, to tell them how much he loved them.

Kyle sighed. To be honest, he'd expected to be sent back to Earth after defeating Xanos a week ago, but it hadn't happened. In fact, Ampir – the man who had almost certainly brought him to this world in the first place – hadn't paid Kyle a visit since Xanos's defeat.

Ampir, the mystery man. A black-armored Runic who'd lived in Ancient times, who'd been so powerful that entire armies had surrendered at the sight of him showing up on the battlefield. A man who had somehow sent his memories to Kyle through Kyle's dreams, and had brought him to this strange land. And for what?

Kyle glanced down at the ring on his left thumb, realizing that he'd forgotten to leave it in his room that morning. He was supposed to leave it in his room's magical safe so that Erasmus's research team could study it during the day. Light glimmered off of the yellow crystal embedded on top. It had been Ampir's long ago, of that there was little doubt. So how had it ended up in Kyle's hands? He'd gotten the ring for his birthday...a lousy gift from his dad, or so he'd thought at the time. Sometimes he wished he'd never gotten it, never been taken from his family and friends back home. Then he remembered Kalibar, Ariana, and even Darius, and knew that he had to be thankful for having met them. They were the most extraordinary people Kyle had ever met, brave and loyal beyond measure.

"Kyle," a kindly voice said from behind. Kyle turned about, and saw Master Owens standing behind the couch. The Weaver gestured to the empty seat on the couch beside Kyle. "May I sit?"

"Sure," Kyle mumbled. Master Owens sat down, smoothing the wrinkles out of his black robes. He hesitated for a moment.

"Kyle, I've been thinking," he stated, his tone suddenly solemn. Kyle felt a creeping dread twist his guts. When an adult mentioned that they'd been thinking, it was almost always about something bad.

"What?" Kyle asked.

"Well...to be blunt, I've been thinking that perhaps Weaving isn't the best fit for you."

Kyle's mouth fell open. He sat there in stunned silence, waiting for Master Owens to laugh, to say he was just kidding. But Owens just sighed.

"I've been talking it over with Grand Weaver Kalibar," he continued. "We both agree on this," he added. Kyle shook his head, righteous indignation rising up in his breast.

"What do you mean?" he protested. "I'm good at weaving," he added hotly. "I learned the patterns a lot faster than Ariana," he added. "If anything, *she* should be the one..."

"Stop," Master Owens ordered, his tone ice-cold. Kyle's jaw snapped shut, and he felt his cheeks turning hot with anger and shame. "I will *not* have you disparaging your friend," Master Owens added, his tone uncharacteristically harsh. "You're better than that, Kyle," he admonished. Kyle felt sudden, hot tears well up in his eyes, and he turned away in shame.

18

"I just don't understand," he protested, shaking his head, then wiping the tears away with one sleeve. "I thought I was doing so well," he added. He felt Master Owen's hand on his shoulder.

"You *are* doing well," his teacher replied gently. "Incredibly so."

"Then why...?" he asked. Master Owens patted Kyle on the knee

"Your ability to memorize patterns is remarkable," he explained. "I've never met someone that had such a knack for learning them. But you..." he paused then, an apologetic look on his face.

"I what?" Kyle pressed, his dread returning. Master Owens sighed.

"Well, you're just not as strong at *applying* those patterns on the fly," he replied. Kyle's eyebrows knit together, and he opened his mouth to defend himself, but Master Owens stopped him with one hand. "You *are* better than Ariana at learning patterns," he conceded. "But you can't deny that, once she's learned them, she's better at thinking on her feet...using her patterns strategically, in real time," he added. Kyle said nothing, lowering his gaze to his knees. Now it was his turn to smooth the wrinkles out of his pants, running his fingers over the coarse black fabric. He couldn't deny what Master Owens was saying; after all, he'd had the very same thought earlier that day. How often had Ariana burst into action during their last adventure, acting decisively while Kyle had frozen? Heck, *everyone* had been braver and more decisive than him. He'd just tagged along, a nobody surrounded by heroes. He'd hoped that becoming a Weaver would change that.

"So you're saying I can't learn magic?" Kyle asked. Master Owens chuckled.

"No, nothing as bad as that," he countered. "In fact, I think you've got an amazing career ahead of you," he added. "One that might be more suited to your strengths." Kyle felt his hopes rise.

"As what?" he asked. Master Owens smiled.

"As a Runic."

"A *Runic?*" Kyle almost spat. Master Owens chuckled again.

"Now, now," he said, patting Kyle on the shoulder. "You make it sound like it's a bad thing."

"It *is*," Kyle countered, pulling his shoulder away. "Runics are boring," he added vehemently. It was true; all of the Weaver students said it. Runics were all loners, hunchbacked nerds wasting their lives making little trinkets for other people to use. Weavers, on the other hand,

19

led exciting lives, filled with action and adventure. While Runics stayed safely behind enemy lines making swords sharper and armor stronger, Weavers led the way, flying through the air and blasting enemies left and right. "All they do is draw runes all day," Kyle complained, "...while Weavers go out to battle and get all the glory."

"You should ask Grand Weaver Kalibar who saved him from dying in battle a dozen times over," Master Owens retorted gently. "Or did you think he did everything himself?"

"He *did*," Kyle shot back, crossing his arms in front of his chest. Kalibar was, after all, the greatest Battle-Weaver the Empire had ever produced.

"He most certainly did *not*," Master Owens countered. "Now, I'll admit that he certainly held his own later in life...and that now there are few who could stand against him – with or without runics. But in his earlier days, Kalibar was every bit as dependent on his Runic as any other Battle-Weaver...or soldier, or citizen of the Empire."

"What do you mean?"

"Ask Grand Runic Erasmus," Master Owens replied. "He's the one who made Kalibar's weaving glasses, his warding staff, the wards for his carriages, the rings he always wears on his fingers, that crisp black uniform with those rows of runic medals...need I go on?"

"Oh," Kyle replied, grudgingly realizing that Master Owens was right. Kalibar had accumulated a vast collection of runic items, all of which he'd used to make himself a more effective Weaver. And of course, as a Weaver, Kalibar couldn't have made any of it himself.

"The dawn breaks," Master Owens said with a grin. "By the way, those 'boring' old Runics built everything you see around you," he added, gesturing up at the upside-down lobby above their heads. "This Tower was entirely built by Runics," he explained. "The levitating carriages on the streets? All made by Runics. Every sword, every scrap of armor each of our soldiers and guards wear?"

"Made by Runics," Kyle answered. "I get it," he added glumly.

"The point is that, well, you're really good with patterns." Master Owens stated. "Memorizing them, understanding them, understanding how one pattern can affect another...*these* are your strengths. Not to mention your unheard-of ability to produce magic. These are the

20

talents of someone who is better suited to learn the art of rune-link-ing."

"Rune-linking?" Kyle asked. He'd never heard of the term.

"Linking sensor and effector runes together in novel ways," Master Owens explained. "It's a process that requires a great deal of creativity, Kyle...and frankly, it can be a lot of fun."

"Uh huh."

"Talk to Grand Runic Erasmus later today," Master Owens urged, patting Kyle on the knee. "I think he'll be able to ease your mind about all of this."

With that, Master Owens stood up, turning to give Kyle one last smile, then walking away. Kyle sat there on the couch, staring at the floor in front of him. Not cut out to be a Weaver! He suddenly wanted to cry. On Earth, he'd never been particularly good at anything. An average student, and the second-shortest kid in his grade, he'd hardly stood out. Then he'd come here, and learned that he had enormous magical potential – even greater than that of the mighty Kalibar, at least when he'd been a kid – and now, after weeks of dreaming of becoming an all-powerful Weaver blasting his way through his enemies with unfettered ease...

Kyle sighed. He should've known that it was too good to be true. He'd failed...and now he was being shipped off to tinkering school. He would never have a chance to be a hero like Kalibar.

"Hey," a voice called out. Kyle snapped out of his morbid thoughts, watching as Ariana sat down next to him, her slender frame sinking into the plush white fabric of the couch. She was scowling, her arms crossed over her chest.

"Hey," Kyle mumbled back. Then he sighed. "I'm sorry for..."

"Forget about it," Ariana interjected, shaking her head. "It's not your fault. I'm just frustrated, that's all."

Kyle couldn't help but smile. Ariana talked – and acted – like a grown-up, even though she was only a year or so older than Kyle. She was quick to forgive and forget, much like himself. As such, they didn't argue much...and when they did, they didn't fight for long.

"What's wrong?" Kyle asked. Ariana's scowl softened, then disap-peared.

"Master Owens told me," she confessed.

21

"Oh," Kyle mumbled, his cheeks flushing. He felt Ariana's warm hand on his shoulder.

"I told him he was wrong, you know," she added. "You're really good at magic, Kyle...*really* good. You're just..." She trailed off then, grimacing slightly. Kyle frowned.

"Just what?"

"Well, you're unsure of yourself," Ariana answered. Kyle immediately felt the heat return to his cheeks, and he turned away abruptly. Ariana was right, and he knew it.

"Master Owens says I can't think on my feet," Kyle blurted out. "I'm slow," he added bitterly.

"Only with some things," Ariana replied with a twinkle in her eyes, shoving Kyle's shoulder playfully. Kyle blinked, wondering what the heck *that* meant. "Besides," she added, "...the Dead Man thought you'd make a great Weaver...and he was a teacher for a lot longer than Master Owens."

Kyle had to smile at that. It was true, after all; the Dead Man, for all of his extraordinary faults, had been the most skilled teacher he'd ever learned from. And at the same time, the most unpleasant. But Ariana's point held; the Dead Man had seen something in him that maybe, just maybe, Master Owens had missed.

But the Dead Man, of course, was dead.

"It doesn't matter," he replied dejectedly. "Master Owens says I'm better off being a Runic, so that's what I'm going to be." Ariana grinned wickedly.

"A lowly tinkerer," she mocked, parroting the typical insults Weaver students lobbed at their Runic counterparts. "Staying at home with the women while the men go off to war!" Kyle scowled.

"You mean while *you* go off to war," he grumbled. Ariana laughed.

"You know, staying home with the women doesn't have to be so bad," she teased. "You might even like it!"

"Whatever," Kyle shot back. But his cheeks flushed yet again, making Ariana laugh even harder. Oh, how he hated his body!

"I'm just kidding Kyle," Ariana said, putting a hand on his shoulder. "You know I'd take you with me," she added, a smile playing at her lips.

"Oh yeah?" he replied warily. Ariana nodded, trying desperately to keep a straight face – and failing.

"I'll need someone to fix my stuff if it gets broken," she blurted out, then burst out into laughter again.

"Oh, go drown yourself," Kyle grumbled back. Ariana kept laughing, her face turning pink, tears rolling down her eyes. At length she stopped, rubbing her moist cheeks with the back of her hand.

"Oh come on," she said. "You know, I think being a Runic could be really cool," she added. Kyle scowled. "No, I'm serious," she insisted. "You'll get to create anything your mind can come up with...anything at all. Think about how amazing that could be! Maybe you'll make those flying machines you were telling me about." Kyle had told Ariana about airplanes yesterday, when she'd asked, as she did every night, about Earth. She never tired of the stories he told about his home world, of guns and computers, of television and cars. It was all as magical to her as...well, as magic was to him.

"Thanks," Kyle mumbled, "...but I never really saw myself sitting in some room, spending all day carving runes and charging gems."

"Just give it a chance," Ariana urged. "For me," she added sweetly. Kyle glanced up at Ariana, at her big brown eyes, strands of brown hair having fallen fetchingly over her face. He felt his anger and shame melt away...as it always did when he was around her. Ariana made everything better, just by existing; she had a special magic all her own.

"Okay," he agreed. He gave a grudging smile. "Thanks," he added. Ariana smiled back, standing up from the couch suddenly.

"Anytime," she replied. "I have to go again," she added, "...but I'll be back later."

"Where are you going?"

"Master Owens wanted to finish teaching me those patterns you already memorized," she answered with a wink. "Don't worry," she added, "I'll catch up to you eventually!" With that, she bolted, running across the lobby toward the double-doors in the distance. Kyle smiled again, shaking his head. Then he felt a pang of guilt. While he had been bad-mouthing Ariana's skills to Master Owens, she had done nothing but support him. What a terrible friend he was! He grit his teeth, vowing to do better by her in the future.

23

Suddenly a horrendously loud screeching sound echoed throughout the lobby. Kyle heard shouting, and spotted a group of black-armored guards running into the Tower through the lobby's double-doors. The men rushed past Kyle, vanishing down one of the hallways beyond the lobby. Kyle stood up, noticing that everyone else in the lobby was doing the same, staring nervously down the hallway the guards had sprinted down. Kyle heard footsteps behind him, and felt a heavy hand on his shoulder. He turned about, seeing a man in black armor – a member of the elite guard – standing behind him. The guard pulled him close, the runes on the man's armor flashing blue. Two more elite guards flanked Kyle, their armor activating similarly.

"What's going on?" Kyle asked, his voice rising with alarm.

"There's been an assassination attempt," one of the guards answered tersely. Kyle frowned.

"On who?" he pressed, fighting back a sudden wave of panic.

"Grand Weaver Kalibar," the guard replied.

Chapter 2

The screeching alarm continued to sound throughout the Tower, so loud that Kyle had to cover his ears with his hands. It was an all-too-familiar sound...he'd heard it when Rivin and Bartholos were murdered over a week ago.

Kalibar!

Kyle had tried unsuccessfully to bolt from the guards surrounding him, wanting nothing more than to run all the way up to Kalibar's suite. He'd asked his guards whether or not Kalibar had been killed, but no one knew the answer. The Grand Weaver had powerful wards to protect him, but with a being as powerful as Xanos...

Kyle stood there helplessly, his heart thumping in his chest. He squirmed under the elite guard's grasp, fearing the worst.

"Kyle!"

Kyle turned to find Ariana running up behind him, a duo of elite guards sprinting after her. She stopped beside him.

"What's going on?" she asked.

"Someone tried to kill Kalibar," he answered, his voice trembling. Ariana's eyes widened, and her hand went to her mouth.

"Is he okay?" she pressed. Kyle said nothing, afraid his voice might crack. Ariana shook Kyle's shoulders. "Come on!" she urged, pulling him toward one of the hallways beyond the lobby. One of the elite guards put a hand out, blocking their path.

"You have to stay here," the man declared. "We're still sweeping the Tower for enemies."

"Kyle's ring is the only thing that can save Kalibar," she retorted, pointing to the ring on Kyle's thumb. Kyle frowned; everyone thought that his ring was an enormously powerful runic, a magical device that protected him from any source of harm...and killed anyone who tried to hurt him. In reality, it had been Ampir himself who had protected Kyle; the ring was just a glorified transmitter. No one else knew that Ampir was still alive...and that's apparently how the man wanted it to stay.

"I don't know," he mumbled. But Ariana would not be denied.

"Remember Darius?" she retorted. Kyle saw the guards waver at that. Darius had been mortally wounded by Xanos, a sword driven through his chest...until he'd been saved by Kyle's ring. Or rather, by Ampir. The guards knew about that, too...and they were likely thinking that if Kalibar had been mortally wounded, then perhaps Kyle's ring could bring him back.

"All right," the guard grumbled. The guards led the way, striding quickly down one of the hallways off of the main lobby. Kyle and Ariana followed, making their way down the wide corridor, which ended with a large, circular platform – the riser. Within seconds of standing on it, the riser began to ascend, catapulting them straight upward with gut-twisting speed. There were no elevator doors to block the view as they sped forty-two floors upward; luckily, gravity fields prevented anyone from stepping off of the platform while it was moving.

The riser came to a halt, the guards leading Kyle and Ariana down a narrow hallway toward Kalibar's chambers. Kalibar spent most of his time there, for two reasons. One, it was the most secure room in the Tower – and perhaps in the Empire. Two, he still had a hard time getting around with his blindness. Without his sight, he was not the warrior he'd once been. If the assassin had somehow managed to get past Kalibar's wards...

They halted at Kalibar's door, and one of the guards pounded on it. Within seconds, the door began transparent, another elite guard peering at them from the other side.

"We have Kyle," the first guard stated, stepping aside so that Kyle was visible. "And his ring," he added. The other guard glanced at Kyle, then turned about, the door becoming opaque once again. A few moments later, the door swung inward, revealing the guard standing beyond.

"Come in," he said, ushering Kyle through. Ariana pushed past as well. Their guards, however, were blocked from coming in, the magical door swinging shut as soon as Ariana had passed.

"Where's Kalibar?" Ariana asked, rushing into the massive suite. Massive glass walls towered over their heads, tapering to a pyramid-shaped peak far above their heads. A dozen black-armored elite guards stood in several clusters around the room. A short, balding man with an impressive white beard draped over his equally impressive belly stood in the center of the room, conversing with one of the guards. The man turned his blue eyes toward Kyle and Ariana as they entered, his bushy eyebrows rising slightly.

"Erasmus!" Kyle exclaimed. The old man nodded grimly, stepping away from the guard he'd been talking to and walking up to Kyle and Ariana. "Is Kalibar...?"

"He's fine, thank goodness," Erasmus replied, his voice clearly shaken. "He's in the bedroom with Darius, examining the body," he added. Kyle frowned.

"Wait, what body?" he asked.

"The assassin's body," Erasmus answered. "Somehow the fool managed to get past my wards, although how, I have no idea. We found his body a few feet from Kalibar's bed."

"Is Kalibar hurt?" Kyle pressed. Erasmus shook his head, putting an arm around Kyle's shoulders.

"Not a scratch on him," Erasmus answered. "Can't say the same for the bastard on the floor, though. Seems he lost his head."

Suddenly the door to Kalibar's bedroom opened, a tall, fit-looking man in a plain black shirt and pants striding through. With his characteristic white military-short hair and neatly trimmed goatee, it was no mistaking who stood before them – even with the golden double-eyepatches covering his empty eye sockets.

"Kalibar!" Kyle cried, rushing forward. Kalibar hesitated, then smiled broadly, extending his arms to the sides. Kyle leaped into the

27

old man's arms, burying his head into Kalibar's shoulder. A normal man – especially a blind one – would have been knocked clean off his feet, but Kalibar didn't even budge. The man was a master-level Weaver, perhaps the most skilled practitioner of magic in the Empire. Kalibar held Kyle for a moment, then gently pushed him away.

"Where is Ariana?" he asked. Ariana stepped forward, and before she could say anything, Kalibar inclined his head toward her, no doubt sensing the magic inside of her. Ever since Kalibar had lost his vision, his sense of magic had become more powerful; he had admitted to Kyle that he could feel the unique magical "signature" that each person radiated, allowing him to know exactly who was nearby...if they were close enough.

"I'm here," Ariana replied, stepping in to give Kalibar a hug. "What happened?" she asked. Kalibar sighed.

"We're still trying to figure that out," he admitted. "We know that an assassin – dressed in a guard's uniform – managed to get into my room. I nearly killed myself falling over his body when I got up this morning," he added with a wry grin. Erasmus snorted.

"That would've been a trip," the portly Grand Runic quipped, his blue eyes twinkling. "Killed by a decapitated assassin...imagine the obituary!"

"That's another mystery," Kalibar stated. "First he managed to get inside my room without triggering any of my wards, and then he was killed before he ever reached me...but again, not by any of my wards. It doesn't make any sense."

"Damn right it doesn't," Erasmus grumbled. "Nothing could've gotten past those wards without tripping them. Hell, a gnat couldn't have made it into your room," he added, clearly frustrated. And for good reason; most of the wards protecting Kalibar had been designed by Erasmus himself, a Runic of formidable talent. The Grand Runic was obviously unsettled by the idea that his handiwork had proven inadequate to the task.

"It's not your fault, old friend," Kalibar stated, putting a hand out toward Erasmus. Kalibar's enhanced magical senses weren't perfect – Erasmus was too far away to touch – but Erasmus stepped forward so that Kalibar's hand landed on his shoulder.

"Bullshit," Erasmus retorted. "It's all my fault, and you know it!" Kalibar smirked at that.

"Fine, it's all your fault, you old hack," the Grand Weaver replied. "I was just trying to make you feel better. You're fired, by the way," he added. Erasmus snorted.

"Oh, go walk out a window," he shot back, swatting Kalibar's hand from his shoulder. "This from a guy who nearly broke a hip tripping over a dead man!" But he couldn't help chuckling, and soon the two were laughing merrily – to the supreme discomfort of the guards around them. After all, the two were the most powerful and respected men in the Empire; hearing them gleefully insult each other had to be quite jarring for those that weren't used to it. Kyle grinned; he'd grown to love the two men dearly, though he'd known both for less than a month.

"Hey, where's Darius?" Kyle asked. He'd assumed that Kalibar's personal bodyguard would've been here by now. Erasmus nodded toward Kalibar's bedroom door.

"He's inside, inspecting the body," the Grand Runic replied jovially. "Cheery bastard, isn't he?" he added with a wink. Kyle smirked; Darius was many things, but cheery wasn't one of them. Rude, callous, abrupt, and insulting, sure, but never cheery. Erasmus had grown quite fond of needling the bodyguard every chance he got...and Darius, never being one to respect rank or privilege, gave as good as he got, much to the horror of the other guards.

"Can we see?" Ariana pressed. Even though they were still technically children, Kyle and Ariana had already seen their fair share of corpses, and unlike on Earth, exposure to the unfortunate realities of life at a young age was heartily encouraged here.

"Of course," Kalibar replied. He led the way, turning about and walking unerringly back to his bedroom door. Erasmus had spent the better part of a day setting various runes about Kalibar's room, marking the location of obstacles and important destinations. Kalibar could quite literally *feel* the entire suite, navigating through his domain as quickly and safely as any other man. At Kalibar's touch, his bedroom door opened, and they all stepped inside.

Kalibar's bedroom was large by any standard, with a comparatively modest-sized four-post bed set back against the wall. The floor was made of polished granite, two-story tall windows allowing the sun's rays to glitter off of the opulent surface. A few feet from the bed, a man in glimmering, golden armor knelt, staring down at a black-armored form lying motionless on the floor. The armored man glanced up as Kyle entered, staring with his startlingly blue eyes. It was Darius, of course...and as usual, he looked remarkably bored.

"What have you found?" Kalibar asked the bodyguard, stopping a healthy distance from the body.

"He's dead," Darius replied, rising to his feet. The man was tall – taller even than Kalibar – and despite the armor covering him from his chest downward, it was clear that he wasn't lacking in the muscle department. Erasmus snorted.

"Hot damn, somebody give that man a raise," the Grand Runic quipped, walking up to Darius and clapping him on the shoulder with a metallic clang. "Not only that, I think we'll add 'Royal Coroner' to his title," he added with sly grin. Darius's expression, as usual, didn't change.

"Nice wards," the bodyguard growled back. Erasmus froze, looking shell-shocked. Then he gave Darius a murderous glare.

"Insolent swine," he grumbled. "Why can't you hire a proper bodyguard, Kalibar?"

Kalibar ignored the two, his expression one of practiced patience. Darius, in turn, ignored Erasmus, turning back to Kalibar.

"Decapitated, probably an hour ago," he stated at last. "Wound was cauterized, no bleeding. Uniform stolen from one of ours...we found another body downstairs."

"So it wasn't a rogue elite guard," Kalibar deduced.

"Not likely," Darius agreed. Kalibar's shoulders visibly relaxed at that. Much of his and Erasmus's time had been spent pouring through the ranks of their guards, ensuring that none were secretly agents of Xanos. Not a single impostor had been found, much to their frustration. Except of course for the man who'd killed Rivin and Bartholos; he'd been an elite guard for over a decade, biding his time until the order had come to strike. Xanos apparently planned for the long-term.

"Any clue as to how he got past my wards?" Kalibar asked.

"Nope," Darius answered. Erasmus frowned, no doubt having expected the bodyguard to insult him again, and having come up with a particularly clever retort that he couldn't use. Darius ignored the Grand Runic, but Kyle noticed the corner of the bodyguard's mouth twitch. The two really were insufferable; much to Erasmus's ire, Darius had consistently proven the more skillful opponent. The man was a master at combat, whether with words or weapons.

"Ass," Erasmus grumbled.

"Without knowing how he got in, it'll be impossible to prevent it again," Kalibar observed, ignoring the two men. "And we still don't know who – or what – killed the assassin before he managed to kill me."

"Agreed," Erasmus stated, his expression sour. "None of this makes any sense. We're missing something, Kalibar."

At that moment, a man in a white cloak strode into the bedroom, flanked by a few of Kalibar's guards. He was quite old, at least seventy by Kyle's estimation, with gaunt, smooth-shaven cheeks contrasting with his quick and calculating brown eyes. He was Jax, the eldest Council member, appointed leader of the twelve-member group that wielded power second only to Erasmus and Kalibar. He ignored the body on the ground, nodding curtly at Kalibar and Erasmus.

"Good morning, Excellencies," he greeted, putting a wrinkled hand on Kalibar's shoulder.

"Good morning, Jax," Kalibar replied.

"We've locked down the Tower," Jax stated crisply. "The top ten floors have been evacuated. As of now, no risers will go past the thirtieth floor," he added. "Not until we figure out how this happened."

"Yes, well," Erasmus replied, rubbing his bald head sheepishly. Jax was one of the few Runics alive more skilled than Erasmus. If anyone would know how the assassin had gotten past Erasmus's wards, it would be Jax. "Any ideas?" Erasmus asked.

"Your wards were excellent," Jax replied authoritatively. "I myself would not have been able to breach them."

"Which can only mean one thing," Kalibar said with a sigh.

"Xanos," Jax agreed. Kyle felt a chill run down his spine. It could have been no other. The self-proclaimed god had power far beyond their understanding.

31

"I can't defend Kalibar against a god!" Erasmus protested, clearly frustrated. "If Xanos can get an assassin within a foot of his bed, what's to stop him from killing us all in our sleep?"

"Nothing," Jax replied darkly. Kalibar frowned.

"Except I'm not dead," he countered. Jax and Erasmus turned to look at him. "Erasmus, your wards failed, but the fact remains...the assassin is dead, and I'm not. Which means *something* was protecting me."

"Good point," Erasmus admitted. They all turned to stare at Kyle. Or more precisely, the ring on Kyle's left thumb. Kyle felt his face flush, and he lowered his gaze to the floor.

"We need to redouble our efforts to decode that ring," Jax stated. "And duplicate it. It may be the only real defense we'll have against our enemy."

"Agreed," Erasmus said. "Everything else – the guards, the wards...hell, even our armies – is pointless against Xanos. He could walk one of his Chosen straight through ten legions of infantry and destroy them all!"

"Don't remind me," Kalibar grumbled. He'd been spending most of his days planning the mobilization of the Empire's vast military, preparing for any assault against Stridon and the Empire's other key cities. Doing so had put him at odds with the Council; each Councilman owned four legions – each containing 10,000 men – of the Empire's military. Any use of military force required authorization by the Council by a majority vote. Getting them to agree to Kalibar's strategies had taken a monumental effort...and as Erasmus had so bluntly stated, that effort had likely been for naught.

"That reminds me," Jax stated. "The Council is requesting a debriefing regarding this assassination attempt...and they're eager to hear how the attack on the Death Weaver base on Crescent Isle went."

"Of course," Kalibar replied. "I assume they'd rather not meet here," he added wryly. Jax smirked.

"Corpses don't bother me," the elder Councilman replied, "...but I doubt such a symbol of our failure would work to our advantage with the rest of the Council." Kyle noticed Erasmus's eyes falling to stare at the floor. The Grand Runic was taking the matter of his wards harder than Kyle had thought. "We could use the War room," Jax offered. Kalibar nodded in agreement.

"Convene them in the War room then," Kalibar replied. "Lead the way," he added. Jax placed one hand on Kalibar's back, walking side-by-side with the Grand Weaver out of the bedroom. Erasmus followed close behind. Kalibar paused at the doorway, turning back toward Kyle.

"You'd better come too, Kyle," he said. "You too, Darius." Then he resumed walking.

"Can I come?" Ariana asked. Kalibar nodded.

"Of course."

With that, they left the room, leaving the headless corpse of the assassin laying on the ground. Kyle glanced back, and noticed the man's severed head laying on its side a few feet from the body. He stifled a shudder.

The dead man's eyes were staring right back at him.

Chapter 3

The twelve members of the Council sat around the huge, circular table in the center of the War room. Kalibar and Erasmus sat side-by-side at one end of the table, Jax at the other, the eleven other Councilmen positioned in-between. They were all older men and women, seasoned politicians that had risen through the ranks to become the most powerful people in the Empire, save for Kalibar and Erasmus. As in the United States, they were split into two parties, the Populists and the Elitists. The Populists championed policies that supposedly favored the lower classes, making them popular amongst much of the populace. The Elitists tended to favor the rich and powerful. Each believed themselves to be possessed of the Truth, and saw the other party as being obviously wrongheaded in their views. From what Kyle could tell, Kalibar tended toward Populist ideals, while Erasmus was an Elitist. Somehow, the two managed to respect each other's differences, unlike the rest of the Council.

The meeting had begun with Kalibar recounting his tale of what happened earlier that morning. When he'd finished, an older Councilman wearing black robes sitting next to Jax leaned his elbows on the table, frowning at Kalibar. He was, Kyle knew, Councilman Goran, the most senior Elitist on the Council. With jet-black hair slicked back over his head, and a full, trimmed beard, he was a handsome and imposing figure. He also seemed to hate Kalibar – and by extension, Erasmus.

"I don't understand," Goran said, his deep voice booming across the table. "How did the assassin get into your bedroom?" He glanced at Erasmus, then turned his gaze back to Kalibar. "Weren't your rooms warded, Grand Weaver?" Erasmus glared at Goran, and leaned forward to respond, but Kalibar stopped him with a hand on Erasmus's arm.

"They were, Councilman Goran," Kalibar answered calmly. "None of the wards had been set off by the assassin," he added. Goran sat back in his chair, clearly unconvinced.

"That's hard to believe," he stated. "Unless of course the wards were deactivated somehow," he added. Even Kyle knew that runic wards could only be deactivated by the person who made them, at least if they were going to be deactivated quickly. It was a dig at Erasmus.

"They weren't deactivated," Kalibar replied. "The wards were still active when I woke."

"So unless our assassin deactivated them, then reactivated them *before* getting decapitated, so that he'd have to deactivate them *again* in order to escape before being caught..." Erasmus shot back, "...then your theory doesn't add up." Goran frowned at Erasmus.

"No need to get defensive, your Excellency," he stated. "I understand your point, but if you're right, and the runes weren't deactivated first, then how did the assassin get to Kalibar in the first place?" A few of the other Councilmen nodded in agreement. It was an excellent point – and one that Erasmus couldn't refute. With his wards active, a gnat couldn't have gotten into the room without being instantly destroyed.

"We still don't know," Kalibar admitted.

"Is it possible that someone deactivated the wards for the assassin?" Goran asked. "And then reactivated them after the assassin died, but before Kalibar woke?"

"It's possible," Jax piped in, nodding at Goran. "In fact, it's the only plausible scenario."

"But that would require someone with intimate knowledge of those wards, to deactivate them so quickly," Goran continued, glancing at Erasmus again.

"Why don't you just say it?" Erasmus shot back, glaring at Goran. But Goran's eyebrows rose, and he looked genuinely surprised.

"Say what?" he asked. "I'm merely suggesting that there may have been two assassins, one with knowledge of your wards. A man on the inside...a traitor."

"A disturbing possibility," one of the other Councilmen agreed.

"But why would this traitor reactivate the wards to hide his tracks, only to leave the body of the assassin?" Kalibar asked.

"Perhaps to send us a message," Jax replied grimly.

"That our defenses are useless?" Goran asked. Jax nodded. Goran shook his head. "Then why not finish the job? That would have sent an even more powerful message."

"Agreed," Jax replied. "No offense, Grand Weaver."

"None taken," Kalibar stated. "I agree with you, Goran," he added. The statement made Erasmus's face change colors; the fiery Grand Runic hated Goran with a passion, and for good reason. While Goran always managed to appear reasonable, and never outright insulted Erasmus or Kalibar – or the other Populists – he was a consummate politician, able to insinuate, manipulate, and aggravate while remaining maddeningly blameless. Erasmus fell for Goran's tricks all the time, constantly trying to catch Goran in the act, and Goran took full advantage of that. Their interactions inevitably left the Grand Runic appearing impulsive, hotheaded, and paranoid...when only the first two were accurate.

"Well the assassin didn't just up and kill himself," Erasmus grumbled. "So either this imaginary accomplice killed him, or someone else did."

"Or some*thing* else," Kalibar interjected.

"Well it certainly wasn't the wards," Goran observed, crossing his arms over his chest. Again, Erasmus held his tongue, stopped by Kalibar's hand on his arm. Jax frowned at Goran disapprovingly.

"Those wards," the Elder Runic retorted sternly, "...were flawless. I reviewed them myself after they were placed. No Runic in the Empire...and certainly no Weaver," he added, giving Goran – a Weaver himself – a particularly withering look, "...could have gotten past them."

"I would hardly characterize them as flawless," Goran shot back, his tone deceptively mild. Then he gestured at the rest of the Council. "How many of you here would trust your lives to those wards?" The other Councilmen stirred uncomfortably in their seats, clearly disturbed by the question. The fact was, *all* of their rooms were protected by wards that Erasmus had devised. And by the looks of it, not a single member of the Council appeared eager to raise their hand. Another master stroke by Goran, insulting Erasmus without anyone being able to fault him for it. Still, Jax glared at the man.

"Be careful, Councilman," Jax warned, clearly losing patience with Goran's antics. Goran uncrossed his arms, nodding almost imperceptibly at the Elder Runic. He, like the other members of the Council, deferred to Jax...at least when it came to maintaining decorum. Kyle couldn't help but feel a bit of satisfaction at watching Goran be censured. Despite having been present at several Council meetings in the two days since Kalibar had won the election, he was still shocked by the undercurrent of hostility between the Populists and the Elitists. It was a polite war, for sure, and often terribly boring to watch, but it was far from the way Kyle would have imagined an Empire would be run. It was more like a sporting event, with two teams bent on beating the other instead of doing what was best for the Empire. Luckily, while Erasmus fought back in kind, Kalibar treated each member of the Council with unflappable politeness...a quality that defused tensions more effectively than the most clever of counterattacks.

"Do keep in mind that I'm not dead," Kalibar piped in, a bemused smile on his face. "I was protected, and I have every reason to believe that any of you would have been, too."

"Explain yourself, Grand Weaver," an elderly Councilman requested. Kyle recognized the man as Ibicus, the second-eldest Runic on the Council, after Jax. Ibicus had long salt-and-pepper hair, with silver eyes and a smooth-shaven face that appeared much younger than his 70-odd years. While Ibicus was an Elitist, and typically sided with Goran, he did not engage in Goran's style of politicking. Indeed, Ibicus hardly said anything at all during Council meetings; when he did speak, everyone listened.

Kalibar turned his head toward Ibicus; the act gave the disturbing illusion that the Grand Weaver could still see.

"Xanos was almost certainly involved in this assassination attempt," he replied. "...and this isn't the first time we've been protected from his magic."

The Councilmen murmured to each other, nodding in agreement. Kyle knew that they were all thinking back to when Xanos had nearly killed them all, cutting them down with a whirlwind of razor-sharp pieces of glass. Yet no one had suffered more than minor injuries from the ordeal, and Xanos had been defeated...if only temporarily. Everyone believed that Kyle's ring was responsible for protecting them. Kyle knew better, but he'd been forbidden from telling anyone the truth.

"An interesting theory," Goran conceded, "...but forgive me if I have reservations about trusting my life...and the lives of my fellow Councilmen...to Kyle's ring." Then he turned to Kyle. "Please understand that I'm grateful to you," he stated rather hurriedly. Everyone had treated Kyle remarkably well since the attack a week ago. No one understood how Kyle's ring worked, but everyone knew about the tests on the prisoners who'd worn the ring. The powerful artifact only seemed to work when Kyle was wearing it...and only protected those that were on Kyle's side. It was ironic that Goran, so ready to dismiss Kyle's ring, was as yet unwilling to cross it.

"We must deal in realities," Kalibar declared. "We would already be dead if it weren't for Kyle, so we must accept that his ring has protected us. I for one am grateful...no more so than today," he added. "In any case, we can review proposed security measures after this meeting. Unless anyone has anything else to add, I suggest that we move on to the debriefing regarding Crescent Lake."

"Agreed," Jax said. "Councilman Goran?" Goran nodded grudgingly. Jax turned to Kalibar. "You have the floor, Grand Weaver." Kalibar stood then, facing the Council with his double-eyepatches. Once again, Kyle nearly fell for the illusion that Kalibar could still see.

"My Battle-Weavers returned from the Arena last night," he stated. "They suffered no casualties," he added. "But not on account of their skill. When they arrived at the foot of the cave entrance to the enemy base, it was unguarded. They found dead bodies everywhere, soldiers and Death Weavers." Kalibar paused, taking a sip from a glass of water on the table, then continued.

"The Battle-Weavers made their way down the tunnels into the Arena itself. They found more bodies...hundreds of them. The Arena itself was deserted."

"So everyone had been killed?" Councilwoman Hess asked.

"Not quite," Kalibar replied grimly. "When my Battle-Weavers searched the dormitories in the Arena, they found dozens of children hiding in the classrooms. They were terrified...they didn't even put up a fight, even though many were Weavers. They were relieved to see us."

"Where are these children now?" Goran asked.

"We've detained them," Kalibar answered. "They're being kept in the maximum-security wing of Stridon Penitentiary. We're treating them well, of course. They're being questioned at this very moment."

"Excellent," Goran stated. "The information they provide may be critical in winning this war."

"I will keep the Council informed, of course," Kalibar promised.

"So what happened to all of the Death Weavers?" another Councilman inquired.

"When we asked the children," Kalibar answered, "...they said that someone – or some*thing* – came for them in the middle of the night. All of the lights in the Arena went out at once...and anyone who tried to weave the light pattern found that it wouldn't work. They were thrust into complete darkness. Panicking, the children made their way blindly into the dormitories. One by one, they heard the screams of the Death Weavers. The students were led into a few classrooms by their teachers, and huddled there in the absolute darkness. Then they heard their teachers scream, and fall to the floor. Every child sat there, terrified, thinking that they would be next."

"What happened?" Jax pressed.

"Nothing," Kalibar replied. "Eventually, one of the children tried to weave the light pattern...but this time it worked. When their classroom lit up, they found their teachers lying on the floor, dead."

"Dear god," Jax exclaimed.

"They'd all been killed," Kalibar explained. "Every last Death Weaver. The children had been spared, for what reason I can only guess at."

"But who would do such a thing?" Councilman Goran wondered. "We're the only ones who knew where the Arena was!" Then he frowned. "Unless you're suggesting that Xanos had his men killed?"

"Not at all," Kalibar replied. "It wouldn't make any sense for Xanos to kill off his own army, unless it was a punishment for allowing us to escape. Even then, why would he let the children live? They'd been left alone in those dormitories for days by the time we'd found them."

"So who then?" Jax asked. Kalibar shrugged.

"I have no idea," he admitted. "But if it wasn't sanctioned by Xanos, it means that we may have an ally in this war."

"Let's not get presumptuous," Goran grumbled. "We can't keep relying on mysterious allies – and rings – to save us," he added. "We need to concentrate on doing what *we* can do...starting with interrogating those children. The information we extract from them might be vital to the survival of the Empire."

"Don't forget that we have one of those children in this room," Erasmus countered, turning to the side to gesture at Ariana. Everyone at the table turned to look at her. While Kyle would have shrunk down in his seat at the attention, Ariana faced the Councilmen bravely, sitting tall in her chair. Erasmus smiled at Ariana. "She has been remarkably cooperative with us, and she's already made it known that the Dead Man kept his secrets...and Xanos's secrets...to himself. I myself doubt that these children will be as critical as you imagine, Goran."

"Perhaps," Goran retorted. "But remember that Ariana was an outsider...the other children shunned her for it. They may have kept information from her, information that could potentially save millions of lives." He shook his head. "Allowing this civilization to crumble for the sake of a few children is a far greater evil than any cruelty suffered at the hands of an interrogator."

"They will be questioned, Councilman," Kalibar stated, "...but it will be done humanely," he added firmly. "I will not compromise the ethics of the Empire by torturing children." Kyle glanced at Ariana, and saw her smile. She'd hated the Dead Man for torching her village and killing her parents and friends. How would she have felt if Kalibar had condoned torturing those children? After all, if she hadn't been rescued, she would've been one of them.

"Of course," Councilman Ibicus piped in. "The children will be handled with dignity. I believe Councilman Goran was simply expressing the urgency of the situation," he added, his silver eyes locking on Goran's. Goran paused, then nodded.

"I think everyone is in agreement," Jax declared. "Grand Weaver, thank you for your report. We look forward to the results of these interrogations. In the meantime, we have a third item in the agenda for today's meeting...his excellency the Grand Weaver's proposal for the consolidation of our legions. Councilman Goran, I believe you had some concerns about this?"

Kyle groaned, realizing that the meeting was about to become painfully boring...and that it wouldn't end anytime soon. He was suddenly desperate to get out of there while he still had the chance. He glanced at Ariana, who in turn gave Darius a pleading look. The dour bodyguard smirked, but stood, gesturing for the two to follow him as he made his way through the door. Darius led them down the hallway, back toward Kalibar's suite. When they'd made it through Kalibar's front door, Kyle let out a sigh.

"Thanks, Darius," he said. "We would've died if we'd had to stay for that!" The bodyguard shut the door behind him, then glanced across Kalibar's huge living room, toward the Grand Weaver's bedroom. The door to the bedroom was open, and Kyle could see the motionless body of the assassin still lying on the ground.

"Don't get your hopes up," Darius grumbled.

* * *

After a long while, the meeting adjourned, and Kalibar and Erasmus joined Kyle, Ariana, and Darius in Kalibar's chambers. Kyle was glad to see Kalibar; ever since the old man had won the election, he'd been too busy to spend much time with his adopted children. Kyle missed the old days, when Kalibar had all the time in the world to spend with him. Of course, that had also been when they'd been imprisoned, tortured, and nearly killed, but still, the moments of peace they'd had before all that had been some of the best days of Kyle's life.

Erasmus didn't seem at all pleased with how the rest of the meeting had gone. He stormed into the room, then began to pace in front of Kyle and Ariana, who were sitting on one of the couches in the corner.

"Obstructionist pigs!" he spat. "Even in the middle of a war, they can't stop with their political bull-"

"Ahem," Kalibar interjected. Erasmus glanced at Kyle and Ariana, then sighed.

"Sometimes I just want to put my thumbs right over Goran's eyes, and just push, just to see what sounds he'd make," Erasmus grumbled.

"You fall right into his traps every time," Kalibar observed, although not unkindly. Erasmus shrugged helplessly.

"I can't help it," he complained, staring down at his thumbs and making wiggling motions with them. "I swear, the bastard makes me ashamed to be an Elitist!"

"I know, old friend," Kalibar replied. "But in the end, it doesn't matter. Goran and the rest of the Elitists don't have a majority vote for the Council. With half the Council on our side, and Jax's tiebreaker vote, we have enough support to get a majority when we need it." And this was true; Kyle didn't understand much of what went on with the Council, but with each member having one vote, and Kalibar and Erasmus having six of the twelve on their side, voting almost always split 6-6. Since Jax was Elder Runic, he had a tiebreaker vote...and usually won them the day.

"The bastard had the gall to accuse me of deactivating your wards to let the assassin in!" Erasmus complained. Kalibar smirked.

"He insinuated," he corrected. "And you know as well as I do that no one in the Council took that comment seriously."

"Maybe I should change up *his* wards," Erasmus grumbled, "...so that they fry him when he walks into his bedroom." Still, the Grand Runic stopped pacing, and sat on the couch next to Kyle and Ariana. Kalibar sat on the couch opposite them.

"In any case," Kalibar stated, his eyepatches pointing right at Ariana and Kyle, "I have some news for you two." Kyle and Ariana stole a glance at each other, then turned back to face Kalibar.

"What kind of news?" Ariana asked, her voice wary. Kalibar smiled.

"I talked to Master Owens yesterday," he replied. "He was very impressed with your progress...both of you," he added. Kyle felt his cheeks burning, and stared down at his feet. Master Owens had seemed far from impressed when he'd spoken to Kyle earlier that morning. Luckily Kalibar couldn't notice Kyle's chagrin. "Master Owens was particularly pleased with your performance during your sparring match yesterday, Ariana."

This time, it was Ariana's turn to blush. She'd had a sparring match with one of the other Weaver students the other night, and had beaten her opponent handily. When the student had shot a flaming ball of *punk* at her, she'd made a big gravity sphere behind the student. The sphere had sucked air into itself so powerfully that her enemy had been sucked back into it as well...along with his flaming *punk*. Luckily, Ariana had woven the water pattern soon after, dousing the flames even before Master Owens could stop the sparring match. It had been an impressive display of strategy...much more impressive than Kyle's match before that. Sure, he'd won handily...but only by virtue of his sheer magical power, not by dint of cleverness.

"Thank you," Ariana replied. Kalibar smiled.

"Thank Master Owens," he countered. "After all, he's the one who recommended that I grant you a waiver to start your specialty training earlier than the mandatory age."

"Specialty training?" Ariana asked.

"Battle-Weaving," Kalibar clarified. Ariana's jaw dropped open.

"Really?" she breathed. Battle-Weaving was a highly sought-after specialty, one that most Weaver students desperately hoped to get into. It took perfect grades – and a great deal of luck – to be accepted into the program. And no one was accepted until they turned 18.

"Master Owens agreed to be your personal instructor until you graduate," Kalibar explained. "Your training will be intense – all day long, instead of four hours a day. With such an accelerated course, you might graduate in a few years...and be able to start your Battle-Weaver training before you turn eighteen."

Ariana cheered, then ran into Kalibar's arms, giving the old Weaver a big hug. Kalibar laughed, embracing her back, then gently pushing her away.

"It won't be easy," he warned.

"I learned under the Dead Man," Ariana countered. Kalibar chuckled.

"You've got me there," he admitted. Then he stood up from the couch. "Now, I'm afraid I have to ask you all to leave," he added. "Except for you, Kyle...and you, Erasmus." Darius and Ariana stood up – Ariana giving Kalibar one last enthusiastic hug – and then they both filed out of Kalibar's suite, leaving Kyle alone with the Grand Weaver and Runic. Kyle had remained seated, as had Erasmus. Kalibar joined them, sitting down beside Erasmus. He faced Kyle, his expression difficult to read. Kyle squirmed under that eyeless gaze, dropping his own eyes to the floor.

"Kyle," Kalibar began, then paused for a moment. His tone was far from jovial. Erasmus rolled his eyes.

"Oh, cut the crap, Kalibar!" the Grand Runic snorted. He shuffled up next to Kyle on the couch, throwing an arm around Kyle's shoulders. Kyle's back, which had been cut through to the bone a few weeks ago, still ached a little with the impact. "The greatest day of my life, and you're acting like someone died!"

"Erasmus," Kalibar began.

"Oh, don't you ruin this for me," Erasmus interrupted, wagging one finger at Kalibar...which of course Kalibar couldn't see. "It's about time we had a talent like Kyle in our ranks," he added, throwing Kalibar a dirty look. "Your wartime heroics sent two generations of young talent straight into Weaving. Kyle's the finest recruit we've had in two thousand years...and I won't have you convincing him otherwise!"

"I was just trying to comfort my son," Kalibar protested. "Are you okay, Kyle?" he asked. Kyle nodded, then blushed...once again, he'd forgotten that Kalibar was blind.

"I'm okay," Kyle replied. And it was true...after talking with Ariana, and with Erasmus so excited to have him on board, he felt a tad better about his sudden career change. He'd much rather be a Weaver, but he wasn't *completely* devastated anymore.

"Good," Kalibar replied. "I still don't necessarily agree with Master Owens," he added. "I do think you'd make a fine Weaver...an exceptional one, in fact. But you may find being a Runic more to your liking. It's worth trying."

"And I have just the teacher for you," Erasmus stated. "One of my former students, in fact," he added proudly. "His name is Master Banar...and I have a feeling you two are going to get along just fine."

Kyle smiled at Erasmus, but didn't say anything. He really had hoped to become a Weaver, flying through the air and throwing fireballs at his enemies. But who said he couldn't still learn that stuff anyway? After all, he was really good at memorizing patterns...and he was pretty sure that Ariana wouldn't mind teaching him if he asked. He could be a Runic first...and a Weaver in secret. Only he and Ariana would know.

Yes, Kyle decided with a smile...it was a perfect plan. He could still become everything he wanted to be, do everything he wanted to do.

That is, if Xanos didn't kill them all first.

Chapter 4

Kalibar stepped into his spacious shower, feeling the magically warmed granite under his bare feet. The shower was powered by magic; with a thought, Kalibar could activate the sensor rune on the ceiling, generating a soothing cascade of water over his head. Activating a rune to the right of the center rune would make the water colder; the left, hotter.

He activated the center rune, feeling water spray down over his head, dripping over his bare shoulders. Though the shower made water by consuming air, there was no cold wind whipped up by its creation. Gravity-field generating runes in the shower stall dissipated the breeze, while others warmed the air, creating a consistent temperature. A miracle of modern runic technology, this shower. And yet it paled in comparison to the simplest trinket from Ancient times.

Kalibar sighed, feeling the weight of the day begin to lift off of his shoulders. He adjusted the temperature with a thought, the water turning from warm to hot. It felt good over his aching head, where he'd struck his temple on a rock fighting the Dire Lurker two weeks ago. Two weeks ago, but it already felt like the distant past.

Kalibar lowered his chin to his chest, letting the water course over the back of his neck. He'd naively expected the Council to be more cooperative during his second term. Imaged them setting aside their differences, coming together under a common goal, against a common enemy. Instead, they bickered as usual, letting old animosities and party lines dictate their allegiances. Goran had run against Kalibar for Grand Weaver almost twelve years ago...a vicious battle of the popular Elitist versus the legendary Populist war hero...and Kalibar had won handily. Twelve years later, Goran failed to secure a second nomination after Orik – also a Populist – had used his considerable influence and unlimited funds to ensure that Goran never got a chance to challenge him. Goran had never forgiven Kalibar for his successes, and had fought against him on almost everything since...and did so even now, when the stakes were at their highest.

Kalibar sighed, mentally *nudging* the sensor rune above his head. The water became hotter still, almost burning hot. He ignored the pain, feeling his heart thumping in his chest, and an increasingly familiar sensation in the pit of his stomach.

Fear.

He was going to fail, and he knew it. The enemy was too powerful, too organized. United under one ruler with one vision. The Empire, on the other hand – the Council with its dual leaders – had been designed to provide inertia, to ensure that no change in its laws was enacted without significant debate. It was an excellent system in times of peace, but terrible in times of crisis.

There *was* one way to get around it, though. The founders of the Empire had anticipated this very situation. In times of crisis, he and Erasmus could enact emergency powers, giving them full control over the military. The Right of Dictatorship, it was called. It was a sure way to win control over the Council, but it would make the rest of his six-year term – if he lived that long – a miserable experience. After the crisis, the Council would almost certainly block any future bills brought forth by himself and Erasmus, effectively shutting down the government until their terms expired. Then, once they were civilians, they could both be tried with war crimes for "subverting the government"...and even be executed.

It had happened before.

Another piece of insurance, that. The Right of Dictatorship could be wielded, but only if the Grand Weaver and Runic agreed together to enact them...and were willing to face the consequences if their actions were later deemed inappropriate. Only the truly desperate would ever resort to using them. Those with nothing left to lose.

47

Kalibar shut off the shower, standing there as beads of water trickled down his body. He stood there for a long moment, mulling it over. Certain failure, or almost-certain execution...with his reputation in shambles, as well as that of his closest friend.

He sighed again, stepping out of the shower, then reaching out blindly for the towel he knew Jenkins had left hanging to his right. He found it, using it to wipe the water off of his body. He winced as it brushed up against the innumerable half-healed cuts and bruises that covered him, being extra gentle over the ribs on his left side. He was pretty sure they had been broken. When he was done, he wrapped the towel around his waist, and felt for the runes Erasmus had placed on the railing next to the wall, the one that led back to his bedroom.

He stepped out of the shower, making his way slowly around the corner, turning right. After six years of living in this room during his previous tenure, he knew that his bed would be straight ahead...even without the runes Erasmus had peppered all over the room. He let go of the railing, and walked forward carefully, sliding his feet forward across the floor with each small step. He could *feel* every object in the room...except the floor. Even though he knew it was level, and that Jenkins would never allow an obstacle to be left for him to trip over, he couldn't help being cautious. He could easily stop any fall with his magic, but a part of his mind refused to believe that. He was still human, after all.

He put his hands out in front of him, feeling his palms to touch soft bedsheets. He found himself tilting his chin up as he walked, and lowered his head. He would have to work on that.

He eased himself onto the bed, his body aching with each movement. His recent adventure had taken more from him than just his sight. Every breath hurt, and he still got awful headaches from time to time. He knew that, at his age, he would never fully recover. Pain was now, and would forever be, an everyday fact of life.

Along, of course, with the blindness.

He'd never told anybody, and he never would, but there had been times in those first two weeks after the Dead Man had ripped his eyes out of their sockets, dark times where he'd stared into that swirling blackness – that terrible nothing – and he'd wept silently. At first he'd been angry, angry that he hadn't just stayed at his home in Bellingham, angry with the fact that some kid from another planet had happened on his doorstep, changing his life forever. If only he'd pawned the boy off on someone else, or stayed in Stridon instead of running off to Crescent Lake, he would still have his eyesight. He missed seeing the morning sky, a brilliant painting that was never the same as the one composed before it. He missed colors, and textures. He missed being able to see people's faces. It was so hard to talk with people when he couldn't see their faces. So much about communication was visual, more so than he'd ever imagined.

In the first two nights, chained to his narrow cot in his prison cell, he'd thought about ending it all.

Of course, he hadn't. He'd suffered through the pain, the realization that his life was now irrevocably changed, and pulled himself slowly together. He'd done it for Kyle, the boy who he now thought of as his son. He'd done it for his *real* son, a boy who'd died at birth because his father had failed to save him. Most of all, he'd done it for himself.

He laid down on the bed, kicking the sheets down with his legs, then sitting up to pull them up over his body. He cursed silently; he should have pulled the sheets down first, before he'd gotten into bed. If he'd been able to see, he wouldn't have made that mistake. Still, it was getting easier to live with his blindness. He'd found himself dwelling on it less and less with each passing day, slowly coming to accept his new reality.

He sighed, trying to find a comfortable position on the bed. His doctors had mixed the extract of a narcotic-producing plant with some herbal tea. He knew without a doubt that a glass of the pain-killing tea had been placed within his reach, on the nightstand to his left. Jenkins had, of course, seen to it. The man was brilliant, in his own way...anticipating Kalibar's every possible need. Even a half-glass would ensure him a pleasant night's sleep.

He left the glass on the nightstand.

He sighed again, bringing his hands up to his face. A nightly ritual, this. He ran his fingers over his lips, then up along either side of his nose. When he reached his lower eyelids, he paused, his heart skipping a beat. He'd promised himself he'd stop doing this, stop torturing himself, but every night he completed the ritual. He continued onward, running his fingertips lightly over his sunken lids, grimacing as they dipped sickeningly, unnaturally inward. When his fingers reached his cheekbones, he stopped, dropping his hands to his sides.

Kalibar had never considered himself a particularly vain man, but now he knew that he'd been deceiving himself. He found himself desperately wishing that he could look in a mirror, just once. He wanted to see what he looked like, and at the same time, he was thankful that he could not.

Kalibar shifted in bed again, rolling onto his right side – his good ribs. It still hurt to take a breath in, but he ignored this as best as he could. His mind went once again to the glass of tea on his nightstand. He almost reached over to grab it, but stopped himself. If he started doing that now, he would do it every night. Then he would do it just to get through the day...would end up *needing* it.

Instead, he lay there, his mind starting to drift. He played with the images in his mind, the only images he had left. The last thing he'd ever seen was the Dead Man's fingers reaching toward his face again, after he'd pulled out the first eye. The bastard had been right about one thing; Kalibar never would be able to forget his face. He shuddered at the memory of it.

He forced his mind away from the ghastly image, the Dead Man's pale, gaunt face staring down at him, the green diamond-shaped crystal in the man's forehead glittering in the dim light of the Arena. It took a long time for his mind to wander again, swirls of color exploding in his mind's eye. Sleep crept over him slowly, pulling him away from his pain.

He jerked awake.

Kalibar laid perfectly still, straining his ears. Had he heard something? A few seconds passed, but the room was silent. He started to relax.

A soft click came from the distance, the sound of a door closing gently.

Kalibar's body went rigid, the hairs on his neck rising on end. No one else was supposed to be in his room. No one could possibly have entered without activating the newest wards Erasmus had just...

A bolt of terror twisted his guts, his heart pounding in his chest. *Of course,* he thought. They'd come for him again. Come to finish the job.

Footsteps echoed off of the stone walls, getting louder with each step.

Kalibar tried to sit up in his bed, but his muscles stayed limp, refusing to obey his commands. He felt a surge of sheer panic, sucking in a deep breath. He could still breath...but he could control nothing else. He could feel the bed beneath him, could sense everything inch of his body, but he could not move.

The footsteps grew louder as they came closer, *clip-clopping* slowly, almost casually toward him.

Kalibar tried to yell out, but his lips did not move, and only a harsh wheeze escaped his mouth. He lay there, a prisoner in his own body.

I'm going to be murdered in my own bed, he despaired, his heart thumping violently in his chest. *And there's nothing I can do about it!*

He heard the footsteps enter his bedroom, then stop.

Kalibar had a sudden flash of inspiration, gathering magic into his mind and weaving it into a tight pattern. His body might be paralyzed, but his mind was still his own! He threw the deadly pattern out in the general direction the footsteps had stopped in.

Nothing happened.

Suddenly Kalibar felt a force slam into his consciousness, an immense power coursing over his body. Waves of pure energy pulsed through his mind, power beyond any he had felt before. This was magic, he knew, but it was boundless, without limit. It filled his being, this power.

The sound of footsteps returned, coming right up to the side of Kalibar's bed, mere feet from where he lay. The power grew stronger, until it all but overwhelmed him. He knew beyond a doubt that whoever was standing at his side was the source of this energy, this unimaginable fount of magical power. It made his own power seem puny in comparison; he was a mere insect compared to this mountain of magic.

If Kalibar could have trembled, if he could have fallen to his knees before this being, he would have.

51

He felt something heavy press down on the bed beside him, making the bed sink slightly lower. A warm, calloused hand touched his forehead. He wanted to jerk away, but he could not. A voice whispered in his mind, soft yet firm.

You wanted to meet me.

Kalibar felt a shudder run through him. He was still paralyzed, only able to breath and swallow. He could not speak. He could not answer this being's statement. He could not ask any questions of his own.

Now you have.

Suddenly he was in rapture. The pain left his body, ecstasy coursing through him. He felt the rough hand slide off of his forehead, then felt a pressure on his face, over his empty orbits. The rapture intensified, and he cried out silently, his breathing fast and shallow. He felt his lips tingle, the tips of his fingers going numb.

Then the rapture left him, and the weight lifted off of the bed. The wellspring of power vanished.

Kalibar lay there for a long while, staring into swirling darkness, unable to move. His heart, still hammering in his chest, began to slow, sweat beading up on the tops of his arms. He listened, waiting for whatever was to come next.

Nothing happened.

Suddenly, Kalibar's left hand twitched, then spasmed, clenching into a fist. His right hand soon followed, and then his legs. One by one, his muscles came back to life, back under his control. He bent his legs, flexing his toes against the soft fabric of the bedsheets. Then he flexed his arms, twisting his wrists in a slow circle. There was none of the usual pain in his joints. He reached over to feel his ribs, and found that they no longer hurt to press on. In fact, there was no discomfort in his body whatsoever.

Kalibar paused, then sat up slowly, placing his palms on the bed to brace himself.

Then, very slowly, he opened his eyes.

A pair of familiar blue eyes stared back at him.

Chapter 5

Ampir stands in the large chamber by the central dais, cradling Vera in his arms. The light cast by the lanterns on the walls gives her pale face an otherworldly glow, and he gazes down at her, tears streaming down his cheeks.

Boom.

Ampir looks up just in time to see the ceiling caving in far above his head, the Behemoth's foot falling through the shattered ceiling toward him, filling the entire chamber with its enormous size.

With not a shred of magic left in his mind or armor, there is nothing he can do.

He looks down at Vera, holding her tightly to himself. Her face is serene, her pale skin seeming to glow the faintest of blues. He frowns, his breath catching in his throat.

Magic!

He lowers his forehead to hers, *pulling* at the magic within her. Cords of power fill him, and he weaves the magic rapidly, forming a tight, throbbing pattern in the center of his mind's eye. He throws it at his feet...just as the Behemoth's foot slams down on him from above.

Ampir cries out, feels himself falling, his feet striking something hard below. He loses his balance, falling onto his back, utter darkness surrounding him. The deafening *boom* of the Behemoth's foot slamming into the floor of the chamber blasts his eardrums, a shockwave pinning him to the hard rock below, blasting the air from his lungs.

He lays there in utter darkness, gasping for air, dust raining down on him, getting into his nose and mouth. He coughs, then sneezes, covering his face with one hand and turning his head to one side. He holds his breath; moments pass, and eventually the dust settles, letting Ampir breathe again.

He lays there in the darkness, Vera atop him, his ears ringing loudly.

Suddenly the earth trembles, and the Behemoth's foot rises upward, rays of starlight piercing through the blackness. They illuminate the pit he'd made in the ground below his feet with Vera's magic, a pit they'd fallen into right before the Behemoth's foot would have destroyed them.

The Behemoth's foot glows a faint blue, rising further upward, until it passes back through the massive hole in the ceiling some forty feet above. It vanishes from view.

Boom, boom.

The chamber vibrates with each of the Behemoth's footsteps as it retreats from the chamber. Ampir grunts, sitting up, then rising to his feet. He sets Vera in the pit beside him, kneeling before her. Starlight outlines her slender form in a ghostly hue, caressing her gentle curves. Ampir gazes at her, taking in her otherworldly loveliness, knowing that this will be the last time he ever sees her.

"I'm sorry baby," he whispers. "I'm so sorry."

He pictures her when they'd first met, so full of life. She'd rescued him from the hopelessness of his final days in the military, softened him with her vivacious spirit. War had transformed him into a heartless killing machine; Vera had turned him back into a man. Made him believe that he was still worth loving, even after all the terrible things he'd done.

She'd saved him in life, and now she'd saved him in death.

He leans over, kissing her on the lips, finding them cooler now. He gazes down at her face, her body, drinking in every detail. Minutes pass, and still he kneels over her, running a gauntleted hand through her hair.

I love you, he states silently. Then he rises to his feet, struggling against the incredible weight of his armor. Without magic, it weighs over a hundred pounds; sweat pours down his chest and flanks, the armor's temperature-regulating runes non-functional. He stands there, gazing down at his wife, picturing their son vanishing through the portal.

I'll find him, he vows silently. *I promise.*

Then Ampir turns away, facing the wall of the pit he'd created, grabbing the ledge to the chamber floor above. He tries to pull himself up, but it's no use...without his armor's numerous gravity-nullifying runes, he's far too heavy. He focuses, gathering what little magic he has left and directing it to a few runes in his armor. He feels its weight lessen slightly, and tries again, pulling himself upward. This time he succeeds, swinging one leg over the edge above and hauling himself upward. His magic runs out just as he rolls onto the chamber floor above.

He lays there in the ruins of the chamber, his breath coming in short gasps, his heart pounding in his chest. The huge room has been reduced to rubble, the circular stone dais in the center reduced to rubble. Renval's teleportation device – the runes within its crystal the only clue to Junior's location – is gone forever.

Ampir closes his eyes, forcing his breathing to slow, feeling an emptiness within his mind's eye. His brain is completed drained of its magic, as are his bones. Any magic his mind creates will be siphoned away by the hungry bones of his skull. Only sheer willpower will allow him to keep magic in his mind where he can use it. With every bit of magic it absorbs, his skull's pull on his magic will weaken, making it easier for him to weave. After his skull becomes saturated, his spine will begin to fill, taking hours to saturate completely. The rest of his skeleton will take days.

He doesn't have that much time.

They'll come for me, he knows. *For confirmation of the kill.*

He lays there, a part of him hoping that the enemy finds him. That they finish the job. He gazes upward at the massive hole the Behemoth had ripped in the ceiling above, seeing the stars winking through a thin haze of smoke above the chamber. A deep, rumbling sound echoes through the night air, followed by a distant *boom, boom.*

The Behemoth has moved on.

Ampir closes his eyes, picturing Vera smiling at him. Remembers their last kiss.

Remember your promise.

55

He grunts, struggling to roll onto his belly. Lifting himself onto his hands and knees, he heaves upward, his armor threatening to pull him back onto the ground. He rises to his feet slowly, then turns to a dark corner of the chamber. There is a mound of rubble there, large enough for him to hide behind; he walks toward it, knowing that he needs time. Time to generate magic, to fill at least a few of his armor's runes.

Step-by-step he moves forward, his metallic boots *clunking* on the stone floor.

He senses a faint vibration in his skull, and glances behind him. Something is descending slowly through the air above the gaping hole in the ceiling. A shadowy silhouette against the starry night...a Weaver.

Shit!

Ampir tries to move faster, but his boots *clunk* loudly on the floor, the sound echoing through the chamber. He slows his pace, angling toward a shadow thrown by the remaining ceiling above. He stops there, turning around to face the Weaver.

The Weaver drops through the hole in the ceiling, stopping a few feet above the rubble-strewn floor. Its back is to Ampir, its black cloak flowing in the slight breeze.

Ampir reaches into his mind's eye, sensing magic blossoming in the center, then flowing in all directions to the bones of his skull. He waits, knowing that the more saturated his bones are with magic, the easier it will be for him to weave.

The Weaver turns slowly in place, hovering above the floor, his face coming into view. His eyes scan the ruins, stopping at the pit in the floor. Then he moves toward the pit, stopping before it. He pauses for a moment, then grabs the edges of his black hood, pulling it back to reveal a bald head. The Weaver's skin is as black as night, tattoos crawling up the temples. Long, raised scars run like bony fingers up the sides of his head. Ampir recognizes him instantly.

Torum.

The dark Weaver stares down at the pit, his black eyes glittering in the starlight. Then he turns away, scanning the ruins. Searching.

He knew we were here, Ampir realizes. Torum had intercepted them just outside of the evacuation tunnels, before they'd taken the tunnels to this chamber. Despite working for the enemy, the dark Weaver had let them go. *The Empire is our enemy, not you*, he'd said.

Torum turns in a slow circle, peering into the darkness. His eyes pass over Ampir, not seeing him in the shadows.

He was the only one who knew where we were.

Ampir feels a flash of rage, knowing that the Weaver had betrayed them, giving away their position so that the Behemoth could find them.

The Weaver continues to turn in a slow circle, his back to Ampir again. Ampir dips into the stream of magic in his mind's eye, pulling a strand out. It comes easier than before; he sends it to a few of runes on his right gauntlet. Then he grabs another strand, sending it to runes on his chest. Slowly, methodically, he fills a few other runes with tiny amounts of magic, just enough for one burst.

Torum stops his circling, and starts moving in Ampir's direction. He searches through the rubble, lifting stones with his magic, scanning the ground carefully.

Ampir steps out of the shadows.

"Looking for something?" he asks.

Torum spins around, his black eyes locking on Ampir. Multi-layered gravity shields appear around the dark Weaver, glowing blue in the darkness. Torum stares at Ampir silently, his expression unreadable.

"We meet again," Ampir states. Torum inclines his head slightly.

"Indeed."

"What a coincidence," Ampir murmurs.

Torum says nothing for a long moment. Then he gestures at the pit.

"My condolences."

"I'll be sure to say the same to your family when I visit them," Ampir replies coolly. Torum's jawline ripples, the gravity shields surrounding him glowing brighter. He gestures at the ruins around them.

"I would say that this is well deserved, don't you think?" he opines. "You certainly thought so the last time we met."

"You could have let us go," Ampir retorts. Torum raises an eyebrow.

"Really? After everything you did?"

"I *spared* your people," Ampir growls. "Or did you forget?"

"I remember," Torum shoots back. "I *remember* you giving the Empire the keys to our kingdom. And I remember what they did to it."

Ampir stares at Torum, clenching and unclenching his fists. He reaches into his mind's eye, filling more runes with bits of magic.

"How was I supposed to know?" he says at last. Torum sneers.

"Ah, the age-old defense," he retorts. "You didn't know," he concedes. "And what did you do once you *did* know?"

"I spent *years* on the Council trying..."

"And yet here we are," Torum interrupts, gesturing at the ruined chamber. "Sabin did what you would not." He points one finger at Ampir. "You're the only one who could have stopped this," he continues. "You had the power to force the Empire to free us."

"By becoming a dictator," Ampir retorts.

"You would have replaced one with another," Torum shoots back. "At least Sabin had the courage to stand up to your tyrant."

"Sabin was a fool," Ampir growls.

"And you're the bigger fool," Torum retorts. "You're the traitor who broke him out of prison."

Ampir says nothing. *Can* say nothing. Torum smirks.

"You see?" he states. "You did this to yourself."

"What about the millions of people that didn't do anything wrong?" Ampir presses. "Why do they have to die?"

"Those people *are* the Empire," Torum answers. "The *idea* of the Empire lives within them. The Empire deserves to die," he adds. "And so do you."

Ampir stares at Torum silently, then at the pit nearby. He clenches his fists, *pulling* magic into his mind's eye, weaving rapidly.

"You're right," he replies. "But my wife didn't."

He *shoves* the pattern outward, leaping toward Torum at the same time, swinging one armored fist at the man's head. Torum's shields vanish, leaving him completely exposed.

A shockwave bursts outward from Torum, shoving Ampir backward violently, his fist missing Torum's head by inches. At the same time, a jagged bolt of electricity shoots outward from Torum, slamming into Ampir's chest. His armor takes the brunt of the attack, his skin tingling, his hair rising on end.

Ampir stumbles backward, catching his balance and raising his right hand toward Torum. A ray of blinding white light shoots outward at the dark Weaver...

...and scatters harmlessly as gravity shields reappear around him.

"Well done," Torum states, nodding his head slightly. "You-"

Something *smashes* into Ampir's right side – a huge slab of stone hurtling through the air – throwing him to the left. He feels his armor react, taking the brunt of the hit, the slab shattering. He grunts, barely managing to keep his footing...just as another slab slams into his *left* side.

Pain lances through his left shoulder, the armor there crumpling under the impact.

Ampir is thrown violently to the side, landing on his back. His injured shoulder hits the unforgiving stone floor, another burst of pain shooting down his left arm. He bites back a scream, clutching his shattered shoulder, feeling a wave of nausea threaten to overwhelm him.

"You're weakened," Torum observes, staring down at Ampir through his layered gravity shields. "How unfortunate."

A force lifts Ampir off of the ground, throwing him backward through the air. He feels his back slam into the stone wall behind him, the rapidly draining runes on his armor barely absorbing the impact. He cries out, falling onto his belly, his shoulder in agony.

"You deserve a slow death," Torum states, levitating motionlessly a few feet above the chamber floor. "But you're too dangerous for that, aren't you?"

Ampir grits his teeth, pushing himself up onto his knees. He can *feel* the power radiating from Torum; the man was possessed of a near-infinite supply of magic, though at great sacrifice. With Ampir's magic rapidly running out, there is no way he'll be able to stand against Torum for long.

A half-dozen huge chunks of rubble rise up all around Torum, hurtling toward Ampir.

Ampir *pulls* at the magic in his skull, streaming it to runes in his armor. He feels his armor become weightless, and leaps upward and forward just as the chunks of rubble reach him, barely clearing them in time. He sails high above the chamber floor toward Torum, streaming more magic to his right gauntlet. He cocks his fist back, aiming right for the Weaver.

Another shockwave bursts outward from Torum, hurtling Ampir backward through the air. He slams into the wall, bouncing off of it and falling onto his side on the unforgiving floor. He hears a *crack*, pain lancing through the side of his chest. He rolls onto his back, gasping for air. Each breath sends stabbing pain through his left side.

Torum levitates toward him, his multilayered gravity shields glowing bright blue against the darkness.

"You *were* too dangerous," he corrects, eyeing Ampir almost pityingly. "Without your armor, you're nothing."

Ampir grunts, steeling himself against the pain, forcing himself to take deep, even breaths.

"The Resistance wants your armor," Torum continues. "They lust for your power." He shakes his head. "Men with too much power caused all of this," he continues, gesturing at the chamber. "I will relish destroying it."

Ampir hears a *crack* from above, and looks up. A huge chunk of what remains of the shattered ceiling breaks off...falling right toward him.

"Goodbye, old friend," Torum mutters.

Ampir tries to get up, but his left shoulder spasms, dropping him back onto the ground. He cries out, clutching his shoulder, watching helplessly as the massive stone slab plummets toward him.

Time slows.

He rests his head on the cold stone, then spots a glittering red object on the floor a few feet away. A fragment of the red gemstone that had been embedded in the center of the dais.

He stares at the fragment, then at Torum.

Ampir closes his eyes, draining what little magic remains in his armor's runes and focusing that power in his mind's eye. He pulls several strands at once, weaving them simultaneously into a complex knot in the center of his mind. An old pattern, one he'd learned long ago.

He thrusts the pattern outward, right at Torum.

* * *

Kyle woke up to a knock on his bedroom door, sitting up in bed groggily. He rubbed his eyes, taking a moment to remember that he had to get up earlier than usual this morning for his class with his new Runic instructor, Master Banar.

Another knock came at the door, and Kyle groaned, rolling out of bed, walking up to it and cracking it open. Apparently, no one had invented alarm clocks yet in this world. A man's head poked through the door – it was Greg, Jenkin's assistant butler. Jenkins had been promoted after Kalibar's coronation, and Greg had been promoted to Jenkin's assistant. Greg was nice enough, but more aloof than Jenkins, if such a thing were possible.

"Time for class," Greg said, opening the door wider.

Kyle nodded, yawning again. He'd had trouble sleeping the night before, and not just because of the Ampir-dream. He'd dreaded the thought that he'd start learning to be a Runic, then realize that he wasn't good at that either. It would be like being on Earth all over again. Even though he'd gotten decent grades in school, he'd never been a straight "A" student, or the best at any particular sport. He wasn't the funniest kid, or the strongest, or the fastest. He'd always been, well, mediocre. When Kalibar had first told him of his magical gifts, Kyle had believed that – for the first time – *he* would get a chance to be the best at something. Master Owens had thrown a cold, cruel dose of reality on that dream.

He changed quickly into the clothes Greg had brought him...a pair of white pants and a white shirt, a poignant reminder of his recent career change. He went to the bathroom, noting that the burned blanket he'd stashed in the bathtub had been removed...replaced by a polite-looking note from Jenkins. Kyle couldn't read it, of course, which was probably for the best.

Kyle washed up, then hurried out of his bedroom, following the butler into the main room of Kalibar's retirement suite. Kalibar slept one floor above, in the Grand Weaver suite on the top floor of the Tower, and Darius had moved into a guest room within that suite after Kalibar's near-assassination yesterday. Kyle thought about waking Ariana, who was still sleeping in her bedroom next to his, but decided against it. Her classes didn't start for another hour or so. He couldn't help but feel a little jealous of her recent promotion.

Kyle glanced down at his ring, remembering that he was supposed to leave it in his magic safe. He did so, closing the safe afterward. Only Kalibar would be able to open it, and Kalibar would hand the ring back to Kyle later in the day, as had become their routine.

Greg led Kyle out of the suite and into the hallway, then down the riser to the lobby. Only two risers had been allowed to remain functioning, at least to reach the top three floors, and they were guarded twenty-four hours a day by several stern-looking Battle-Weavers. Greg led Kyle past them, walking through the silent lobby and out into the crisp early-morning air. Kyle followed Greg down one of the cobblestone pathways, until the Tower of the Secula Magna was far behind. The sun started to peek over the trees in the distance, sending rays of brilliant color across the sky. In the distance, Kyle spotted a tall, thin man in a white cloak sitting in mid-air – on nothing at all – reading a book by a tall tree.

"Your student, Master Banar," Greg stated with a short bow, gesturing for Kyle to continue walking toward the white-cloaked man. Master Banar looked up from his book, extending his legs and straightening his back, after which he slowly floated to the ground until he was standing on it. He closed his book, depositing it into one of the deep pockets in his cloak, then walked up to Kyle, extending a hand.

"Kyle!" the man greeted warmly. "A pleasure to finally meet you...I'm Master Banar," he added. "But please, call me Banar." Master Banar was a surprisingly young man, with short, curly black hair and gray eyes. He was smooth-shaven, with a broad, easy smile. He was almost disturbingly thin, with skin so pale it was almost translucent. Kyle was relieved; he'd been expecting an old, crotchety teacher like Jax.

"Yes sir," Kyle greeted back, bowing just as Jenkins had.

"I've heard a lot about you, Kyle," Banar stated. He looked Kyle up and down, then nodded approvingly. "I have to say I'm plenty impressed," he continued. "You've got a lot of potential."

"Maybe," Kyle mumbled, feeling uneasy. People kept doing that...telling him he should have a ton of talent, only to realize that he wasn't all he was cracked up to be. He decided he would be brutally honest with Banar. "I failed out of Weaver school," he admitted, blushing with shame.

"Nonsense!" Master Banar retorted. "You did just fine at Weaving, Kyle," he added. "In fact, Master Owens was sorry to lose you."

"But..."

"Being better off as a Runic doesn't mean you failed *anything*," Master Banar interjected. "It just means we didn't find the best fit for you the first time."

"But I haven't even *tried* being a Runic yet," Kyle countered, his frustration mounting. They'd thought he'd make a great Weaver, and they had been wrong about that, so how could anyone possibly know whether or not he'd make a good Runic?

"Fair enough," Banar conceded. "You're probably sick of people expecting you to be the next great thing, huh?" Kyle nodded silently. "All right, then how about we make a deal...I'll do my best to teach you, and you'll do your best to learn, and I'll be honest with you about how you're doing." Kyle smiled.

"Deal," he agreed, extending his hand. Banar shook it, then clapped Kyle on the shoulder.

"Okay, first thing's first," he began. "I know what you're thinking, and it's not true. Runics aren't inferior to Weavers. Period. And I can prove it."

"I didn't say..." Kyle began, but Banar waved him off.

"You don't need to," he countered. "Every kid thinks so, and most adults, too. Weavers are awesome, Runics are boring. It's all bull," he explained. "First, name one thing a Weaver did two thousand years ago."

Kyle frowned.

"Um," he began, then stopped. "I have no idea," he admitted. Master Banar grinned.

"Me neither," he agreed. "But I can think of a thousand things Runics did. They built the first Tower, all of the technology that people used, the armor and weapons for the military, the armor you won at the awards ceremony two weeks ago..."

"You were there?" Kyle asked.

"Sure was," Banar replied. "But seriously, think of what Runics have done...even in the last two hundred years. We rebuilt the Tower, defended it with a magical gate, built an entire city filled with magical technology, outfitted everyone with jumpsuits and levitating carriages, built a bridge across a massive river – with no physical structural supports, mind you – and created a military so advanced that no enemy has been able to withstand our might. And Weavers...well, they made

63

a few craters in the ground," he added dismissively. Kyle couldn't help but grin.

"Well, when you put it *that* way," he conceded.

"I'm just saying," Banar said with a wink. "Weavers are cool...they really are, there's no doubt about it. It feels good to make things go boom. And let's be honest, Runic school *does* tend to attract the...less sociable, to put it kindly. But for a hard-working, creative, motivated student, learning to make runic technology can be an amazing, rewarding experience."

"I see," Kyle stated, not quite sure how else to respond. Master Banar smiled.

"I've got something for you," he stated, reaching down into a large bag at his feet. He pulled out a pair of black boots, handing them to Kyle. "Your gravity boots, courtesy of Grand Weaver Kalibar."

Kyle looked down at the two boots; they went up all the way past the ankles, and had strips of silver metal going down the sides, with tiny runes etched into the surface. A few gems were embedded into the leather. They were identical to the gravity boots that Kalibar had worn a week ago, after their escape from the Arena.

"Thanks," Kyle replied. "Are they like feathergrass?"

"No, they're *much* better," Banar corrected. "Put them on," he insisted. Kyle did so; the boots were exceedingly comfortable, and a perfect fit.

"Now, push a stream of magic into the blue crystal on the top of each boot," Banar commanded. Kyle did so, immediately sending a stream to each boot. The crystals began to glow faintly. "That activates the boots," Master Banar explained. "Now, send a third stream to the orange crystal on the left side of your left boot." Kyle complied, activating the gem. He lurched upward a foot, crying out in surprise, and immediately dropped both magic streams. Instead of falling onto his butt like he'd expected, he floated gently downward. Master Banar chuckled.

"Notice how slowly you fell," he stated. "Your boots will never allow you to fall quickly, as long as they still have magic stored in them," he explained. "The center crystals store and provide the magic power for the rest of the boot. They're all connected inside."

"Then why do I have to send magic to the side-crystal?"

"Those side crystals control the gravity fields generated by your boots," Master Banar answered. "Putting magic into the left boot strengthens the up-going gravity field, while the right boot strengthens the down-going field. The left boot goes up, the right goes back down."

"Oh," Kyle mumbled. He still didn't get it.

"It's complicated," Master Banar admitted. "I'll explain how it really works in mind-numbing detail later, believe me. But for now, just trust me. Now put more magic into that left crystal."

Kyle did so, sending a burst of magic to it. He felt himself lurch upward, flying well above Master Banar's head. He cried out, swinging his arms out to the sides to catch his balance...and found that he didn't need to. He was standing perfectly upright in the air, without even a smidgen of wobbling. Having once again halted his magic stream, he floated slowly back to the ground.

"Whoa there," Master Banar exclaimed. "I forgot who I was talking to! Here, put a slow, tiny stream of magic into the left boot. *Tiny*," he insisted. Kyle obeyed, sending a much smaller stream of magic to his boot. He began to float upward slowly, until he was about a foot off of the ground. He stopped streaming to the side-crystal, his ascent slowing, then stopping. He remained where he was, levitating in mid-air, feeling a thrill run through him. He was flying!

"Sorry about that," Banar apologized. "I'm not used to dealing with a powerhouse like you. So anyway, you get the idea. Notice how you're only streaming magic to the center crystal on each boot now, and you're not falling. If you stop putting magic into a side crystal, the boots will keep you at whatever elevation you're at...as long as you maintain the stream to the center crystal."

"I think I got it," Kyle said. Activate the boots by constantly streaming magic to the main crystals, and go up and down by sending magic to the side crystals. It was simple...in theory, at least.

"Good," Banar replied. "You look like you could use a break."

"Already?" Kyle asked. He was eager to get a handle on learning how to fly.

"I don't want to overload you with information," Banar explained. "Learning is best done in small doses."

"Okay."

"Here, why don't we sit down for a bit," Banar suggested, sitting cross-legged on the grass. Kyle joined him, stopping his magic stream to his boots and sitting down himself. He felt cool moisture soak through his pants, the grass still wet with the morning's dew. "So, Kyle...tell me, where do you come from?"

Kyle hesitated. He couldn't very well tell him the truth – that he was from another planet. But it wouldn't hurt to tell Banar *part* of the truth.

"Earth," he answered at last. He smiled at Banar's puzzled expression. "It's pretty far away," he admitted.

"It must be," Banar agreed. "I've got a fair knowledge of the world, and I've never heard of it." He cocked his head at Kyle then. "I don't mean to pry...and please feel free to refuse to answer this question...but I'm curious. How did you meet Grand Weaver Kalibar?"

"He uh, took me in after I got hurt," Kyle answered. Which was true; Kalibar had saved Kyle after he'd been nearly killed by a vicious beast, a wolf-like creature called an Ulfar.

"How did you get hurt?"

"I was lost in the woods," Kyle explained. "I was attacked by an Ulfar, and barely escaped. I passed out trying to find help, and when I woke up, I was in Kalibar's house."

"I see," Banar replied. "You're lucky to have Kalibar as a father," he added. "He's a good man. Not many politicians would take in an orphan."

"An orphan?"

"Well yes," Banar replied. "I assume that your parents are...no longer with us."

"Oh," Kyle replied, not quite sure what to say. On the one hand, he didn't want to give anyone the impression that his real parents were dead. But he couldn't think up of any other explanation for why they weren't around, so he shrugged, lowering his gaze. "Yeah," he mumbled.

"I'm sorry," Master Banar apologized. "I didn't mean to upset you."

"It's okay," Kyle replied. But it wasn't; he felt terribly homesick all of a sudden. Kalibar was a good surrogate father, and the closest friend that Kyle had ever had, but he couldn't replace his real dad.

"You've gone through a lot for someone your age," Banar observed. "Do you have anyone to talk to about it?"

"I talk to Kalibar, sometimes," Kyle answered. "When I can," he added. "He's pretty busy now."

"That he is," Banar agreed. "Well, I know we've just met, but if you ever need someone to talk to, I'm here."

"Thanks," Kyle replied, smiling at his new teacher. Banar seemed sincere, and Kyle realized that it *would* be good to talk to someone. But how much could he really say without telling the whole truth? Only Kalibar, Darius, Ariana, and Erasmus knew that he was from another planet. And Kalibar had made it quite clear that Kyle was to tell no one else.

"Come on," Banar stated suddenly, rising up to his feet and offering Kyle his hand. Kyle grabbed it, and Banar hauled him to his feet. "It's about time I taught you how to *really* fly!"

* * *

Master Banar levitated a few feet off of the lawn of the Secula Magna, looking down at Kyle, who was still standing safely on the ground. The sun peeked over the horizon, sending a splash of red and purple light across the feathered clouds far above, making the dew-tipped grass glitter like tiny diamonds.

"Okay," Banar stated, folding his arms in front of his chest. "Stream magic to the blue center crystals in each boot to turn them on." Kyle did so, and saw each crystal glow a slightly brighter blue. "Now," Banar continued, "...send magic to the 'up' crystal."

Kyle paused, concentrating on creating a third magic stream while maintaining the first two. He did so successfully, feeling himself rising up off of the grass. He stopped the third magic stream, and levitated in mid-air just like Master Banar.

"Excellent," his teacher stated. "Now, look down at your right boot...see that orange crystal on the right side of your right boot?" Kyle glanced downward, spotting it instantly. It was identical to the one on his left boot.

"That's the 'down' crystal, right?" Kyle guessed. Banar nodded.

67

"Send a little magic to it," he instructed. Kyle did so, and immediately felt himself dropping downward, until his feet were once again on the ground.

"Perfect," Banar stated. "So left goes up, right goes down. Got it?"

"Got it."

"Okay, let's show you how to move forward," Banar said. "See that crystal, the red one at the tip of your boot, at the toes? You only have it on your left boot."

Kyle nodded, spotting the small red crystal.

"Send some magic to your left boot again, to clear the ground," Master Banar ordered. "Then send a *small* amount of magic to the toe-crystal." Kyle complied, levitating off of the ground a few inches, then sending a magic stream to the toe-crystal. He began to move forward through the air. Once again, he brought his arms out to catch his balance...but there was no need. His entire body felt stabilized somehow.

"No need to balance yourself," Master Banar explained. "The boots create a weak cylindrical gravity field along the axis of your body, surrounding your torso. It sucks inward toward the center of your body...that prevents you from tipping over."

"Wow," Kyle breathed. He stopped the magic stream to the crystal, and he slowly came to a stop in mid-air. Master Banar grinned.

"Wow is right," he agreed. "The crystal on the heel of your right boot goes backward. Got it?"

"Yeah, I think so," Kyle replied.

"Good!" Master Banar exclaimed. "Now, let's have some fun. Send a stream to your toe-crystal, then slowly increase the intensity, until you get the speed you want. Then just hold the stream at that level, and you're good to go."

Kyle tried it, and soon he was accelerating forward at a brisk pace, as fast as he could run. At first he was apprehensive, afraid he'd fall, or run into something. He'd felt the same way the first few times he'd gone snowboarding with his uncles, until he'd gotten used to it. At least with gravity boots he didn't have to fall down to stop!

Master Banar sped alongside Kyle, and it wasn't long at all before they'd reached the Tower. Banar grabbed Kyle's arm, and swerved to the side somehow, pulling Kyle around the Tower, staying clear of the road where students were beginning to travel from their dormitories

68

to the Tower itself for their lessons. They passed by the Tower, levitating over the well-manicured lawn.

Eventually Master Banar slowed down, pulling Kyle backward with him. Kyle fumbled, then stopped the magic stream to his toe-crystal. He decelerated slowly, until they had come to a stop above the grass, over a mile from the Tower. Master Banar grinned at him, his gray eyes twinkling merrily.

"Fun, eh?" he said. Kyle nodded, matching his new teacher's smile. It had been a *lot* of fun, actually...once he'd gotten over his fear. Banar pointed at Kyle's feet, at a yellow crystal on the inner side of each ankle. "These crystals move you side-to-side," he explained. "It's counter-intuitive...the left crystal moves you right, and vice-versa. Once you get used to it, it's not so bad." He demonstrated then, strafing left and right while levitating above the ground. Kyle tried it, and soon he too was sliding from side-to-side. Banar was right...it did take a bit to get used to.

"Okay," Master Banar declared, deactivating his own gravity boots, sinking gently to the grass below. Kyle did the same. "Now that you've had a taste of what Runics can build, it's time I showed you how we do it!"

Chapter 6

Kalibar squeezed his lids shut, then opened them again, squinting against the dazzling white light forming a miniature corona around the shadowy face that stared down at him from above. He groaned, bringing his hand up to shield his eyes from the assault, tears welling up and dribbling down his cheeks. He closed his lids again, then opened them, seeing two blue eyes staring down at him.

"Kalibar?" a voice called out.

Kalibar groaned again, rolling onto his side on the bed, squeezing his eyes shut and covering them with his hands. Even the slightest light caused a deep, aching pain to shoot through his eye sockets.

"Kalibar," the voice called again.

Something cold and metallic grasped his bare arm, and Kalibar flinched, pulling back from that grip. Kalibar curled up into the fetal position, pulling his bedsheets over his face. The pain gradually lessened, and he forced himself to slow his breathing, to uncurl his body, extending his feet out in front of him on the bed. He clutched the bedsheets to his face, his tears soaking into the thin fabric.

"Kalibar, what's wrong?"

Slowly, Kalibar brought the sheets down from his face, keeping his lids shut. His eyes still hurt, but now the pain was tolerable. He took a deep breath in, then let it out slowly.

Then he opened his eyes.

A pair of blue eyes stared back at him, surrounded by smooth, tanned flesh. Short brown hair...a glimmer of gold below the neck.

"Darius?" Kalibar blurted, his voice filled with disbelief.

"Kalibar!" Darius exclaimed, his head jerking backward, his metal-gauntleted hand releasing its grip from Kalibar's arm. The bodyguard backpedaled, his jaw dropping. "Your eyes!"

Kalibar blinked, then slowly sat up in his bed, bringing his hands up in front of his face. He stared at his fingers, at the innumerable wrinkles carved into their surfaces, the familiar swirls of his finger-prints plain to see. He turned his hands over, his eyes devouring the pearly surface of his fingernails, the shimmering metallic rings encircling his fingers.

A great sob threatened to burst out of him.

"Go!" Kalibar shouted, feeling the tidal wave of emotion coming, refusing to allow anyone – especially Darius – to see him when it arrived. "Go!" he repeated, waving Darius away with one hand. Darius hesitated, then hurried out of the room, shutting the door behind him.

And then, Kalibar wept.

* * *

Kalibar stared at the surface of the table, marveling at the honey-brown swirl of its grain, the mirror-like quality of its polished finish. He couldn't get over it, this feast of texture and color. Everything he laid his eyes on was beautiful, filled with infinite detail. Everything was perfect.

Just perfect.

He glanced up from the table at last, knowing that Darius, who was seated opposite him, was still staring at him, waiting for him to say something...anything. But Kalibar found it impossible to concentrate, distracted by everything around him. He thought back to the moments after Darius had left the room, when he'd wept uncontrollably, over-whelmed by the miraculous return of his vision. Eventually he'd re-gained his composure, emerging from his room. He'd seen Darius sit-ting at the small round table at one corner of his suite, and had sat down opposite the silent bodyguard, saying nothing at all. How long they'd sat there in silence, he didn't know.

Thank god it had been Darius, and not someone else, Kalibar thought. He'd never met another man more comfortable with spending his days saying nothing at all, merely patiently observing while everyone else chattered away. A rare skill, to hold one's tongue.

How Kalibar appreciated that silence now!

Minutes passed, and Kalibar finally sighed, his hunger for the sights around him sated for the moment. He turned his gaze to Darius, who was still staring at him.

"This isn't a dream," Kalibar observed. It wasn't a question, merely a statement of fact. Darius smirked.

"Not unless I'm the man of your dreams," he quipped. Kalibar chuckled, then glanced down at his hands for the umpteenth time, mesmerized by the horizontal wrinkles at each knuckle, and the three veins coursing over them. How had he lived so many decades without ever having noticed that?

"What happened?" Darius asked. Kalibar shrugged.

"I have no idea," he admitted. He paused for a moment, then burst into laughter, his shoulders heaving up and down.

"What?" Darius pressed. Kalibar kept laughing, tears streaming down his cheeks, then finally shook his head.

"I thought I was going to be murdered," he answered, wiping his eyes with his sleeve. "Here I was, lying in my bed, paralyzed...literally paralyzed! And all I could do was wait for death. For some assassin to come out of the shadows and end it all. And you know what went through my head at that very moment?"

"Nope."

"Whether or not I'd put clean underwear on!" Kalibar replied. "Here I am, inches from death, and I'm worried about my corpse being found with dirty underwear. Don't laugh!" he protested as Darius's shoulders heaved up and down, a rare grin on the bodyguard's face.

"Seriously?" Darius remarked.

"Damn right I'm serious!" Kalibar retorted. "How could I possibly make that up? Why would I?" Darius chuckled, shaking his head.

"It all happened so fast," Kalibar continued, rubbing his hands together. "One minute, I was lying down to go to sleep, consumed by my thoughts...then I think I may have started to drift off. I heard a noise..." he paused, then nodded. "Yes, and it woke me up. Then I heard the door to my suite close, and then footsteps. I couldn't move, I was paralyzed. Then something...some*one*...sat on the bed, and I felt a hand over my face. Then..." he trailed off, staring past Darius, remembering that feeling.

The rapture.

Kalibar shook his head, snapping himself out of his reverie. He glanced up at Darius, realizing that the bodyguard was still staring at him.

"Then I got my eyes back," he continued. "I heard footsteps leave, then I laid there for a while, until my muscles came back to life. The next thing I remember, I was opening my eyes, and saw you." Then he frowned. "Wait, what time is it?"

"Sunrise," the bodyguard answered. Kalibar's eyes widened.

"I just went to sleep a few minutes ago!" he objected. Then he shook his head. "I must have fallen asleep at some point." Then he frowned. "The question is, how did this thing get past my wards?"

"The assassin did," Darius pointed out.

"Yes, true," Kalibar admitted. "It..." he began, then stopped. He struggled to find the right words, then gave up. "He...I think it was a he, I mean he spoke to me, in my mind...he was the most unbelievably powerful being I have ever sensed. More powerful than anything I could have even *imagined* sensing. These wards...you're right. They would have been nothing to him." He glanced at Darius then. "Did you see anything?" he asked. Darius shook his head.

"I heard you yell," the bodyguard replied. "Got up, saw your door was open. Figured something was wrong, so I ran in, hoping one of Erasmus's wards wouldn't cook me before I got to you."

"They're all deactivated," Kalibar stated. And it was true; all of the wards in Kalibar's bedroom had been completely depleted of magic. Not a single one was still active. "So you didn't see anyone come or go?" he pressed. Darius shrugged.

"Sorry," he replied. Kalibar sighed, but was unable to keep a smile from his face for very long.

"Ah, what does it matter?" he decided. "Whoever it was sure didn't want to kill me...and if they *had* wanted to, there wouldn't have been a damn thing anyone could have done to stop him. I can at least assume he's on our side."

"You don't think it could have been Xanos?" Darius asked. Kalibar shook his head.

"Unlikely," he opined. "He said that I'd wanted to meet him...that I'd *said* that I'd wanted to meet him, and that now I had. I don't recall ever having said I wanted to meet Xanos," he added with a wry grin. "But then again, I don't remember who I might have said that about."

"Hmm," Darius mumbled. The bodyguard pushed himself back from the table then, standing up. He lent a hand to Kalibar, who waved the bodyguard away.

"I hardly need that anymore," he stated, standing up from his chair with one smooth motion. An hour ago, that movement would have taken three times as long...and would have brought on a veritable symphony of aches and pains. "I think the rest of me healed too," he added, shaking his head. "It's as if everything I suffered as a result of being a prisoner of the Dead Man...every injury I was dealt, every insult...has been erased. Hell, I feel better than I did *before* I left my home in Bellingham."

Kalibar turned away from Darius, glancing around his suite, when he froze suddenly.

"What?" Darius asked. Kalibar said nothing, staring across the room. There was something different about it, and until now, he hadn't figured out what it was.

Everything was glowing.

The runes marking the marble columns, the suits of armor hanging on the walls...even the rings on Kalibar's fingers. They were all glowing a pale blue. Faintly, almost imperceptibly, but definitely glowing. He could even see a faint blue haze coming from himself. He turned to Darius, and saw no blue coming from the bodyguard. He frowned, then wove magic in his mind, throwing out a small gravity field into the center of the room. He saw the blue haze around himself ripple, a faint blue line shooting outward right where he'd sent the field. A shimmering blue sphere of light-bending gravitational force appeared in the middle of the room.

"My god," he whispered.

"What?" the bodyguard repeated. Kalibar turned to glance at Darius silently. Then he turned back to the gravity field.

"I can *see* magic!"

"So?" Darius grumbled. Kalibar shook his head, realizing that the bodyguard would have no idea how magic should be normally be sensed.

"We Weavers *feel* magic," Kalibar explained. "Like a vibration. I can *see* magic now, with my eyes...it's kind of like being able to see sound." He stared at the rings on his fingers again, taking a closer look. He could see the tiny runes carved into their surfaces, the magic storage crystals behind each set of runes glowing ever-so-faintly. Even though the crystals were covered by the metal of the rings' bands, he could still see the magic radiating from them...meaning he could see magic *through* solid surfaces. He glanced upward, scanning the walls of his room. He couldn't, however, see any magic coming from behind the walls; that must mean that magic couldn't penetrate easily through solid materials, if they were thick enough. An observation that was certainly consistent with his experience.

Kalibar shook himself from his near-trance, glancing at Darius. He had a sudden idea. "Can you keep this between you and me?" Kalibar requested. Darius nodded.

"My lips are sealed."

"They usually are," Kalibar replied. Then he nodded to himself. "If I keep my sight a secret — at least for now — it might give us an advantage when it comes to the Council. And more importantly, if Xanos has spies within the Tower, it might make them careless around me."

"You planning on seeing through your eyepatches?" Darius asked. Kalibar frowned.

"I suppose we'll have to let Erasmus in on our secret," he admitted. "He'll be able to make me some one-way mirror eyepatches. Then I'll be able to see how my opponents are reacting to me, especially if I get their guard down by talking to them in private." He nodded then. "In politics, knowing what your opponents *really* think is critical information. Perhaps I can make more use of this gift than was intended."

Darius shrugged, clearly uninterested in politics.

"I'm going to check up on Kyle," he stated. Kalibar nodded.

"Good idea," he replied. He watched his bodyguard leave, then stared at a suit of ceremonial armor hanging on one wall, almost hypnotized by the sparkling array of blue lights emanating from the magical armor's surface. It was going to take a while for him to get used to this.

Kalibar sighed, looking about his room, not quite sure what to do with himself. He wanted desperately to wake Erasmus up, to describe to his best friend what had happened. The Grand Runic would be as fascinated as Kalibar. Darius had been predictably underwhelmed by the morning's events, no doubt because Darius appeared underwhelmed by just about everything...but also because the bodyguard, unable to sense or use magic, had no concept of how incredible Kalibar's experience had been. Kalibar longed to share his experience with someone who could fully appreciate it.

Suddenly, there was a loud, high-pitched wail sounding throughout the room. Kalibar turned almost immediately to the front door of his suite. The sound, he knew, was the emergency alarm. It had to have been activated by Erasmus, one of the Council members, or the elite guard...and only in the event of a catastrophe. He sprinted to the front door, which was always translucent from the inside, and saw Erasmus appear on the other side of it. The Grand Runic was dressed in a simple robe; judging by his appearance, he'd clearly just woken up. Kalibar activated a crystal embedded in the side of the door, and saw Erasmus's eyes focus on Kalibar as the door became translucent from the outside.

"Kalibar," the Grand Runic yelled, banging his fist on the door. He drew back sharply as Kalibar's face became visible. "What the...!"

* * *

Erasmus and Kalibar sat on a U-shaped white couch, resting their elbows on the circular glass table in the middle.

"I don't believe it," Erasmus was saying, staring into Kalibar's eyes, appearing mesmerized by them. Kalibar shrugged.

"And yet I have eyes, and I can see," he replied. Erasmus shook his head.

"God, what I wouldn't give to have met this fellow," he breathed. "If what you're saying is true..."

76

"It's true, trust me," Kalibar insisted. "This...being, he was indescribably powerful. You can't imagine it, the power he radiated...it was absolutely amazing."

"So who the hell is this guy?" Erasmus asked. "And why did he decide to stroll into your room and give you your eyes back?"

"He only said two things, if you can call it speaking," Kalibar answered. "'You wanted to meet me,' and 'now you have.'"

"So who did you want to meet?" Erasmus pressed. "With a guy that powerful, the list of candidates is pretty damn short."

"That's what I've been asking myself all morning," Kalibar admitted. "There's no one alive that I want to meet that I already haven't...and like you said, no one I know could be that powerful. It doesn't make any sense."

"It sure doesn't," Erasmus agreed. "Anyway, we have more pressing matters to attend to right now."

"Yes, about that," Kalibar said. Erasmus had been so surprised to see Kalibar's new eyes that he'd almost forgotten about the emergency that had brought them together in the first place. "So you're saying that someone freed some of the criminals from Stridon Penitentiary?" The prison included the highest-security jail cells in the Empire, specializing in the detainment of criminals who happened to be powerful Weavers and Runics.

"That's right," Erasmus replied gravely. "No one realized it until the morning shift arrived, and found all of the night guards on the floor, dead. Not a mark on any of them, either. The bars to each cell had been ripped from the walls, the magic containment fields destroyed. At least eighty of the prisoners are missing...we can only assume they escaped somehow."

"I still don't get it," Kalibar stated. "How could any of the prisoners have escaped...in broad daylight...without anyone noticing?" It was a good point; all of the prisoners had been wearing blue and orange prison jumpsuits, and the prison's only entrance led out into a busy street. Yet there had been no eyewitness reports of a breakout.

"We *did* hear from a man," Erasmus replied, "...a passer-by on his way to work at the time, that the two guards at the entrance had let an old man into the prison. A beggar, by the eyewitness's description."

"A beggar? Why would they let a beggar into Stridon Penitentiary?" Kalibar exclaimed. "That doesn't make any sense." The prison was on constant lock-down, with no visitors allowed. Only officials with the proper clearance were admitted into the prison, and even then only with advance notice. "Do we have a description of the beggar?" Kalibar pressed. Erasmus nodded.

"In process," he answered. "The eyewitness is working with our sketch-artists to render a likeness. It should be completed within the hour."

"Good," Kalibar replied. "We'll notify the city guard to copy and distribute it once it's finished. I want the public to know what this man looks like...we need to bring him in for questioning."

"There's something else."

"Isn't that enough?" Kalibar asked. Erasmus sighed.

"Orik was found..." he added, shaking his head. "He was in pieces." Kalibar frowned.

"I wouldn't have thought him shaken up so easily," he remarked. Erasmus smirked.

"No, I mean he was literally *in pieces*. Someone slaughtered the bastard and left him to rot in his cell."

"Damn," Kalibar swore. "We weren't done interrogating him."

"He certainly deserved what he got," Erasmus opined. "But there's more...the guards at the entrance were killed, like I said before, without any sign of violence to their bodies...at least not externally."

"Go on."

"We ordered emergency autopsies on the two guards at the entrance to the prison," Erasmus continued. "I got a report – right before I came up to talk to you – from the coroner about his findings."

"So quickly?" Kalibar asked. A coroner's examination usually took days to weeks.

"As I said, there were no external signs of trauma," Erasmus repeated. "But the guards' armor – and the guards themselves – were completely drained of magic. Not a lick of power left in them. And when the coroner removed the top of the guards' skulls, their brains poured out."

"*Poured* out?" Kalibar exclaimed. Erasmus nodded.

"They'd been liquefied," he explained. "The rest of their bodies were intact."

"How were their brains liquefied?" Kalibar pressed, rubbing his goatee fiercely. "I know of no pattern that would allow for that without causing external damage," he added. "Or one that would allow anyone to *completely* drain magic from a full suit of armor so quickly...not even Verhanian technology can do that." But of course Erasmus knew this; if anyone would know about the armor the guards wore, it was the Grand Runic. Erasmus had, after all, been instrumental in designing that armor, before he'd gone into politics.

"It appears that whoever is attacking us," Erasmus replied, giving an apologetic look, "...is once again capable of circumventing my work." Kalibar knew what his old friend was thinking. First, his runic wards failed to stop an assassin from nearly ending Kalibar's life, and now his designs had failed to save the prison guards from having their minds literally destroyed.

"It's not your fault," Kalibar interjected quickly, putting a hand on Erasmus's shoulder. "No one doubts that your work is among the finest the Empire has seen," he added. "We have to remember that our enemy is resourceful in ways that we haven't begun to understand. We're dealing with a man who can raise the dead, and take on an entire room full of Weavers and Runics and win easily."

"Small consolation," Erasmus grumbled. "But you're right...it has to be Xanos, or one of his Chosen." He sighed heavily, shaking his near-bald head. "We're dealing with people far more powerful than we are," he added wearily. "I hate to be the one to say this, but I'm not sure we can win against such an enemy." Kalibar said nothing, but he knew that Erasmus was only stating what they'd all been thinking...indeed, what he himself had thought just last night, while taking his evening shower.

They were going to fail, and there was nothing they could do about it.

"But we have to try," Erasmus stated. "I refuse to roll over and die for these bastards. We won against Xanos once, we can do it again!"

"*We* lost," Kalibar corrected, feeling suddenly exhausted. "Kyle's ring is the only reason we're still alive having this conversation," he added. "How are we on decoding his ring?"

"Closer," Erasmus answered. "But the blasted thing is maddeningly complex," he added. "Most of the runes are completely foreign to us...I mean, I've never seen anything like them. We've isolated two dozen of them or so, and we've had our Weavers try them out. So far, all the runes have done is generate some sort of harmless energy beam. We're trying to link together the runes just like they're linked in the ring, but it'll take more time."

"At least we're getting somewhere," Kalibar said, rubbing his eyes tiredly. Then he stretched his arms out to his sides. "What I wouldn't give to get a good night's sleep," he added wistfully. Erasmus snorted.

"You're a politician now," Erasmus reminded him. "You won't get a good night's sleep until your term's over."

"Or until I'm dead," Kalibar replied. "Now, about those eyepatches..."

Chapter 7

The morning sun shone in full force as Kyle sped alongside Master Banar, easily keeping pace with the Runic as they raced across the massive lawn of the Secula Magna. Master Banar had spent the better part of an hour explaining how Ancient Runics had discovered the unique properties of crystals to store and channel magic. Apparently, weaving had been discovered first, and it wasn't until much later that runic technology had been invented. Kyle's new instructor had not spared a single opportunity to show Kyle the many miraculous inventions that Runics had created in the past two thousand years. Master Owens had been right; Weavers were flashy and cool, but the Empire itself had been built by Runics. He still felt lousy about his failure to succeed as a Weaver, but he had to admit that Master Banar had managed to make Runics seem like a pretty cool alternative.

"Did you have breakfast this morning?" Master Banar asked, slowing down, then stopping. Kyle followed suit, shaking his head. "Well then, time to eat!" the Runic exclaimed, dropping to the ground. "Come on, I've got plenty of food in my pack." He slung his bag off of his shoulder, rummaging through it until he found what he was looking for – a small sack. "I've got bread, and vegetables," Master Banar offered, pulling a loaf of bread out of the sack. "I don't eat meat," he added. Kyle smiled, remembering the countless meals of bread soaked in soup he'd had during his last adventure.

"That's okay," Kyle replied, taking some bread from his instructor. He munched on it, surprised at how moist and flavorful it was. It was certainly much better than the rations Darius had fed him on the way to Crescent Lake.

"While we're here," Master Banar continued, throwing his pack back over his shoulder, "...I might as well start teaching you the basics about runes." He took another bite out of his loaf of bread, chewing vigorously. "Now, you already know how to Weave, which is going to make this much easier," he added. "Magic, as you know, is created in the brain, and must be woven into certain patterns to have a desired effect. Well, at some point, it was found that the patterns didn't have to just be woven in the brain. As long as magic was moved in a particular pattern – within the brain or outside of it – the effect was the same."

Kyle nodded; Kalibar had mentioned something similar previously, at Crescent Lake.

"So the question is...how do we get magic to move in a particular pattern? And the answer lies in minerals," Banar continued. "Some minerals store magic, that everyone knows. But other types of minerals are better at *conducting* magic."

"What do you mean?" Kyle asked.

"Well, if you take certain minerals, and form them into a long wire of sorts, magic will flow from one end of it to the other," Banar explained. "And if you make that wire into a certain shape – a pattern – it's just like weaving magic in your mind."

"So runes are made of crystal wires?" Kyle asked. Master Banar hesitated.

"Sometimes," he replied. "It's complicated," he added ruefully. "In any case, there really isn't much difference between patterns in the mind and patterns drawn outside of it...except that with runes, a pattern can be used over and over again, nearly effortlessly. All you have to do is supply the magic, and the rune does all the rest."

"Kalibar showed me how to make runes once," Kyle offered. Master Banar's eyebrows rose.

"Really?" he replied. "I can't say I'm too surprised," he admitted. "Grand Weaver Kalibar is an exceptional academic...few Weavers ever deign to learn how the other side operates. So you know how it works?"

"Well...not really," Kyle admitted. "I just remember him carving stuff into some metal," he added. Master Banar smirked.

"Not quite," he corrected. "Here, let me show you how we do it," he added, pulling something from his pocket. It was a small brown cube.

"What's that?"

"A storage crystal," Banar answered. "We're going to create a rune on it," he added, handing it over to Kyle. The cube felt warm in his hand.

"How?" Kyle asked.

"Well, as hard as it may be to believe, that cube is made up of many smaller cubes," Banar replied. "In fact, it's made up of cubes so small you'd need a magnifying glass to see them."

Kyle smiled; being from Earth, he knew that everything was made up of tiny atoms. Crystals were just clumps of particular atoms that formed a certain shape. There was no way that Master Banar could know that, of course.

"This cube is good at holding onto magic," Banar continued, "...but terrible at making magic move." He gestured for Kyle to hand the cube back, and Kyle did so. "In order to make a rune, we have to make a wire, remember?"

"How do we do that?" Kyle asked.

"By using magic to change parts of the cube," Banar replied. "There's a magic pattern that will change the nature of the crystals that make up that cube," he added. "That will make them better at conducting magic." He paused then. "It's actually a lot more complicated than that," he admitted. "But let's keep it simple for now."

"Sounds good," Kyle agreed. His head was already starting to hurt with all of the information Banar had taught him.

"There's a pattern that'll change the structure of this storage crystal," Banar continued. "You just weave the pattern in your mind, then throw it out to the area on the crystal you want to alter." He demonstrated then, leaning over the cube, his forehead nearly touching the surface of it. A faint blue dot appeared on the face of the crystal, then faded. Banar handed the cube to Kyle, who glanced at it. Where the blue dot had been, the cube had changed color, turning bright orange. Kyle frowned at the orange dot.

"That's not a rune," he observed.

"True," Banar agreed, taking the cube back from Kyle. "But if you took a powerful enough magnifying glass, you would see that the orange part of the cube had a different structure than the rest."

"Making it better at conducting magic," Kyle guessed.

"Correct," Banar confirmed. "And can you imagine what would happen if, instead of making a simple dot, I were to create a magical pattern on the surface of the cube?"

"It would make a wire that would conduct the magic," Kyle replied. "A rune," he added, suddenly getting it. He felt a sudden giddiness. "Wait, so it's that simple?"

"Well, in theory, yes," Banar answered. "In practice, it can get a lot more complicated. But yes, that's how the simplest runes are made."

"Cool," Kyle breathed. He stared at the orange dot on the cube, suddenly eager to try his hand at making a rune of his own. But Master Banar put the cube away.

"Let's take another break," he stated, stretching his arms up and outward. His bony shoulders popped with the motion.

"Already?" Kyle asked. He wanted to continue, now that he finally understood how runes were made. Master Banar smiled.

"The next part is a bit complicated," he warned. "And I don't know about you, but I could use a breather."

"Okay."

They both sat down on the grass, as they had during their previous break. Kyle gazed up at the clouds, now only barely tinged with a purplish hue as the sun rose above the trees in the distance. Then he sighed, dropping his gaze to his lap.

"What's wrong?" Master Banar asked. Kyle shrugged.

"I'm still upset about failing as a Weaver," he admitted. "Not that I don't like the idea of being a Runic," he added hastily. He hardly wanted to offend his new teacher, especially since they were getting along so well. But Banar didn't seem offended.

"It's hard to take criticism," he replied. "Especially when it comes from people you admire," he added. "But you have to understand that Master Owens thought you'd make a good Weaver...he just thought you'd make a *better* Runic."

84

"Yeah, well it seems like everyone's good at something except for me," Kyle muttered. And it was true; Ariana had not only proven herself a better Weaver, she'd also been more responsible, showing up to class on time every time, except for yesterday, of course. And she'd saved his life on more than one occasion, leaping into action while he froze.

"You *are* good at something," Banar countered. Kyle frowned, not understanding what Banar was getting at. "Let me show you," Banar added. He stood up then, reaching into one of his many pockets and pulling out a small, transparent sphere. It almost immediately turned yellow.

"What's that?" Kyle asked. It looked familiar.

"A Finder stone," Banar answered. Kyle nearly slapped his forehead, recognizing the crystal ball.

"That's how Kalibar showed me I could make magic," Kyle recalled. And it was true; the stone had turned green when Kyle had touched it, indicating that he could make nearly as much magic as Erasmus...unheard of for a young boy.

"Do you remember what color you made it turn?" Banar asked.

"Green," Kyle replied. Banar gave a low whistle.

"Impressive," he murmured. "Well, as you know, the Finder stone changes color based on how much magic whoever is touching it makes. The colors go from least to most magic: gray, red, orange, yellow, green, blue, and violet. Each color change indicates an exponential increase in magic production."

"Right," Kyle replied. "Kalibar turned it violet," he added. Kalibar was not only the most acclaimed Battle-Weaver in the Empire, but also the man able to produce more magic than anyone else.

"He's quite powerful," Banar agreed. "Here, why don't you hold on to this for a second," he added, tossing the Finder stone to Kyle. It turned clear almost immediately after it left Banar's hands, then shifted to gray after Kyle caught it, cycling rapidly through red, yellow, green, and then a dark blue, slowing as it went. Kyle looked up at Banar, a grin on his face.

"Hey, it's blue now!" he exclaimed.

"People make more magic as they go through puberty," Banar explained. "And by using lots of magic – and forcing your body to make more to replace it — you can drastically increase the rate at which you produce magic," he added. Then he gave Kyle a strange smile. "Look down," he ordered. Kyle did so, glancing at the Finder stone cradled in his palms.

It was black.

Kyle blinked, staring at it. The crystal was utterly black, and no longer translucent. It may as well have been a cannon ball. He glanced up at Master Banar questioningly.

"That's what I thought," Banar murmured, staring at the Finder stone for a moment, then taking it from Kyle's hands. It gradually reverted back to a pale yellow hue.

"What?" Kyle asked.

"I've never seen that before," Banar admitted, "...but I've read about the possibility."

"What?"

"The designers of the Finder stone included another color after violet, even though they never believed that anyone would be able to produce that much magic," Banar explained. "But you just did."

"What does it mean?"

"It means that you make more magic than Grand Weaver Kalibar," Banar explained.

"*What?*"

"You *are* good at something, Kyle," Banar stated, placing the crystal ball back in his pocket. "In fact, you might just be the best in the world at it...at producing magic."

* * *

Kyle stared at Master Banar, his mouth agape. Master Banar chuckled at Kyle's shocked expression, patting him on the shoulder.

"You alright?" he asked with a grin.

"How?" Kyle blurted out at last.

"What do you mean?"

"I mean, how can I make so much magic?" Kyle clarified. "Just a few weeks ago, I could only turn it blue," he added. Banar shrugged.

"You're growing, Kyle," he replied. "People gain magic the quickest during puberty," he added. "You're maturing in more ways than

86

one." Kyle nodded, but he hardly felt comforted by his new-found ability.

"So what?" he muttered. "What's the point of being able to make a lot of magic if I can't *use* it?"

"But you can," Banar insisted. "Magic powers everything in the Empire," he added. "We need producers like you to keep everything running."

"Great," Kyle muttered. "So I'm gonna be a glorified generator."

"Well, no," Banar replied. "But you'll be very helpful in keeping the city's storage crystals filled with magic."

"What crystals?"

"Stridon has massive crystals stored below ground," Banar explained. "Giant cables conduct magic from the storage crystals to everything in the city...the street lights, the Tower, and the Gate Shield, for example."

"So Ariana will be flying around fighting wars and saving lives while I stay home filling crystals with magic?" Kyle sighed. "Great."

"Don't give up hope just yet," Banar counseled. "You have a great gift, but it doesn't mean you're doomed to a fate you don't want." He put a hand on Kyle's shoulder. "And you know, you don't have to be a warrior to be a hero...or a hero to be important."

"I guess," Kyle muttered.

"Come on," Banar said, "...let's get back to your lessons." He took his hand off of Kyle's shoulder. "Now, remember how Weavers can sense when another Weaver is weaving a particular pattern?"

"Yeah," Kyle replied. Kalibar had said as much at Crescent Lake. "Like Kalibar's glasses," he added. Kalibar had worn a pair of glasses that had symbols flash on the inside whenever a particular pattern was being cast by a nearby enemy. Master Banar nodded.

"Yes, but even without the glasses, Grand Weaver Kalibar could still sense these patterns, if not as easily," Banar said. "To Runics, that meant that the brain could somehow sense when a pattern was being thrown outward. Ancient Runics discovered that runes made of a certain mineral generated a magical current when exposed to a pattern woven in the same shape. So if a rune made of this mineral was in the shape of the light pattern, and a Weaver wove the light pattern, magic – an admittedly small amount – would flow through the rune."

"Sensory runes," Kyle stated, suddenly understanding. Kalibar had taught Kyle about effector and sensory runes at Crescent Lake. Sensory runes sensed magic, while effector runes generated a magical pattern in response to a sensed pattern. Kalibar's staff could sense an enemy using the fire pattern, and automatically create a blast of wind to counteract it, for example.

"Exactly!" Master Banar exclaimed, clearly pleased. "Now, if you attach a sensory rune to another rune – a rune that weaves the light pattern, for example – activating the sensory rune will send magic into the light rune, and it'll glow. That's how Grand Weaver Kalibar's glasses work."

"Got it," Kyle replied.

"We call that rune-linking," Banar explained. "That's when you attach a sensory rune to an effector rune...a rune that *does* something."

"So if I weave a pattern, the sensory rune makes a little magic, and that flows across a crystal wire to the effector rune, which weaves another pattern," Kyle deduced.

"Correct," Banar confirmed. He finished his bread, taking Kyle's half-finished loaf and placing it back within the sack it came from. Then he placed the sack back in his pack. "I need a change of scenery," he proclaimed suddenly. "How about we get back to flying?"

Banar activated his gravity boots, levitating a few inches above the ground. Kyle did the same, eager to finish learning how to fly. He couldn't help but grin like a fool...it was pretty cool, being able to levitate with a whim. Runic items were awesome, that was for sure. The idea that he would be able to build his own inventions – limited only by the power of his imagination – was starting to sound even better than being a Weaver. Imagine going back to Earth, and building magical boots for his parents! Or watching as Big Joe, the infamous bully at school, had his big meaty fists bounce off of Kyle's magical shields? Kyle could even sell his inventions, and become a millionaire! Heck, he could become a *billionaire*...and then he could have a massive mansion just like Kalibar, with plenty of rooms for his family and friends. He would never be able to do that as a Weaver, but as a Runic, his inventions could make him rich...and benefit mankind, of course.

"Let's go," Banar urged, rising upward and forward. Kyle followed suit, finding it easier to match his teacher's trajectory now that he'd had some practice. It wasn't long before they were both levitating slowly forward a dozen feet above the campus. Kyle marveled at how quickly he'd gotten used to being so high up; not even an hour ago, he'd been nervous about floating a foot or two above the ground.

"One more bit of theory," Master Banar stated as they flew side-by-side. "Pure crystals can hold more magic than plain old rocks, probably because of their perfect geometry. Rocks can still hold magic, but not nearly as much as a diamond, for example. That's why crystals are so valuable – and expensive. That and the girls think they look pretty," he added with a grin. Kyle smiled back; crystals *did* look pretty, as long as they were attached to a girl.

"Now," Master Banar continued, "...if you take any old rock or crystal from the ground, you'll find that the ones nearest the surface are almost completely filled with magic. Can you think of why?"

Kyle frowned, mulling it over. If rocks on the surface had more magic, that had to mean that they were exposed to magic from another source...something that leaked magic from nearby.

"From people?" he asked.

"You're on the right track," Banar replied. "It's actually magic-radiating plants that feed the minerals," he added. "Animals do too, but plants make up the vast majority of magical life. Just look around you...what do you see?" Kyle did so, glancing around himself. Other than the road, and a few mountains far in the distance, the landscape was covered in nothing but grass, shrubs, and trees.

"Makes sense," Kyle remarked.

"So in nature," Master Banar continued, "...most minerals are filled to the brim with magic. Now, there are some plants that *extract* magic from crystals, just like humans can. The Ancients believed that these plants – and human brains – had tiny crystals within their flesh, crystals that had a higher magic vacuity than anything around them."

"Magic what?" Kyle asked with a frown. Master Banar smiled.

"Magic vacuity," he repeated. "Think of it as how much a crystal 'wants' magic. Crystals that store lots of magic – like diamonds – have high magic vacuity...they suck magic into themselves very strongly."

"Okay."

"So what would happen if you took a rock that was filled with magic, and put it next to a diamond that had no magic?"

Kyle frowned again, knitting his eyebrows together.

"You'd find magic streaming from the rock to the diamond...until the diamond had sucked almost all of the magic out of the rock."

"Oh."

"A mineral without much magic in it creates a vacuum of sorts, pulling any magic available into it. We call that magic vacuum 'magic vacuity.'"

"I think I get it," Kyle stated.

"So what would happen if you did the opposite?" Banar pressed. "What if you put a magic-filled diamond next to a depleted rock?"

"Well," Kyle replied, "...wouldn't the empty rock pull magic out of the full diamond?"

"A little bit, sure," Master Banar admitted. "But the diamond has a much higher magic vacuity than the rock," he explained. "The diamond *wants* magic more. If their vacuities were identical, like if you had two diamonds, the empty diamond would suck magic into it until they both were filled half-and-half. The reality is, magic streams to-and-fro from crystals all the time, in both directions. But crystals with extraordinarily high magic vacuities essentially stream magic away from everything else. When you begin to fill a gem, however, the vacuum lessens, until it stops completely when you've saturated it."

"So empty crystals act like magic-suckers," Kyle deduced.

"Exactly!" Banar exclaimed. "You're a natural, aren't you? In fact, the Ancients believed that the only reason people could suck magic out of any known crystal was because they must have crystals with extraordinarily high magic vacuity in their own minds. In fact, one of the most famous Runics of all time was the foremost researcher on that very subject."

"Ampir?" Kyle asked. The Ancient Battle-Runic had been the best of his generation, and had been widely considered to be the most powerful Runic who'd ever lived. But Master Banar shook his head.

"No," he replied. "It was actually a contemporary of Ampir's, a Runic named Sabin." Kyle frowned.

"Wasn't Sabin the guy who created the Behemoths and destroyed the Ancient Empire?" he pressed. Master Banar nodded.

"Unfortunately so," he confirmed. "But the man was a genius in his own right, and his work on finding what he called the 'void mineral'...the crystal with the highest magic acuity, one that could drain any other substance of its magic...was extraordinary."

"Did he ever find it?"

"No," Master Banar admitted. "Perhaps if he hadn't been so ambitious with his other pursuits, he would have had enough time to finish his work. Unfortunately, the vast majority of written works from that time were destroyed. We only have bits and pieces of what remain." He sighed then, much as Kalibar had done when he'd contemplated the tragedy of the Ancients. Then he glanced at Kyle, giving him a rueful smile. "Is your brain full yet?"

"Kind of," Kyle admitted.

"Well then, enough talking," Banar decided. He sped up suddenly, shooting ahead of Kyle. He spun around as he did so, facing Kyle as he went. "Come on, I'll race you to that hill!"

Chapter 8

Kalibar paced back and forth down the length of his enormous suite, his bare feet making little noise on the magically warmed granite. He looked up, seeing Jenkins, his loyal butler, trying not to stare back at him. Kalibar was wearing the special eyepatches Erasmus had crafted for him; no doubt Jenkins was clearly unnerved by the "illusion" of his Grand Weaver staring right at him. The man had arrived moments ago to bring Kalibar his lunch, which sat steaming upon a silver tray that Jenkins held before him.

"Not now, Jenkins," Kalibar stated, waving the tray away. Jenkins bowed.

"Would you like me to leave the tray, sire?" he inquired.

"Yes," Kalibar answered. "...and thank you, Jenkins," he added. His tone had been abrupt earlier; Jenkins was not the source of his frustration, and he hardly wanted to sour his relationship with the man over a misconception. Jenkins was, after all, the finest butler he'd ever had. The man had been instrumental in smoothing out the wrinkles in Kalibar's minute-to-minute existence, ensuring that Kalibar had whatever he needed...often before he realized he needed it. Such devotion to one's work was a rare quality indeed, in any walk of life. Kalibar knew that his position gave him an extraordinary power over Jenkins. He was responsible not only for his butler's employment, but for his very self-worth. A Grand Weaver's praise was as valuable to Jenkins' disposition as was his salary, and by recognizing his accomplishments, he could vastly improve Jenkins' satisfaction with his work. It was a responsibility Kalibar had seen far too many men in positions of power ignore, or worse, abuse.

Kalibar watched as the devoted butler set the tray down on a nearby table, along with a tall glass of water.

"Jenkins, what's your salary?" Kalibar inquired. The butler froze, then glanced up at Kalibar.

"Twenty-six thousand per year, your excellency," Jenkins answered, stepping back from the table. Kalibar frowned, taken aback. He'd thought that Jenkins would have been granted a more robust salary after his recent promotion; twenty thousand was barely three times the poverty level...enough to live a moderately comfortable middle-class lifestyle, as long as the man had no children.

"Do you have children?" he pressed. Jenkins smiled, his eyes lighting up.

"Yes sire, two girls and a boy," he answered proudly. Kalibar shook his head.

"Jenkins, you're far too good at what you do to make that little," he replied firmly. "Money should not worry a man of your excellent qualities. I'm doubling your salary effective immediately."

"I appreciate your generosity, your excellency, but I can't..." Jenkins protested. Kalibar raised one hand.

"No buts," he interjected. "You must be paid in proportion to your worth. I don't know what I'd do without you," he added with a smile. Jenkins smiled back, bowing once more.

"Thank you, sire," he replied. "And thank you again for my promotion," he added gratefully. Then he blinked, realizing that he was still carrying Kalibar's tray. He set it down on an end-table, then bowed to Kalibar once again. "Is there anything else you require?"

"No, thank you, Jenkins," Kalibar replied. Jenkins nodded, then turned about, leaving the room as quickly as he'd come. Kalibar watched the butler go, then sighed. He resumed his pacing, leaving the steaming tray on the end-table. The meal was almost certainly delicious – Jenkins and his assistant Greg had grilled Kalibar extensively on his food preferences, and had never failed to deliver a culinary master-piece with every meal – but Kalibar was too distracted to enjoy even the tastiest of delicacies. No one had yet been implicated in the prison break earlier that morning. Even so, he had a good idea of who was ultimately responsible.

He stopped his pacing, closing his eyes.

The children from the Arena had been there, of course. And Kalibar's guards had just informed him that they too had vanished from the prison. While the children might not have had any useful information about Xanos or the Chosen, now the Empire would never know. And worse yet, the Council would be outraged at the loss. Even with a narrow advantage over Goran in the Council, their meetings had become increasingly difficult. If Kalibar and Erasmus lost just one of the Councilmen's support, they would lose their majority, and be rendered effectively powerless.

And that, he knew, would force them to invoke the Right of Dictatorship.

He sighed in frustration, resuming his pacing. The nerve of the enemy, to walk right into Stridon and completely nullify any benefit his raid of the Arena had conferred! It was a show of strength as much as anything else, he knew. Xanos was sending them a message, telling them that even their victories were ultimately futile.

Kalibar stopped pacing, walking toward one end of the spacious room. The walls and ceiling were made of huge sheets of magically-reinforced glass – glass that acted as a one-way mirror, allowing Kalibar to see out, but no one to see in. To people on the outside, his room was a giant crystalline pyramid, sparkling like a gem in the sunlight. He had, as a result, a breathtaking view of the southern half of the city. He walked to the transparent wall, placing both palms on the smooth, cool glass, staring down at the city below. From here, he could see the commercial district, hundreds of squat, rectangular buildings flanking the winding city streets. Innumerable blue and red squares littered the streets and flat roofs of the buildings, landing zones for citizens wearing jumpsuits, allowing anyone to leap from rooftop to rooftop, or rooftop to street. It was possible for a man to traverse the entire city without touching the ground, and the fact that rooftops were usable space for pedestrians had made Stridon different than any other city in the Empire. Rooftops had gardens, pools, and sometimes even storefronts for various peddlers. Every inch of the city was usable space, all because of recent advances in runic technology. Kalibar could only imagine what the city must have looked like in Ancient times, over two thousand years ago. Their runic technology had been far more advanced, with flying vehicles, weapons that shot deadly beams of energy, and even entire buildings that levitated high above the ground.

Kalibar gazed at the cityscape below, knowing that he would never live long enough to see such a spectacle...the re-creation of the Ancient Empire. He'd read nearly every book that existed on the Ancients, devouring the texts in his youth, fascinated to the point of obsession. He'd read all of the Ancient biographies of the giants of those times...Renval, Sabin, Gogan, Ampir. How many times had he wondered what the Empire would look like if Sabin and Ampir hadn't betrayed their people, setting civilization back two thousand years?

It was a futile line of thinking, Kalibar knew. His whole life had been devoted to slowly rebuilding what Ampir and Sabin had destroyed.

He sighed, taking his palms off of the glass wall in front of him, then stepping backward. He reached up with the same hand, gazing at his pink, wrinkled flesh. He'd nearly forgotten that, just a few hours ago, he'd been living in a world of pure darkness. How quickly the mind adapted...he was already having a hard time remembering what it was like to be blind. He flexed his fingers, marveling at the faint blue rays emanating from the magic rings on his fingers.

What a remarkable gift, he thought.

A sudden boom rocked the Tower, making the glass windows vibrate. Kalibar frowned, looking beyond the transparent panels, down at the buildings far below.

There, in the distance – right in the center of the commercial district – a massive cloud of dust and smoke rose above a large building. It was Stridon Central Bank, the headquarters for the wealthiest banking company in the Empire. As he watched, its stone walls collapsed inward on all sides, the roof breaking apart and falling downward. Massive chunks of stone shattered as they converged in the center of the building, forming a crude sphere. Debris sucked into the sphere, nearby carriages and people sliding across the street and flying upward into that vortex. Everything that was sucked into its vacuum was torn apart near its center, then shoved outward, only to be sucked back in

95

again. The sphere undulated for a few moments, the fragments of stone and wood getting smaller and smaller as they were torn asunder, and then the whole thing suddenly collapsed, hunks of rubble dropping straight down onto the street below. A massive cloud of dust shot up with the impact, and seconds later, another shockwave rattled the Tower. Kalibar stared at the expanding cloud of gray, at the pile of rubble below it, in disbelief.

The bank had been utterly destroyed.

Kalibar heard the high-pitched emergency alarm, and turned around, spotting Jax and Erasmus behind the transparent front door. Kalibar walked up to the door, opening it...but not before he remembered that he wasn't supposed to be able to see.

"What the hell is going on?" he asked as Erasmus rushed into the room. Jax followed him in, along with a few elite guards. Kalibar closed the door behind them, activating its defensive wards.

"Stridon Central Bank has been attacked," Erasmus stated grimly. "You heard the shockwaves?"

"I...yes, I did," he replied. "I want my Battle-Weavers mobilized. Jax, get me High Weaver Urson." Jax nodded, go to the communication half-globe, activating it. He turned to one of the elite guards. "Debrief the captain of the elite guard, have his men seal the Tower. No one comes in, no one goes out. No one is to come in or out of the Gate Shield either, except for my Battle-Weavers." The guard nodded, rushing out of the room. He turned to another guard. "I want the captain of the city guard. Tell him to set a perimeter around the bank," Kalibar demanded. "We need to protect the people from the wreckage."

"Agreed," Erasmus piped in. "If this is an isolated attack – a terrorist attack – we'll need disaster crews in after the area is declared safe. We'll need medical teams to separate the dead from the wounded, the dying from the well. I'll contact the governor."

"Good idea," Kalibar stated. Erasmus turned about, replacing Jax at the communication orb. Jax walked back to Kalibar.

"Battle Weavers are conducting aerial surveillance," Jax stated. "They'll move in to neutralize any further attacks."

"Thank you," Kalibar replied. "I want High Weaver Urson here as soon as possible," he added. Urson was the commander of the Battle-

Weavers, second-in-command to Kalibar himself...and despite his relatively young age, one of the finest tacticians in the Empire. Jax nodded silently. Erasmus came back from the communication orb.

"The governor's courier is coming," he informed. "I'll have him organize mobile medical units. We'll set up evaluation and treatment tents beyond the perimeter of the attack, and set up carriages to bring seriously wounded victims to our hospitals."

"Good," Kalibar replied. Then he shook his head. "This feels like a terrorist attack," he muttered. "They're trying to turn our own people against us, by playing on their fears. First the prisoners, now this...some of the wealthiest citizens in Stridon had their fortunes tied up in that bank."

"Myself included," Jax stated with a sigh. "It's a good thing I'm so close to death that I don't give a damn."

"I doubt others will be so understanding," Kalibar muttered. "We'll have to help finance the rebuilding of the bank, and guarantee our citizens that their fortunes will be preserved."

"Agreed," Jax replied. "And we need to prove that Xanos is responsible for this," he added. "But if he is, I don't see how we can stop him."

"We always knew this was a losing battle," Kalibar muttered. Erasmus snorted.

"Well, the damn Council isn't exactly making our jobs any easier," he interjected. "Present company excluded," he added hastily. Jax sighed.

"The government was designed for inertia," he admitted. "Not for this kind of situation."

"The founders *did* anticipate this," Kalibar countered. Jax's eyes narrowed.

"You mean the Right of Dictatorship," he stated warily. "There's no turning back from that, Kalibar. You know what they'll do to you if you go down that path."

"It's starting to look like it's our only remaining option, Jax."

"Give me some time," Jax requested, suddenly looking even older than his seventy-two years. "Let me speak to Goran and his followers...make them see reason. Leave the Right of Dictatorship off the table," he insisted. "If you invoke it, you *will* be hanged, Kalibar."

"If the Council decides to hang me for saving my people," Kalibar replied, "I'll put the damn noose around my neck myself."

"Give me some time," Jax repeated. Then he turned away, walking out of the suite. Kalibar watched the old man leave, then sighed, glancing back at the cityscape beyond the suite's massive, transparent walls. He knew that his citizens would be in shock for some time. They would still believe that the government would protect them. That this disruption in their lives would be the last, and life would return to normal soon. But when the attacks *didn't* stop, when it became clear that the Empire was powerless against this new enemy, the lofty ideals of the Empire would succumb to the sheer instinct to survive. The citizens of Stridon would submit to Xanos, offering Kalibar's head to the enemy themselves if it meant they would be spared.

He'd seen it happen before. Had used the tactic himself against his enemies long ago, much to his mentor Marcus's dismay.

If Kalibar didn't find a way out of this mess, Xanos wouldn't need overwhelming power or an army of Death Weavers to defeat him. With a few well-placed attacks, and a little patience, the Empire would end up destroying itself.

Chapter 9

Kyle sped along in his gravity boots, following Master Banar as he flew between some trees, over a mile from the Tower. The going was slow, requiring a great deal of concentration to steer around each tree. That was the point, of course; Master Banar was teaching Kyle finer control over his gravity boots. At first, Kyle smacked into more than one tree, but eventually he managed to avoid the obstacles. It was an exhausting exercise, at least mentally. Eventually Master Banar stopped in mid-air, rotating to face Kyle.

"Getting tired?" he asked with a grin. Kyle nodded. "All right, fly up above the treetops," he ordered. Then the Runic flew upward through the air, dodging branches as he went. Higher and higher he soared, until at last he stopped a dozen feet above the tallest tree.

Kyle gulped, staring up at his instructor. He'd always had a healthy respect for gravity, particularly the way in which that most unforgiving of forces could pull you down to your death if you dared to defy it. But Master Banar was insistent, gesturing for Kyle to levitate upward. Kyle gathered his courage, then streamed magic gently into his left boot. Upward he rose, the ground shrinking below him.

"Careful!" Master Banar warned. Kyle stopped his magic stream, halting in mid-air. Looking up, he saw that there was a large tree branch right above his head. He went around it, then rose up until he was level with Master Banar.

"Sorry," Kyle told Banar.

"No problem," he replied. "We need to protect that precious brain of yours," he added with a grin, ruffling Kyle's hair playfully. "Alright, time for more learning! Where were we?"

"Uh, magic vacuity?"

"Right," Banar stated. "Crystals pull magic into them unless they're full, and the emptier a crystal is, the hungrier they are for magic around them."

"And my brain has crystals that can pull magic out of just about anything," Kyle added. Banar nodded.

"So we assume. Now, no one can pull magic out of your mind," he explained. "...at least not without great difficulty. But you *can* pull magic from other parts of peoples' bodies."

"Like what?" Kyle asked.

"Like their bones," Master Banar answered. "Bones are made of minerals, and they're good at storing magic. Magic flows from the brain and into the skull bones, filling them up until they're saturated. Some magic is leaked into the surrounding air. This is the magic you can sense coming from Weavers and Runics."

"How can I use the magic in my bones?" Kyle pressed.

"It's used automatically," Master Banar answered. "When the stores within your brain are depleted, magic streams from the nearest bones – those of your skull – to the brain. That's why Sabin assumed that the brain must contain small amounts of his 'void mineral.' When the magic in the skull starts to get used up, magic from the next nearest bones – the spine – streams to the skull, and so forth. The opposite happens when you use up all of the magic in your body."

"How do you mean?"

"Well," Banar answered, "...when you use up every last bit of magic in your bones, magic still gets produced in your brain. However, re-member that, the emptier a mineral, the greater its magic vacuity. Bone has a high vacuity, so when its completely empty of magic, the vacuum is quite powerful. In fact, it's so powerful that it's almost impossible to keep much magic within the brain, at least at first. As magic continues to get produced, the bones fill up...first the skull, then the upper spine, and so forth. Once the skull is filled again, using magic is easier."

"I think I get it," Kyle said. Master Banar beamed.

"Good," he replied. "The reason I'm teaching you this is because vacuity becomes extraordinarily important when making runics," he added. "Imagine creating an incredibly powerful item, one with a massive amount of stored magic. Then imagine someone found a crystal with greater magic vacuity, emptied it of its magic, and placed it near your amazing invention. Guess what would happen?"

"It would get drained," Kyle answered.

"Exactly," Banar agreed. Kyle frowned.

"But wait," he asked. "Kalibar said most storage crystals had a 'password' on them, so people couldn't just take the magic out of anyone's stuff."

"True," Master Banar replied. "There are ways to protect storage crystals from being drained. One is to keep them only partially saturated...that way they'll still have a high vacuity, resisting the pull of other crystals. In fact, the vast majority of storage crystals are purposefully kept at about 20% capacity, for this very reason."

"And the passwords?" Kyle pressed.

"Well, that's complicated," his teacher admitted. "The 'passwords' Grand Weaver Kalibar described are sensory runes. These runes don't do anything...they're just randomly created by the maker of the storage crystal. But weaving the password pattern activates the sensory runes, which in turn activate effector runes on the crystals...runes that break up the crystalline structure."

"I don't get it," Kyle replied. "How does that make it possible to pull magic from the crystal?"

"You can *always* pull magic from crystals," Master Banar corrected. "Even a diamond with an impossibly complex password is vulnerable. It's just that the diamond's vacuity is so high that it takes a great deal of time and effort to extract any magic from it. But if you make lots of tiny fractures within the diamond – by a magically reversible process – its magic vacuity will decrease. Then you can pull almost all of the magic out with ease. And when they're done, all they have to do is re-lock the gem, and the process reverses."

"Wow," Kyle replied, shaking his head slowly. "How did anyone come up with this stuff?"

"Well, I'll give you a hint." Master Banar replied with a wink. "It sure wasn't a Weaver that figured it all out." Kyle couldn't help but smile. Still, he felt a bit overwhelmed by it all.

"Yeah, I don't think I'll be coming up with anything so creative," he muttered. "I'll be lucky just to carve a rune," he added glumly. Master Banar laughed, clapping Kyle on the shoulder with one hand.

"Oh, don't you worry," he replied with his characteristic grin. "Have a little faith in yourself, Kyle...you'll be doing far more than that, and sooner than you think!"

* * *

Kyle and Master Banar zipped forward over the treetops, the Tower behind them growing ever smaller in the distance. The Gate Shield glimmered in the distance, rising up in a massive dome over the three-story tall black fence surrounding the Secula Magna, now only a quarter mile away. Kyle glanced down, spotting two figures dressed in black walking on the grass far below. It was Ariana and Master Owens, already preparing for their morning lesson. Master Banar called out after the two, descending smoothly toward them.

"Master Owens!" Banar greeted, landing gently on the grass beside the Weaver. Master Owens grinned, embracing the younger Runic and clapping him on the back.

"Master Banar," Owens replied. Then he glanced at Kyle, who had halted in mid-air above them. "Kyle," he added with a nod. Ariana stared up at Kyle, a huge smile on her face.

"You're flying!" she blurted out, rather enviously. "How are you doing that?" Kyle shrugged, unable to hold back a smile of his own. He descended through the air gracefully, landing beside Ariana.

"Oh, just tinkering," he replied casually. But he beamed at her, and even gave her a wink. Ariana shook her head, her jealousy plain to see.

"Are those Gravity boots?" she pressed. Master Banar nodded.

"A miracle of runic technology," he answered, extending a hand for Ariana to shake. "Master Banar," he stated, introducing himself. "I'm Kyle's Runic instructor. And you must be Ariana, Master Owens' prized student."

"Nice to meet you," Ariana replied, shaking Banar's hand. She stepped back then, admiring Kyle's boots once more. "Can I try them?" she asked. Master Owens frowned.

"Perhaps later," he stated. "We have a lot of ground to cover today."

"Yes Master Owens," Ariana murmured. But she turned to give Kyle a peculiar look, and he knew what that meant...he was going to teach her how to use the boots later that night, whether he wanted to or not. He certainly didn't mind; any excuse to spend time with her was more than welcome. She had a peculiar power over him, such that any time he was around her, he felt a marvelous giddiness come over him.

He sighed then, suddenly gripped with an anxious desire to be alone with her. If only there was a magical pattern for speeding up time, so he could fast-forward to tonight! Unfortunately, no new patterns had been discovered since Ancient times, so Kyle would have to wait.

"Hey Master Banar," he asked suddenly. "Why hasn't anyone discovered any new patterns?" The fact that people had been using the same patterns for centuries, never daring to experiment to find new patterns, baffled Kyle.

"Well, it's dangerous to try new patterns," Master Banar began. "More than a few Weavers and Runics have died...or suffered terrible injuries...attempting it. There's no way to predict what a particular pattern will do until it's woven. A few brave scholars have tried it, and none have lived long enough to produce more than a pattern or two." He smiled ruefully. "It's a pretty messy way to get into the history books."

"What about magical animals and plants?" Kyle pressed. "They must weave patterns to make their magic, right?"

"True," his instructor conceded. "Nature employs a remarkable variety of patterns," he added. "The Ancients knew of some of them, but unfortunately, most magical patterns have been lost to history." Kyle frowned.

"How did *they* figure out all these patterns?" he pressed. Master Banar glanced at Master Owens, who shrugged.

"No one knows, Kyle," he answered. "We may never know."

Kyle lowered his gaze to the grass below, continuing to frown. Then an idea struck him.

"Wait," he exclaimed. "Couldn't you figure out what animals and plants were doing by making sensory runes?"

"What do you mean?" Banar asked.

"Well," Kyle explained, "...Kalibar had glasses that lit up whenever a particular pattern was woven. What if you made a bunch of random patterns – as sensory runes – and made a plant weave a pattern...if you had hundreds of random sensory runes, maybe one particular rune would be triggered, and light up. That way, you could figure out what pattern the plant was weaving."

"You mean, have a runic that had hundreds of random sensory runes, and expose the runic to multitudes of animals and plants, and see if any of the sensory runes are triggered?" Banar asked. Kyle nodded.

"That way, you would know what pattern they were using," Kyle replied. "You could do that for hundreds of animals and plants, and learn tons of new patterns."

"Interesting," Master Banar murmured. But Master Owens frowned.

"I don't know," he interjected. "There are so many different possible patterns, it could take millions of guesses to find one that matched."

"True," Master Banar admitted.

"Well what if you use *parts* of sensory runes?" Kyle pressed. "Wouldn't they still light up if something wove part of a pattern? Then you could put them together afterward."

Banar frowned, glancing at Master Owens.

"I don't understand," he replied. "What do you mean?" But Master Owens cleared his throat.

"We really should get back to our lesson," he stated. Master Banar nodded.

"Right," he agreed. He turned to Kyle. "Good thinking, Kyle," he stated. "You might be on to something."

"It *is* a novel idea," Master Owens admitted. "Well done, Kyle," he added, gazing approvingly at his former student. Kyle felt his cheeks flush.

"Well, I don't know," Kyle replied sheepishly, glancing at Ariana. She was staring at him, a strange smile on her lips. Kyle felt a swell of pride, a giddy sensation he'd never quite experienced before. He knew immediately that the idea would work. Why it hadn't occurred to someone else, Kyle couldn't fathom. It was so obvious, now that he thought about it!

"Let's go back to the Tower," Banar stated, turning to Kyle. "I think I know what you meant by using parts of runes," he added rather excitedly. "We need to tell Grand Runic Erasmus about your idea!"

"Wait, you really think it'll work?" Kyle asked, suddenly doubting himself. What if Master Owens was right, and his idea ended up not being all that useful? Or worse, what if it didn't work at all? Kyle was flattered by Master Banar's confidence in him, but he didn't want to have to suffer the shame of discovering that he wasn't as great as everyone thought he was. Again.

"There's only one way to find out," Banar answered. "Let's go back to the Tower."

"Don't forget the Aegis," Ariana reminded, pointing to Kyle's chest. He glanced down, seeing his white shirt, and realized he'd forgotten to put on his silver armor – the Aegis of Athanasia – this morning. If Kalibar ever found out, he'd be furious. Kyle nodded, giving Ariana a grateful smile.

"Thanks, I will," he replied. Then he felt Master Banar tugging on his arm. Banar was already levitating a foot above the ground. Kyle activated his own gravity boots, quickly rising through the air – to Ariana's obvious delight – and flying after his instructor. Kyle waved as he flew upward, turning and catching up with his new teacher, who'd sped a few dozen feet ahead, his white cloak rippling in the wind. Kyle accelerated to catch up with his instructor, the wind blowing through his hair, sending a chill through him. The morning was early still, the sun having yet to bake the earth with its warming rays. He ignored the cold, concentrating on following behind Master Banar. Within minutes, they'd left Ariana and Master Owens far behind, the Tower only a mile or so ahead.

Suddenly, Kyle heard a deafening boom, and felt something slam into him, making him lurch to the side. The world spun crazily around him, and he cried out, flailing his arms. The awful sensation of free-fall gripped his gut, and screamed as he saw the ground rising up toward him at breakneck speed. He closed his eyes at the last minute, feeling a terrible pain as his shoulder slammed into something hard, knocking the wind out of his lungs. Then he was rolling madly through something cold and wet, until at last he came to a stop, lying on his back.

He lay where he was, gasping for air.

A shrill wailing noise assaulted his ears, a sound that was instantly recognizable. It was the same sound Kyle had heard when Rivin and Bartholos had been murdered. And when Kalibar had been nearly assassinated.

Kyle rolled onto his side, realizing that he was lying on cool, wet grass. He tried to roll onto his left side, but a sharp pain lanced through his shoulder, and he cried out, flopping onto his back. He laid there for a moment, struggling to catch his breath. After a few seconds, he tried to roll again, this time onto his right side. He saw a figure in white roll into his field of field.

It was Master Banar!

The Runic tumbled across through the grass, coming to a stop a dozen feet from Kyle. Banar groaned, then rolled onto his stomach, pushing himself up onto his hands and knees. His eyes focused on Kyle, and Banar reached out toward him. Then something slammed into the Runic's back, shoving the man's belly violently onto the ground.

It was a boot. A black boot.

Master Banar yelled out in pain, a shimmering gravity shield erupting around him. Then it vanished as quickly as it had appeared; the boot on his back hadn't even budged.

"Hello, Kyle," a deep, resonant voice murmured.

Master Banar struggled to push himself up against the weight on his back, the veins on his forehead bulging with the effort. Then something slammed into the back of his head, burying his face into the grass.

Blood welled up around a long, metallic shaft embedded through the back of the Runic's skull.

Master Banar's arms jerked once, then again, and then he lay perfectly still in the dew-tipped grass. The boot on his back lifted up, then stayed in the air, hovering an inch above the ground. Another boot came into view, also floating above the grass. A corner of black fabric rippled sinuously in the still morning air, ornate gray symbols woven into it.

Kyle felt terror grip him, choking the air from his lungs. His gaze went upward, despite every fiber of his being screaming for him to look away. Goosebumps rose over every inch of his body, a cold sweat pouring down his arms and dripping down his flanks. Still, his gaze went upward. Two black boots, and then black pants. A black shirt, with an endlessly rippling cloak wrapped around it.

Master Banar's head jerked upward as the long, metal pole impaling it was pulled free, the sharpened end crimson with blood. Kyle followed the length of the pole, seeing the pale hand that gripped it. He saw a pale face, black eyes sunken deep within its skull, a thick, knotted scar on its left temple. Short black hair. And in the center of the forehead, a lone, shimmering, diamond-shaped green crystal.

Kyle tried to scream, but nothing came out.

"I warned you about defying me," the Dead Man said, his low, smooth voice sending chills down Kyle's spine. Then his pale lips twisted into a smile. "But I forgive you."

Kyle felt something wet and sticky press against the back of his neck, and then darkness took him.

Chapter 10

Kalibar stared out of the glass windows of his suite, at the ant-sized people swarming through the streets around the site of the attack. Where the bank had once stood, regal and imposing, there was only rubble now. The response to the disaster had been nothing short of amazing. It had been less than a half-hour, and already his Weavers had removed the majority of the debris, using large gravity spheres to suck in tons of stone at a time, then sending the debris-laden spheres beyond the city limits. Runics had already placed wards around the site, preventing passers-by from looting, and from interfering with the cleanup process.

Kalibar lowered his gaze to his feet. Combined with the prison break earlier that morning, he'd thought that the attack on the bank would've caused a near-panic within the city. In fact, the exact opposite had happened; people from all over the city had responded to the blast. Doctors had immediately set up tents to treat victims, sending the sickest to the surrounding hospitals. Others had organized crews to help find victims stuck in the rubble. Surrounding grocers had offered to bring food and water to help the relief crews stay nourished. The governor himself had just returned from giving a speech a few blocks from the site, praising the efforts of the people. It had been enormously gratifying to know that, far from resulting in terror, the strike against Stridon had brought its people closer together.

Still, Kalibar knew that his citizens would demand answers as to who had done this...and whether or not their government would protect them from another attack. He'd wanted to travel to the site to give a speech addressing these concerns, but his elite guard had cautioned against it out of concern for his safety. Speculation abounded on whether some of the escaped prisoners from the jailbreak earlier – many of them powerful Weavers themselves – were responsible for destroying the bank. Kalibar didn't particularly care; he assumed that Xanos was behind both events, regardless of the specifics. It was a classic strategy when laying siege to an enemy; promote chaos, induce panic, reduce morale. Make the populace question the effectiveness of their elected officials. Make them feel unsafe. It hadn't worked this time, but after enough attacks, the will of the people would break.

Terror, Kalibar knew all too well, was a very effective weapon.

A knock came at his door. Kalibar pushed aside his annoyance at the interruption, walking up to the magical door guarding the entrance, seeing one of his Battle-Weavers standing on the other side. Kalibar activated the door, making it translucent for the Weaver.

"Your excellency," the Weaver greeted, bowing stiffly. "Grand Runic Erasmus requests an audience with you in the Runic Archives."

Kalibar nodded, opening the door and allowing himself to be led down the hallway to the riser. This brought them swiftly to the 32nd floor. where the Runic Archives was located. It represented the largest repository of magical artifacts in the Empire. Surprisingly, many of these artifacts had been found on one small island hundreds of miles west of Stridon...an island that was responsible for the recent renaissance in runic technology, and the international dominance of the Empire.

No one knew the Archives better than Erasmus, who had, until recently, been the Head Archivist for the Secula Magna. He'd stepped down after beginning his second term as Grand Runic, but everyone assumed that Erasmus would resume being Head Archivist after his term ended...if he lived that long.

In addition to the Archives, there was the Testing Chamber...a room designed for testing both Ancient runic artifacts and new runic inventions. The Testing Chamber had powerful magical shields on every surface – walls, floor, and ceiling – and an attached viewing room

109

that allowed for remote activation of the runic item being tested. The room had been designed that way after more than one Runic had been blown to bits experimenting with Ancient runic relics.

And, quite appropriately, that was where Erasmus's most skilled Runics had attempted to decode Kyle's ring.

When the riser stopped, Kalibar and his Battle-Weaver escort walked to the front door of the Archives. Erasmus was there, standing just outside of the door. When he saw Kalibar, he rushed forward, grabbing Kalibar by the arm.

"I need to show you something," Erasmus urged.

"What's wrong?" Kalibar asked. Erasmus said nothing, but opened the door to the Runic Archives, pulling Kalibar inside. Kalibar, wearing his eyepatches, continued the act of being blind, allowing Erasmus to guide him into the room. It was truly massive, with dozens of rows of shelving standing several stories tall, each stuffed to the brim with thousands of magical artifacts. To one side of Archives was a door that opened to reveal a long hallway, at the end of which was the Testing Chamber; that's where Erasmus led Kalibar. The chamber was thirty feet long, thirty feet wide, and had ceilings 30 feet tall. The walls were a light blue color to Kalibar, due to his newfound ability to see magic in the shields protecting the walls. They were, in actuality, stark white.

Erasmus led Kalibar toward the center of the chamber, to a small white table there. On top of the table, Kalibar saw a familiar object: Kyle's ring.

"We've done it," Erasmus stated, his tone oddly neutral. Kalibar frowned.

"Done what?" he asked. Erasmus gestured to the ring.

"We've decoded Kyle's ring."

"You did it?" Kalibar asked, taken aback. Erasmus gave a slight smirk.

"The three dozen Runics may have helped," he replied wryly. "I've had them working three rotating shifts around the clock. Each was assigned a few runes to decode." He gestured to the white table; next to the ring sat a long, rectangular crystal with dozens of runes inscribed onto its surface. "After they decoded the runes, I had them copy the runes in the proper sequence onto that crystal slab."

"That's a pretty big slab," Kalibar noted. It was true; the ring was dwarfed by the two-foot-long crystalline block beside it.

"Yeah, well the runes on that ring were so small we couldn't see them without using a series of magnifying lenses," Erasmus replied. "Never mind tracking the connections between runes...they were inscribed in three dimensions inside main crystal. We laid them out in straight lines – all two hundred of them."

"Two *hundred?*" Kalibar exclaimed. His magical staff – the latest in modern runic technology – was nearly six feet long, and carried a similar number of runes. The center gemstone of Kyle's ring was two carats, at most. To think that all of those runes could be packed into such a small area...it gave him goosebumps. The Ancients had truly been masters of runic technology...and Ampir had stood head and shoulders above them.

"Tell me about it," Erasmus muttered. "In any case, if I trigger the sensory rune on our runic copy over here," he stated, walking up to the rectangular crystal, "...it'll reproduce the functionality of Kyle's ring."

"You've already done it," Kalibar guessed. Erasmus nodded, but to Kalibar's surprise, his friend's expression was hardly joyous. Kalibar's brow furrowed. "What's wrong?"

"See for yourself," Erasmus answered. He closed his eyes for a moment, and re-opened them. "There," he stated.

"There what?" Kalibar asked. "Nothing happened."

"Exactly what we thought...at first," Erasmus agreed. "But I assure you that it *is* doing something. We were about to give up on guessing what that something was until one of our brighter Runics noticed that the last rune in the activation sequence doesn't code for any magic effect at all."

"What?"

"You know how password runes are just sensory runes with a particular shape? And if you weave that shape, it will activate the sensory rune?" he asked. Kalibar nodded. "Well," Erasmus continued, "...it turns out that the last rune in the sequence is meant to send a password to a sensory rune far away."

"Wait, so the ring just transmits a message?" Kalibar asked. "Surely it does more than that!"

111

"Afraid not," Erasmus replied. "Other than a few runes to protect the ring from being destroyed, that's all it does."

"Impossible!" he exclaimed. He stared at the ring on the table, then turned his gaze back to Erasmus. "You're sure?"

"As sure as I can be," Erasmus replied. Then he gave a rueful smile. "You know, I didn't remember it until now, but Xanos himself had called the ring a...what was it?"

"A glorified transmitter," Kalibar recalled. He'd completely forgotten about that as well. "He knew it all along," he realized.

"That's right," Erasmus stated. "And you know what really terrifies me? That Xanos figured that out in seconds, and it took almost forty of my best Runics over a week to confirm it."

They both stood there silently for a long moment, staring at the ring laying in the center of the white table. Finally, Erasmus looked up at Kalibar, rubbing a hand over his shiny, bald head.

"So this brings up the obvious question," Erasmus said. Kalibar nodded, tapping his goatee with one finger.

"Right," he replied. "If the ring is a glorified transmitter, then what's been protecting Kyle – and all of us – all this time?"

"My thought exactly," Erasmus agreed. Kalibar stared at Kyle's ring, the center gemstone glittering a faint yellow-blue in the harsh light of the magical lanterns bolted to the walls. He idly remembered that it had been pure yellow before he got his new eyes; now it had a yellow center, with a light blue tint at the edges. He shook his head slowly, considering the ramifications. If the ring was just a transmitter, then it couldn't have protected Kyle from anything...and it couldn't have teleported Kyle to this world.

A glorified transmitter, he mused. *So who is the ring transmitting to?*

He turned away from the ring, staring at nothing in particular.

"I need time to think," he muttered.

* * *

Kalibar sat down on his bed, staring at the spot where the assassin who'd tried to murder him yesterday had lain. The body had finally been moved a half hour ago, the forensic evidence collected. Not that there had been any evidence to collect, other than the body. It had been a clean kill, with no damage at all to the surrounding furniture. Not a bloodstain on the carpet, or on Kalibar's bedsheets. The assassin's body and head had been transferred to the Royal Medical Examiner's office, where a careful autopsy would be performed.

He glanced at the full glass of greenish liquid on his nightstand. It was the narcotic drink Jenkins had prepared for him – and that Kalibar had declined – since he'd become Grand Weaver. If he hadn't needed the pain-killing drink before, he certainly didn't need it now.

Kalibar shook his head, realizing he was woolgathering. He'd come up to his room to get away for a while, to strategize, but his meeting with Erasmus had shaken him.

He sighed, rubbing his eyes wearily. Ever since he'd met Kyle, Kalibar had wondered how the boy had been transported here. At first, he hadn't really believed that Kyle was from another planet. Such an idea had seemed preposterous, laughable. But then he'd seen Kyle's timepiece...the "watch" with such amazing technology, such minute, perfect craftsmanship, powered by a mysterious, non-magical energy...it had convinced him that Kyle was for real.

An alien from another planet.

Yet he was so inexplicably human...indistinguishable from any other boy, save for the enormous amount of magic he generated. And Kyle had somehow recognized horses, which were also apparently on his planet...Urth, he'd called it. None of it made much sense.

Kalibar shook his head; he was woolgathering again. But why not? He laid down on his bed, still fully clothed, staring up at the ceiling. The real question was how Kyle had gotten here. Of course, the fact that Kyle's ring was a powerful transmitter was an obvious clue. If the signal were capable of traveling far enough, it could conceivably reach from one planet to another. The ring, then, might allow someone to determine its precise location from an enormous distance.

Kalibar closed his eyes, thinking back to what Kyle had said about his dreams. He'd only been half-listening at the time, what with his numerous head injuries, his blindness, and the threat of Orik's plot to overthrow the Empire hanging over him. Now he wished he'd been paying closer attention. The dreams had all been of Ampir, his wife, and his son. Of them experiencing the final hours of the Ancient war that had destroyed the Empire. Ampir had taken his family to a chamber, and had supposedly created a portal to another world, teleporting his son to safety, right before a giant magic death-machine had stomped the life out of him.

But before that, he'd given the child a ring...

According to Kyle, it had been *Ampir's* ring. And Erasmus had confirmed that Kyle's ring was indeed of Ancient origin. Which meant that Ampir's son had traveled to Urth, and somehow, over the next two thousand years, it had gotten into Kyle's hands. It was extraordinarily unlikely that Kyle had any blood relation to Ampir's son...after all, a lot could happen in two thousand years. The ring must have changed ownership countless times through the hundred or so generations that had passed. So why would anyone want to bring Kyle – a complete stranger – to this world? And why the dreams?

Kalibar frowned, stiffening suddenly.

The *dreams*! He sat up suddenly, slamming his fist into one palm. Then he got up from the bed and began to pace. The *dreams*...how could he have overlooked that? They were, without a doubt, Ampir's memories. Kalibar had assumed they'd been stored in the ring, and somehow Kyle had triggered their release. But if the ring was just a transmitter, then where had the memories come from?

Kalibar stopped, running a hand through his short, white hair. Then he looked down, staring at the tips of his boots. They were black, with numerous crystals embedded in the surface. Blue wisps of magic glowed faintly from each crystal. What an incredibly simple but powerful gift, to see so precisely what others could only feel vaguely. Sensing magic the traditional way – *feeling* the patterns with one's mind – was difficult and slow, requiring years of practice. If he'd had the ability to visualize the patterns as a child, to *see* magic streaming to these patterns in real time, he would have become a prodigy. Magic would have been so easy and intuitive, he would have become the most gifted Weaver in history...perhaps the greatest wielder of magic who'd ever lived. Like...

He felt goosebumps raised up on his arms, and a chill run down his spine. He closed his eyes, remembering the voice that had reverberated in his mind mere hours ago.

You wanted to meet me.

114

Kalibar felt his heart pound in his chest, and he stared off into the distance, at nothing at all.

And now you have.

"Dear god," he whispered.

It came to him then. He'd been at Crescent Lake with Kyle, talking about Kyle's dreams. He remembered staring at the waterfall in the distance, watching the countless droplets glitter in the morning sunlight. They'd been talking about Kyle's dreams.

What I wouldn't give to meet the man, he'd said.

Kalibar brought his trembling fingers to his eyelids, closing his eyes and passing his fingertips over them. His heart thumped rapidly in his chest.

Of course!

"Dear god," he repeated, another chill running through him. He sat down on his bed, resting his palms on his knees. It was so obvious now! How hadn't he figured it out earlier? But no, it was impossible...the man had died over two thousand years ago. Or had he? If he'd somehow managed to survive all these years...

Kalibar stared at the communication half-orb sitting on the end-table, the one he'd used to summon the guard previously. Runes shone on its surface, dozens of glowing blue patterns that only he could see.

Someone *had* been able to see magic like this, long ago. And they'd become the most powerful wielder of magic of all time. The most powerful Battle-Runic of all time.

It *had* to be Ampir!

Kalibar put a hand to his face again, running his fingers over his eyelids, feeling the swell of his eyeballs underneath. He lowered his hand, opening his eyes.

Of course Ampir wouldn't know any other way of seeing. It was all he knew, this amazing sight...and now he'd given Kalibar the gift of his perspective. Which meant, of course, that the man he'd met...that unthinkable wellspring of power...

But he died, Kalibar told himself, shaking his head slowly. *Even in Kyle's last dream, Ampir had died...*

But he knew it wasn't true. It could be no one else. And only a man as brilliant as Ampir could have found a way to fend off the greatest enemy of mankind...death.

You wanted to meet me.

Kalibar laughed suddenly. He'd wanted to meet Ampir, that much was true. And for some unknown reason, through some impossible stroke of luck, the most powerful Runic ever known had come to him, giving him back his sight.

Suddenly the doorbell rang. Kalibar flinched, then got up from his bed, striding into the main suite and peering to see who was behind the door. To his surprise, it was Master Owens, followed by a shaken-appearing Erasmus. Master Owens — usually preternaturally calm — looked uncharacteristically distraught, his face pale and drawn. Kalibar grabbed his eyepatches from his breast pocket, putting them on. Then he rushed to let the two men in.

"What's wrong, gentlemen?" he asked. Neither Erasmus or Master Owens said anything, but Owens shook his head, his lower lip quivering slightly.

He looked terrified.

Kalibar felt his guts twist, knowing that the fact that Owens himself had come to bring him news meant that it had to be about one of two people. And judging by the look on Owens' face...

"What is it?" he demanded, grabbing the man by the shoulders, struggling to stay calm.

"It's Master Banar," Master Owens replied, his voice quivering. "Kyle went to train with him this morning."

"And?" Kalibar pressed, his toner harsher than he'd planned. Owens paled, and Erasmus stepped in, putting a hand on Kalibar's shoulder.

"Master Owens found Master Banar a half-mile from the Tower," Erasmus interjected. Then he dropped his gaze to the floor. "Banar is dead."

"*What?*" Kalibar exclaimed. "How?"

"Murdered," Master Owens replied. "Impaled through the back of the head by the looks of it."

"And Kyle?" Kalibar pressed, dread coming over him. Master Owens shook his head mutely. Kalibar swallowed in a dry throat. "Is he...?"

"Missing," Owens replied.

"Damn it!" Kalibar swore. He turned from Erasmus and Master Owens, clenching and unclenching his fists.

116

They've taken my son!

He closed his eyes, feeling suddenly numb. The cold, calculating part of him examined the possibilities, and came up with only two. *They've taken him, or killed him,* he deduced. A vision of Kyle lying on the ground, eyes staring lifelessly upward, appeared in his mind's eye. He shook his head to clear it of that horrid image, opening his eyes. Master Owens and Erasmus were both staring at him. He turned away, unable to face them.

I was supposed to protect him, he thought, a familiar shame creeping over him. *I was supposed to protect my son, and I failed.*

Again.

Kalibar felt a hand squeeze his shoulder, and he turned to see Erasmus standing there. His old friend was one of the only people who knew about Kalibar's long-dead son. One of the few who understood what Kyle had really meant to him.

"We'll get him back," Erasmus promised. "I've already mobilized the guards. Say the word, and a dozen Battle-Weavers will fly out to find him."

Kalibar nodded mutely, knowing that if he spoke now, his voice would crack. He had the sudden, desperate urge to fly out of the Tower, to scour the Empire for Kyle himself. But he knew that he could not. He was Grand Weaver now...the entire Empire was his to protect. He could not endanger the lives of millions to save one, no matter how precious that one life might be.

But that was exactly what Ampir had done.

Kalibar turned back to Master Owens; the Weaver was still staring at the floor, clearly struggling to maintain his composure. Kalibar sighed, putting a hand on the man's shoulder.

"Send Battle Weavers to find him," he ordered. Master Owens nodded silently. Then Kalibar paused, a chill running down his spine. "Where's Ariana?"

"I sent her to her room in your retirement suite," Owens answered. "Erasmus took the liberty of asking a few Battle-Weavers to guard her until more formal arrangements could be made."

"Thank you," Kalibar replied, relieved. "Thank you both. If you could double the wards in her room," he added, glancing at Erasmus.

"Consider it done," Erasmus replied. Kalibar gave his old friend a weak smile, then walked over to the communication orb and activated it. At the same time, he turned back to Master Owens.

"No more outdoor lessons," he stated firmly. "Teach Ariana in her room." Master Owens nodded silently. He stared at Kalibar for a long moment, fidgeting restlessly. Kalibar frowned. "What is it?" he asked.

"We..." Master Owens answered, "...Ariana and I were only a mile away...we'd talked with them minutes before it happened." He lowered his gaze to the floor, shaking his head slowly. "I'm sorry, Kalibar." Kalibar put a hand on Owen's shoulder.

"It's not your fault," he replied. Master Owens nodded, but he did not look convinced. Kalibar sighed. "I can only hope Kyle's Aegis will protect him."

Owens swallowed visibly.

"He wasn't wearing the Aegis," the Weaver murmured, refusing to look up from the floor. Kalibar paused, a chill running through him. He felt suddenly as if the world were crumbling around him, and struggled to maintain his composure.

"I see," was all he could manage. He felt a sudden anger building within him, and tried to suppress it, without success.

Not wearing his armor!

He turned away from Master Owens, feeling the anger growing, turning into a cold fury. He grit his teeth, wondering how Kyle could possibly have forgotten to wear his armor, the Aegis of Athanasia, a breastplate so powerful that it would have made him nearly invincible. Perhaps not to Xanos, but still...

Not wearing his armor!

He closed his eyes, then turned back to Master Owens, using every ounce of self-control he had to stop himself from screaming.

"Explain how this happened," he ordered, his voice icy calm. He saw the blood drain from Master Owens' face, saw the man's hands trembling slightly at his sides. Owens opened his mouth to respond, but nothing came out. Kalibar stared at the man for a long moment, watching him struggle. "Name the guard who woke Kyle this morning," he commanded.

118

"Kalibar," Erasmus replied, stepping forward and placing a hand on his shoulder. "One of Jenkins' butlers woke Kyle this morning, and got him ready."

"What? Who?" Kalibar asked. Then he waved the question away. "I *specifically* stated that an *elite guard* was to accompany Kyle to and from the Tower," he growled, pulling backward so that Erasmus's hand fell from his shoulder. He clenched his fists, turning back to Master Owens. "Is a butler an elite guard?" he asked, his tone ice cold. Master Owens shook his head mutely.

"No sire," he mumbled.

"*Damn it!*" Kalibar shouted. A burst of magical patterns shot forth unbidden from his mind, and the glass table to his left exploded, shards of glass and metal flying across the room in all directions. He stared at Owens, spotting the gravity shield springing up around the Weaver, and felt a sudden desire to lash out at the man. Owens was a master-level Battle-Weaver, considered among the finest alive. But Kalibar was better – far better – and he had the sudden, mad desire to hurt Owens. To unleash his power, to show people what happened when they invited his rage.

Not wearing his armor!

He felt a warm hand on his shoulder, and turned, seeing Erasmus still there at his side. The Runic's blue eyes were gentle, his expression sad.

"Don't," he mouthed.

Kalibar paused, staring into his best friend's eyes, the rage draining from him. A part of him regretted its leaving, wanted to hold on to that anger, to sate its blood-lust. To feel the pleasure of giving in to it. But he nodded, knowing that Erasmus was right. He took a deep breath in, then let it out slowly, turning to Owens. He felt a sudden shame, knowing that Owens hadn't been responsible for Kyle not having his armor, and that he'd lashed out at the poor man – already wracked with grief over Banar's death and Kyle's absence – without provocation. Kalibar had not lost his temper in years; being possessed of enormous and deadly power had a way of instilling patience, out of necessity. At least in the just.

"I'm sorry," Kalibar apologized, putting a hand on Owens' shoulder. "You didn't deserve that. I hope you can forgive my temper." Master Owens glanced up at Kalibar, a weak smile on his lips.

"I'd forgotten you had one," he replied. Kalibar had to smile at that; Owens had served in the military with Kalibar, and had witnessed Kalibar losing his temper – to sobering effect – on the battlefield more than once.

"Yes, well, I'll save it for my enemies," Kalibar countered. "Not for you, old friend."

"You love your son," Owens stated with a shrug. And that, Kalibar knew, was true. Despite only having known Kyle for a few weeks, he'd grown terribly fond of the boy, a testament to the strange power that love could wield.

"Speaking of Kyle," Erasmus interjected, "Master Owens was just telling me that Kyle had told them of an idea he'd come up with, something that Master Banar had gotten very excited about." Kalibar frowned, only half-listening. Despite having regained his composure, his anger had not completely left him. He would have to have a conversation with that butler – and the elite guard who'd been scheduled to escort Kyle – to get to the bottom of their failure to protect his son.

"What was it?" he asked absently.

"Kyle had come up with an idea for finding new magical patterns," Owens answered. "He asked why we didn't just put random sensory runes into a crystal, then place magical plants or animals nearby, and see which runes lit up."

"What?" Kalibar asked. Owens repeated what he'd said, and this time Kalibar paid attention, frowning slightly. "Interesting idea," he murmured, turning to Erasmus. "What do you think?"

The Grand Runic frowned, running a hand through his thick white beard. Then he shook his head. "Not very practical," he opined. "Don't get me wrong...it would probably work, but it'd be a damn slow process," he added. "Probably take years just to stumble upon one pattern."

"That's what Banar and I said," Owens agreed. "But then Kyle said something...something about using parts of runes instead."

"Yes, well," Kalibar muttered. "...I don't have time for this right now. We need to find Kyle."

Erasmus put a hand on Kalibar's shoulder.

"I'll get my Runics involved," he promised. Then he turned to Owens, nodding at the man. They both left Kalibar then, closing the door behind them. Kalibar watched them go, then stood there in the empty room, the most powerful man in the most powerful Empire in the world, feeling anything but.

Kyle isn't wearing his ring, he brooded. He dismissed the thought almost immediately. It didn't matter, of course...the ring was useless. Unless of course...

Kalibar frowned. Unless of course Ampir – or whoever it was that was protecting the boy – needed the ring's transmitter to find him.

He walked across the massive suite, to the thick glass wall at one end of the room. He gazed out over the city, past the expanse of lawn, past the countless buildings in the distance, past the massive bridge crossing the Great River.

Then a thought occurred to him; Darius had gone looking for Kyle earlier that morning! Kalibar spun around, sprinting up to the communication globe, signaling the head of the elite guards. He resuming pacing, intermittently glancing at the front door to his suite, waiting impatiently. If Darius had gotten to Kyle in time...

A man appeared in front of the door – one of the elite guards. Kalibar made his door translucent for the guard, watching as the man's eyes focusing on him.

"Your Excellency," the guard greeted.

"I want Darius found," Kalibar ordered. "He left to find my son a few hours ago, when he was with Master Banar." The guard's eyes widened at that. News traveled quickly in the Tower; no doubt everyone knew of the Runic's fate. The guard bowed crisply.

"Yes Grand Weaver."

"And..." Kalibar added, willing his voice to remain calm. "...get me the guard that was supposed to wake Kyle this morning."

"Yes, sire."

Kalibar dismissed the man with a wave of his hand, and the guard went immediately to his task. Kalibar turned away from the door, running a hand through his hair. He began pacing yet again, considering the possibilities. If Darius had gotten to Kyle before Master Banar was attacked, then there was hope for Kyle. Then again, despite the body-guard's skill, he wouldn't stand a chance against a group of Weavers. But if Darius hadn't gotten there in time, he would have found Master Banar's corpse himself, and one would hope that the bodyguard – un-predictable as he was – would have returned to notify Kalibar before running off to find Kyle.

Kalibar sighed, feeling the weight of his son's fate on his shoulders. It felt every bit as heavy as that of the Empire he'd sworn to protect.

Not wearing his armor!

Kalibar grit his teeth, feeling the enormity of his failure. He'd vowed to protect Kyle at any cost, to do for the boy what he'd failed to do for his own son, so many decades ago. Now the boy was gone, kidnapped or worse, and he had no idea where Kyle was...or if he was even still alive.

And despite his immense magical power, and the influence he wielded, all he could do now was wait.

Chapter 11

Ampir closes his eyes as the slab of gray stone falling from the ceiling falls toward him, draining the last of the magic from his armor's runes and weaving strands of power into a complex knot in the center of his mind. An old pattern, one he'd learned long ago, one he'd taught to Renval.

Teleportation.

He thrusts the pattern outward, right at Torum.

The air around Torum *rips*, the very fabric of space and time bending to Ampir's will. The dark Weaver vanishes...then reappears behind Ampir. Torum's multilayered gravity shields intersect with Ampir's back, throwing Ampir bodily forward...and out of the path of the falling stone slab.

Torum doesn't even have time to register what has happened before the slab slams into him from above.

Ampir stumbles forward, losing his balance and falling onto his belly on the stone floor. He cries out, his shattered left shoulder and broken ribs screaming in pain. Stars float in the periphery of his vision.

He lays there in agony, his breaths coming in short gasps. Then, slowly, painfully, he rolls onto his back. He raises his head, staring at the pile of rubble where the slab had fallen...where Torum had been standing.

Two black boots protrude from the rubble.

Ampir stares at the boots, then lowers his head to the floor, closing his eyes and taking long, slow breaths. Each breath sends stabbing pains through the left side of his chest.

Focus.

He grits his teeth, then rolls back onto his belly, biting back a scream as more pain shoots through him. He spins around slowly until he's facing Torum's boots, then pushes himself onto his hands and knees. Using his good arm, he crawls forward.

Slowly, painfully, he reaches Torum's exposed legs. They're covered in a tight, black, almost woody fabric. Ampir spots a tear in that uniform at mid-shin; a jagged, pearly white shaft of broken bone protrudes through Torum's skin there. Blue light emanates from it.

Ampir pulls himself forward until he's directly over the exposed shin bone, then lowers his forehead until it is almost touching it. He *pulls*, feeling magic flow into his mind's eye, then redistribute to his starving skull bones. He lets them fill, knowing it will be easier to weave if they're sated.

After a few minutes, the bone is drained. Ampir redirects some of his magic into his armor's runes, feeling its incredible weight immediately vanish as its gravity fields come back online. He activates its ventilation and temperature-control runes, then fills a few runes on his gauntlets.

He needs magic. So much more magic.

Ampir reaches down, clearing large chunks of rubble from Torum's body with his right hand, shoving the heavy stone aside as if it weighs nothing. He exposes the Weaver's shattered corpse, finding islands of blue light glowing from tears in that black uniform. Slowly, methodically, he drains the magic from Torum, redirecting it to the critical runes in his armor.

Then he stands up, turning away from the Weaver. With a thought, the armor covering his left arm becomes immovable, forming a virtual cast around the broken limb. It still aches terribly, but at least it's bearable now. He glances at the pit in the ground nearby, then weaves magic, a huge hunk of rubble rising up from the floor. It floats forward until it levitates directly over the pit, lowering itself to seal Vera's final resting place.

Torum was right, he knows. It was *his* fault that Vera was dead. And that the Empire lay in ruins.

He gazes up at the massive hole in the ceiling, at the stars far above. With a thought, he rises through the air, passing through the hole. Above ground, he sees the vast campus of the Secula Magna spread out before him. The Great Tower is nothing more than a pile of rubble, the shattered cityscape beyond the campus covered in a thick layer of black smoke.

Ampir rises high above the ground, staring at the devastation around him, feeling numb. Millions of lives had been lost in mere hours, many of them his colleagues, a few his friends. All because of Sabin.

Ampir opens his eyes, lowering his gaze and using his visor to magnify his vision, staring at the countless blackened corpses lying in the streets. At the bodies floating in the Great River. He knows what most of them had been thinking before their deaths.

Ampir will come. Ampir will save us.

He turns his head, spotting the Behemoth in the distance, now wading across the Great River. The dark water comes only to its mid-thighs, massive waves shooting upward from each leg as they move forward through the water. The fact that the Behemoth isn't flying across the river is telling; it means that its magic capacity is limited, that it is conserving its remaining power.

Ampir flies forward toward the Behemoth, passing over the campus of the Secula Magna. He crosses the Gate shield, flying over the ruins of countless buildings, until he lands on what remains of the roof of Stridon Penitentiary. He closes his eyes, picturing Sabin's small cell back in this very prison years ago. How pathetic Sabin had looked, how utterly defeated.

I should've let him rot in there.

He stares at the Behemoth, using his visor's power to study the Behemoth. A slight vibration buzzes the back of his head, and he turns to see a black-cloaked Weaver descending through the air toward him. Like Torum, he is bald, with tattoos on his face and skull. Multi-layered gravity shields surround him.

Ampir just stands there, staring at the Weaver as his feet touch down on the roof, his black cloak rippling in the wind. The Weaver stares back.

"Where's..." he begins.

Ampir reaches out with his good hand, the runes on his gauntlet flashing bright blue. The Weaver's head lurches forward, flying toward Ampir's open palm. Ampir's hand and arm go right through the Weaver's shields, and Ampir grips the man's face, a burst of white light shooting from his palm.

The Weaver's head disintegrates, his body falling with a *thump* at Ampir's feet.

Ampir kneels down before the headless corpse, leaning over until his forehead is inches from the stump of its neck. He closes his eyes, *pulling* magic from its bones, feeling his mind's eye fill with power.

Minutes later, when he's had his fill, Ampir stands, turning to face the Behemoth in the distance. Slowly, methodically, he fills his armor's runes, studying the monstrous machine as it finishes crossing the Great River miles from where he stands. A pale white spotlight shoots outward from its lone eye, scanning the buildings in the other half of the city beyond the River. A burst of green light shoots outward, reducing several buildings to red-hot rubble.

I started this.

He uses up the last of the magic he'd taken from the Weaver, his armor still only filled to a fraction of its full power. Hopefully it will be enough.

Now I'm going to end it.

* * *

Kyle opened his eyes.

He squinted against a bright light shining on him, putting a hand between his face and the offending rays. He groaned, his shoulder aching with the movement. Slowly, it came back to him...traveling with Master Banar back to the Tower. Tumbling to the ground. Master Banar's...

Kyle squeezed his eyes shut, tears dripping down his cheeks. He'd known the man for only an hour or two, yet even in that short span of time, he'd grown fond of the Runic instructor.

Then he felt a spike of fear in his belly, a horrible, sickening hopelessness coming over him.

The Dead Man.

Kyle forced the fear away, opening his eyes and blinking against the light. He was in a rectangular room, with metallic walls, ceiling, and floor. There were slit-like windows on the sides, letting in narrow beams of light. He was sitting up against one side-wall, a small rectangle of white gauze-like material laying on the ground beside him.

The room looked familiar somehow.

He braced his hands against the cool metallic floor, ignoring the pain in his shoulder as he pushed himself to his feet. Swaying a little, he walked to the narrow, horizontal window in front of him, peering out. He saw only blue light, nothing more. Turning away from the window, he noticed a man slumped against the wall.

Kyle froze.

The man was dressed in a simple white shirt and gray pants, his biceps bulging out of his short sleeves, the sinews of his forearms clearly visible underneath his tanned skin. His feet were bare, the calloused soles caked with dirt. He was asleep – or worse – his hands bound in front of him with metal cuffs. Kyle frowned, not recognizing the man...at first. Then he felt his heart skip a beat.

"Darius!" he shouted, running to the bodyguard. He grabbed the man's broad shoulders, shaking them. "Darius!" he repeated, shaking harder. The bodyguard said nothing, his eyes remaining closed. Kyle felt a pang of fear, and reached for Darius's neck, feeling for a pulse at his carotid. Kyle's parents, both emergency room doctors, had showed him how to do this years ago. To Kyle's relief, he felt a slow, steady pulse there. Darius was alive!

Kyle shook Darius again...but it was no use. He stood up, looking around. Where were they? In a prison cell? He walked up to the slit-like window above Darius's head, peering out. He saw more blue, as before, but this time he spotted a faint wisp of white all the way to the left. He frowned, staring at that wisp, realizing that it was moving

127

slowly, from left to right in his field of view. He blinked, then stared at it again; sure enough, it was still moving.

Then it came to him...that wisp was a *cloud.*

Kyle spun about, taking in the four metallic walls, the narrow windows. He suddenly realized why this room had seemed so familiar earlier. It wasn't a room at all...it was a carriage. A *flying* carriage.

Kyle stepped back from the window, a chill running through him. He'd flown in a similar carriage after the Dead Man had defeated Kalibar at Crescent Lake...the carriage that had taken them to the Arena.

He stood on his tip-toes, trying to look as far downward through the narrow window as possible. Sure enough, he saw treetops below the sea of blue, moving slowly in the distance. He felt his knees weaken, and he sat down with a thump, despair coming over him. After everything he'd been through – the harrowing escape from the Arena, nearly dying at the feet of the Dire Lurker, and the final battle with the Dead Man – he'd thought that the whole experience had been far behind him. Now he knew that his escape had been temporary...a cruel taste of freedom before returning to the depths of Hell.

Kyle slumped over, burying his head in his hands. He was doomed to live underground, to be viciously and systematically molded into a servant of the Dead Man's dark lord. But this time, Ariana wouldn't be there. Kalibar wouldn't come to save him. He would be utterly alone.

Wait...

He looking up to see Darius there, still fast asleep against the wall. No, he wasn't alone...not yet. He felt a glimmer of hope, knowing that if he could just get the bodyguard to wake up, the man would know what to do. He *always* seemed to know what to do, after all. Kyle got to his feet, walking up to the bodyguard and grabbing his shoulders again.

"Wake up!" he shouted, shaking Darius. No response. Kyle hesitated, then raised his hand until it hovered over Darius's face. He held it there, knowing that he had to wake Darius up somehow...but slapping the man in the face was something he just couldn't bring himself to do. Then he remembered when he'd first met Darius, how the man had yanked him out of his chair, treating him like a mutt. How he'd called Kyle useless, and laughed when he'd nearly killed himself flying through Kalibar's gravity shield.

Kyle swung his arm, slapping Darius full across the face.

Then he shrieked, launching himself backward against the opposite wall. He grabbed his right hand, shocked at the pain lancing through his palm. He always figured the bodyguard had a thick skull, but that *hurt!* He shook his hand, massaging it gingerly. Then he stared nervously at Darius, half-expecting the man to jump up and give Kyle a royal beat-down. But Darius hadn't so much as flinched.

Suddenly, the carriage tilted, nosing downward. Kyle braced himself against one wall, feeling his stomach flip. He turned to look out the window, seeing the carriage dip below the treetops.

Kyle knew what the descent signified. It was the end of his flight, and the beginning of his trip into the bowels of the earth.

The carriage leveled off, winding through the forest, until the trees became more sparse. Then it dipped downward again, very gently, until it leveled out once more, and stopped.

Kyle backed up against the front wall of the carriage, facing the double-doors on the opposite side. Then he turned to Darius, sprinting to his side and grabbing his wrist. He pulled on it, straining to move the burly bodyguard, but the man was impossibly heavy...he didn't budge an inch. Kyle tried again, pulling as hard as he could, leaning backward. Darius slid toward Kyle, then rolled onto his side, his head slamming into the metal floor below with a dull thud. Kyle cringed, letting go of Darius's wrist and backing up against the front wall again. But not even that woke the bodyguard.

Kyle felt a subtle buzzing in the air, the familiar sensation of magic being woven. Suddenly, the rear doors of the carriage swung open, bright sunlight bursting into the carriage, making Kyle's eyes sting. He squinted, pressing his back against the cool metal wall. A tall, bald-headed man in a red shirt and pants stood beyond the double-doors. The man wore a black sash with a green diamond in the center, the uniform of a Death Weaver.

"Get out," the man growled. Without warning, he lunged forward, grabbing Kyle's wrist and yanking him out of the carriage. Kyle stumbled onto the rocky ground beyond, nearly falling onto his face. He righted himself, looking around. In front of him stood the sheer vertical face of a mountain, its tall peak hidden in dense clouds far above their heads. A huge entrance had been cut into the face of the rock wall before them, some twenty feet wide and ten feet tall.

"Wake the man," a deep voice commanded. The bald Death Weaver let go of Kyle's wrist at once, walking back toward the carriage behind Kyle. Kyle turned about, realizing that there were over a dozen other carriages hovering inches above the ground behind the one he'd emerged from. All of them, save for the one he'd come from, were empty. He turned forward again, and nearly jumped; the Dead Man stood before him.

"Are you hurt?" the dark Weaver asked, gesturing toward Kyle's left shoulder — the one he'd smacked into the ground when he'd fallen earlier. Kyle shook his head mutely, then glanced back at the carriage. The bald Death Weaver was inside, kneeling over Darius's motionless body.

"Your friend will be awake soon enough," the Dead Man promised. "You've both been sleeping since yesterday," he added. Kyle blinked, wondering how he'd managed to sleep for so long. The bald Death Weaver reached under Darius's shirt, peeling something thin and white from his chest. It was a white gossamer square, almost translucent, and rippled in the warm breeze. It was, Kyle realized, identical to the one he'd seen at his feet when he'd woken up earlier. It had to be dreamweaver silk, woven by the deadly dreamweaver spider; the substance could make its victims sleep indefinitely.

The Death Weaver threw the silk patch aside quickly, stifling a yawn as he did so, then grabbed Darius's arm, pulling upward. The bodyguard didn't budge.

The Death Weaver stood back, then placed both of his hands under Darius's armpits, bending his knees, then hauling the bodyguard upward. The veins on the Weaver's forehead bulged as he strained, managing with great difficulty to lift Darius into a sitting position against the wall. The Dead Man watched for a few moments, then sighed.

"Lift him with magic, Ethan," he instructed. The bald man nodded, but before he could comply, Darius's eyelids fluttered open, and he groaned, bringing his hand to his right temple.

130

"Get up," the bald Weaver – Ethan – ordered, kicking Darius in the hip with one booted foot. Darius turned his piercing blue eyes on the man, then looked out of the carriage at Kyle.

"I said get up!" Ethan yelled. Darius glanced back at the Death Weaver.

"You need a nap," he grumbled, rising to his feet in one fluid motion. He glanced down at the metal shackles around his wrists, then at Kyle and the Dead Man standing beyond. Ethan shoved Darius forward, or tried to; Darius twisted his shoulder forward at the last minute, causing Ethan to stumble forward into him. Then Darius snapped his shoulder backward, catching the Death Weaver square in the jaw with it.

The man dropped like a stone.

The Dead Man glanced down at the fallen Ethan, then looked back at Darius.

"Join us," the Dead Man ordered. Then he shifted his gaze to Kyle. "Come," he ordered, extending a pale hand. Kyle glanced at it, then back at the Dead Man's black, sunken eyes. Despite every fiber of his being screaming for him to obey, knowing what might happen to Darius if he didn't, he couldn't move. His mind would not let him go forward into the cavern, to that underground prison.

"We both have...unpleasant memories to face," the Dead Man murmured. "I assure you that mine are harder to bear." His jawline rippled. "He took everything from me."

Kyle lowered his gaze, swallowing in a dry throat. He glanced at the Dead man's hands, noticing that the left hand was different than the right; the fingers were longer, the skin slightly darker. He pictured the Dead Man as he had last seen him, his feet crushed by Kalibar's magic, his left arm missing, the left side of his face blackened and charred. Kyle looked up at the Dead Man's face, at the white scars spreading like pearly fingers across his left temple. He wondered what dark power had revived the Dead Man, breathing life back into his shattered body.

"We will face our demons," the Dead Man stated, "...and our fates." He gripped Kyle's shoulder with his icy fingers, then turned toward the huge cavern opening, gliding forward silently, his boots levitating

131

inches above the ground. He pulled Kyle with him. Kyle stumbled forward, then matched the Dead Man's pace. He glanced back, seeing Darius step out of the carriage, following close behind. In this way, they made their way toward the cavern together, until the rocky ceiling blotted out the sun above, the cave's shadows swallowing them whole.

* * *

The tunnels were just as Kyle remembered them.

They walked silently through the massive main tunnel, the ground sloping gently downward into the bowels of the earth. Magical lanterns hung on the walls on either side, gently illuminating the massive cavern. Kyle couldn't help glancing back the way they'd come, past a silent Darius, watching as the mouth of the cave retreated in the distance. The sun's rays splashed on the gray rocks jutting out of the cavern walls near the entrance, but none dared venture deeper in. Kyle stared at those illuminated rocks, wondering with a sinking heart if he would ever see the sun again. As the three continued their onward and downward trek, the cave entrance disappeared, hidden by the downward-sloping cavern floor. Kyle turned forward, and he didn't look back again. He felt as if a chapter of his life had just ended, and a new, darker one was about to begin.

No one spoke as they traveled for what seemed like an eternity down the massive underground tunnel, passing countless magical lanterns on either side. The air became cooler as they moved downward, and damper, the powerful stench of dirt making Kyle sneeze more than once. His mind wandered, and he found himself imagining being back on Earth, getting picked up after school, telling his dad about his day. Playing with his best friend Ben in the backyard, the sun shining on them as they pretended to be spies on the roof outside Ben's bedroom window, tracking the other kids as they played in their own yards. He pictured himself in his own bed, his mom stroking his hair as he slowly fell asleep.

Kyle jerked himself out of his reverie, realizing the tunnel had suddenly ended. An all-too-familiar stone ramp extended along the rightmost wall, to a small tunnel hewn in the rock. Kyle followed the Dead

Man up the ramp and into that dark tunnel. There were no magic lanterns in this tunnel; the Dead Man stopped, turning to Kyle.

"If you would," he prompted. Kyle nodded, weaving the light pattern rapidly and casting it outward. A bright ball of white light appeared, casting a gentle glow throughout the long tunnel. The Dead Man smiled. "Thank you," he said. Then he moved forward again, gliding above the smooth stone floor, his black cloak rippling endlessly behind him. Kyle noted absently that the grayish patterns on the cloak were different than they had been before. It made sense, of course; Darius had taken the original cloak and given it to Ariana after beheading the man.

Kyle glanced up at the back of the Dead Man's neck, spotting a thin, purplish line in the pale flesh. He felt queasy, picturing the man's head lying on the ground, black eyes staring lifelessly outward, the body several feet away. He stared at the Dead Man's neck, wondering just how securely it had been reattached. He couldn't help running his fingers over his own neck, imagining what it would be like to know that it had been welded back to his body.

They continued down the tunnel silently, until it opened up into a huge, well-lit cavern. Everything was exactly as it had been when he'd been there not even two weeks ago; the rows of stadium seating, the circular, dirt floor of the Arena below. The twin pairs of dormitories surrounding the perimeter of the far side of the cavern, their walls carved out of the very rock itself. The dark waters of a pond between each pair, underneath which Kyle knew the secret underwater chamber the Dead Man had called "the Void" lay. Even the Timestone was there, a massive glowing sphere levitating halfway between the floor of the Arena and the ceiling a hundred feet above.

Everything was the same...except that it was empty. Whereas before the lair had been bustling with people, now it was utterly deserted.

The Dead Man stopped abruptly, staring down at the Arena, his expression unreadable. Darius stopped ten feet behind them, having said nothing the entire time.

"Welcome home," the Dead Man muttered. Kyle couldn't tell if the dark Weaver was talking to him...or to himself.

Kyle said nothing, staring at the dormitories below instead. He noticed a dark figure emerging from the leftmost dormitory entrance, moving slowly toward the Arena floor. The figure made its way across the Arena to one of the many stairways traveling upward between rows of seats. As it shambled toward them, Kyle saw that it was an old man carrying a beaten-up wooden cane in his right hand. No, old was an understatement; the man was *ancient*, his skin as thin and dry as wrinkled parchment. Deep lines crisscrossed his forehead, then fell in sharp crevices cutting into his sunken cheeks. He had a large, irregular white scar running across his forehead, with countless smaller scars running the length of his stick-like arms. Odd bumps rose from his flesh, scattered over his body. The man's clothes were too large for his thin frame, the fabric torn and soiled.

The old man hobbled up the steps of the Arena, until at long last he stopped a few feet before Kyle and the Dead Man. Kyle shrank back, wrinkling his nose in disgust; a foul odor rose from the old man, a stench so revolting that it almost made Kyle gag. The old man's eyes — nearly hidden beneath the folds of his eyelids — were sharp and lively, the only part of him that seemed alive.

"Your remaining children are safe," the old man stated.

"Thank you," the Dead Man replied, bowing slightly. The old man paused, then sighed, putting a wrinkled hand on the Dead Man's shoulder.

"Your family deserved better."

"It was my failure," the Dead Man murmured, lowering his gaze.

"And that failure led to necessary consequences," the old man lamented. "Faith in the Chosen must be absolute. I only hope the children can be rehabilitated." He sighed again. "We are dealing with a force beyond your abilities," he added, patting the Dead Man's shoulder. "Xanos will see to it that you and your family are avenged."

"Thank you," the Dead Man replied, bowing again.

The old man turned to Kyle then, and Kyle shrank under his gaze.

"Ahhh, *this* is the boy," he murmured, looking Kyle over. "A remarkable specimen...he would have been exceptional even in Ancient times, as you call them now."

Kyle said nothing, nearly gagging at the awful stench emanating from the old man.

"And this must be the bodyguard," the old man proclaimed, turning to Darius, who was standing behind the other two. He reached out

134

with one misshapen finger, gesturing for Darius to come forward. "Come closer...my eyes aren't what they used to be." Darius complied, stepping forward until he was standing between Kyle and the Dead Man. The old man looked Darius up and down.

"I've heard a lot about you," he stated, reaching out with one withered hand and patting Darius on the side of the face. The bodyguard didn't react. "I particularly enjoyed the lesson you gave poor Ethan," he added. "Too many Weavers fail to understand that magic is just a tool. And, like any other tool, it can be taken away. The man makes the tool...and you, my friend, have made great use of what little you have."

"You have no idea what that means to me," Darius muttered.

The old man leaned forward, hunching over his cane.

"You look familiar, my boy," he murmured. "Have we met before?"

"Would've remembered the smell," Darius replied. The old man chuckled.

"I suspect so," he agreed. Then he sighed, turning back to the Dead Man. "Well, as much as I'd like to stay and chat, I must be going."

"Xanos be with you," the Dead Man stated, bowing slightly. The old man smiled – or smirked. It was difficult for Kyle to tell.

"Indeed," he replied. He hesitated, then put a hand on the Dead Man's gaunt cheek. "Your faith will be rewarded."

The Dead Man lowered his gaze, saying nothing.

"The seeds of the future grow from the fertile soil the dead leave behind," the old man mused, lowering his hand and rapping the butt of his cane on the stone floor. Then he turned away, hobbling down the steps one at a time, slowly making his way back down to the Arena floor. The Dead Man watched the old man leave, saying nothing. Kyle watched as the man crossed the Arena, limping toward the pond between the dormitories. He waded through the water, his knees, then his waist vanishing below the dark surface. Still, he continued forward, until his head had disappeared, only slow ripples marking where he had been moments ago.

The Dead Man stirred, turning to face Kyle and Darius, his expression unreadable.

"Come," he stated. He glided forward then, down the stairway. Kyle and Darius followed the Dead Man, passing rows of seats on

135

either side until they reached the bottom. They crossed the packed dirt floor of the Arena, the Dead Man guiding them toward the pond between the dormitories, stopping before the gently rippling waters. He turned toward the dormitories on the left, gazing at them wistfully.

"I knew them all," the Dead Man stated softly. "Every single one of them. And their fathers, their mothers. Their grandparents. I raised all of them. I was there when they were born, and for every birthday they celebrated. But I wasn't there for them when they were sacrificed." He turned back to Kyle, his pale lips thin and tight on his face. "Six generations, Kyle. My life's work."

They stood there for a long moment, in complete silence.

The Dead Man tore his gaze away from the empty dormitories, turning to stare at the empty stands of the Arena. He stood there for what seemed like an eternity, not so much as blinking. At long last, he stirred, turning to face the pond again.

"Come close," he ordered. Kyle and Darius complied, flanking the Dead Man. A faint blue gravity sphere appeared around them all, and the Dead Man levitated forward, the globe moving forward with him into the pond. The dark waters parted around the impenetrable sphere, and before long they were descending rapidly. The pond completely engulfed them, faint rays of light shimmering from the now-turbulent surface above. Soon it was so dark that Kyle could see nothing at all. Kyle felt the Dead Man's hand on his shoulder.

"If you would," he murmured.

Kyle wove the light pattern, and a bright light appeared within the sphere, revealing a sea of blue in all directions. Downward they went, until Kyle spotted gray, irregular stone below. He looked forward, seeing a familiar arched doorway carved into the sheer stone wall ahead. A rippling mirror made of water filled the doorway, a portal into the secret room beyond.

The Void.

They floated toward the doorway, their reflections growing larger and larger, until the magical sphere contacted the silvery surface, parting the water and revealing a narrow tunnel beyond. Soon they had passed all the way through the doorway. The shimmering sphere vanished, and the Dead Man dropped to the floor, his black boots clicking on the metal platform below. His cloak fell limply around his body, its perpetual rippling coming to an end.

Kyle looked down the narrow hallway, seeing huge white crystals lining the walls and ceiling, forming a glittering, pulsing arch above their heads. A narrow metallic platform ran down the length of the tunnel, clanging dully with every footstep. The Dead Man stepped forward, making his way down the tunnel, not bothering to look back. Darius and Kyle followed. Darius, having never seen the tunnel, walked more slowly than the other two, gazing upward at the massive crystals.

"There's something I want to show you," their pale captor said without turning, his tall, black-clad form contrasting brilliantly with the perfect whiteness of the Void crystals surrounding him. They followed him down the long platform, until the tunnel opened up into a dome-shaped room, the walls and ceiling made of more huge, glittering white crystals. The floor was a continuation of the metallic platform from the tunnel behind them; in the very center of the floor, a series of green crystals of various lengths jutted out at a forty-five-degree angle. The Dead Man walked up to the green crystals, putting a hand on one of them. They began to glow faintly, bathing the Dead Man in their sickly light. He turned to face Kyle.

"You're cold," he observed, watching as Kyle shivered in the icy air of the Void. Kyle nodded mutely, crossing his arms over his chest and stuffing his hands in his armpits. He cleared his throat.

"Can I make a fire?" he asked. "To warm my hands." The Dead Man nodded.

"Of course."

Kyle concentrated, pulling magic from his mind's eye...and couldn't find any. He frowned, concentrating harder, and *pulled* a thread of magic from his brain, twisting it into the fire pattern. Then he threw it outward, and...

It vanished.

He opened his eyes, giving the Dead Man a bewildered look.

"Now you can see," the Dead Man stated, gesturing at the white crystals all around them. "The Void crystals absorb all magic. You can't weave in this room...no one can. As soon as the magic leaves you, the crystals absorb it. Even now, the Void is drawing out the magic from your mind and your bones. It is a perpetual vacuum...in another minute, there will be no more magic left within you...or within the earring you wear."

Kyle touched the yellow earring in his right earlobe, remembering how it had stopped working the last time he'd been in the Void. He glanced up at the green crystal in the Dead Man's forehead.

"What about *your* crystal?" he asked.

"An excellent question," the Dead Man replied. Then he sighed. "You have such potential, Kyle. If only we'd been able to realize that potential together." He gestured at his black cloak. "My cloak prevents my bones from losing magic," he stated. Then he lifted his right hand, bringing his fingertips to the gemstone on his forehead. "And there is a Void crystal in the center of my shard, as small as a grain of sand. It ensures that a small amount of magic will remain within, so that I can live to recharge my shard here, at that terminal," he added, gesturing toward the green crystals jutting up from the metallic floor. "It also pulls in magic from my surroundings, should my crystal become critically low on power."

"But isn't the magic being pulled from it right now?" Kyle pressed. The Dead Man nodded.

"Very astute," he replied. He turned his back to them, gesturing at the small chamber with one hand. "I came here to show you something."

The platform beneath them vibrated, then began to rise. The domed ceiling above opened like the petals of a flower, revealing an utter blackness above. They rose through that opening, ascending into utter darkness. Soon, the ceiling of the Void closed below them, forming the floor upon which the platform rested. Without warning, their ascent stopped.

Kyle glanced about; the green crystals continued to glow, illuminating a large circle in the gray stone floor below. The Dead Man turned back to face them.

"You're about to witness something only the Chosen are privileged enough to see," he declared, his deep voice echoing in the blackness. "It is Xanos's will that you see it," he added, resting his hand on the green crystals.

138

A sudden burst of light exploded before Kyle's eyes, forcing him to squeeze them shut. He thrust his hands in front of his face, grimacing against the unexpected assault. Slowly his eyes adjusted, and he opened them, squinting in the bright light.

His breath caught in his throat.

The room they'd entered was massive...as big as an airplane hangar. All around them were row upon row of huge, metallic constructions, standing at least ten stories tall, and as wide around as a large building. Kyle stared at one of the monstrosities, gazing at the jet-black metal, trying to figure out what exactly it was. The thing stood on four huge limbs, that much was clear, but beyond that, Kyle could only guess. There were nine of the monstrous contraptions placed in neat rows of three in the chamber.

Kyle glanced at Darius, who was looking around the room; the bodyguard seemed just as perplexed as Kyle.

"Behold my sacred duty," the Dead Man declared, spreading his arms out wide. "Xanos has tasked the Chosen with serving as His avatars, so that He may maintain His army beneath the earth." He lowered his arms, his black eyes staring into Kyle's. "We work in the darkness, unknown and unseen, guiding and protecting humanity from its greatest enemy."

"What enemy?" Darius asked. The Dead Man smiled.

"Itself."

Darius said nothing, staring at the metallic constructs filling the chamber.

"Xanos guides humanity," the Dead Man continued. "He will bring it back to the power and sophistication of the Ancients...and far beyond."

"Right," Darius grumbled. The Dead Man smirked.

"Men fear what they don't understand," he lectured. "They react to their fear with violence. Old men resist change, clinging desperately to their way of life, and old men carry the power in this world. Change is always accepted by the next generation...after their elders grow old and die."

"Or are killed off," Darius countered. The Dead Man sighed.

"That was not the original intent," he countered. "Had Orik followed orders, he would have become Grand Weaver, and instituted sweeping changes to magic education, governmental policy, and every other aspect of life. The renaissance of runic technology would have continued at an incredible pace, transforming the world, bettering the standard of living for poor and rich alike."

"So why all this?" Darius asked, gesturing around the chamber.

"This army," the Dead Man answered, "...was created to protect humanity."

"From what?" Darius pressed.

"Only Xanos knows."

"Isn't that convenient," Darius muttered. The Dead Man ignored the comment, lowering his eyes to the platform below.

"You think us the enemy," he stated. "But we far from it. Xanos wished for a peaceful transition to Orik's rule...but Orik failed Him. Failed *me*. That necessitated my intervention. Kalibar was a casualty to preserve the original plan...one casualty to prevent millions. He, of course, did not see it that way. He is, after all, one of the old men I spoke of earlier. Despite my explaining what I've just told you to him, he remained predictably defiant."

"So you tore out his eyes."

"He presented a danger to my daughters, and resisted his duties...at first," the Dead Man explained. "I couldn't guard him twenty-four hours a day, not with my other responsibilities. And he was most certainly planning to escape, to warn the Empire. And now that very thing has occurred, despite my efforts to stop it...and Kalibar himself is leading the Empire toward a pointless war with us." He shook his head. "We offered a peaceful solution. You chose war."

"We're not the bad guys!" Kyle protested. "You killed Ariana's parents. You kidnapped us. You ordered me to set Darius on fire!"

"Ah yes, Ariana," the Dead Man replied calmly. "A gifted student...something we have too few of," he added. "We didn't have any difficulty getting such students before the New Empire was formed...and it wasn't until Kalibar's first term as Emperor that the Secula Magna's monopoly on children with the gift became complete." He shook his head sadly. "The only way to get access to a pool of students was to take them before the Secula Magna could...none would go willingly to us with the incentives the Empire gave parents for allowing their children to be enrolled. We had no choice."

140

"You're wrong," Kyle retorted. "You can say whatever you want, but you're still evil!"

"You're young," the Dead Man countered. "You don't understand that there's no such thing as 'good' and 'evil,' Kyle." He turned to Darius then. "Don't you agree?"

"It's you versus him," the bodyguard replied, gesturing toward Kyle. "I'm on his side."

"Fair enough," the Dead Man replied. "I see I'm not going to convince either of you." He placed his hand back on one of the green crystals in the center of the platform. "Again, you force my hand."

The green crystals glowed brighter, and the crystal in the Dead Man's forehead flashed briefly. The Dead Man removed his hand from the depression in the green crystals, and they went dark.

"Xanos is..." the Dead Man stated, "...curious about the deaths of His Chosen. No Weaver alive should be powerful enough to destroy any one of them, much less several. So you can imagine how eager Xanos is to discover the identity of the person responsible."

Kyle said nothing, swallowing in a dry throat.

"I have been tasked with solving this mystery," the Dead Man continued. "There *is* a pattern to their deaths. Only three people were present for the first killing, four for the second...mine, in fact. We believe that one of you three...Kalibar, Darius, or you, Kyle...is responsible." He turned to Kyle, staring with those unblinking eyes.

"You, Kyle, are very special indeed," he stated. "And you are gifted, if inexperienced, in magic. While it is unlikely, it is still possible that you are the one."

"I'm not," Kyle protested. The Dead Man ignored him, turning his glittering eyes on Darius.

"You," the Dead Man continued, "...I have consistently underestimated. No magic ability, yet you managed to kill many of my soldiers...and mastermind Kalibar's escape from the Arena. And despite being mortally wounded by one of the Chosen at the Tower, here you are, alive and well."

"You skipped my favorite part," Darius replied with a smirk. The Dead Man's mouth twitched, and he reached one hand to the angry scar on his neck.

"Indeed."

"We had some help," Darius countered.

"Ah yes, you must mean Kyle's ring," the Dead Man replied. "A magical relic of enormous power, they say. A lost artifact from the Ancients." He turned to Kyle. "When you wear it, it protects you from any serious harm...am I right?"

Kyle nodded silently, feeling the blood drain from his face.

"I can't help but notice that you're not wearing it now," the Dead Man murmured. Then he sighed. "Not that it matters," he continued. "Xanos has examined your ring. It does nothing you claim it does." He turned his gaze back to Darius. "Kyle has been lying to you all along."

Darius turned to Kyle, staring at him silently. and Kyle lowered his gaze, shame coming over him. He *had* been lying to his friends all along...and they'd believed in him, in his ring's ability to protect them. They'd counted on it.

"You knew it, didn't you," the Dead Man murmured. Kyle said nothing, his eyes locked on the floor. The Dead Man turned to Darius. "Kyle's ring didn't heal you," he stated. "It didn't defeat me, or the other Chosen."

Darius continued to stare at Kyle, his jawline rippling.

"Which means that something else did," the Dead Man continued. "Some*one* else." He stepped forward, lifting Kyle's chin with one icy hand. Kyle stared up into those cold, dead eyes, his stomach twisting into knots. "Who?"

Kyle said nothing.

"Perhaps it was Kalibar," the Dead Man murmured.

"It wasn't," Kyle blurted out, pulling away from the Dead Man's touch. "It wasn't him, I promise!"

"And why should I believe you?" the Dead Man inquired. "You're a liar, Kyle."

Kyle glanced at Darius, realizing the bodyguard was still staring at him. He swallowed in a dry throat.

"Yes, Kalibar could be the one we're looking for," the Dead Man continued. "Especially considering how he – a blind man – managed to kill the highly skilled assassin we sent to his room."

"He's not," Kyle insisted.

"We'll see," the Dead Man countered.

"Wait, what does that mean?" Kyle asked, a chill running down his spine.

"Kalibar will be tested," the Dead Man answered. "As will you both," he added, gesturing at Kyle and Darius.

"Tested?" Kyle pressed. The Dead Man smiled, turning to Darius.

"You decapitated me, Darius...based on Kyle's admission to the Council."

"Wait, how do you...?" Kyle began.

"Xanos knows all," the Dead Man interjected.

"Not all, apparently," Darius retorted. The Dead Man gazed at the bodyguard impassively.

"Given that *you* beheaded me, and that, by all accounts, *you* beheaded the third Chosen..." he paused, placing one hand back on the shallow depression formed by the green crystals beside him. "I cannot rule out the possibility that *you* are the one Xanos is searching for."

"I saw my opportunity and took it," Darius replied.

"Indeed," the Dead Man agreed. "That appears to be your talent." The crystal on his forehead flashed bright green for a moment, then faded, the green crystals in the center of the platform responding with their own burst of green light. "I'm going to give you one more opportunity to use it," the Dead Man stated.

The underground chamber shuddered then, a loud, deep vibration resonating through the air, so powerful that Kyle felt it in his bones. There was a piercing shriek, and then one of the massive metallic structures near Kyle began to move. Kyle stepped backward, watching as metallic limbs slowly unfolded, a dome-like structure the size of his house back on Earth swinging upward between two massive pillars. The thing rose higher into the air as it unfolded, until the huge dome had swung all the way upright. Kyle made out two gargantuan feet, each four times his height, attached to massive jet-black legs that rose to meet at a torso over a hundred feet up. They supported a squat body and a huge, domed head that nearly touched the ceiling far above.

Kyle stared up at the thing, his eyes widening. Sheer terror gripped him.

A single, green, diamond-shaped eye gazed outward from the center of the domed head. A beam of light shot from the eye, forming a massive spotlight on one of the walls beyond. The beam narrowed, then swept down the wall, traveling across the floor until it locked onto Kyle and Darius.

Kyle felt his legs turn to mush, and he fell onto his butt on the metal platform below, his heart hammering in his chest. He tried to scream, but nothing would come out.

The Dead Man stared at Kyle impassively, removing his hand from the crystals beside him.

"Behold," he proclaimed, gesturing grandly upward, "...the destroyer of the Ancients." He gazed upward at that massive domed head, at the diamond-shaped eye far above, his own green crystal glittering in its spotlight.

"Behold the Behemoth!"

Chapter 12

The traitor walked slowly down the long hallway, his feet padding silently on the rug overlaying the gray granite floor below. He glided past door after door, making his way toward the end of the hallway.

Second-to-last door on the left, he knew. He'd long ago memorized the maze-like passages of the Great Tower, having worked there for decades now. It had been highly successful, this charade. Mingling seamlessly with the elite of Stridon, coming in and out of the Great Tower with ease, an enemy in the perfect disguise...one that made him effectively invisible to everyone around him. And given his occupation, there were few places that were closed to him. He went everywhere without being questioned, allowed into every room without arousing suspicion. He found it fascinating, how people took him for granted. He imagined what it must be like, for those who lived their lives like this, toiling for those who thought themselves superior, doing so much for so little recognition.

It was pathetic.

The traitor reached the second-to-last door on the left, pausing before it. He closed his eyes, sending a pulse to the churning cauldron of magic in the center of his forehead. A few seconds later, he felt his will, his very *being* forced into a corner of his mind. His limbs went rigid as he lost control of them, as he became a spectator in his own body. He remembered the first time he'd felt that sensation, so alien at the time. Now he witnessed impassively as his arms moved without his volition, as the great God took control. He felt Xanos's mind there inside of him, a fragment of the great one's consciousness. He could not sense the God's actual thoughts, but what he did feel was alien, and ancient.

It was a privilege, to have such a mind within him...and to have been freed of the eternal prison of the Void.

He watched as the door's magical locks and wards were dismantled, a process that would have taken the traitor days, but took Xanos seconds. And this from a divided consciousness; he shuddered to think of what Xanos could do if He were to apply His full will.

The traitor felt Xanos leave him, felt his own mind regain control, his limbs once again his own. He pressed one palm against the door, silently pushing it open.

The room beyond was blanketed in shadow, but he could see easily...another gift from Xanos. He could *feel* the wards all around the room, and knew at once that they had been neutralized by his Master.

The traitor stepped into the room, allowing the door to close slowly behind him. He made it all the way to the other end of the room without making a single sound, stopping before a closed door. This too had been locked only moments before, he knew. Xanos had unlocked all doors, and neutralized all wards, in a matter of seconds.

He felt a chill run through him, feeling like a lowly insect next to his God. And grateful that he had been granted such an important role in preserving His kingdom.

The door opened under his touch.

He passed silently through the doorway, guiding the door to a silent closing with one hand. Beyond, there was a bed pressed up against the back wall of the room, centered between two tall windows. No light passed through the windows. They were made of magical glass that, with a thought, could turn opaque, blocking all light from coming through.

The quiet sound of a man's breathing came to his ears.

The man on the bed was asleep, judging by the cadence of his breathing. Xanos had ordered that he be taken in his sleep, much to the traitor's disappointment.

The traitor walked up to the side of the bed, hearing the man's breathing much more clearly now. A soft, gentle sound, unlike the vulgar snoring of the fat or infirm. The man had managed to stay in remarkable health for his age, the traitor knew. A paragon of virtue, everyone in the Tower believed. A man who lived by his principles. But the traitor knew better. This was just another old man playing at ruling the world, no different than the countless others that had come before. Xanos had shown the traitor that.

The traitor paused, standing by the foot of the bed, closing his eyes. The half-dozen wards around the bed were already neutralized, of course. Pathetic, that these men fancied themselves experts of magic, when all they had was a child's grasp of the power. They'd accomplished so little in the last two centuries, barely scratching the surface of their potential. They were primitives, these people.

The traitor stood there over the bed, listening to the man before him sleeping peacefully for a moment longer. He took a moment to reflect on where he was and what he was doing. He'd waited a long, long time to serve God, hiding in plain sight among the enemy.

He wanted to savor this moment.

He reached into a hidden pocket on the inside of his jacket then, his fingers closing around the cool, textured handle of the knife he'd placed there. He drew the blade out, holding it before him, silently moving to the side of the bed. He was standing directly over the sleeping man now. He could feel the magic emanating from the man's bones, outlining his skeleton. The man was powerful for his generation, the greatest and most skilled among his peers.

And that, the traitor thought, was a shame.

He leaned his knees against the side of the bed, raising the knife above his head. Stood there for a long moment, marveling at how easy it was to take away the most glorious gift of all. Too easy, he thought. Far too easy. He would have preferred a challenge.

The traitor brought the knife down, hard, plunging it straight into the sleeping man's heart.

The man cried out once, his limbs jerking violently, and then lay still. Blood welled up around the blade, buried to the hilt in the man's chest. A long sigh escaped his lips, the release of his final breath.

The traitor let his fingers uncurl from the handle of the knife, straightening his back, then stepping away from the bed. He felt a giddiness come over him, and smiled down at the dead man laying before him.

"For Xanos," he murmured.

Chapter 13

Ariana woke up with a jolt, hearing the high-pitched wail of the Tower alarm echoing through her bedroom. She glanced quickly about her room, then shoved her blanket from her body, swinging her legs over the side of her bed. She grabbed the black pants and shirt that had been neatly folded on the nightstand beside her bed, slipping out of her pajamas and putting the clothes on. Then she ran out of her room and into the living room of Kalibar's retirement suite, sprinting to the magical front door. Without thinking, she wove the light pattern, a softly glowing globe appearing above her head. She searched for her black boots on the shoe rack on the wall near the door, finding them and tugging them on. Then she unlocked the door, opening it and stepping silently into the hallway.

It was empty.

The alarm continued, much louder in the hallway than it had been in her room, making Ariana cover her ears with her hands. Something was wrong...she was supposed to be guarded by two Battle-Weavers. They'd been posted outside of her door ever since the attack on the bank yesterday. Ever since Kyle...

She closed her eyes for a moment, willing that horrible thought away.

She opened her eyes again, peering down the empty hallway. The siren was only used when the highest government officials – the Councilmen and the Grand Runic and Weaver – were threatened. So whatever was going on had to be happening either one floor above or below her. The Councilmen had living chambers on the 40th floor, and Kalibar and Erasmus on the 42nd.

She paused, then ran down the hallway, toward the riser at the end. She glanced at the painted statues carved into the walls on either side as she passed, spotting Kalibar's likeness there. She felt a chill go down her spine.

She ran faster, sprinting to the end of the hallway, and stopping in the center of the riser. She sent a single magical pulse to one of the forty-two crystals on the floor of the riser, the one that would send her upward, to the 42nd floor.

Nothing happened.

Ariana frowned, trying again. Still, the riser did not move.

That's weird...

She paused, thinking it through. Someone must have deactivated the riser's ability to travel to the topmost floor...to protect Kalibar and Erasmus.

Or to prevent anyone from reaching the scene of the crime, she thought with another chill.

She heard a shout behind her, and spun around, spotting two black-clad men running down the hall toward her. She took a step back instinctively, then realized that they were Battle-Weavers. They ran up to her side, both panting with the exertion, their foreheads slick with sweat.

"Ma'am," one of them blurted out. "Get back in your room now!" He grabbed Ariana's shoulder, turning her about and pushing her toward Kalibar's suite.

"What's going on?" she half-asked, half-demanded, resisting the man's attempts to get her back into her room.

"Someone's been assassinated," the Weaver replied. "If you don't get back in your room willingly..."

"Okay, okay," Ariana replied, allowing herself to be led back into Kalibar's suite. The two men followed her in, letting the magical door close behind them. They ushered her to one of the many large, white couches in the living room, motioning for her to sit down. She did so, knowing it was no use resisting two experienced Battle-Weavers.

"Someone's been killed?" she asked. The two Battle-Weavers sat down, one on a couch opposite her, the other beside her.

"Assassinated, yes," one replied.

"Who?" she pressed, fear growing within her. She shoved it aside, knowing that panicking wouldn't do her any good. A year with the Dead Man had taught her that.

"I can't say," the Weaver answered. When Ariana glowered at him, the man shifted in his seat uncomfortably. While Ariana was still only a teenager, she was the daughter of a living legend. Adopted or not, everyone knew how Kalibar felt about her...and no one wanted to get on Kalibar's bad side, particularly his Battle-Weavers. All of them practically worshiped the Grand Weaver, knowing that he'd been the greatest of their kind since Ancient times. "I don't know," the Weaver admitted. "When we responded to the alarm, we were ordered to come right to your room."

"Is it Kalibar?" she asked bluntly, immediately regretting the question. If he had been killed, she didn't want to know.

"I'm sorry," the Weaver replied. "I just don't know. It must be someone important," he added. "I've never seen Grand Runic Erasmus so distraught."

"*What?*" Ariana blurted, bolting up out of her seat. "What did you say?"

"Grand Runic Erasmus," the Battle-Weaver repeated, almost apologetically. "He was...weeping," he added. "I've never seen him like that before."

"What did he say?"

"He was overwrought," the Weaver replied, shrugging helplessly. "I'm sorry, I don't know anything more," he added. Ariana paused, then sat back down on the couch, closing her eyes. For some reason, all she could picture was Master Banar's corpse, lying on its stomach, a gaping hole in the back of the poor man's head. How Master Owens had reacted as they'd come upon the scene, how utterly pale her instructor had become.

She opened her eyes, staring at her kneecaps for a long moment. Then she glanced up at the Weaver facing her.

"What do we do now?" she asked.

151

"We wait," the Weaver answered. Noting Ariana's incredulous expression, he shook his head. "We haven't found the assassin yet," he explained. "Until we do, everyone is a potential target...including you."

Ariana sighed. The man was right, of course. She just wished she knew what was going on. She needed to know that her loved ones were okay. Kyle had already been taken from her, as had Darius, apparently. Kalibar was the only one left, the only one who had been there with her in the Arena, who had helped her escape that hell. She couldn't bear the thought that she'd escaped at last, only to lose her second family the same way she'd lost her real parents.

For the first time since Kyle had been taken, Ariana felt tears welling up in her eyes, and she turned away, brushing them with the back of her hand. But still they came, and she broke down, thinking of that poor boy lost in some terrible prison, alone as she had been only a few weeks ago, wondering if anyone would ever find him. A sob escaped her lips, and she fought it back, her shoulders heaving up and down silently. She felt a warm hand on her back, and gave in, noisy, awful sobs escaping her. She hated the sound of them, the helplessness they conveyed. But try as she might, she couldn't hold them back any longer.

Suddenly, there was a knock at the door, followed by the sounds of boots clicking on the granite floor. Ariana looked up, hastily wiping the tears from her eyes, and saw Erasmus walking quickly toward her, a line of Battle-Weavers and elite guards in tow. The portly Grand Runic's expression was furious, his eyelids puffy. He stopped in the center of the room, turning about and facing a man dressed in white – one of the Councilmen, Ariana realized.

"So you just want to give up?" he shouted at the man. "Run with your tail between your legs?" The man's face paled, but he stood his ground.

"If they can get in *his* room, with all of his wards, and murder him in his sleep, what's to stop them from killing us all?" he retorted. Erasmus rolled his eyes.

"You've got to be kidding me," he muttered. "It's all well and good when *other* people are dying, but the minute your lives are on the line, you fold!" He shook his head. "You're pathetic, you know that?"

"Calm down, Erasmus," the Councilman pleaded. Erasmus spun on him.

"That's *Grand Runic* Erasmus to *you*," he retorted. "Or have you forgotten your place here?" The Councilman raised his palms into the air, backing up a step.

"My apologies," he stated, his face paling even further. "I'm just trying to tell you how we feel," he added. Erasmus laughed bitterly.

"Oh yes, I know how you *feel*," he shot back. "I also know that the first time your Grand Weaver was threatened by an assassin in his bedroom, *he* didn't act like a coward, begging for surrender!"

"That assassin died," the Councilman countered. Erasmus shook his head.

"You and I both know it wouldn't have mattered," he replied angrily. "You're nothing but cowards!" he spat. The Councilman's expression hardened.

"Don't accuse us of lacking patriotism," he warned, his voice suddenly cold. "None of us has run off in the middle of the night. We're considering *options* here."

"Consider a different one," Erasmus shot back.

"Gentlemen!" a voice boomed, reverberating off of the walls. Everyone in the room started, then turned to face the front door. A tall man dressed in black silk pajamas entered the room, his short white hair mildly askew. His eyes were covered with double-eyepatches, his lips turned in a fierce frown.

"*Kalibar!*" Ariana blurted out, leaping off of the couch and sprinting toward the Grand Weaver. She jumped into his arms, tears flowing down her cheeks. "Kalibar!" she cried again, burying her face into his chest. "I thought..." she stopped then, choking up. She felt Kalibar wrap his arms about her, giving her a gentle squeeze.

"I'm fine," he replied, pushing her back gently. "I'm afraid there's been a murder," he added gravely.

"Who?" Ariana asked. She felt a little guilty knowing that, whoever it was, she would still feel glad that her adopted father was all right. Kalibar grimaced.

"Jax," he answered, then sighed. "He was late for a morning meeting, so one of the Councilmen went to find him. He was still in his bed," he added solemnly.

"You won't believe what Councilman Hewes was just suggesting to me," Erasmus interrupted, pointing one finger at the younger

153

Councilman in white. Kalibar reached out, lowering Erasmus's hand with his own.

"I can guess," he replied calmly. He turned to face Hewes. "There will be a great deal of fear and sadness today," he stated, "...and our initial reactions will not be our best. We must all give ourselves time to calm down, so we can plan the future rationally."

Erasmus glared at Hewes, then turned away from the Councilman. "His *first reaction* says a lot about him," he growled. Kalibar shook his head.

"I wasn't talking about him," he chided gently. Erasmus blinked, then lowered his gaze to the floor. Kalibar sighed, putting a hand on Erasmus's shoulder. "I've seen war heroes that did the right thing the first time, and those that hesitated first," he added. "Both deserved the title."

"All right, all right," Erasmus muttered. "What do *you* suggest we do?"

"Surrender is an option of last resort," Kalibar answered, "...but we cannot leave it off of the table. Nor can we consider it until our doom is otherwise sure. We must investigate Jax's murder, determine who was involved. As tragic as his death is, I have reason to believe that our own deaths will not follow. But I, for one, am willing to give my life for my country," he added firmly, his eyepatches locking on Councilman Hewes. The younger Runic lowered his own gaze, unable to face Kalibar's disapproval. Everyone knew that Kalibar *had* risked his life for the Empire – many times over – as a Battle-Weaver.

"As you say, Grand Weaver," he murmured. Kalibar nodded briskly.

"Councilman, I want an emergency meeting of the Council, in the War Room, in ten minutes. We must elect a new Elder Councilman, and deal with the former's death."

"Yes your Excellency," Hewes replied, turning about and striding out of the front door. A few of the guards followed behind him. Erasmus watched him go, then turned to Kalibar.

"I still think..." he began, but Kalibar cut him off.

"Cowards by instinct," he interjected, "...can yet be made into brave men. That," he added, "...is the purpose of leadership."

There was a knock on the front door, and Kalibar turned about, seeing a man in a simple gray shirt and pants standing outside of the door, carrying a large envelope in his arms. He recognized the uniform, if not the man; it was of the Medical Examiner's office. One of the elite guards glanced at Kalibar, who nodded. The guard opened the door, letting the man in.

"Your Excellencies," the man stated, bowing deeply. Sweat glistened on his forehead, and he was breathing heavily. Erasmus frowned.

"What is it?" he asked.

"The pathology report on the man who tried to assassinate you, Grand Weaver," he answered, nodding at Kalibar. He offered Kalibar the large envelope, and Ariana watched as Kalibar opened it, pulling out a sheath of papers. Then he paused, handing the papers to Erasmus.

"Sometimes I still forget," the Grand Weaver muttered, pointing to his eyepatches. Erasmus smirked, then glanced down at the papers. He scanned through the first page, then his eyes widened, his face turning very pale.

"Dear god," he whispered, staring off into space. Then his eyes focused on Kalibar, and he shook his head mutely.

"What is it?" Kalibar asked. Erasmus glanced at the papers again, then put them back into the envelope, re-sealing it.

"We're in deep trouble," Erasmus replied.

* * *

The eleven remaining members of the Council sat around the circular table in the War Room, with Kalibar and Erasmus in their customary positions. Where Jax had presided for over three decades, only an empty chair remained. Erasmus had debriefed the Council on Jax's murder, right down to the grisly details, his voice breaking more than once as he did so. Erasmus had been as close as any man could get to the aloof Jax, having had him as a mentor so many years ago.

"So this assassin," Goran stated grimly, "...was able to unlock Jax's master-level door lock, built by Jax himself...perhaps the most skilled Runic in the Empire?" Councilman Goran asked. "And then deactivated all of his wards, *and* all of his personal defensive runics...in a single night?"

"That's correct, Kalibar confirmed. "The elite guard does daily checks of all wards and locks, and they were intact when Jax went to bed last night." Councilman Ibicus, sitting beside Goran, shook his head.

"Well, if that's the case, what's to stop this assassin from coming into any one of our bedrooms, and killing us while *we* sleep?" he asked. Several other Councilman nodded in agreement.

"We're all sitting ducks," Goran agreed. He turned to Kalibar then. "And we all know now that Kyle's ring won't protect us either." he added coldly.

"We don't know much about Jax's assassin," Erasmus admitted, showing remarkable restraint in not taking Goran's bait. "But we *have* learned more about Kalibar's."

"Do tell," Councilman Ibicus prompted. The man was hardly a fan of Erasmus, despite them both being Elitists, because he believed that the Grand Runic had allowed Kalibar to overshadow him in their first term. Ibicus was of the opinion that Kalibar's overt popularity over Erasmus had caused hundreds of potential Runic students to go into Weaving instead.

"We received the official medical examiner's report on the first assassin's autopsy right before this meeting," Erasmus continued. He paused for a moment, glancing at Kalibar, then turning back to face the Council. "It was most revealing," he added grimly.

"Paraphrase, if you will," Ibicus replied.

"The assassin had been killed by decapitation, as well all know," Erasmus stated. "Other than that, there were no other findings...except for one."

"Spare the theatrics," Goran grumbled. "What did they find?" Erasmus tossed the envelope with the medical examiner's report across the table at Goran.

"See for yourself," Erasmus retorted. Goran grabbed the envelope, opening it up and taking out the sheath of papers within. He scanned the document, his eyes growing wider as he did.

"Dear god," he gasped. Erasmus gave Goran a grim smile.

"That's what I said," he replied. "Would you do the honor of...*paraphrasing*, Goran?" Goran looked up from the papers he held, then nodded.

"There was a green crystal embedded in the assassin's skull," the Councilman revealed. "Nestled within the brain, just as with the late Grand Weaver Rivin."

"*What?*" Councilman Ibicus exclaimed. "This assassin was one of these Chosen?"

"Apparently so," Goran stated, handing the papers to Ibicus.

"How did we miss this?" Councilman Ibicus half-asked, half-demanded, scanning the papers for a moment, then shaking his head. "I ordered extensive background checks and physicals on every person living within these gates!" It was true, Kalibar knew; as the most senior Councilman other than Jax, Ibicus had been in charge of organizing and implementing the screening process for the entire Secula Magna. Ibicus's work had been exhaustive; no one could fault his efforts.

"The crystal," Erasmus answered, "...was embedded so far into the assassin's brain that the base wasn't visible on the forehead." He shook his head, rubbing one hand over his bald pate. "From what we can tell, the skin on his forehead had been peeled back, the crystal embedded through the skull, and then the skin was replaced over the wound...which sealed itself perfectly."

"Barbaric," Ibicus muttered.

"So this assassin," Goran interjected, "...was able to summon Xanos at any time, with all of his power?" Erasmus nodded.

"I assume so," he replied. "The crystal was identical to the one Rivin had. Unfortunately, it also self-destructed after the assassin was killed. But yes, we have to assume you're correct."

"That's it," Goran stated, standing up and throwing his arms up into the air. "It's over, gentlemen."

"Hold on," Kalibar countered. "Remember that my assassin was killed."

"Jax's wasn't," Goran shot back. "You insisted that we have faith in Kyle's ring, that we would be protected as you were, and what happened?" He jabbed a finger at Kalibar angrily. "You were wrong about Kyle's ring, you were *wrong* about our safety, your excursion to Crescent Isle *failed*, there are eighty powerful criminals loose in the city, our most prestigious bank is in ruins..." He lowered his hand, slamming both palms on the top of the table. "Xanos is making a *mockery* of this Empire!"

"I agree," Ibicus concurred. "We're severely outclassed, gentlemen. But we've known that from the beginning...we all knew this was a losing war."

"So what do you suggest?" Erasmus nearly shouted. "Surrender? Evacuation? Head for the hills and hope we're lucky enough not to be hunted down and killed one-by-one?"

"Hold on," Councilman Mudd – a stalwart ally of Kalibar's – interjected, standing up slowly. He turned to Kalibar. "If Kyle's ring didn't kill this assassin, do we have any idea what...or who...did?"

Erasmus glanced at Kalibar, who grimaced, lowering his gaze to the well-polished tabletop. He had two options...reveal the mystery man who'd given him his sight, or say nothing. There was no way of knowing how the Council would react to the former...but at this point, the Council was near its breaking point. He had to do whatever it took to keep the Empire together.

Kalibar stood.

"Someone extraordinarily powerful," he answered, leaning forward and placing his palms on the table. "Someone more powerful than any of you could ever imagine."

"Like Kyle's ring?" Goran shot back snidely. Kalibar felt anger rise within him, and paused for a moment to let it fade. Councilman Ibicus leaned forward, his interest clearly piqued.

"Hold on Goran," he admonished. "Let Kalibar talk."

"Thank you Councilman," Kalibar stated, nodding at Ibicus. "I have proof," he added calmly. "I met him."

"Are you saying you met your assassin's killer, and you've been keeping this information from the Council?" Goran pressed. Ibicus turned to glare at him.

"Let him explain, Goran," he interjected sternly. Goran frowned at his ally, then nodded, folding his arms across his chest.

"It was only yesterday that I met him," Kalibar explained. Then he recounted what had happened...him going to sleep, the paralysis, the enormous outpouring of magical power...and then the rapture. Goosebumps rose on his arms at the memory.

"That's all well and good," Ibicus stated when Kalibar had finished, "...but it could have just been a dream." Erasmus smirked, shaking his head.

158

"Doubtful," he retorted. Kalibar sighed, taking his palms off of the table, then grabbing his eyepatches, one in each hand. He peeled them off slowly, his eyes remaining closed, then tossed the eyepatches on the table.

Then he opened his eyes.

* * *

Councilman Ibicus burst upward from his chair, followed by Goran, Hewes, Mudd, and the rest of the Council. Their eyes went wide, their jaws dropping as they all stared into Kalibar's regenerated eyes.

"Impossible!" Goran breathed. Ibicus stared silently at Kalibar for a long moment, then got up out of his chair, walking to the Grand Weaver's side.

"May I?" he asked. Kalibar nodded, and Ibicus leaned in to stare at Kalibar's eyes. "You're saying this man gave you your eyes back?" he pressed. Kalibar nodded.

"He did," he confirmed. "And I have every reason to believe that he was the one who protected me from the assassin...and who saved all of us from Xanos when he attacked the Tower."

"Do we know anything else about this man?" Ibicus pressed, walking back to his own chair and sitting down. Kalibar shook his head.

"Not really," he admitted. "Anything else is pure conjecture. But the point remains...we have a powerful ally, one that's already saved us, and the Empire, from certain death."

"We have no proof of that," Goran countered. "All we really know is that someone gave you your eyes back." He held his palms out in front of him as Erasmus scowled. "That's a miracle, no one is denying it," he added hastily, glancing at Ibicus. "I'm just saying that you can't prove this man was involved in anything else other than that."

"I agree," Ibicus stated. "After all, where was this mystery man when Jax was being murdered? Or when Master Banar was killed? Or when Kyle was kidnapped?" He shook his head. "He let that prison outbreak happen, and the destruction of the Central Bank. We can hardly count on him to save us." Several of the other Councilmen nodded their agreement.

"So what would you suggest we do?" Erasmus asked Ibicus, pointedly ignoring Goran.

"We need to protect the government," he answered. "First and foremost, we need to protect our Grand Weaver and Grand Runic...and those serving in the Council. I suggest that each member of the Council sleep in a secret location known only to that Council member and a select few others, and that these locations are changed on a nightly basis."

"An excellent idea, Councilman Ibicus," Goran agreed. "I think I speak for all of us when I say I won't go to my room here, waiting to be murdered in my sleep."

"I say we take a vote," Councilman Mudd suggested. Goran nodded, raising his hand.

"All in favor?" he asked. All eleven hands joined him. "Then it's decided."

"Our next act," Erasmus stated, "...as much as it pains me to say it, is to vote for a replacement Runic for the Jax's seat on the Council." Goran nodded.

"And an Elder Councilman to lead us," he added. "As Jax's replacement will not be eligible for elder Councilman, I suggest we choose the most senior – and eldest – Councilman here...Councilman Ibicus."

"Of course you would," Erasmus retorted angrily. Kalibar put a hand on Erasmus's shoulder, making him pause. Kalibar certainly knew why his old friend was furious; Ibicus was on Goran's side. With Ibicus as elder Councilman, the balance of power would shift away from them, making the Council far more difficult to work with. In fact, it could render them all but impotent, if the Council elected a Runic that was also sympathetic to Goran's cause. The Council was already split 6-6 in terms of those sympathetic to the Grand Weaver and Runic, and those sympathetic to Goran. A tie vote on any issue would be decided in favor of the elder Councilman's vote; with Jax on their side, Kalibar and Erasmus had won consistently on their proposals. With Ibicus, they wouldn't have that edge...and if the Council chose a Runic sympathetic to Goran, the Council would be split 5-7 in Goran's favor, with Ibicus swinging any occasional tie votes Goran's way.

Either way, it would be disastrous.

Kalibar sighed, knowing that a 5-7 split was all but inevitable. He'd thought through the implications of Jax's murder as soon as he'd heard of it...after the initial shock had passed. Ibicus was a shoe-in for Elder Councilman. No other would be chosen. This would bring the Council 5-6 in favor of Goran. Voting for a new Councilman entailed each member of the Council submitting the name of their nominee, then counting the votes for a majority.

Kalibar closed his eyes for a moment, then looked across the table at nothing in particular.

Goran had undoubtedly already conferred with his fellow Elitists on the Council, letting each know his preference for a nominee. They would all choose the same person, to maximize their chances of winning. Even if there happened to be a tie, Ibicus, also an Elitist, would decide the vote.

A master stroke, by a master strategist, Kalibar thought. Xanos had bested him yet again.

He and Erasmus had lost the Council, even if Erasmus hadn't realized it yet. As brilliant as his old friend was, he was not a superb strategist. Erasmus's strength lay in his ability to execute a plan, not to come up with one. Conversely, strategy came easily to Kalibar, whether it was on the battlefield or in the political arena. He was always thinking a half-dozen steps ahead, considering every possible attack and counterattack.

This battle had already been lost.

* * *

"Those bastards!" Erasmus roared, slamming the door to his suite. Kalibar said nothing, walking to one of the many white couches placed throughout the room and sitting down in it. Erasmus didn't follow suit, pacing back and forth in front of Kalibar instead.

"Can you believe the guile of that man?" he seethed, complaining about Goran. "Jax's body isn't even cold yet, and he's already scrambled to take advantage of his death!" Erasmus turned to Kalibar then, pointed one chubby finger at him. "And you didn't even put up a fight," he accused. "You just sat there as it happened!"

161

Kalibar sighed, being careful not to seem too nonchalant. Doing so would just irk Erasmus more.

"It was inevitable, Erasmus," Kalibar replied evenly. "And we have no say in who is elected to Council...you know that," he chided gently. Erasmus threw up his hands.

"So we roll over and die?" he shot back. Kalibar paused for a moment, then shook his head.

"Consider what we've lost," he stated. "With the Council against us, at best we've got an uphill battle with every decision. At worst, we lost control over the military...save for our Runics and Weavers."

"Oh, that's all?" Erasmus stated sarcastically. Kalibar raised an eyebrow.

"Has it occurred to you," Kalibar asked, "...what would happen if our soldiers encountered a single Chosen like the Dead Man?" Erasmus snorted.

"Of course," he replied. "They'd get slaughtered, without Battle-Weavers backing them up."

"Even with backup," Kalibar agreed, "...our Battle-Weavers would be no match for a Chosen with Xanos possessing them."

"You're making me feel better already," Erasmus grumbled. "What's your point? Should we all grab shovels and start digging our own graves?"

"Not yet," Kalibar answered with a smirk. "I have a better idea."

"Better than laying down and dying? You don't say," Erasmus retorted. But the steam had been taken out of him...some of it, anyway. Kalibar motioned for Erasmus to sit on the couch opposite where he was sitting, and the Grand Runic sighed, plopping his plump frame down on the soft cushions. Kalibar leaned forward, propping his elbows on his knees.

"I've been thinking," Kalibar stated, "...about that idea Kyle had. You know, the one about reverse-engineering naturally occurring magical patterns."

"I remember."

"I think I figured out what Kyle was talking about," Kalibar stated. "Do you have any fresh crystals on you?"

Erasmus frowned, thrusting his hands into his pockets. Eventually, he retrieved a small yellow crystal, handing it to Kalibar. Kalibar shook

162

his head, giving the crystal back to Erasmus. "Embed the gravity-sphere rune into it," he commanded. Erasmus shrugged, and soon a small rune began to form itself on the mineral's surface.

"Stop," Kalibar ordered.

"It's not finished," Erasmus protested. Kalibar smiled.

"Precisely," he agreed. "Now, runes in the natural world are too complicated to stumble on by random, right?" he asked. Erasmus nodded.

"Only the simplest runes could be discovered that way," he agreed.

"But when I weave the gravity-sphere pattern in my mind," Kalibar continued, "...magic theory states that I must be doing the same thing in my mind that magic does in a rune...travel in a tight loop, forming a pattern that, in whole, triggers a similarly-shaped rune."

"Right," Erasmus replied. "It's entry-level Runic theory," he added rather indignantly. Kalibar smirked.

"I'm an entry-level Runic," he remarked. "In any case, it stands to reason that, if I weave the gravity-sphere pattern near this incomplete sensory rune, when I've completed weaving the pattern up to the same point as this rune, it should be triggered."

"No," Erasmus countered. Then he frowned. "I mean, I don't think so," he added. He scratched his bald head, thinking it over. Then he shrugged. "Actually, I have no idea."

"Make another sensory rune," Kalibar instructed. "The second half of the gravity-sphere rune, as a separate rune from the first." Erasmus did so, completing the task within seconds. "Now," Kalibar continued, "...make each sensory rune trigger a light-emitting rune, like we talked about." Erasmus complied again, shaking his head at Kalibar.

"Dementia finally kicking in, old buddy?" he quipped. "I'll give it a bit longer before I have you write your will. I always liked your mansion in Bellingham." Kalibar ignored the comment, knowing full well that Erasmus hated Bellingham, and waited for his friend to finish his task.

"Now, weave the gravity-sphere pattern," Kalibar commanded.

"Do I look like a Weaver to you?" Erasmus protested.

"Humor me," Kalibar insisted. Erasmus sighed, closing his eyes. Kalibar frowned. "No, keep your eyes open," he insisted. "Watch the crystal," he added. Erasmus complied. A second later, a small gravity sphere appeared between the two men, winking out after a few seconds.

And, right before it had appeared, two bursts of light flashed from the surface of the crystal in Erasmus's hand, one after the other.

"What?" Erasmus exclaimed, blinking at the crystal. "Well I'll be dipped in..."

"Not quite demented yet, am I old friend?" Kalibar said with a grin, clapping Erasmus on the shoulder. Erasmus stared at the crystal for a moment longer, then frowned.

"Alright, so what?" he asked. "I still don't see how this is going to help us."

"Well," Kalibar replied, "...say we take a long crystal slab, and put a bunch of random sensory rune fragments on it."

"Okay..."

"What if, instead of having you weave the gravity sphere pattern, we took some feathergrass, and put it near the sensory runes?"

Erasmus frowned, thinking it over.

"If the sensory rune fragments matched whatever pattern the feathergrass wove, they would light up," he answered.

"Exactly."

"But they'd light up incredibly quickly," Erasmus pointed out. "Unless you could slow down time, there would be no way to figure out the correct sequence of pattern fragments to make the whole pattern."

"Except there is," Kalibar countered with a grin. Erasmus frowned.

"No there isn't," he insisted. Kalibar's grin widened, and Erasmus frowned. "Don't even *tell* me you figured it out," he warned, jabbing a finger at Kalibar. "You're a damn Weaver, Kalibar...not a Runic!"

"You're right, I'm not," Kalibar agreed. "I'll need your help if it's going to work," he added. Erasmus continued to frown, and then he leaned forward as well, his blue eyes narrowing.

"Alright, tell me."

"So, we put a bunch of short, random patterns on a sensing board," Kalibar began. "Feathergrass extract continues to weave its magic pattern – that of affecting gravity – even after the death of the plant."

"Yes, yes, I know," Erasmus replied impatiently.

"Bear with me," Kalibar insisted. "Now, I put the extract near the sensing board, and a few dozen runes lit up, almost all at once. If I could just slow down time, I could see each rune lighting up, figure out the sequence of runes as they were triggered, and recreate the complex pattern."

"But you can't slow down time, so it won't work," Erasmus concluded rather smugly. Kalibar shook his head.

"Imagine if we had a long sheet of paper," he explained. "...and we had it on two rollers."

"Okay..."

"Say we rolled the paper quickly from the right to the left on these rollers," Kalibar continued. "And that we had a long, single line of effector runes right below the paper that could each burn their unique pattern fragment into the paper."

"Right," Erasmus mumbled.

"And say that each sensory rune on the array, when triggered, was linked to one of these effector runes...and burned their specific pattern into the paper."

"So the paper would record which runes were triggered," Erasmus reasoned.

"Exactly," Kalibar confirmed. "And if you moved the paper quickly from one roller to the other while the sensory runes were being triggered..."

"Then you could figure out which runes were triggered when!" Erasmus exclaimed, his eyes widening.

"...because the patterns would be burned from one side of the paper to the other, in the order they were triggered," Kalibar confirmed. "Then you'd just have to string the printed fragments together..."

"And you'd have your full pattern!" Erasmus nearly shouted. "You lousy bastard," he declared, punching Kalibar in the shoulder, making him grunt. "Damned if you're not onto something!" Then he frowned. "But what does this have to do with winning the war?" he asked. "Learning the feathergrass pattern isn't exactly going to strike terror into the hearts of our enemies."

"Agreed," Kalibar conceded. "But I believe there are other naturally occurring patterns that would prove far more suited to that task."

He leaned forward then, whispering into Erasmus's ear. The pudgy Grand Runic's eyes lit up almost instantly.

"Brilliant!" he exclaimed, clapping his hand on his knee. "Kalibar, you're a genius!"

"No, I'm not," Kalibar countered. "Kyle is." He shook his head slowly. "He had it all figured out...on his first day as a Runic. And it took us this long to follow his train of thought."

"For *you* to follow his train of thought," Erasmus grumbled. "I didn't even take his idea seriously."

"Yes, well," Kalibar stated. "We need to get working on a prototype of Kyle's invention so that we can create the weapon I was thinking of."

"That, my friend," Erasmus replied with a wink, "...is where I come in!"

Chapter 14

Kyle gazed up at the massive, hulking form of the Behemoth, staring at that singular green eye, a jet-black monstrosity plucked from his very nightmares and placed before him. It was larger than he remembered, and the details were different...the arms were more streamlined, the angles sharper...but the overall look was the same.

The Behemoth's lone eye stared down at Kyle and Darius, its narrow white spotlight held motionless over them. The Dead Man stood beside them, his cold black eyes having never left Kyle's, his expression unreadable. His cloak had resumed its sinuous rippling, despite the still air inside the massive cavern.

"I have a proposition for you both," the Dead Man stated, his sunken black eyes lit with glowing semicircles from the Behemoth's light. "If either of you tell me the nature and location of the one Xanos is looking for, you both will be freed immediately. You will not be killed, or harmed in any way. In fact, you will be returned to Stridon, if you choose."

Kyle glanced back at Darius, but the bodyguard wasn't even paying attention; he was staring up at the Behemoth, his blue eyes scanning the monstrous creation. Kyle turned back to the Dead Man, unnerved at the ghoulish Weaver's unblinking stare.

"However," the Dead Man continued calmly, his smooth, deep voice sending a chill down Kyle's spine, "...if no one chooses to come forward, then Xanos will kill you both. And then He will come for

Kalibar, and for your friends. And if they don't talk, He will come for the Empire itself."

"That's not fair!" Kyle protested, finding his voice at last.

"Agreed," the Dead Man replied. "But it is my offer, Kyle. Xanos demands it."

Kyle stared back up at the Behemoth, squinting in the face of that intense spotlight, recalling the vision of Ancient Stridon burning under its deadly gaze. There would be no victory against such an enemy, he knew. The Dead Man was powerful, it was true. But the Behemoth had leveled entire cities, destroying a civilization with magical defenses far advanced of their own. They would be helpless before it.

He turned to Darius, finding the bodyguard staring back at him silently. Still handcuffed, without his trademark golden armor, the man looked uncharacteristically vulnerable. Kyle thought back to all of the times that Darius had risked his life to save him, thought of what it would feel like to have Darius die here...and knew he could never live with that on his conscience.

He turned back to the Dead Man.

"I'm the one you want," Kyle declared, squaring his shoulders. His heart pounded in his chest, a cold, slick sweat dripping from his armpits down to his flanks. But he forced himself to stand tall. He glanced at Darius, who continued to stare at him silently. Then he turned back to the Dead Man, who merely stared at him for a long, uncomfortable moment.

"Are you?" he murmured. He continued to stare at Kyle, his dead eyes unblinking. Kyle wilted under his gaze, and wondered, not for the first time, if the ghoulish Weaver could read his thoughts. "Then show me," he stated.

"Show you what?"

"Prove it," the Dead Man answered. Kyle stood there, staring back at the Dead Man, his mouth going dry. Then he lowered his gaze to the floor.

"I'm not from around here," he replied at last, trying not to shiver in the cold air. He didn't want the Dead Man – or Darius – to think he was afraid...even though he most definitely was.

168

"And where are you from, Kyle?" The Dead Man asked, his voice almost gentle again. Kyle glanced at Darius, who shook his head almost imperceptibly. But there was no other way.

"Another planet," Kyle stated. He caught Darius rolling his eyes, and blushed. The Dead Man, however, did not appear amused.

"Another planet," he stated flatly. "Is that so."

"It *is*," Kyle insisted, trying his best to sound convincing. "We have technology there that you can only dream of," he added, more defiantly now. "Bombs that can destroy entire cities...medicines that can cure almost any disease!"

"I see," the Dead Man replied. "It's a shame you couldn't have been more honest with me...and more loyal."

Kyle felt the color leave his cheeks, his guts twisting in his belly. He'd heard that tone of voice once...right before the Dead Man had ripped Kalibar's eyes out. He took an involuntary step backward.

"But it's true!" he protested, feeling every muscle in his body tense up. "I'm not lying!" The Dead Man ignored him, turned to face Darius.

"Do you have anything else to say?" the Dead Man asked. Darius said nothing, his blue eyes locked on the Dead Man's. They stared at each other for a long moment, until the Dead Man turned away with a sigh. "Very well then," the ghoulish Weaver stated, turning to the green crystals jutting out from the platform at his side. "I suppose it's only fair that I give you a head start."

He placed his hand back on the green crystals, and they flashed brightly for a moment, then went dark. A massive circular portion of the ceiling far above their heads began to open up, dilating like an iris until it had opened up to a diameter of over a hundred feet. Kyle stared upward into that massive circular opening, seeing only darkness beyond.

Kyle felt his stomach lurch suddenly, felt himself rising upward through the air, pulled by an invisible force. He cried out as his feet lifted off of the metallic platform; the Dead Man and Darius rose upward with him. Kyle looked downward, seeing the platform they'd been standing on shrinking as they flew slowly upward. He felt his guts squirm; despite his recent experience with his gravity boots, the height – they were well over a hundred feet high and still climbing – was nerve-wracking. He imagined himself being dropped, falling helplessly to his death. If the Dead Man wanted to kill Kyle and Darius now, it would be as simple as that.

Instead, a strong breeze whipped through the massive chamber, chilling Kyle to the bone. The blackness beyond the iris-shaped opening in the ceiling began to swirl, like a whirlpool of water in an upside-down pool. As they drew closer, he realized that the blackness *was* water, churning like the surface of the ocean during a storm. The whirlpool intensified, creating a watery funnel above their heads. The funnel deepened and widened as the whirlpool grew ever stronger, forming a long, dark tunnel. Suddenly, a blinding ray of light shot downward from the end of the tunnel, far above their heads. Kyle squinted against the brightness, watching as the tunnel widened, until it was well over a hundred feet in diameter. Its walls were made purely of churning, flowing water that spiraled madly, roaring with the fury of a dozen waterfalls.

Kyle stared down the length of that awesome channel, gasping as he realized what lay beyond...white, puffy clouds against an impossibly blue sky!

The watery tunnel stopped expanding, sunlight glittering off of the foaming water. The Dead Man continued to rise, carrying Darius and Kyle with him. They ascended through the tunnel, a cold wind tearing at their clothes. Kyle shivered involuntarily, staring into the dark waters as they rose, spotting dark shapes moving from deep within, darting rapidly away from the maelstrom. The roar of water was deafening, forcing Kyle to cover his ears with his hands. Still upward they went, until they reached the end of the tunnel at last, the cold wind dying away as they rose above the water. Kyle stared downward, seeing a large lake below. The whirling tunnel below slowed, shrinking rapidly, water pouring violently inward to fill the void the tunnel had created. The water at the lake's surface churned wildly, water spraying high into the air, until the tunnel had closed at last. Only the agitated surface of the lake remained.

Their ascent stopped suddenly, a few dozen feet above the surface of the lake. Kyle looked about, staring at the mountainous terrain beyond the lake, feeling the sun's hot rays on his scalp. The chill he'd felt in the chamber below had already begun to dissipate, and despite everything, he felt renewed under its glow. He scanned the rocky mountainside beyond the lake, spotting a shadowy entrance of a cave there. It was instantaneously familiar; it was the same cave they'd escaped from a few weeks ago, the one the Dead Man had ambushed them at...and had been supposedly killed near. Now Kyle knew how the Dead Man had gotten to them so quickly back then; he'd used the water-tunnel to get to the surface, intercepting them as they'd escaped.

The Dead noted the direction of Kyle's gaze, and nodded approvingly.

"Very observant, Kyle," he murmured. They began moving forward then, toward the shore in the distance, summoned by the Dead Man's power. "You have so much potential," he added wistfully.

They reached the shore in a matter of minutes, the Dead Man dropping them gently onto the grass beyond the sandy shoreline. Kyle glanced at Darius, who was staring back at him. The bodyguard's mouth was set in a grim line.

"You have one last chance," the Dead Man stated solemnly. "If you reveal the identity of whoever is killing the Chosen, the others will be spared."

Kyle glanced at Darius, then looked down at his feet. He grit his teeth, knowing that he could end this with one word, could save Darius and perhaps even himself, if he told the Dead Man who'd really been responsible for saving the Council. Kyle had promised not to tell, but that promise seemed insignificant compared to what was at stake. He knew, however, that there was a good chance that the Dead Man would kill them both even if Kyle *did* tell the truth.

But at least there was a chance he wouldn't.

"Very well," the Dead Man stated with a sigh. "The Behemoth will take some time to arrive," he added, turning his head to gaze at the lake behind them. "I suggest you start running now."

"Wait," Kyle protested, stepping forward. But the Dead Man ignored him, lifting up into the air gracefully, then flying across the rippling waters of the lake, his black cloak flowing sinuously behind him. The surface of the lake began to churn violently, a depression forming in the center. The depression grew wider and deeper as Kyle watched, and he felt his heart leap into his throat.

"No, wait!" he shouted, bolting forward. "Wait, I'll tell..." He felt a strong hand grip his forearm, stopping him in his tracks and spinning him about. He found Darius standing before him.

"Run," the bodyguard commanded, pulling Kyle forward toward the tree line. Kyle resisted, turning to stare at the Dead Man, still hovering above the center of the lake. A massive whirlpool was already forming below the dark Weaver.

"Now!" Darius shouted, shoving Kyle forward.

They broke into an all-out run, bolting madly for the forest beyond. Kyle pumped his legs as hard as he could, the grass and dirt crunching under his boots. Darius ran alongside Kyle, easily keeping pace despite the fact that he was barefoot.

Boots, Kyle thought, glancing down at his feet. Black leather boots covered his feet, with strips of silver metal going down the sides. A few blue gems sparkled on the surface of the leather.

"Darius!" Kyle called out, skidding to a stop. Darius frowned, stopping beside him. Kyle pointed down at his own feet. "I have gravity boots! Grab onto me!"

Darius glanced down at Kyle's feet, then wrapped an arm around Kyle's waist from behind. Kyle concentrated, sending a stream of magic to the blue gem on the top of the boot. Then he sent a burst of magic to his left boot. Almost immediately, he rose up into the air, carrying Darius with him. Just as Kyle had hoped, the wide cylindrical gravitational field surrounding him – the one preventing him from tipping over – kept Darius from falling away as well. They both soared into the air, flying up above the treetops. Kyle sent a stream of magic to the left toe crystal, and he bolted forward, feeling his guts twist as they accelerated rapidly. Within seconds, they were zooming over the treetops, far faster than he had ever gone with Master Banar. Still, he struggled to send even more magic to his boots. Depleted after his stay in the Void, he barely had any magic left to work with. If it hadn't been for the Void crystals, he would have been able to fly much faster.

Kyle glanced back over his shoulder, at the roiling surface of the lake far in the distance. The tunnel was completely formed now, a greenish glow coming from deep within. As Kyle watched, a dark shape began to rise from the depths of the lake...a black, metallic dome. It was, he realized, the massive head of the Behemoth rising from the watery tunnel. Its green eye cleared the surface of the lake, followed by its black, armored body. The Behemoth continued to ascend, until at last its massive legs had cleared the surface of the waters. Still upward it rose, flying higher into the sky.

"It's *flying*!" Kyle shouted in horror. "Darius!"

"So are you," Darius retorted. "Go faster!"

Kyle struggled to dredge up more magic into his mind's eye, feeling sweat bead on his forehead with the effort. He'd already nearly depleted what little magic he had left; the sheer force of will it took to conjure up more was simply too great. He shook his head, gritting his teeth.

"I can't!" he cried. He glanced backward, spotting the Behemoth. Its upper body leaned forward, and it began to move, slowly accelerating away from the lake – and toward them. Kyle was still traveling much faster than the monstrosity, but it was gaining speed remarkably quickly. Darius tightened his grip about Kyle's waist.

"There!" Darius shouted, pointing at something in the distance ahead of them. Kyle squinted, following Darius's finger; the bodyguard was pointing to a break in the forest perhaps two miles away, where a huge spiral of shattered rock had been carved into the earth. It looked like pictures of mining excavations Kyle had seen back on Earth. Kyle squinted, noticing a truck-sized hole carved into the side of one rocky wall.

"What about it?" Kyle asked.

"The mine shaft," Darius shouted back. "It's too small for that thing to fit in!"

Kyle nodded, swerving toward the excavation site. It had to be one of the many mines near Crescent Lake that had been abandoned long ago. Even after all that time, the forest had barely begun to regrow around the site. Kyle glanced back again at the Behemoth; it was still far away, but it was moving quickly now...almost as quickly as Kyle was.

And that, he realized, was far slower than he'd been going a minute earlier. The magic stream he'd been powering his boots with had nearly petered out; he'd spent so much energy blasting ahead as fast as possible that he'd used up nearly all of his reserves. Now he didn't have much of anything left...and not only were they beginning to slow down, they were also losing altitude at an alarming rate.

"What are you doing?" Darius shouted in Kyle's ear. "Go faster!"

"I'm *trying!*" Kyle protested.

"Try harder!"

Kyle pushed himself as hard as he could, the veins on his forehead bulging with the strain. He grabbed at wisps of magic desperately, shoving them toward his boots. But it was hopeless; the stream was not even powerful enough to keep them afloat now. They dropped down toward the treetops, sinking until leaves and branches were slapping at their feet. Kyle struggled valiantly, but still they dropped. A tree branch slammed into Kyle's shin, threatening to flip him head-over-heels. He cried out, seeing another branch coming for him, pushing a wisp of magic toward his boots to dodge it. It clipped his thigh anyway, sending him into a mad spin through the air. A kaleidoscope of green, brown, and blue flashed before his eyes, and he felt Darius's arm slip from his waist. Kyle screamed as he fell, closing his eyes and throwing his arms in front of his face. Something slammed into his chest, and the air exploded from his lungs. Stars floated before his eyes, and his body went numb. Time slowed as he rolled onto his back, realizing that he'd stopped falling – that he was on the ground.

Kyle tried to take a breath in, but his body refused to obey his commands. He felt his head swim sickeningly, and stifled the urge to vomit, instead rolling slowly back onto his belly. He tried to breathe again, this time managing to suck some air into his burning lungs. He exhaled, then took another breath, the stars in his vision fading slowly. He got to his hands and knees slowly, feeling a sharp pain in his left shoulder as he did so. He rose to his feet, staggering to his left and slamming his already injured shoulder against a tree trunk. He howled in agony, clutching his shoulder and nearly falling back to his knees. Tears streamed down his cheeks, dripping onto the bed of dead leaves and dirt below.

"Kyle!" a harsh voice shouted from behind. Kyle turned about, blinking through his tears, seeing a man running toward him. It was Darius; the bodyguard's shirt was a tattered mess, a large rent exposing the thick muscles of his chest. Darius ran up to Kyle on his bare feet, ignoring the sharp branches and pebbles littering the forest floor.

"Darius!" Kyle shouted back, nearly buckling again as another surge of pain spread from his shoulder to his arm. Despite this, he felt a wave of relief wash over him. "You're alive!"

"For now," Darius grumbled back. He ran up to Kyle, grabbing him by the right arm and pulling him forward. "The mine is ahead," he added, breaking out into a run. Kyle clenched his teeth, forcing his legs to match Darius's pace. Kyle's lungs burned with each breath, and it wasn't long before he was struggling to keep up with the bodyguard. His foot struck a small rock, and he stumbled, landing on the ground with one knee. Darius ignored Kyle's plight, dragging him across the forest floor. Kyle scrambled to his feet, each step sending sharp pain through his knee.

"Damn it," Kyle swore, trying his best to keep up with Darius. But the bodyguard's pace was too much for his knee, and it gave out from under him. The bodyguard gripped Kyle's wrist hard, yanking him to his feet.

"I got you," Darius stated, wrapping an arm around Kyle's waist and hauling him forward. Kyle grimaced, stumbling along as best he could, dodging tree trunks as they ran. Kyle spotted a hint of bare rock through the trees in the distance, and realized that it was the excavation site, only a hundred or so feet ahead. He felt a surge of hope then, his limbs filling with a second wave of energy. He caught up with Darius, matching his long strides. It wasn't long before they burst through the tree line, the massive rocky spiral of the excavation site opening up before them. There, on the far side of the site, halfway down the long spiraling pit, stood the entrance to the mine shaft Darius had spotted earlier.

"There!" Kyle blurted out, pointing at the mine entrance. Darius ran along the now-rocky path, his torn shirt rippling in the wind. Kyle glanced backward, but from his vantage point, he could see no sign of the Behemoth. They were still a few hundred yards from the mine entrance, but with a little luck...

Kyle felt Darius skid to a sudden stop, one muscled forearm barring Kyle's way forward. Kyle nearly lost his balance, his gravity boots sliding over countless scattered pebbles. He glanced at Darius, but the bodyguard was staring off into the distance, his eyes sweeping the area ahead.

"What?" Kyle asked. Then he noticed the air around them shimmering ever-so-slightly, like the air rising off of a sun-baked parking lot on a hot summer day. A dark shape materialized out of the air in front of them. It was a tall man in a red cloak, a black sash tied about his waist. A green diamond-shaped symbol had been woven into the center of the sash, the all-too familiar symbol of the Death Weavers.

Kyle felt his mind go blank with terror.

Darius shoved Kyle backward, moving to stand guard in front of him. The bodyguard stared coldly at the lone Death Weaver, his blue eyes unblinking. The Death Weaver smirked, the air around him shimmering with the might of his multi-layered gravity shields. The air near the Death Weaver warped, and another man appeared beside him, and then another. More and more red-cloaked figures popped out of thin air, until more than a dozen Death Weavers stood before Kyle and Darius, blocking the way to the mine shaft ahead.

"Turn around!" Darius barked, grabbing Kyle's arm again and pulling him away from the line of Death Weavers, sprinting back toward the tree line. Kyle ran alongside Darius, his heart pounding in his chest. The forest was only a hundred feet away, maybe if they reached it, they could find a place to hide...

A massive black dome rose above the tree line ahead.

Darius skid to a stop, pulling Kyle to his side. Kyle's eyes widened as he stared upward, beyond the treetops, at the huge metallic dome lifting through the sky like a dark sun. Upward it went, leaves whipping about madly, branches waving violently in the wind of its passage. A huge, diamond-shaped eye rose into view, peering from atop the treetops, its green light aiming right at them.

Kyle stared at the Behemoth, his mouth agape.

"Come on!" Darius yelled, spinning Kyle around again, then stopping dead in his tracks.

A tall man in a rippling black cloak stood before them, pale, bone-thin hands extending beyond his loose sleeves. A brilliant green gem embedded in the man's forehead shimmered in the sunlight, splaying spots of verdant light across his ebony cloak.

"I'm disappointed, Kyle," the Dead Man stated, his pale lips pulled into a frown. He gazed down at Kyle with his piercing black eyes. "I was hoping for something...unexpected."

176

Kyle felt his knees buckle, felt his bottom strike the rocky ground below. He barely felt the pain of the impact, a numbness coming over him. He stared mutely at the Dead Man, too terrified to speak. The Dead Man sighed, dropping down to one knee before Kyle, his face only inches away. Kyle drew backward, but was unable to turn away; the ghoulish Weaver's eyes were almost hypnotic, pinning his own gaze to them.

"I had such hopes for you, Kyle," the Dead Man lamented, putting an icy cold hand on Kyle's shoulder. "You were so different from the others...so pure." He shook his head sadly. "It's tragic, the process that Xanos demands." He gestured at the line of Death Weavers standing behind him. "Preparing men for war necessitates taking a piece of their humanity from them, Kyle. I took this from my students, just as Xanos took it from me."

Kyle felt the coolness of the Dead Man's hand seeping through his shirt and into his flesh, and stifled a shudder.

"But I did not take it from you," the Dead Man continued. "I treated you gently, in hopes that you would retain some measure of your humanity, your enthusiasm. I thought that I could mold you into what Xanos required without ruining what made you special to me."

Kyle shook his head angrily, tears forming in his eyes.

"You tried to kill me!" he blurted out, pulling back from the Dead Man's hand. "You tried to kill my friends!"

"I never tried to harm you," the Dead Man countered. "Think back...when did I ever threaten to hurt you? I had to take you by force...I threatened your friends because it was the only way to ensure your loyalty. If circumstances had been different, I'd like to think you would have joined me voluntarily."

"Never," Kyle retorted, shaking his head. "I hate you," he growled, feeling something snap inside of him. He grit his teeth, rising to his feet and clenching his fists in a sudden rage. "I hate you!" he screamed.

The Dead Man stared at Kyle impassively, his black eyes unblinking. The ground shook suddenly, a massive *boom* exploding from behind them. Kyle whipped about, seeing two black, metallic legs in the distance, right in front of the forest line. There the Behemoth stood, many times the height of the trees behind it, its green eye staring down at him. Kyle stepped backward, feeling something cold touch the back of his neck. He spun around again, seeing the Dead Man standing there, staring down at Kyle, his face expressionless.

"Xanos is wise," he stated softly. Then he turned to face Darius, who was standing silently beside Kyle, his blue eyes darting from Death Weaver to Death Weaver. The bodyguard's eyes met the Dead Man's, stopping there.

"You," the Dead Man stated, lifting one pale hand to point at the bodyguard. "I believe this is long overdue."

A bright flash of light shot out from the Dead Man's palm, slamming into Darius's chest. Darius didn't even have time to cry out as he flew backward at breakneck speed, his shirt exploding into flames. He careened through the air almost too quickly for the eye to follow, slamming with a loud *crunch* into one of the Behemoth's feet. He ricocheted off of the hard metal, landing in a limp heap on the dirt below, his chest and back engulfed in red-hot flames. Darius's shirt shrank and blackened with the heat, his flesh hissing and popping as the fire spread.

"Darius!" Kyle screamed, lunging toward his friend.

A cold hand grabbed Kyle's left shoulder from behind, fingers digging into the already-injured flesh. Kyle howled in pain, unable to break free from that iron grip.

Darius stirred, rolling slowly, agonizingly onto his stomach. Something was terribly wrong; he wasn't moving his legs, Kyle realized with horror. The man's back had been broken.

The Dead Man stared impassively at the bodyguard, his iron grip unyielding on Kyle's shoulder. He gazed upward at the Behemoth.

"Show the man some mercy," the Dead Man commanded disapprovingly. "Put him out."

The Behemoth stirred, leaning slightly to one side. One leg rose up slowly into the air, dirt and pebbles cascading from the bottom of its monstrous foot. Kyle saw Darius reach out with one hand toward Kyle, his blue eyes locked on his own. The bodyguard's lips were moving, but only a tortured moan managed to escape them. Kyle choked out a sob, tears pouring down his cheeks, reaching out to his friend with his own hand, held back by the cruel grip of the Dead Man.

The Behemoth's leg paused for a moment, then dropped downward through the air, its massive foot crashing down on Darius from above.

Chapter 15

A huge plume of dust shot up from around the Behemoth's foot as it crushed the rocky ground beneath it, sinking a full foot into the earth. An ear-shattering blast nearly threw Kyle backward, a burst of air from the shockwave of the foot's impact tearing at his clothes. Kyle stared mutely at the massive foot, at the spot where Darius had been only moments before.

Darius, the ever-faithful bodyguard. The man who'd risked his life countless times to save Kyle. The only true hero Kyle had ever met.

His friend.

Kyle stared at the Behemoth's foot, unable to comprehend what had just happened. Unwilling to believe that his friend was gone.

The Behemoth's foot stirred, the mass of black metal rising slowly, a shower of dust and pebbles falling from its sole. Kyle watched it rise, unable to look away, unable to help noticing the charred remains of Darius's shirt still stuck to the bottom of it. Along with...other things.

Kyle turned away then, feeling the Dead Man's grip loosen on his shoulder as he did, and vomited.

"Well," the Dead Man stated calmly, gazing upward at the flattened, bloodied corpse still stuck to the Behemoth's foot. "He's certainly not the one we're looking for."

Kyle waited for the sound of the Behemoth's foot striking the earth once more, then turned forward again. The Behemoth stood motionless in front of him, its glowing green eye locked on him. He felt the Dead Man's hand back on his shoulder; this time, his grip was gentle.

"I'm sorry, Kyle," he murmured. Kyle said nothing, feeling a horrible sob burst from his lips. He wept then, his shoulders heaving as he did. He fell to his hands and knees, his tears staining the parched rock below, not even bothering to shrink away from the Dead Man's touch.

He didn't even feel it.

The Dead Man said nothing, his hand remaining on Kyle's shoulder. He'd dropped to one knee by Kyle's side as he'd fallen, his cloak ever-rippling around him. He remained silent, holding a hand up as one of his Death Weavers made a snide comment, stopping the man in mid-sentence. The only sound afterward was the wind blowing through the trees, the soft, gentle whistling of air running its fingers through the grass at the forest's edge.

Kyle wept, feeling the tears drain from him, until he had no more.

He sat back on his butt then, staring at the huge hole left by the Behemoth's foot, at the wet crimson staining the rock in the middle of it. He'd never been particularly religious, his parents never raising him to be, but he felt that he needed to pray. Not for himself, but for his friend. For all of his friends.

Despite himself, he prayed that their deaths would be as quick as Darius's. And he hoped that he would not be alive to see it when it happened.

"Come, Kyle," the Dead Man ordered, grabbing Kyle's arm under his armpit and lifting him to his feet. Kyle did not resist. "It's almost over," the Dead Man added, patting Kyle on the shoulder. "You've suffered a great deal because of my failure. If I had been wiser, I would have killed Kalibar instead of wounding him. Orik would have become Grand Weaver, and I would not have had to hurt you."

Kyle laughed bitterly at that, the sound surprising even him as it came from his lips. He turned to face the Dead Man.

"I hate you," he spat.

"I know," the Dead Man replied. He withdrew his hand from Kyle's shoulder, turning his eyes away from Kyle's and staring up at the Behemoth. "I had hopes for us, Kyle. You've been given a remarkable gift." He turned back to Kyle then, his black eyes boring through

Kyle's. "Not your ability to generate magic," he added. "Your teachers at the Tower are obsessed with that, so much so that they're blind to your true gift."

Kyle swallowed in a dry throat, wondering how the Dead Man had known about Master Owens and Master Banar.

"The ability to generate a lot of magic has its uses," the Dead Man continued. "...indeed, the fact that you could weave magic so soon after being drained by the Void is unprecedented. But recall that I myself cannot generate any. It's the ability to weave magic...to *understand* magic...that is truly valuable. Your intuition. You grasped the fundamentals of magic more quickly and completely than any of my other students." He shook his head then. "When I heard that your teacher declared you unfit to become a Weaver, I laughed. The fools don't even understand what they have in you."

Kyle lowered his gaze, unable to look into the Dead Man's eyes any longer. The black-cloaked Weaver sighed, turning away from Kyle once more. He stared at Darius's remains, his black eyes glittering in the sunlight.

"Death is not so bad," he murmured. Then he turned back to Kyle. "When I died...before I became one of the Chosen...it was only painful for a moment. Then it was like that feeling you get before you pass out. Lightheadedness, a short struggle against the final slumber, and then...nothing." He turned back to face Kyle.

"It was anticlimactic," the Dead Man continued. "Only significant in that it marked the end of something. For me, it marked the beginning of a new life, but now that I've died – twice – I do not fear an eternity of nothingness. When my time comes, if it comes, I will be ready."

"I don't care," Kyle mumbled, feeling only a faint fear of what the Dead Man might do to punish him for such insolence. But to his surprise, the Dead Man did nothing.

"I know you don't care about *me*," he replied, his deep voice almost gentle. "But I do care about you." He paused for a moment, then sighed. "Kyle, I want this to end as peacefully as possible for you. For your sake, and for mine."

Kyle felt his pulse quicken, felt his heart begin to pound in his chest.

182

"What do you mean?" he asked, gooseflesh rising up on his arms. The Dead Man said nothing for a long moment, staring off into the forest beyond the Behemoth, his expression unreadable. When he turned back to Kyle, his eyes were sad.

"You're going to die today, Kyle."

Kyle felt the blood drain from his face. He licked his lips, his heart hammering in his chest.

"Today?" he croaked. The Dead Man nodded.

"This is how it happens, Kyle," he replied apologetically. "It's no different when you're older. The days go by, one after another, and you assume there will always be more. One day, you're wrong. There's no fanfare, Kyle. Time doesn't slow down. It just keeps going, pushing you along with it, no matter how hard you dig in your heels."

He paused for a moment, then smiled.

"I think I lived more vibrantly in the few minutes before my death than I had for most of my life before it...those moments were the most pregnant of my adult life. I never missed the process of *being* more than when I realized I was about to lose it. You see, I didn't realize that I was to be reborn. Xanos did this purposefully, I think, in order to allow me to fully comprehend what a treasure the moments of my life were."

Kyle stared mutely at the Dead Man, unable to speak. He knew the Dead Man was saying something, heard the words, but the man might as well have been speaking gibberish. The only thought he was capable of now was that of his own impending death.

"We fear our deaths as soon as we realize it will happen to us, but we live as if it will never happen," the Dead Man observed. He stared at Kyle for a long moment, then wrapped a slender arm around Kyle's shoulders. "I'm telling you this because I wish it had been told to me. And because I don't want your death to seem unimportant."

"I don't want to die!" Kyle blurted out, finding his voice at last. The Dead Man grimaced.

"I don't have a choice, Kyle...and neither do you," he countered. "Xanos has demanded your death."

"But why?" Kyle pressed.

"Someone is killing His Chosen," the Dead Man answered. "This should not be possible. This person is protecting you, or it *is* you. I

183

believe you are not the one Xanos is looking for, but He is wiser than I. If your protector is near, they will reveal themselves in saving you. If not, then you will be proven to not be the one He is searching for."

Kyle turned to stare at the pit created by the Behemoth's giant foot, his eyes drawn to the red-soaked rock. The Dead Man noted the focus of Kyle's gaze.

"Xanos is thorough," he explained. Then he stood up, staring down at Kyle. "It's time, Kyle. Stand up."

Kyle stared up at the Dead Man, terror gripping him. He stayed where he was, sitting on the ground, paralyzed with fear.

"Don't make this more unpleasant than it needs to be," the Dead Man warned.

Kyle bolted then, leaping up from the ground and sprinting as fast as he could away from the Dead Man and the line of Death Weavers, running into the depression created by the Behemoth's foot. He jumped over the bloodied portion of rock, pumping his legs hard, aiming for the large space between the Behemoth's feet. He half-expected one of those feet to rise up and smash down on him, finishing him off as they'd done to Darius, but they didn't move. He ran between them, seeing the edge of the forest only fifty or so feet ahead now, his lungs burning with the effort. He sprinted as fast as he could, pushing his body to its limit.

And then the Dead Man struck.

Kyle felt a vibration in his skull, then felt a powerful force yank him backward, his heels sliding across the ground. He struggled against that invisible grip, digging his heels into the dirt, but it was no use. Backward he went, passing between the Behemoth's legs again, then flying over the foot-shaped depression in the ground. A bolt of terror passed through him.

No!" he screamed out.

Without warning, the force pulling on him vanished, and he dropped to the ground with a loud *thump*, sliding to a halt on his back. He grunted, then rolled onto his stomach, pushing himself up off of the ground with his palms.

Then he looked down and noticed the blood soaking his shirt, spreading rapidly across his chest.

184

He took a deep breath in, and screamed again, his legs feeling like lead. He stumbled to the ground, crawling on his hands and knees, clutching his bleeding chest with one hand. His head swam sickeningly, a wave of nausea threatening to overcome him.

A cold hand gripped his shoulder.

Kyle tried to pull away from that horrible grasp, but it was impossibly strong. The hand pulled back, spinning Kyle around; he screamed a third time, shielding his face with one forearm, knowing that he was about to die.

His distorted reflection stared back at him.

Kyle's eyes widened, and he scrambled backward, feeling the hand on his shoulder slip away.

A man was kneeling in front of him on one knee, a tall man in jet-black armor, countless tiny runes carved into the metallic surface. Blue light arced through the runes in slow, random patterns, casting the man's face in a pulsing glow. The man wore a silver, mirrored visor across his eyes, sunlight reflecting off of the curved surface. His short brown hair rippled in the gentle breeze that blew across the open pit mine.

Kyle sat there on the ground, resting back on his palms, his eyes wide, his jaw slack with awe.

Rise.

The voice – there but not there, heard but without sound, echoed through his mind. Kyle rose slowly to his feet, his eyes locked on that mirrored visor. Then he glanced down at his chest, remembering the blood dripping from his shirt. He blinked, realizing that the blood wasn't his; he'd fallen onto the puddle of blood on the rocks, the one created by the Behemoth.

Darius's blood.

Kyle lifted his gaze upward, spotting something in the distance...the Dead Man, standing some thirty feet away, his black cloak ever-rippling. He was staring at the black-armored man, his pale lips drawn in a frown.

"And who," the Dead Man inquired, "...are you?"

The black-armored man turned slowly, facing the Dead Man, blue light rippling down the runes on his black gauntlets in rhythmic pulses. He remained silent.

185

"I asked you a question," the Dead Man warned.

Suddenly, Kyle felt something *slam* into his mind, an immense power coursing over his body. A shockwave of blue energy flared outward from the armored man, blinding in its intensity. He gasped, feeling energy coursing through him. The magic flowed through his bones, filling them instantly, recharging all that had been lost to the Void earlier.

Kyle squinted against that ocean of blue, watching it shoot outward in all directions, striking the Dead Man and his Death Weavers. The Dead Man's eyes widened, his jaw dropping. The Death Weavers fell to their knees.

And then the wellspring of power vanished.

The black-armored man strode slowly toward the Dead Man, his black boots cracking the very stone beneath them with each step, the green crystal on the Dead Man's forehead reflecting off of that silver visor. The armored man stopped a few feet from the Dead Man, who stood there levitating an inch above the ground, his black cloak rippling sinuously around him. Blue spherical gravity shields appeared around the Dead Man in a dozen shimmering layers. The Death Weavers scrambled to their feet, activating their own gravity shields.

The black-armored man stood before them, unafraid.

"*I*," he stated, the word echoing through Kyle's mind, but this time also heard, the sound sending a chill down Kyle's spine. The Death Weavers stepped backward almost as one, no doubt sensing the voice as Kyle did. Only the Dead Man remained unmoved by it.

"*...am*," the voice continued, rolling across the pit mine. Kyle felt goosebumps rise on his arms, the hair on the back of his neck rising on end. The black-armored man raised his right gauntleted fist into the air, blue light coursing through its runes.

"*Ampir.*"

He slammed his fist onto the ground, his black gauntlet crushing through the rock with ease, the very earth rising up in a shockwave around him. The stone rippled outward in front of him in an expanding wave of crumbling rock ten feet high, crashing through the Death Weavers' shields and throwing them backward onto the ground like rag dolls. Only the Dead Man remained untouched, rising up through the air over the moving wall of stone.

Then the shattered earth rose into the air in a storm of pebbles and stones, the Death Weavers flying up into the air with them, soaring into the sky until they came to a stop some fifty feet in the air. Their shields vanished as one, obliterated instantly by an unseen power, each Death Weaver flying apart from the other until they formed a loose circle in the sky. The air in the center of that circle *ripped*, a dark hole appearing there. It expanded rapidly, strange white pinpoints of light glimmering against that blackness.

Then, the Death Weavers – every last one of them – shot inward with blinding speed, vanishing into the void above.

Kyle stared upward, watching as the dark hole in the sky shrank, then vanished. A powerful gale slammed into him, making him stagger to one side. He righted himself, bracing himself for more, but the wind dissipated as rapidly as it had arrived.

And there was silence.

The Dead Man remained levitating ten feet in the air, staring down at the black-armored man, the one who called himself Ampir. He descended slowly, the green crystal in his forehead glittering in the sunlight, until he was mere inches from the ground. His eyes were cold, his expression unreadable. His shields glowed powerfully around him, warping the light at their edges like a magnifying glass.

"You're the one we've been searching for," he deduced. Ampir said nothing. He stood there in front of the Dead Man, arms at his sides, no shields surrounding him. The Dead Man glanced upward. "What did you do to them?" he asked. "Where did you send my children?" Ampir's lips curled into a slight smirk.

"Orbit," he replied. This time, he spoke only with his voice. No sound echoed within Kyle's skull, as it normally did when Ampir communicated with him. The Dead Man's eyes narrowed.

"What?"

Ampir said nothing, but took a step toward the Dead Man, his gauntlets glowing brightly now. The Dead Man glided backward, the crystal embedded in his forehead flashing bright green, casting a harsh glow over his pale, gaunt features. Kyle stepped back involuntarily, a spike of fear twisting in his belly.

Then the shard's light went out.

187

Ampir took another step forward, bringing his hands to the sides of his head, his gauntleted fingers resting on the sides of his visor. The visor was held in place by a black metal band encircling the back of Ampir's head; when his fingers touched the band, it flashed bright blue, then vanished.

"Don't bother," Ampir said, stopping some twenty feet from the Dead Man. The Dead Man reached up to touch the gem in his forehead with one hand, his eyes widening.

"How are you doing this?" he asked, his voice filled with awe. "Who *are* you?"

Ampir didn't answer, instead grasping his visor with both hands, then slowly pulling it away from his face. Kyle stepped forward to get a better look, then stopped in his tracks. Ampir removed his visor, turning his head to face Kyle.

Kyle froze.

A pair of blue eyes stared into his, so startlingly blue that they seemed almost to be glowing. They were framed by well-tanned skin, a face both handsome and ageless.

And unmistakably familiar.

"Darius!" Kyle gasped, his legs giving out underneath him. He slumped to the ground, landing on his butt on the hard rock below. He didn't even feel the pain of the impact, his whole body numb with shock. It *was* Darius, back from the dead...but why was he wearing Ampir's armor?

"You!" the Dead Man exclaimed, staring in shock at Darius. "I thought I killed you!"

"Ditto," Darius shot back. "Nice talk, by the way. Very touching." He put one arm under Kyle's armpit, pulling Kyle up from the ground. "Almost made me think twice about killing you," Darius added. He smirked then. "Almost."

The Dead Man stared at Darius, then glanced back at the crimson stain on the ground, left by the Behemoth's massive foot. Darius followed his gaze.

"One of your Dead Weavers," Darius explained. The Dead Man turned back to face Darius, his jawline rippling.

"I'm not sure what you hope to accomplish by releasing so much magic from your armor," he stated, his tone ice-cold. "But I assure you it pales in comparison to the power of Xanos's creations." Kyle heard the Behemoth stir behind them, and spun around, watching as its green eye moved to focus on them. The eye began to glow brightly, nearly blinding in its intensity. Kyle cried out, ducking down low and covering his face with one arm, feeling the air around him heat up, his skin beginning to burn.

Then the air around the Behemoth's head rippled.

A perfect line split the Behemoth's head, running diagonally from one end to the other, bisecting its diamond-shaped eye. Then the upper dome pulled away, vanishing into thin air. Half of its head remained, green crystal glinting in the cross-section that was revealed.

The Behemoth's head tipped backward, bringing its body with it, sending it into a slow fall. It struck the ground with a deafening *boom*, sending a plume of dust into the air. Its upper body smashed into the trees at the edge of the forest, snapping the thick trunks like so many twigs under its incredible weight.

Darius, his eyes having never moved from the Dead Man's, shook his head.

"If you want to kill someone without scaring the crap out of them, try not telling them first," he offered. Kyle heard a low whistling sound coming from above, almost imperceptible at first, then getting louder and louder. Darius smirked. "Like this."

A shockwave struck Kyle, a cloud of dust slamming into him, thrusting him backward. If it hadn't been for Darius's arm about his shoulders, he would have been knocked clear off of his feet. The dust cloud shot upward in front of Kyle and Darius, rising dozens of feet into the sky. Small pebbles fell toward them from above, clattering on the ground around them. Kyle shielded his eyes with one forearm, protecting them from the flying dust. Then he realized that none of it was reaching him, a gravity shield having appeared around him. He lowered his arm, watching as the dust cleared slowly, until he realized that he was looking at something huge and black embedded into the ground. He stepped backward, feeling Darius's arm slip from his shoulders as he did so. A breeze blew the remainder of the dust cloud away, and Kyle realized what he was looking at...the top half of the Behemoth's head, having fallen through the sky, slamming into the rocky terrain.

Right where the Dead Man had been standing.

Kyle turned to the fallen body of the Behemoth, having decimated a huge swath of trees in the distance. Then he turned back to stare at Darius.

The bodyguard stood there silently, calmly regarding Kyle. The air around the bodyguard's face wavered, the mirrored visor reappearing suddenly, hiding his eyes once again. He walked up to the fallen half of the Behemoth's head, grabbing the rim of the house-sized half-dome with one gauntleted hand and pulling it upward with frightening ease, peering at the crystalline innards.

"Interesting," Darius stated, staring for a long moment, then letting go of the rim. The half-dome crashed downward, the ground it lay on sinking slightly under its countless tons of weight. Kyle stared at Darius, then back at the Behemoth's head, his jaw slack. Darius ignored Kyle, turning to glance at the Behemoth's fallen body a few dozen feet away. Kyle followed the bodyguard's gaze, then turned back to Darius, finally finding his voice.

"How?" he asked, flabbergasted. Darius turned to regard Kyle.

"How what?"

"How are you still alive?" Kyle pressed. "And why are you wearing that armor? And how did..." he turned to the Behemoth's fallen body, gesturing limply. "How did you do *that*?"

"Magic," Darius answered.

"I know *that*," he replied impatiently. "I mean, how did *you* do it?"

"I dropped a head on him," Darius replied, pointing to the Behemoth's severed skull. Kyle rolled his eyes.

"How did you do *that*?" he pressed.

"Magic," Darius repeated.

"But *how*?" Kyle pleaded, now exasperated with the bodyguard. Then he paused, realizing that he'd somehow gone from missing the bodyguard terribly to *almost* wishing the man had been mashed into goo by the Behemoth...all in a few minutes. Kyle had to give the man credit; Darius certainly had a gift for making others wish he didn't exist.

"I'm Ampir," Darius replied.

Kyle started to respond, then felt the breath stop in his throat. His mind blanked, and he stared at Darius in confusion.

"What?"

190

"I'm Ampir," Darius repeated.

Kyle stared at Darius for a long moment. The bodyguard tolerated this for a short time, then turned away, walking toward the body of the fallen Behemoth. Kyle hesitated, then ran to catch up with Darius, following him as he circled around one of the monstrosity's massive feet.

"You're *what?*" Kyle pressed. Darius didn't slow down, striding past the fifty-foot-tall foot, forcing Kyle to jog to keep up. "No, seriously," Kyle added. Darius stopped, turning to face Kyle. Kyle stared at his own face reflected in that visor.

You've shown me who you are.

The voice reverberated in Kyle's skull, instantly familiar, identical to what he'd heard only a few weeks prior, after jumping from the Tower to save Ariana.

Now I've shown you who I am.

Kyle stared at Ampir's visor, his mouth agape. He found himself speechless again, unable to process what he was hearing. How could Darius be Ampir? The bodyguard didn't make any magic! And he was just a bodyguard, after all...a good one, but nothing more.

Wait, he was a *bodyguard*...

Kyle felt a chill pass through him.

What if Darius was never Kalibar's bodyguard, but *Kyle's?*

Kyle stared at Darius, his mind working furiously. Darius had been with Kyle every step of his adventure, after all. And every time Kyle had been threatened, Darius had been the one to protect him. From the soldiers and the Death Weaver at Crescent Lake, from the Dire Lurker in the caves, even from the Dead Man...Darius had ultimately been the one to kill them all.

Even Xanos.

Kyle stared at Darius mutely, taking a step backward.

When that man attacked Kyle during the carriage ride to Stridon...Darius had been there to protect Kyle, not Kalibar. It had been Darius, after all, that had killed the leader of the Death Weavers during that attack, beheading him and displaying that gruesome trophy to the survivors, causing one of them to betray Orik. Kyle could picture that disembodied head – the first dead body he'd ever seen – with its vacant eyes, that disturbing hole in the center of its forehead...

191

A single hole in the forehead, just large enough to fit a green crystal in...

Kyle took another step backward, feeling his legs wobble underneath him. He fell backward, landing on his bottom on the hard rock below.

How could he have missed that? How could *Kalibar* have missed that?

The answer, of course, was that Darius had been behind Kalibar when he'd displayed the head...Kalibar had never seen it. But Kyle had.

He licked his lips, clearing his throat noisily.

"Why?" was all he could muster.

Darius said nothing, stepping forward instead and offering one gauntleted hand. Kyle paused, then reached out slowly, grabbing onto the cool metal. Darius hauled Kyle to his feet in one smooth motion, then turned away, facing the Behemoth. He resumed his quick stride past the Behemoth's long leg, to the torso, and then past the arm and shoulder. Kyle followed along, walking until they'd turned the bend around that massive shoulder, walking toward the ruined head. When they reached the top of the head, they saw a gaping hole, big enough to fit a small house in, filled with green crystal. Kyle peered inside, absentmindedly creating a small light hovering in the air above, to better illuminate the innards. Darius stepped right up to the machinery, running a hand over the crystal.

"Interesting," the bodyguard murmured. Then he stepped away from the head suddenly, striding back toward the half-dome that had buried the Dead Man. Kyle followed right behind the man, his mind racing. Darius had worked for Kalibar's mentor, and only switched to working for Kalibar after his former employer had died. But Darius – Ampir – must have planned to work with Kalibar all along, so that he could protect Kyle once Kyle was brought to this world. Did that mean Darius had arranged for his previous employer to die? Or had that been a coincidence?

Kyle picked up his pace, jogging behind Darius again as they made the long trip back to the Behemoth's severed head – and the Dead Man's final resting place.

Of course, Ampir had been the one to bring Kyle here in the first place, protecting him from the rip-vines, the killerpillar, and the Ulfar.

192

Kyle felt an ache in his back where the Ulfar had attacked him, the wound still not completely healed. Kalibar had been confused by the fact that the sap of a balm-tree had been placed in Kyle's wound...that must have been Darius's doing as well.

They slowed down as they reached the Behemoth's severed cranium, Darius's visor vanishing into thin air, revealing his blue eyes, which inspected the large half-dome for a long moment. Then the bodyguard's eyes unfocused for a moment.

The head vanished.

A rush of wind struck Kyle from behind, so powerful that it thrust him forward into the vacuum created by the head's absence. Darius's black-clad arm shot in front of Kyle, preventing him from flying forward; the vacuum filled quickly, the violent wind reduced to a strong breeze within seconds. Kyle stared at Darius.

"What happened?" he asked. "Where did it go?"

"Storage," Darius replied, lowering his arm. Kyle frowned, clearly quite confused. "All in good time," Darius promised. Kyle paused, then turned to the Behemoth's massive body.

"What about..." he began, and then the massive body vanished.

Kyle felt himself lurch forward again, sucked into the vacuum left by the Behemoth's absence, but this time a shimmering blue half-sphere surrounded him – and Darius – instantly protecting them. The trees that had been near the Behemoth's fallen body flew forward violently, fifty-foot trunks ripping from the ground and flying past the tree line. A whirlwind of dust and rocks were sucked from where the Behemoth's body had laid on the open pit mine, mixing with the flying trees. The whirlwind dissipated rapidly, scattering rocks and trees across the landscape.

"Right," Kyle mumbled. "Storage." He stared at the huge impression the Behemoth had left in the rocky ground and the forest beyond, then turned back to Darius. "Where exactly *is* storage?" he asked. Then he turned about, realizing that Darius had vanished...the bodyguard was nowhere in sight! Kyle panicked, frantically searching the landscape for his friend. "Darius?" he called out.

"Same place we're going," a voice replied from behind. Kyle jumped, spinning around and seeing Darius behind him. He stared at the bodyguard, taking an involuntary step backward.

"Wait, how...?" he asked, but Darius cut him off with a gesture.

"We're going home," Darius declared. His visor reappeared, the open pit mine reflecting off of that mirrored surface. Kyle's eyes brightened.

"Back to Stridon?" he asked. Then he felt a surge of hope. "...or Earth?" Darius shook his head.

"Nope," he replied. "*My* home."

Chapter 16

Ariana walked to the center of Kalibar's retirement suite, Master Owens at her side. The main room of the suite had been emptied of most of its couches and tables, leaving a large expanse of granite flooring. The numerous bedrooms – including Kyle's and Ariana's – had been left untouched, but the main room had been converted into a sparring chamber. Ariana had not been allowed to leave the suite after Kyle's disappearance; the necessity of her continued training had prompted the suite's conversion. It was an ideal location for sparring, actually. The room was quite large, with high ceiling tall ceilings, and the walls and windows were protected by powerful runic wards.

Master Owens stopped Ariana, turning to her and taking a step backward. He was dressed, as per his usual, in a simple black robe. Ariana had spent the better part of the day practicing her gravity spheres and *punk* generation, in anticipation for her next sparring match. She'd never considered herself a very competitive person...that is, until she'd had her first sparring match. She'd never gotten to an advanced enough level to spar while in the Arena, but after her first sparring match here – which she'd won handily – she'd found her competitive juices flowing with surprising abundance. She'd won a string of victories against subsequent opponents, and was determined to win any future matches against her fellow students.

"Now," Master Owens stated, putting a hand on Ariana's shoulder. "This next sparring match will be a bit different than the others. First, its confined to this room, limiting our mobility compared to the campus lawn."

Ariana nodded, feeling familiar butterflies flit around in her stomach. She always got them before a match, and hated the feeling every time. She found herself bouncing on her tiptoes, and forced herself to stand still.

"Second, we're only to use four patterns," Owens continued. "Water, gravity, fire, and *punk*. No other patterns are acceptable."

"Got it," Ariana replied. That left out the light pattern...no blinding her opponent, then. That certainly didn't bother her; as long as she got to use gravity fields, she would be okay.

"Lastly," Master Owens stated, "...victory is determined by subduing an opponent long enough for a mortal blow to be issued...but as usual, please don't kill your opponent." Then Master Owens gave a slight smile. "Not that I'm concerned about that in this case," he added.

"I'm ready," Ariana stated, finding herself bouncing on her toes again. This time, she didn't bother holding herself back. "Where's my opponent?" she added, glancing about the room.

"Your opponent," Master Owens replied, "...is me."

Ariana stopped cold, feeling the hairs on the back of her neck rise.

"What?" she blurted out. Master Owens was a teacher now, having retired years ago. But in his prime, he'd been a master-level Battle-Weaver, fighting in the same wars that had made Kalibar a hero. And while Owens would not be able to stand toe-to-toe with Kalibar and have any hope of winning, he was still one of the finest Weavers alive.

And, Ariana knew, Master Owens taught the most advanced Battle-Weaver classes the Secula Magna offered, personally sparring – and almost always soundly beating – the best Battle-Weavers every day. He'd taught almost all of the active Battle-Weavers in the Empire, and knew every one of them by name. It was a gift that Owens had agreed to teach Ariana and Kyle at all...a favor for Kalibar, no doubt. That was why Ariana – a future Battle-Weaver student, if she did well – was so keen on impressing the man.

"Don't worry," Owens reassured her, his voice gentle. "I'm certainly not going to hurt you, as long as you agree to do the same."

"Of course," Ariana stammered. "Sorry, I just didn't expect..."

196

"No pressure, Ariana," Master Owens interjected gently. "This is a learning exercise, not a test."

"Okay," Ariana replied, only slightly relieved. Master Owens took a few steps backward, gesturing for Ariana to do the same. After they'd put about twenty feet between them, Master Owens gestured for her to stop.

"Remember, we'll both be using only the four patterns," he stated. "The match will be decided on how well we can use those patterns." Ariana nodded, feeling almost sick to her stomach. She closed her eyes for a moment, taking a deep breath in to center herself. Then she let it go slowly, opening her eyes.

"Ready?" Owens asked.

"Ready."

Almost instantaneously, a ball of *punk* appeared in front of Master Owens, bursting into flames, then shooting outward with unnerving speed...right toward her! Ariana reacted instinctively, activating her gravity shield – which promptly vanished. She leaped to the side frantically, the projectile missing her shoulder by mere inches. She stumbled, catching her balance after a few seconds. Master Owens had attacked so quickly...and had abolished her gravity shield with a reverse-polarity field of his own. Ariana was immediately grateful that she'd kept on her toes before the match; if she'd been caught flat-footed, that would have been the end of it.

A second ball of *punk* appeared in front of Owens, bursting into flames and shooting toward Ariana. This time, she kept her wits about her, weaving the gravity pattern reflexively, creating a powerful *pulling* sphere in front of her and to the right. The projectile fell under the gravitational field's sway, arcing rightward mere feet from where Ariana stood. She poured as much magic into her magic stream as she could then, multiplying the gravitational pull of her sphere. The flaming *punk* tightened its arc around the sphere, swinging around and reversing direction rapidly. Ariana waited for the exact right time, then cut off the magic stream, abolishing the gravity sphere. The *punk* flew away from her with enormous speed – and right toward Master Owens.

It passed over his left shoulder harmlessly.

"Ambitious," he noted approvingly. Ariana said nothing, conjuring up her own hovering ball of *punk*. She'd gotten faster at it since learning the sequence of patterns a few days ago. First the gravity sphere, then create the *punk* in the center of it. Then set it on fire. Lastly, create a second, much more powerful gravity sphere, but this time pushing *outward* instead of inward. The reverse-gravity field caused the *punk* to shoot outward. Aiming it depended on the proper placement and strength of the reverse-gravity field – and was extraordinarily difficult.

But she'd been practicing.

Ariana's *punk* shot forward, slower than Master Owen's had, but her aim was true. The burning projectile flew toward her instructor's head unerringly.

Suddenly, a ball of water appeared around the *punk*, snuffing the flames instantly. The doused projectile veered off to the left at the last minute, missing Owen's head by a few inches, then falling to the floor in a sticky wet mess.

He didn't so much as flinch.

Ariana didn't pause, creating a second ball of *punk* immediately after she'd sent out the first, setting this one on fire and sending it out again. This time, Master Owens stepped to the right as it approached, dodging out of the way. Ariana immediately created a gravity sphere to the right of the *punk's* path, sucking the fireball to the right...and right at Owens.

"Good!" Owens exclaimed, creating a gravity sphere of his own, pulling the projectile in a quick orbit and flinging it back at Ariana. His aim was perfect, the *punk* flying right at her. She dodged to the left, but not quickly enough. In a last-ditch effort, she created a gravity field a few feet to her left, so powerful that it sucked her violently into it...and out of the way of her own fireball.

Until the fireball arced right into the same gravity sphere...and into her.

Ariana cried out, throwing her arms in front of her face. The gravity sphere vanished, dropping her onto her left side on the unforgiving granite below. She grabbed at her own clothes, desperately trying to brush off the burning *punk* from her body. She screamed then, instantly transported back to that horrifying moment only days ago, when the Dead Man had tried to burn her alive. She felt the burning in her legs, smelling the smoke as her clothes burned, her flesh blackening, then cracking, fluid spilling out from the cracks and spitting and crackling in the fire...

"Ariana!"

She stopping flailing her arms, opening her eyes. Master Owens was rushing toward her, his face filled with concern. She blinked, then looked down at herself, realizing that the *punk* had never even hit her. There wasn't a single mark on her.

"Ariana, are you okay?" Owens asked, stopping at her side. Ariana felt the color rise in her cheeks, and turned away, mortified.

"Sorry," she mumbled. Master Owens dropped to one knee before her, putting a hand on her shoulder.

"What happened, Ariana?" he asked gently. "I've never seen you react that way," he added. Ariana shook her head, fighting back sudden tears. She'd tried to forget that horrible moment – when she'd truly thought she was dying, burning alive at the hands of the man who'd burned her family – and her entire village – alive. She hadn't even thought about it until now, having buried the memory in the past with all of the other terrible things the Dead Man – and his Death Weavers – had done to her.

She hated that those memories could still make her cry...that the Dead Man could still have power over her, even after his demise.

It wasn't fair.

"Ariana?" Master Owens pressed. She sighed, wiping her eyes with the back of her hand, then looking up at the kindly instructor. She thought about deflecting the question, but something in Owen's eyes – his genuine concern – stopped her.

"I have a...problem with fire," she admitted.

"I'm sorry," Master Owens stated. "I didn't know..."

"It's okay," she replied, standing up suddenly. Master Owens paused, then slowly got up to his own feet, his knees popping loudly. Ariana gave a weak smile. "I'll get over it," she added.

And that much, she knew, was true. All she had to do was bury it deep enough, so that it couldn't hurt her anymore.

"Well," Master Owens replied, returning Ariana's smile, "...you certainly did a good job today. You're ambitious, Ariana...that trick of yours, redirecting my own *punk* back at me...that's an advanced technique."

"I missed," Ariana countered. Still, she flushed with pride. She'd been practicing that ever since she'd thought of it, the day she'd been taught the gravity pattern.

"Not by much," Owens said. "You've clearly been practicing on your own. And thinking – *really* thinking – about all of the possible uses of each pattern." He smiled again, patting Ariana on the shoulder with one hand. "I'm proud of you."

Ariana felt her cheeks burning, and she lowered her gaze. "Thank you," she mumbled.

"Keep practicing," Owens instructed. "And remember that gravity can work for you...and against you. Next time, keep your gravity shields up."

"Yes sir."

"I'd like to go another round," Master Owens said. "...but I've got another class to teach." He turned toward the entrance to the suite, walking to the front door and opening it. He turned around then, glancing back at Ariana. "And Ariana..."

"Yes?"

"If you ever want to talk," he stated, "...about what happened...I'm here."

* * *

Ariana threw herself onto her bed, pulling her sheet and blanket over her legs and up to her belly. She'd spent the better part of the evening after her sparring match taking a small coin and practicing the trick she'd tried on Master Owens earlier. She'd thrown the coin across the room with her left hand – her dominant hand – and then tried using a gravity sphere to sling it back toward her, catching it with her hand. She'd caught the coin with her face a few times as well; a poignant reminder to do as Owens had recommended, and keep her gravity shield up at all times.

She'd performed the exercise at least a hundred times, until she'd gotten so hungry that she'd summoned Jenkins. The butler had come almost immediately, bringing Ariana her favorite meal – roasted duck.

200

She'd never even had the meal before coming to the Tower. The night after their battle with Xanos had been the first time she'd tasted it. It had been, for many reasons, the best meal she'd ever had. This time, however, it hadn't been the same. Then she'd had Kalibar, Darius, and Kyle with her, laughing and joking, enjoying each other's company. Tonight, she'd eaten alone; Kalibar was off with Erasmus on some unknown errand, and Darius was still missing from yesterday.

And Kyle...

Ariana closed her eyes, feeling a sinking despair come over her. She'd filled the day with magic practice, so that she wouldn't have time to think about Kyle. She could still see Master Banar's lifeless body, face-down in the grass. She could only hope that Kyle hadn't suffered the same fate; the fact that Kyle's body hadn't been found with Banar's was encouraging.

Although Ariana knew all too well that death was not the worst thing that could happen to someone.

She rolled onto her side, fearing that tonight would be the same as last night...sleepless. She dreaded this, being alone with her thoughts. She couldn't help but imagine Kyle lost in some dark place, terrified and hopeless. Wondering if anyone would ever find him...if anyone was even looking. That was how she had felt, after all, after being torn from her family.

She sighed, rolling onto her other side, pulling her blankets up to her chin. She vividly remembered the first time she had met Kyle, in the classroom in the Arena. He'd been unlike any other boy she'd met there...shy, naïve, and sweet. And he'd rescued her from the Arena; even though Darius had been the mastermind, the bodyguard wouldn't have thought twice about leaving her there to rot. Kyle had vouched for her, refusing to leave if she wasn't freed as well. For that, she owed Kyle a debt she could never repay.

And if he was truly lost, or worse, then she would never even get the chance to try.

Ariana's vision blurred as tears welled up unbidden in her eyes. She blinked, the tears rolling down her cheeks. This was far worse than dying in the Arena would have been, this slow death. She'd been saved only to have her new home – her new friends – taken from her one by one. No matter where she was, Xanos could reach her. Until the god was destroyed, she would never feel truly safe.

Ariana closed her eyes, pulling her blankets over her face. She could only hope that her utter exhaustion would force her to finally fall asleep, so that she wouldn't have to feel this pain anymore.

* * *

Kalibar sighed, stretching his neck to either side, then back, to get the kinks out of it. Then he walked across his bedroom, turning to sit on the edge of his bed. He'd been with Erasmus for most of the day – and night – in the Testing Chamber, racing to complete a prototype of the sensory rune array. They'd nicknamed the prototype "the Rune Seeker," which seemed appropriate enough. The Rune Seeker had seemed pretty straightforward in theory, but it was hardly straightforward in practice.

First, they'd needed to find the right rune fragments to put in their sensory array. That meant writing down every possible magical pattern known, then separating those patterns into common fragments. If the fragments were too short, they'd light up whenever *any* pattern was woven. But if they were too long, they'd be too specific to a particular pattern, and light up only when that one pattern was woven.

Then, after creating a list of the best pattern fragments, they'd tested them to make sure they worked. Erasmus was a remarkably quick rune-linker, and had generated the first sensory array within a few hours or so. Kalibar had then woven every pattern he knew near the array, and about half had lit up the correct sensory runes.

Then it was back to the drawing board.

Ten hours later, they'd finally done it, creating a sensory array that worked. Erasmus had immediately sent for Jenkins, who'd met them in the hallway with two glasses of red wine. One toast and two empty glasses later, they'd gone back to the Testing Chamber, ready for round two – bringing in the magical creature that held the pattern they wanted to learn.

That had been...difficult.

But despite the extraordinary risk they'd taken by having the creature brought in – the risk to the hunters who'd gone out to find it, not to mention the personal danger to Kalibar and Erasmus themselves – everything had gone smoothly. With the specimen secured, the first round of testing had gone remarkably well. A few dozen rune fragments had lit up, and Erasmus was busily combining the fragments to form complete runes.

During the majority of this, Kalibar had found himself to be mostly useless. Erasmus was far more creative and skilled in developing the sensory array, and Kalibar had left to attend to the running of the Empire. As expected, Councilman Ibicus had been sworn in as Elder, and the opposition had chosen a new Runic to replace Jax that was not particularly fond of either Kalibar or Erasmus. The power of the Council had shifted in Councilman Goran's favor 7-5, with Ibicus as a tiebreaker.

Not that a tie vote was very likely any longer.

Kalibar sighed again. He couldn't help but hold a grudging respect for Xanos, whoever or whatever the man was. Despite possessing extraordinary power, Xanos had effectively neutered the highest levels of the government in the Empire in a matter of days, without a single battle being fought. Kalibar had expected an epic battle with a massive army, a show of overwhelming force; instead, the self-proclaimed god had shown himself a superior tactician.

It was all exceedingly depressing.

He glanced at a timekeeper hanging on the wall by his bed; it was a few minutes before midnight. Erasmus had promised to meet Kalibar here at midnight, to give an update on his progress. Sure enough, there was a knock on the front door to his suite. Kalibar stood up quickly, walking to the door to answer it. But when he opened the door, it wasn't Erasmus standing on the other side...it was Councilman Ibicus.

"Grand Weaver," Ibicus greeted, bowing slightly. Kalibar recovered quickly from his surprise, gesturing for the Councilman to come in.

"Councilman Ibicus," he replied. "Come in." He walked Ibicus to a pair of couches facing each other, sitting down opposite the Councilman. "And please, call me Kalibar in private," he insisted.

"Thank you," Ibicus replied. "I apologize for visiting so late, but I admit to having a hard time sleeping," he added. "We both know that my appointment has changed the dynamic of the Council."

"We're hamstrung," Kalibar stated bluntly. Ibicus grimaced.

"Not quite the way I would have phrased it, but yes, I suppose so."

"You know so," Kalibar corrected. Ibicus frowned, but Kalibar smiled. "I don't enjoy the artifice of politics, Ibicus," he stated gently. "We've never seen eye to eye, and we each have different views on how to take the Empire forward. I do believe, however, that we both want the same thing...what we feel is best for the Empire."

Ibicus paused for a moment, then nodded. "Agreed," he replied. "That's why I came tonight. And while we're being honest with each other," he added, "...I've always felt that your decision to go to war with our neighbors, instead of attempting a more diplomatic solution, was immoral."

"I still lose sleep over that decision," Kalibar admitted. "I often wish I were a less introspective man."

"So you didn't come by it easily?" Ibicus pressed. Kalibar shook his head.

"I've seen what war does," Kalibar stated. "It's a tragedy for everyone involved. I knew that declaring war with the remaining tribes would create horrors that would echo through generations. But I did not declare war without provocation, and I weighed the consequences of war against my vision of a lasting peace for the Empire."

"A lot of people disagreed with you," Ibicus countered. "Populists and Elitists both. Goran, myself, even Jax fought you on that," he added. "I don't know how or why Jax made peace with you, but he did." He sighed, running a hand through his hair. "I suppose that's why I couldn't sleep tonight," he added. "Jax started off like me – he was one of your bitterest opponents – and yet somehow he became a staunch ally. As his successor, I feel like I owe it to him to find out why."

Kalibar frowned, lowering his gaze for a long moment, then looking back up at Ibicus.

"I respect your candor, and your temperance," he stated. "But Jax never gave me a reason for his support. I can only guess as to his motives." And that, Kalibar knew, was true; the late Councilman had been sparse with his words, telling more with his actions, much like Darius. Kalibar regretted not having more conversations with the Elder Councilman.

"And what would be your guess?" Ibicus pressed. Kalibar shrugged.

"I told Jax that in conquering our neighbors, I would be preventing countless future wars...by taking nations that had been warring with each other for centuries and making them one people. But I don't think that was what swayed him. I simply think Jax knew that I was genuine," he continued. "That I was thoughtful, and considerate of the impact of my decisions. I do think he disagreed with me – and Erasmus – on many things, but he never took our disagreements personally. And when we disagreed, we talked through it until we understood each other."

"Until you convinced him?" Ibicus asked. Kalibar snorted.

"Hardly. Just until we knew where each other stood. We never had to guess, or assume the worst about each other. We spoke our minds, kept it professional, and went from there."

"I see," Ibicus stated. He regarded Kalibar for a long, silent moment, then nodded slightly. "I hope that we can have a similar relationship, Grand Weaver."

"Kalibar," Kalibar corrected. Ibicus smiled.

"Kalibar."

"I don't expect you to change your opinions – or your vote – to maintain our relationship," Kalibar said.

"I had no intention of doing so," Ibicus replied with a wry smile. Then he stood up, and Kalibar stood with him. Ibicus reached out with his right hand, and Kalibar clasped it in his own.

"Good night, Ibicus," he said. Then he smiled. "I'm glad you came."

"Good night, Kalibar."

"I think," Kalibar ventured, "...that Erasmus would appreciate a visit like this." Ibicus winked.

"Already done," he replied. Then he turned and left the room, leaving Kalibar standing by the couch, staring at his translucent door long after the man was gone. After everything that had happened between them, he'd never expected Ibicus to extend him an olive branch.

Kalibar couldn't help but think that if he had been a better Grand Weaver, he would have done it first.

Chapter 17

Kyle stood beside Darius on the yellowed stone of the open pit mine, a strong breeze whipping through his hair. All that remained of the Behemoth was the massive impression it had left in the ground after it had fallen, a pit nearly three feet deep in the shattered rock. Kyle stared at Darius, clad in Ampir's armor, his mirrored visor reflecting a panorama of the landscape before them.

"We're going to *your* home?" Kyle asked. Darius nodded, the runes on his armor no longer glowing their customary blue. Kyle thought the legendary armor looked strange without that constant, pulsing glow. "Where's that?" he pressed.

"It's complicated," Darius answered. "Come on," he added, gesturing for Kyle to step closer. Kyle did so, and Darius wrapped a cold, metallic arm about his shoulders. "Don't move," he ordered.

Suddenly there was a flash of brilliant blue light, followed by a vibration deep within Kyle's mind, building in intensity until it was so powerful that he felt his brain would explode. He cried out, clutching his head with his hands, trying to keep his skull from flying apart. He felt something squeeze his shoulders, and he opened his eyes, seeing Darius looking down at him, the runes on his armor glowing so brightly that Kyle's eyes ached. The bodyguard glanced upward, and Kyle followed his gaze, his eyes widening.

The sky above their heads rippled like waves from a rock thrown into a pond, then split open, an expanse of infinite black growing from the tear. The void grew ever larger, chewing through the bright blue sky and fluffy clouds. At the same time, tiny points of light flashed against the darkness, then streaked outward in all directions from the center of the void, until they expanded and coalesced into a single, blinding white light. Kyle shielded his eyes with one hand, squinting against the glare, then saw a bright gold disc appear in the center of it all. The disc grew downward and outward, forming a dome some twenty feet above their heads. Still it grew, blotting out the bright white light that had come before it, until it surrounded them on all sides. The open pit mine, the forest – they were gone, replaced by walls of gold.

Then Kyle felt a *shift*, and there was darkness.

* * *

The pain was sudden, and agonizing.

There was an unbelievable pressure in Kyle's chest, as if someone had stepped on it, pain lancing through his chest and back, then shooting up his neck. He tried to yell out, but no sound escaped his lips. He opened his eyes wide, but he could not see; the world was bathed in blackness. His hearing went next, followed by a loud, high-pitched ringing. He clutched his chest, feeling his legs threaten to give out on him.

And then it all stopped.

Kyle's senses returned, the pain in his chest vanishing instantly. He stumbled to one side, his legs still wobbly, but Darius caught him with one black-clad arm. Kyle righted himself, then looked around, his eyes widening.

They were standing in a circular room some twenty feet in diameter. Above their heads was a large dome made of hundreds of thick, golden metal bars arching upward toward a brightly glowing disk above, in the center of the dome. The bars were set back against equally glowing walls with countless runes etched into them, each rune glowing a soft blue. As Kyle watched, the runes began to fade, until their light went out altogether. The disc above continued to glow bright white, illuminating the room.

Looking down, Kyle saw another glowing disk at his feet, as large as the one above, surrounded by a jet-black metallic floor. The runes between the metal bars of the ceiling continued on the floor, forming hundreds of lines of runes radiating from the disc on the floor, like the rays of a dying blue sun.

"Whoa," Kyle breathed, feeling goosebumps rise on his arms.

Darius said nothing, letting go of Kyle and stepping off of the glowing disc on the floor, toward the wall in the distance. Kyle hesitated, then hurried to catch up with the man.

"Where are we?" Kyle asked as he reached Darius's side.

"The Gateway," he answered. "This room is a gateway to the outside world, the only way in – or out – of my home."

Kyle glanced back at the glowing disk in the center of the floor, marveling at how futuristic the room looked. It was very unlike the architecture of the Tower, which was rather old-fashioned with its granite floors and ornate trappings. The Gateway, Kyle decided, looked more like something out of a science fiction movie.

"Did you build this?" Kyle asked. Darius nodded, walking up to the wall, which was simply a continuation of the ceiling, made of the same alternating golden bars and inset strips of carved runes. Darius's armor lit up suddenly, runes on his right forearm glowing bright blue for a moment before fading quickly. A curved section of the wall in front of them rippled, a hole appearing in the center. The hole widened quickly, revealing a long, curved corridor beyond. Darius stepped through the hole into the corridor, gesturing for Kyle to follow. Kyle hesitated, then stepped forward until he'd cleared the hole. There was a sudden rush of air at his back, and he turned about, seeing...a long hallway behind him.

"What the..." he blurted. "Where did the room go?"

Darius said nothing, putting a hand on Kyle's shoulder and pushing him forward. Kyle began walking down the long hallway, Darius at his side. The walls and floor were nearly identical to those of the Gateway, but instead of a glowing disk above their heads, a long glowing strip ran down the length of the ceiling. As they made their forward, Kyle realized that the floor angled upward slightly, curving gently to the right. There were a few large glass windows on either side, and Kyle stopped at one of the windows on his left, peering through the glass. He saw a large room beyond, with big, squat tables. The tables were littered with countless metallic contraptions, most of which were unrecognizable. A few, however, looked rather familiar.

"Are those *guns*?" Kyle asked, pointing at a few black, gun-shaped objects lying on one table. They looked vaguely like long, black rifles, only they were covered in glowing runes.

"Something like that," Darius replied.

Kyle peered more closely at the room beyond, noting what appeared to be black suits of armor hanging on the walls. They looked suspiciously similar to Darius's – or rather, Ampir's – armor.

"Are those...?"

"Come on," Darius grumbled, pulling Kyle away from the window and back down the hallway. Kyle frowned, but didn't resist, knowing that with Darius resistance was futile. They made their way ever upward and rightward, traveling in a loose spiral.

"Where are we going?" Kyle pressed. But Darius said nothing. Kyle sighed, following the taciturn warrior. They passed more windows, but with Darius's quick pace, Kyle only had a moment to glance through them. To the left, there were more rooms, also with tables strewn with strange contraptions. To the right, however, there was an expanse of pure yellow-green. Kyle slowed, peering out of the window, trying to figure out what exactly he was looking at.

"Come on," Darius prompted, pulling Kyle away from the window. Onward they went. Kyle pushed down a rising annoyance, unable to help feeling slighted by the man's silence. He rubbed his chest, remembering the pain and crushing pressure he'd felt when traveling from the pit mine to...wherever this was. Not to mention the blindness; the experience had been terrifying, even if brief.

"What was that feeling when we came to the Gateway?" Kyle asked. "It really hurt, and I couldn't see."

"Traveling between times," Darius answered. Kyle's eyebrows raised.

"Wait, we just did *time* travel?"

"No," Darius replied. "Time travels faster here than it does in Doma."

"Doma?"

"The planet we just came from," Darius clarified.

"So it *is* another planet," Kyle stated. "How far away from Earth is Doma?" Darius shrugged, which made Kyle's brown furrow. "Wait, how can't you know?" he asked. "You traveled there to get me, didn't you?"

"I just followed the signal from my ring," Darius explained.

"*Your* ring?" Kyle asked. Then he remembered who he was talking to; he was so used to thinking of Darius as...well, Darius...that he'd forgotten he was also speaking to Ampir. And of course Kyle's ring was really Ampir's ring. Ampir had sent the ring with his only son to Earth over two thousand years ago...and it had somehow gotten into Kyle's father's possession.

"How did my dad get your ring?" Kyle pressed. That had confused him ever since he'd learned the ring had been Ampir's. It had been over two thousand years since Ampir's son had been sent to Earth, after all. A hundred generations had passed since then.

Darius continued to lead Kyle further up the curved hallway, not answering the question. Kyle sighed, trudging forward. To his dismay, it seemed that, other than his armor and his extraordinary power, Ampir was exactly like Darius...a jerk.

Another set of windows – one on the left, one on the right, appeared ahead. Kyle glanced out of the rightward window as he passed by, seeing another expanse of yellow-green. He heard Darius stop, but this time the man didn't tell Kyle to keep moving. Kyle stared into the endless greenness for a long moment, then turned to Darius.

"What's in there?" he asked.

"Milarite," Darius answered. Kyle frowned.

"Milarite?" he pressed. "What's that?" But Darius didn't elaborate, turning away from Kyle and continuing forward down the seemingly endlessly curving hallway. Kyle sighed, giving one last glance out of the window, then joining Darius. Upward and onward they went, passing yet more windows on either side. The rightward ones always showed the same expanse of yellow-green, while the left held various rooms, among other things. One window appeared to be an aquarium, with tiny silver fish darting about randomly in the blue water. Kyle paused before the tank, staring at the fish; most were of the same type, with streamlined silver bodies, far smaller than a goldfish. Their bodies were so small that they were translucent, and they glowed the faintest blue at the edges. For the most part they just floated in the water motionlessly. But from time to time, one would dart through the water so quickly that if he blinked, he'd miss it.

Kyle sighed, thinking of his grandfather – on his mother's side, of course. He was an avid fisherman, having learned the trade in Vietnam before coming to the states to save his family from the Communists. Kyle suddenly wished his grandfather were here now, so that he could see this. Or at least that he had a camera to record his adventures. As it was, he had nothing to show for the last few weeks, no proof that anything he'd seen or experienced had been real. If he ever got home – to his *real* home, on Earth – no one would ever believe his wild stories.

"They're extinct on Doma," Darius explained, nodding at the fish. "I preserve them."

"Why?"

"I owe them."

"Huh?" Kyle asked, perplexed. Darius stared at the fish tank for a moment, then turned back to Kyle.

"I learned more in a few weeks from those fish than others have learned in a lifetime."

"From their magic patterns, right?" Kyle guessed. "That's what I was telling Master Banar," Kyle added, recalling his idea for the sensory rune array. Then he sobered, remembering what had happened to the poor Runic. Darius must have noticed Kyle's somber expression, slipping a hand off of the window and placing it on Kyle's shoulder.

"By the time I'd found you, he was already dead," he apologized. "Even I can't bring people back to life."

Kyle nodded silently, feeling suddenly choked up. He closed his eyes for a moment, a vision of the Dead Man standing over Master Banar's corpse burned into his mind's eye. Then he opened his eyes, looking up at Darius questioningly.

"Why didn't you just kill the Dead Man right away?" he asked. "Why let him capture us like that? You're so powerful, you could have destroyed the Dead Man – or anyone else that threatened you – without even trying!" And it was true, Kyle knew. Even in Ancient times, Ampir had been formidably powerful, leaps and bounds above the skills of his peers. Weavers today were nowhere near as sophisticated

211

or powerful as they were back then...and Ampir had had two thousand years to build his power. The man was a veritable ocean of magic, when he chose to reveal it.

"You tell me," Darius replied.

"How would *I* know?" Kyle protested. Darius nodded.

"Right," he agreed. "You're useless."

Kyle blinked, then glared at the man.

"What's that supposed to mean?"

"What'd you do when Kalibar's carriage was attacked?" Darius asked.

Kyle frowned, recalling the harrowing attack. He'd nearly been killed...*would* have been killed if Darius hadn't saved him.

"Nothing," he mumbled.

"What did you do when the Dead Man's soldiers attacked us?"

"Nothing."

"When the Dire Lurker attacked?"

Kyle glared at Darius, crossing his arms over his chest.

"Fine, I get it."

"When the Ulfar attacked you?" Darius pressed.

"I blinded Mr. Tenson," Kyle countered rather indignantly. "And I grabbed Ariana before she fell from the Tower!"

"Yup," Darius agreed. "And then you dropped her."

"I used your damn amulet so you could stab Xanos, didn't I?"

"Took you long enough," Darius shot back. Kyle just stared at the man, his face burning with anger and shame.

"Fine, I'm useless," he spat. "Why even bother with me?" Darius smirked, putting a hand on Kyle's shoulder.

"You're getting better."

"Gee, thanks," Kyle mumbled. But Darius turned away from the window, walking down the hallway once again. Kyle stared at the man's retreating back. "You didn't even answer my original question!" he protested.

"Did too."

"You didn't kill the Dead Man right away because I'm useless?" Kyle pressed. "How is that an answer?"

"*Were* useless."

212

Kyle gave up, trudging after Darius dejectedly. When the man didn't want to answer a question, there was no forcing him. But the thought that Darius had let himself and Kyle be captured by the Dead Man, then faked his own death back at the Tower...*and* with the Behemoth...it just didn't make any sense. In fact, now that he thought about it, it seemed incredibly – and unnecessarily – cruel.

"I thought you'd died back there," Kyle protested. "Why'd you scare me like that?"

"You don't truly appreciate what you have until you lose it."

"So you wanted me to appreciate you?" Kyle asked, unable to help smiling at the thought of the dour bodyguard craving some attention.

"The people you love can be taken from you if you don't fight back," Darius replied.

Kyle sighed, following behind Darius, staring at the man's armored back. The countless runes adorning the armor, pulsing a faint blue in constant, random patterns, reminded Kyle a bit of the Dead Man's eternally rippling cloak. Even in death, the Dead Man's image raised goosebumps on Kyle's skin. It was remarkable how a mere few days with the dark Weaver had made a more powerful impression on Kyle than any other bad experience he'd had in his life. Particularly considering that the Dead Man had never once physically harmed him. His Death Weavers had, though. Right before Kalibar had been brought in, and held down on that table.

Right before he'd had his eyes ripped out.

Kyle shuddered; most of the memories of his life were a little vague, but his memory of that day was crystal clear. All he had to do was close his eyes, and he could see the Dead Man's pale fingers digging into Kalibar's eye socket, hear the muffled popping sounds as the Dead Man twisted his wrist, snapping the muscles anchoring the eye in place. Could see the brilliant white of the freed orb glistening in the glow of the Timestone above.

Kalibar falling off of the table and onto the dirt below, clutching his bloodied face, rocking back and forth in agony.

And Darius, standing there in the middle of the Arena, watching it happen.

Kyle felt a chill run through him, and he opened his eyes, staring at Darius's back. He'd completely forgotten that the bodyguard had been there the entire time. At the time, Kyle had thought him helpless to intervene. But now...

He stopped walking, standing there in the middle of the hallway, watching as Darius continued onward for a moment, then stopped. Darius turned his head, glancing at Kyle.

"What?" he asked.

Kyle stared back at Darius, his eyes wide. Darius had been there all along, standing idly by as Kalibar got mutilated, even though he could have killed the Dead Man and every Death Weaver present with ease. And now Kalibar was blind – permanently handicapped – because of it.

"What?" Darius repeated, taking a step toward Kyle. Kyle backed up, shaking his head.

"You were there!" Kyle blurted out, taking another step back. "In the Arena," he continued, pointing at Darius with one finger. "You were there when they took Kalibar's eyes!" Darius stood there, staring at Kyle with his intense blue eyes for a long moment. Then he nodded.

"I was."

"You let it happen," Kyle accused, his voice rising in anger. "You could have stopped it, but you let it happen!"

"I did."

"How *could* you?" Kyle shouted, feeling tears spring unbidden to his eyes. "He was your friend!"

"I had my reasons," Darius countered. His voice was gentle, but firm. If he had any remorse at all for what he'd done, however, he didn't show it.

"Like what?" Kyle retorted incredulously, raising his hands out to either side. "To find Xanos?" he added sarcastically.

"No."

"Then *what?*"

"You'll know soon enough," Darius promised. "Be patient."

Kyle shook his head, turning away and wiping the moisture from his eyes. He suddenly wanted desperately to get out of this hallway, to get as far away from Darius as possible. He didn't even want to look at the man anymore.

"I want to go home," he stated, his voice cold. He heard Darius's footsteps echo from behind, coming closer.

214

"You will," came the reply.

"I want to go *now*," Kyle insisted, not turning around. "To Earth," he added firmly.

"We're not done here," Darius countered. Kyle spun around, feeling a flash of anger course through him.

"*I'm* done here," Kyle yelled, pointing at Darius again. "And I don't want anything to do with you!"

A sudden burst of blinding blue light surged outward from Darius, slamming into Kyle with such force that it nearly knocked him off his feet. Kyle reeled backward, feeling sheer power pulse through his skull, making it impossible to think – or feel – anything else. Then the feeling vanished as quickly as it had come, leaving Kyle feeling disoriented.

Darius stared down at Kyle, now only a few feet away, his blue eyes suddenly hard.

"You don't have a choice."

Kyle froze, feeling a chill run through him. The way Darius had said it – cold and hard, almost cruel – there was no doubt that he meant it. Kyle felt his anger slip away almost instantly, replaced by something even more powerful.

Fear.

Darius stared at Kyle, the runes on his black armor pulsing lazily, a blue glow flowing from rune to rune in random patterns. The man's cold eyes held Kyle as if they were needles pinning a moth to a board. Then he turned away, continuing up the hallway.

"Come," Darius growled, not even bothering to see if Kyle was following behind. Kyle watched the man stride up the hallway, swallowing in a dry throat. He thought briefly about staying where he was, of defying Darius – *Ampir* – once again, but knew it was futile. Darius was right, of course...Kyle *didn't* have a choice. The only way he'd ever get home was through Darius. He was, in effect, the man's prisoner.

Kyle stepped forward, following Darius. This time, however, he allowed himself to lag behind, no longer making any attempt to walk at the man's side.

That, at least, *was* his choice.

* * *

215

The long spiraling hallway ended after a few long, silent minutes, terminating in a nondescript wall. Kyle had maintained his distance from Darius for the remainder of the walk, refusing to even look at the man. He could hardly believe that Darius had been capable of such a betrayal; after all, Darius had protected them – both as a bodyguard and as Ampir – from harm at every other juncture. Of course, Darius's escape from the Arena, and his heroic defeat of the Dire Lurker and the Dead Man, seemed diminished by the knowledge of his extraordinary power. Had Kyle known that Ampir himself had been there the entire time, their capture – and escape – would not have been nearly as harrowing.

When Darius reached the end of the hallway, he stopped by the wall, turning about and watching Kyle as he reluctantly trudged up alongside. Or rather, ten feet away or so. Those blue eyes regarded Kyle silently for a long, uncomfortable moment. The man's expression, as usual, was unreadable. Then he turned back to the wall, putting his hand on it. His armor lit up, runes on his forearm glowing blue just as they had in the Gateway before, the light fading quickly. The wall in front of them rippled, a hole appearing in the center, then widening. Beyond, Kyle saw another gray stone wall some five or six feet away, with a granite tiled floor leading up to it beyond the rift. Darius stepped through without hesitation, then turned, gesturing for Kyle to follow. Kyle hesitated, then stepped through, feeling a sudden rush of warm air as he did. The air – oddly sterile in the hallway and Gateway before – was suddenly sweet, bringing to mind late spring afternoons in his mother's flower garden. He inhaled deeply, feeling invigorated despite himself, then glanced at Darius; the bodyguard – Kyle had a hard time thinking of him as anything but – was standing in front of Kyle, facing him silently.

Kyle frowned, feeling uncomfortable under that intense gaze. He glanced past Darius's shoulder, at the nondescript stone wall only a few feet away. Overcome by curiosity, or perhaps the sheer pleasantness of the air around him, he momentarily forgot his anger.

"Where are we?" he asked, then gestured at the wall in front of him. "What's this?"

Darius said nothing, but his eyes shifted, now looking over Kyle's left shoulder. Kyle frowned, then turned around.

His jaw dropped.

They were standing on a wide, stone-tiled porch perched at the base of a mountain, staring out at a lush valley lay far ahead in the distance. A small city could be seen in the distance, perhaps a half-mile away, white buildings with golden roofs shining under the light of the sun above. Looking upward, Kyle saw a brilliant blue sky, puffy white clouds floating far above their heads, the sun's rays peeking out from between them. A long staircase led from the porch to a lush garden some twenty feet below, with two large stone water fountains flanking a wide stone walkway.

Kyle stared out at the wondrous sight, his eyes sweeping across the landscape. Then he felt a heavy hand on his shoulder. He turned about, and saw Darius standing at his side, gazing off into the distance.

"This," he stated, gesturing with a broad sweeping motion of his arm, taking in everything around them, "...is my home."

Kyle nodded mutely, a warm, gentle breeze massaging his scalp. He glanced at one of the stone water fountains below; it had a tall statue of a fish in the center, its mouth agape. Water shot from that mouth high into the sky, spreading outward in all directions, then falling in a dozen small streams back to the ground. Each stream curved through the air as it fell, undoubtedly under the influence of magic, creating a twisting mid-air waterfall around the fish statue. The streams flowed back into the wide bowl of the fountain, only to be sucked up by the fish statue once again.

"Did you make that?" Kyle asked, pointing to the fountain. Darius nodded. "You sure like fish," Kyle observed, almost hypnotized by the endless flow of water. He never would have pegged the surly bodyguard as a marine enthusiast. Then he frowned. "Hey, it looks the same as those fish in that tank."

"They're blinkfish."

"Oh," Kyle replied. "How'd they go extinct?" he asked. Darius said nothing, staring at the fountain for a long moment. Then his mirrored visor appeared out of thin air, hiding his blue eyes.

"Blink," the bodyguard ordered. Kyle frowned, his eyebrows furrowing.

"What?"

Darius lunged forward suddenly, right toward him. Kyle lurched backward in surprise, closing his eyes and throwing his hands up to protect himself. He cried out, falling onto his rear on the hard stone below. Then he opened his eyes, realizing at once that Darius was no longer standing in front of him. In fact, the man was nowhere to be seen.

"Come on," a voice shouted from below. Kyle scrambled to his feet, rubbing his bruised posterior with one hand. He glanced about, but still couldn't see Darius. Then he turned, looking down from the porch, and saw the man sitting on the edge of one of the fountains twenty feet below – and some fifty feet away – his arms crossed about his armored chest.

"How'd you...?" Kyle asked. Darius gestured for him to walk down the stairs, and Kyle did so numbly, descending step-by-step down the stone stairs until he was only a few feet from where the man stood.

"The blinkfish," Darius stated, "...is the only known creature that can create bridges across spacetime."

"Bridges across what?"

"Teleportation," Darius clarified.

"Oh."

"When I was ten, I finished my training as a Runic, and started my graduate studies as a Battle-Runic," Darius stated. Kyle's eyebrows rose.

"Wait, *ten?*" he exclaimed. Master Owens had said that Runics and Weavers – in Ancient times as in the present – were only allowed to graduate when they turned eighteen. Darius smirked.

"I was...different," he explained. "Anyway, it was mandatory to choose a mentor for a year of research, so I chose a man named Renval."

"The guy who invented teleportation," Kyle recalled. Kalibar had mentioned about Renval in the Tower library long ago, a few days after they'd first met. Apparently Renval's father had been ridiculed for his obsession with teleportation, and Renval – a well-respected Runic – had hidden his own passion for continuing his father's research.

"No, that was me," Darius corrected. "Renval had already spent twenty years researching teleportation, reading his late father's notes, and searching for a clue as to how it could be accomplished." Darius shook his head. "He got nowhere."

"Wow," Kyle mumbled. Twenty years was a long time...having nothing to show for it must have been devastating.

"When I first started working with him," Darius continued, "...Renval could only see a little kid, an inconvenience to be suffered. He set me to doing simple, mind-numbing tasks...like copying textbooks. I used magic to make quick work of it, and spent the rest of my time bored out of my mind."

"Like school," Kyle observed. Darius ignored the comment.

"Renval's uncle had been a naturalist," he continued. "Searching the world for new species. Renval enjoyed tropical fish, so his uncle would often send shipments of rare specimens from across the seas. Renval had several tanks in the basement of his lab, and one day, a shipment came in, a fish I'd never seen before."

"Let me guess," Kyle ventured. Darius nodded.

"A blinkfish," he confirmed. "It was tiny – a fraction of an inch from mouth to tail, just as you saw. I watched it as you did, floating motionless in the water, then darting forward a few inches through that huge tank, moving so fast it was impossible to track. It kept doing that, standing still for a long time, then moving in the blink of an eye."

Kyle frowned, remembering the tiny fish in the aquarium he'd seen earlier. He wanted to ask Darius if those were the same blinkfish Renval had owned, but, as this was the most he'd ever heard Darius say in the last month or so, he stifled the urge to interrupt the man, not wanting to give the taciturn bodyguard any reason to clam up.

"I must have stared at that fish for weeks," Darius continued. "I spent more time studying that fish than anyone alive – even Renval's uncle, who had discovered it. It took that long for me to realize the fish wasn't just darting forward...it sometimes moved to the side, or even backward. The blinkfish was too small to see if it was using its fins to move, so I did the obvious."

"What's that?" Kyle asked, nothing obvious coming to mind.

"I created a gravity sphere around it," Darius replied, "...trapping it in place."

"Oh," Kyle mumbled. It *was* obvious, he supposed, but only after Darius had mentioned it. Kyle recalled his failure as a Weaver, and wondered again if he had any real talent in the magical sciences. Memorizing runes and making lots of magic weren't very useful in and of themselves, not without skill in *using* magic.

"The fish darted right out of it," Darius continued, seemingly oblivious to Kyle's sudden despair. "As if it weren't even there. So I deduced that the fish had either nullified my gravitational field, or it wasn't swimming at all...it was teleporting."

"Ohhh," Kyle breathed.

"Right," Darius replied. "Luckily, with my...gift, I quickly confirmed that the fish wasn't nullifying my gravitational field. So, over the next few weeks, I figured out how the fish was teleporting, and mimicked the pattern."

"*That's* how you invented teleportation?" Kyle asked. Darius smirked again.

"It wasn't that easy," he countered. "First of all, the blinkfish masked the teleportation patterns with other, nonsense patterns sprinkled in between...a tactic I used later with the runes on my armor. And the patterns were always slightly different, depending on where the fish was at the time – and which direction it was traveling in." He stood up from the edge of the stone fountain, turning around and facing the fish statue. It was over eight feet from water-spouting mouth to underwater tail...far larger than the pipsqueak of a fish it represented.

"But," Darius continued, "...I did figure out that the fish moved the same distance every time – regardless of direction. So I assumed that the changes in the fish's patterns had something to do with current position and direction of travel only. And I was right; when I finally tested one of the patterns on one of the books Renval was having me copy at the time, it worked...sort of. Only a blinkfish-sized piece of the book moved, and only a few inches away at that. But it proved that my theory was correct."

"How did Renval find out about it?" Kyle inquired. Darius turned away from the fish-statue, stepping onto the stone walkway, then starting a slow walk away from the stairway they – or rather, Kyle – had walked down. Kyle joined the bodyguard, for the moment forgetting his anger toward the man, walking at his side.

"The book I had taken a chunk out of was one of Renval's father's notebooks," Darius answered. "He was furious when he found out about the damage, and would have had me whipped if I hadn't revealed how I'd done it." He shook his head at the memory. "At first, Renval was...unconvinced. But after a demonstration..."

"Funny that you ruined one of his father's books on teleportation by teleporting it," Kyle observed. Darius smirked.

"Renval said the same thing," he agreed. "And when I told him how I'd figured the patterns out, he nearly crushed every rib in my body embracing me. After that, I never copied another book; we worked together, Renval and I, spending the rest of my year with him attempting to create a runic machine that could duplicate the blink-fish's power."

"The red crystal on the dais," Kyle breathed. It had been there in his dreams — Ampir's memories — all along. A single red crystal embedded in a circular stone dais, the device that had teleported Ampir's son to Earth over two thousand years ago. It was all starting to make sense now.

"That was an advanced prototype," Darius countered. "The initial prototypes were far less sophisticated. By the time I was done with my research year, we'd managed to teleport a stone some ten feet or so. I left to continue my Battle-Runic training, and Renval was already well on his way toward perfecting the technology."

"Did he show everyone?" Kyle asked. After all, Renval's father had been mocked for his obsession with teleportation, and Renval had been forced to study the matter in secret. If he'd been Renval, he would have run into the streets, shouting at the top of his lungs. And pointing and laughing at his father's critics. But Darius shook his head.

"Nope."

"Well why not?" Kyle pressed. "He could've been rich and famous!"

"He already *was* rich and famous," Darius countered. "Besides, Renval's focus was never on teleportation for teleportation's sake," he added. "It was only one step toward completing his ultimate goal...and he didn't want to reveal his findings until he'd reached that goal."

"Which was?"

"Origin," Darius answered.

"Origin?" Kyle asked.

"Origin," Darius repeated. Kyle frowned, wondering if Darius would say it again if he did. But he resisted the urge, wanting the man

221

to continue his tale. If there was one thing he knew about the man, it was that Darius had little patience for inanity.

"What is Origin?" Kyle pressed.

"Where magic comes from," Darius replied. Kyle frowned; he'd always assumed that magic came from people, not from any particular place. He told Darius as much.

"True," he replied. "But where do people come from?"

Kyle's eyebrows knitted together, and he frowned at Darius. The answer, of course, was obvious.

"Earth," he answered. "We evolved there," he added.

"There are people on Doma," Darius countered. "And horses, and dogs," he added. Kyle couldn't disagree; when he'd first seen Kalibar's levitating carriage, pulled by two powerful horses, he'd wondered how an alien planet could have horses and people on it. It had seemed unlikely that they both had evolved to be the exact same on each planet.

"How is that possible?" Kyle asked.

"You tell me," Darius replied.

By this point, they'd been walking for quite some time, the paved walkway leading them forward and downward. The garden by the porch, with its blinkfish fountains, was far behind, replaced by tall trees with glowing leaves flanking the path. Kyle glanced at one of these leaves, seeing a familiar pattern of green and blue dots pulsing on its surface. They were identical to the trees that Kyle had seen when he'd first awoken on Doma. There was a veritable forest of them here, interspersed with short grass and the occasional bush. There were, he noted, no rip-vines or killerpillers here. Before long, the walkway took a sharp turn, and the forest suddenly opened up. Kyle stopped in his tracks, the breath catching in his throat.

"Whoa," he breathed.

The stone walkway continued forward, meeting a much wider stone road some twenty feet in the distance. This road was flanked by large, well-kept buildings three stories tall, their perfectly white stone walls carved with ornate patterns. Stately windows reflected the sun's rays, the light shimmering as it reflected off of the golden, metallic roofs. Beyond these buildings stood a giant, U-shaped structure, a mansion some eight stories high, its walls constructed of the same white stone as the other buildings. In the center of the U-shape, between the arms of the mansion, there was a courtyard complete with an elegant, three-tier fountain made of solid gold. In the center of the fountain stood a golden statue some twenty feet tall, of a man clad in armor from neck to toe, a silver mirrored visor obscuring his eyes. The statue's right arm was raised high into the air, gauntleted hand with its palm facing upward. A miniature island – also made of gold – floated a foot or so above that outstretch hand, only slightly bigger than the palm itself. Kyle stared at the statue, giving a low whistle.

"Nice statue," he observed, turning to glance at Darius. The resemblance was uncanny.

"A gift," Darius grumbled. "They insisted."

"Who?" Kyle asked. Darius gestured outward with one hand.

"Them."

It was only then that Kyle realized there were people in the distance. An old man stood by one of the three-story tall buildings, staring at Kyle and Darius silently. A middle-aged woman sat on the front steps of the building across from the old man, staring at something in her lap. A few people could be seen walking in the courtyard of the mansion beyond.

"Who are they?" Kyle asked. "And why are they staring at us?" Darius waved at the old man, and the old man waved back, a smile brightening his face. He sprinted toward them with remarkable swiftness; The woman, on the other hand, stayed right where she was, apparently oblivious to their presence.

"They're not staring at *us*," Darius corrected. "They're staring at *you*."

* * *

"Ampir!"

Kyle watched as the old man strode purposefully toward them, extending a hand out to Darius. Darius extended his own gauntleted hand, and shook the other man's hand briskly.

"Nalin," Darius replied. The old man – Nalin – looked to be about eighty, with short white hair scattered about his head. He had brown eyes, with tanned skin crisscrossed with wrinkles so deep that Kyle imagined he could fit quarters in them. He wore a simple white shirt and brown pants, and nondescript sandals, and by the looks of him, he wasn't one to care very much about his appearance. He sported a scraggly beard, and his clothes were impressively wrinkled.

"And who is this?" Nalin asked, gesturing at Kyle. Kyle smiled weakly at the old man, his nose wrinkling as it was struck by the sudden, pungent odor of armpit.

"This is Kyle," Darius answered, patting Kyle on the shoulder. Nalin extended his hand, and Kyle shook it dutifully. The old man peered at Kyle rather disapprovingly.

"A bit young to come here, don't you think?" he asked, glancing up at Darius. "Was he struck by cancer?"

"No," Darius replied. Kyle frowned at that; why would Nalin bring up such a horrible thing?

"Well then what use is he?" Nalin pressed. Darius shook his head.

"He's visiting."

"*Visiting?*" Nalin exclaimed, his untamed eyebrows rising, compressing his forehead into a dozen horizontal wrinkles. He glanced at Kyle again, his eyebrows furrowing. "I thought only you could do that."

"Kyle's different," Darius replied. "Where's Marcus?" he asked. Nalin shrugged, apparently unperturbed by the change in topic.

"At home, I think," he answered, rubbing his grizzled chin. "We don't get many politicians here," he added. "I wanted to hate the man, I'll admit it, but I can't. He's very personable."

"He's valuable in his own field, as you all are," Darius stated. Then he patted the old man on the shoulder. "Goodbye Nalin."

"Ah, just a moment," Nalin requested, holding up his left hand, within which he was clutching a large book. Kyle was surprised to see that he recognized the letters printed on the front cover; it was written in English, a language he hadn't read in weeks. After all, Doma's language – both spoken and written – was completely different than anything Kyle had encountered back on Earth. The only reason Kyle could understand anything people were saying was that he wore Kalibar's universal translator – a small yellow earring – on his right earlobe.

But this book's title he recognized. "Introductory Physics" the cover read in bold capital letters. How on earth had Nalin gotten a copy of a physics textbook, written in English no less?

"I have to thank you again for getting me this," Nalin said, beaming at Darius. "We've all been spending months trying to learn the language. Fascinating stuff, really."

"Thought you'd like it," Darius replied.

"Oh I do," Nalin agreed. "But the theories aren't even the best part," he added, opening the book and flipping through the pages rapidly. He stopped suddenly, rotating the book around, and showing it to Darius and Kyle. "Look at these paintings!" he gushed, pointing to a photograph of a city – Manhattan, it looked like – on one of the pages. "Such incredible detail! The artist must have painted them with a magnifying lens." He shook his head then, glancing up at Darius. "Do you suppose such cities actually exist?"

"They do," Darius confirmed. Nalin gave a low whistle, rotating the book again and peering at the photograph.

"What I wouldn't give to go there," he murmured. Then he looked up at Darius. "I suppose you've been there, haven't you?" He shook his head. "You've lived a hell of a life, Ampir."

"We should go," Darius stated. The old man shut his book with a loud clap, and shook hands with Darius one more time.

"I want to show you my newest creation before you leave again," he stated, his eyes bright. "I've been playing around with magically powered electrical circuits ever since I learned about the things. Genius, using electricity to make lights!" he exclaimed. "I'm also working on an electric motor," he added. "Powered by magic, it could conceivably run for weeks without recharging. Imagine the applications!"

"I'll stop by later," Darius promised. Then he ushered Kyle away from the unkempt old man, walking past the middle-aged woman still sitting on the front steps of one of the buildings. She was hunched over what looked like a thin sheet of stone. Unlike Nalin, the woman made no attempt to talk with them.

"Who's that?" Kyle asked, trying not to stare at her.

"Samb," Darius answered. "She designed the city."

Kyle stared at the thin sheet of stone in the woman's lap, standing on his tip-toes to get a better look. To his surprise, there was an intricate carving on the surface of the sheet, of a house, it appeared. As he watched, the thinnest of lines carved itself into the stone as the woman stared intently at its surface.

"Is she doing that?"

"Similar process to carving runes in crystals," Darius affirmed. Kyle nodded, then frowned at the woman – Samb – as they passed by her. She hadn't so much as moved since they'd arrived.

"Does she even know we're here?" he asked.

"Doubtful."

They made their way down the street to the courtyard, turning left toward another street paralleling the giant mansion nearby. More buildings lined this street, colorful banners hanging from golden poles jutting out from the second-story walls. There was lettering written down the length of the banners, but Kyle couldn't understand the language. The streets were mostly deserted, with only one elderly man sitting in a chair on the sidewalk next to one of the buildings. The man waved to Darius as they walked by, stroking his long gray beard slowly as he stared at Kyle.

"Ampir!" the man shouted, rising from his chair and intercepting them on the sidewalk. "Where have you been? It's been what, three months?"

"Something like that," Darius replied. The two men shook hands, after which the elderly man turned his gaze back to Kyle. The man was dressed in a simple gray cloak, with sandals similar to Nalin's.

"My name is Tek," the old man introduced, holding a wrinkled hand out to Kyle. Kyle paused, then clasped it in his own, trying not to wince at the dry, leathery feel of the man's skin. "And who are you, young man?"

"Kyle."

"Well," Tek stated, "...it's nice to meet you." He let go of Kyle's hand, turning to Darius. "Been a long, long time since I've seen someone so young," he added. His expression became grave. "Was it cancer?"

"He's just visiting," Darius corrected. Kyle frowned at Tek, then glanced up at Darius. Why did everyone think he had cancer? But Darius didn't seem to notice Kyle's questioning look.

"Isn't that against the rules?" Tek pressed.

"Kyle's different," Darius explained. Tek frowned, grooming his beard with his fingers.

"Oh really?" he asked. "How so?"

226

"Later," Darius promised. That seemed to be enough for Tek, who shrugged amicably, then stepped out of their way.

"Well, I look forward to hearing more about that," he said, gesturing for them to be on their way. "Nice to meet you, Kyle," he added. Kyle mumbled goodbye, then followed Darius down the street once again. The road curved to the right, the buildings lining it painted in bright colors. This area of the city appeared to be abandoned; despite a good five minutes' worth of walking, they ran into not a single other person.

"Where is everyone?" Kyle asked as the road ended suddenly at a tall black gate. It was made of black metal bars some twenty feet high, and was at least a hundred feet across. The road terminated at T-shaped intersection, and Darius turned leftward. Another empty street greeted them, with tall trees lining the left side. The black gate continued as a tall fence on the right.

"Working," Darius answered.

"Working?" Kyle pressed. "Everyone here's really...old." And it was true; Tek had looked to be at least eighty years old, and Nalin...well, if he was younger than ninety, Kyle would have been shocked.

"Age doesn't matter here," Darius replied.

"What do you mean?"

But Darius, being Darius, said nothing. Which of course, meant that he *wouldn't* say anything, even if Kyle pressed the matter. The man was hard-headed, that was for sure. Of course, for being two thousand years old and possessing god-like powers, yet being forced to spend all of his time babysitting a bed-wetting kid, Kyle supposed Darius was doing pretty well.

The road curved to the left slightly, and they followed it silently for the next few minutes, until at last it ended in a small cul-de-sac. At the end of this stood a one-story home, light brown in color. It was well-kept, surrounded by a short white fence with a small gate. Darius led Kyle up to this, opening the gate and gesturing for Kyle to walk through. Kyle did so, but Darius did not, closing the door behind Kyle.

"Wait, aren't you coming?" Kyle asked, feeling suddenly apprehensive.

227

"I'll be back," Darius replied. He gestured down a small path to the front door of the house with one gauntleted hand. "Go on," he urged. "He's been waiting for you."

"Who?" Kyle asked, not budging. The thought of not having Darius at his side made him feel...vulnerable. Darius said nothing, only staring at him with his intense blue eyes.

And then he vanished.

Kyle blinked, staring in disbelief at the spot where Darius had been standing. A sudden cool breeze whipped through Kyle's hair, then abated as quickly as it had come.

"Darius?" he called out. But there was no answer.

He turned about, staring at the front door of the ranch before him, feeling fear twist his innards. Then he glanced back at the gate, wondering where Darius had gone. Why had he left? And who was waiting for Kyle beyond that door?

Kyle took a deep breath in, then forced himself to walk forward, his gravity boots clicking on the stones of the walkway. Tiny insects buzzed about his face, thirsty for the sweat that had begun to drip down his forehead. He swatted them away, reaching the door. It was a simple wooden door, with a brass doorknob and no keyhole. He paused before it, glancing back over his shoulder, hoping to see Darius standing there by the gate. No such luck.

"Do come in," a deep voice bellowed. Kyle jumped, backpedaling hurriedly from the door, glancing about. The voice seemed to have come from the door itself, but no one was there.

"Don't be afraid," the voice called out, again coming from the door. "Darius is far more likely to hurt you than I," it added with a chuckle. Kyle couldn't help but smile at that. Still, it was with trepidation that he walked back up to the door and twisted the doorknob. The door swung open, revealing a long, narrow hallway beyond. The interior of the house was remarkably cozy, with wood floors and white-painted walls. A tall ceiling with bare wooden beams formed a triangle above his head. He stepped forward into the hallway, the floor creaking under the soles of his gravity boots. There were closed doors on either side of the hallway, and a partly open one at the end, some ten feet away. Kyle walked up to the partially open door, and gathering his courage, pushed it open with one palm.

Beyond he found a large room, perhaps thirty feet square, with a cathedral-style ceiling made of more bare wooden beams. The room appeared to be a combination of a kitchen and dining room, with a few round tables in the center surrounded by short wooden chairs. At the far end of the room was an older-appearing man standing by a large stove, stirring something in a pan with a long wooden spoon. The delicious aroma of stewed meat reached Kyle's nostrils, and his stomach growled almost painfully. It was only then that he realized that he hadn't eaten in well over a day. The man by the stove turned about.

"Ah, there you are!" he exclaimed, taking the pot off of the stove and carrying it to one of the tables in the center of the room. He set it down carefully, then motioned for Kyle to come forward and sit on one of the chairs by the table. "You must be starving," the man added. "You're in luck, I just finished your stew."

Kyle hesitated, staring at the old man. He was perhaps seventy, with long salt-and-pepper hair, and a neatly-trimmed mustache and beard. He was remarkably handsome for his age, with twinkling gray eyes and an infectious smile. Kyle felt his unease drain away almost immediately, and he obeyed the man's request, walking up and sitting down on the offered chair. The old man grinned, setting down a large bowl in front of Kyle, and spooning a generous helping of steaming-hot stew into it. Kyle's mouth watered almost to the point of drooling, and his stomach growled again, so loud that the old man had to have heard it.

"My name," the man stated, taking off the apron he'd been wearing and placing it neatly on the back of his own chair, then sitting down opposite Kyle, "...is Marcus." He extended a hand, and Kyle took it. Marcus clasped Kyle's hand in both of his own, then let go, spooning some of the stew from the pot to his own bowl. "Dig in," he stated, promptly following his own advice.

"I'm Kyle," Kyle replied, taking a spoonful of stew and bringing it to his lips. It was steaming ferociously, and Kyle blew on it a few times before sipping. The stew was hearty, meaty, juicy, and mouth-wateringly perfect. He had never tasted anything quite like it.

"I know," Marcus replied merrily, sipping his own stew. His gray eyes narrowed, and he rolled the stew in his mouth for a long moment, then nodded approvingly. "I think my little experiment was a success," he stated happily. Then he watched as Kyle slurped his own strew greedily, shoving steaming spoonful after spoonful into his mouth. "Try the ambrosia."

"Huh?" Kyle asked. Marcus gestured toward a cup by Kyle's bowl, filled with a pale green liquid. Kyle hesitated, then raised the cup to his lips, sipping the fluid cautiously. It was cool, slightly sweet, and instantly soothing to his burning mouth...all in all, a perfect complement to the stew. Kyle gulped it down greedily, then put the cup down with a satisfied sigh.

"Good, isn't it?" Marcus asked. Kyle nodded, spooning more stew into his mouth. It wasn't long before he'd finished the entire bowl, swallowing another gulp of the ambrosia, then sitting back in his chair with a contented sigh. With his hunger and thirst quenched, he felt a buzzing pleasantness come over him.

"Thank you," Kyle said, nodding at Marcus. The old man grinned.

"Forgive Darius for forgetting to feed you," he requested. "I suspect he has no need of sustenance anymore, and sometimes forgets that others still do." He regarded Kyle silently for a moment, sipping on his own glass of ambrosia, then leaning back in his own chair, like Kyle. "How are you feeling, Kyle?" he asked.

"Good," Kyle responded automatically. Marcus raised an eyebrow.

"You've been through a lot, I'm sure," he said. "So young, but already nearly killed by an Ulfar, attacked by assassins, kidnapped by a sadist, stood up to a god...in addition to whatever Darius put you through since then." He chuckled at Kyle's surprised look. "Darius told me all about your adventures."

"It's been interesting," Kyle admitted. Marcus smiled.

"You're made of stern stuff, Kyle," he said approvingly. "You're a credit to your family."

"Thanks," Kyle mumbled, his cheeks flushing. He immediately thought of his mom and dad, back on Earth. They'd probably already had the funeral, having given up on finding him weeks ago. He felt immediately depressed at the thought, and pined for home. Would Darius ever bring him back? And if he did, what then? He'd be behind in school, and probably need to stay back. And he'd end up missing Kalibar and Ariana as much as he missed his parents now. Kyle lowered his gaze, letting out a long sigh.

"You miss your family," Marcus observed, rubbing his beard with one hand. Kyle nodded mutely, afraid that if he said anything, his voice might crack. "An unfortunate necessity," Marcus stated with a sigh of his own. "Darius's methods may seem...remarkably cruel," he added, "...but I assure you, he has nothing but your best interests at heart."

"Yeah, right," Kyle grumbled. "I don't think he *has* a heart." Marcus laughed.

"Trust me, my friend," he replied, his gray eyes twinkling. Kyle shrugged.

"But I don't even know who you are."

"Ah, but you do," Marcus corrected. "You just don't remember."

"Huh?"

"Kalibar told you about me," Marcus offered. Then he chuckled as Kyle gave him a blank stare. Kyle squirmed as Marcus continued to look at him, no doubt waiting for him to remember.

"Sorry," Kyle mumbled, breaking the silence. He was pretty sure he'd never heard of – or seen – the man before.

"He did only mention me once," Marcus mused. "Personally, I've found that memory is something that can be vastly improved, with a bit of practice," he added, not unkindly. "It's all about knowing what information is important, and what isn't." He took another swig of his ambrosia, then folded his arms across his chest, peering at Kyle. "I do suspect you've missed quite a few clues along the way."

Kyle lowered his gaze to the tabletop, feeling, once again, deficient. Marcus chuckled.

"Don't take it personally," he replied good-naturedly. "Paying attention is hard...living passively is easy." He leaned forward again. "Would you like to know who I am?"

"Yeah."

"Very well," Marcus stated, leaning back. "I," he declared, "...was Darius's previous employer."

231

Chapter 18

Ariana opened her eyes, her heart pounding in her chest.

The ceiling above was hidden in darkness, the large window by her bedside magically darkened to block out the starlight. She yawned, stretching her arms out wide, wondering what time it was. It felt like she'd just fallen asleep.

She lay there for a moment, vaguely recalling the dream she'd just been woken from, yet another nightmare. She'd been trapped in a burning house, someone familiar calling out her name. Her mother.

She sighed, closing her eyes. She knew she would have a hard time sleeping after such a nightmare. She always did. She thought about getting out of bed, maybe to get something to eat. Nothing made her sleepier than a full belly; Jenkins had become quite accustomed to Ariana's night-time snacks. All she had to do was activate the magical communication orb on her nightstand, and he would come. It made her wonder just how much sleep the butler got each night, having to cater to so many at odd hours. She hated to inconvenience the man, but Jenkins never complained.

She turned to her side, staring at the orb on her nightstand. Her stomach growled.

She sighed, sending a pulse of magic to the communication orb, then swinging her legs over the side of the bed, sitting upright at the edge. She stretched again, yawning a second time, then hopped onto the floor, walking toward her bedroom door. Kalibar's suite had plenty of tables to eat at, but her bedroom did not; she didn't want to get her bed dirty and force Jenkins to have it cleaned in the morning. She reached for the doorknob, twisting it and opening the door.

A tall man stood in front of her.

Ariana screamed, backpedaling quickly, then feeling the back of her legs strike the bed behind her. She stared at the man in front of her, magic twisting automatically in her mind, a gravity shield bursting to life around her.

"Relax, child," the man said. He stepped forward then, toward her. Ariana realized that the man was dressed in the blue shirt and black pants typical of the Tower's butlers. Even in the relative darkness of the room, she could tell that it was only Jenkins.

"Oh, sorry," Ariana mumbled, feeling her cheeks flush. She stepped forward from the bed. Jenkins smiled weakly.

"I didn't mean to frighten you," the butler replied. "I was about to open the door when you did."

"Of course," Ariana replied. She paused then, staring at Jenkins. The man's face was pale, and drawn. He looked strikingly unwell.

"What can I do for you?" he inquired. "A late night snack again for your nightmares?"

"Um, yes please," Ariana requested.

"The usual?"

Ariana nodded, and Jenkins bowed slightly.

"I'll have Greg bring you a tray," he stated. Then he turned about, walking out of the room and closing the door behind him. Ariana watched the butler go, feeling her heart slowing at last. There was something...off about the man, although she couldn't put a finger on why.

She sat down on her bed, taking a deep breath in, then letting it out. Her stomach growled again, more insistently this time, and she realized she was starving. She'd hardly eaten since Kyle's abduction, picking at her meals, leaving most of the food on the plate. Luckily, she didn't have to wait long; before she knew it, there was a knock on the door. She opened it up.

"Good evening, Ariana," the man beyond said. It was Greg, Jenkin's assistant butler. Ariana smiled, glancing at the tray of food in the butler's hands. The silver dome covering the food could hardly contain the delicious aromas within, and Ariana's mouth watered instantly upon smelling them. Greg gestured for Ariana to follow him into Kalibar's main suite; they walked up to one of the many glass-topped tables there, and the butler placed the tray on top of it. Then he turned about, facing Ariana.

"Do you require anything else?"

"No, thank you," Ariana replied. She sat down on the white couch facing the table, and Greg raised the silver dome from the platter, revealing a wondrously bronzed portion of duck. Ariana rubbed her hands together, then she unrolled her silverware from the rolled-up napkin at her right, ready to dig in. She took out a fork, and a spoon, then frowned, glancing about her plate. Her knife was missing.

Suddenly the couch jerked backwards, sliding out from underneath her. She cried out, silverware flying as she fell onto her back on the hard granite below. Her head slammed into the unforgiving stone, stars exploding in the periphery of her vision. Her entire body felt as if it were underwater, everything moving in slow motion.

She looked up, dazed, and saw Greg standing over her, a long, serrated knife clutched in his hands high above his head, the cruel point aiming down at her heart. His face was twisted, his teeth bared like an Ulfar's.

He thrust the knife downward.

Ariana wove without thinking, creating a gravity sphere to her left. It pulled her to the side at the last minute, the blade missing her right shoulder by a fraction of an inch. The knife bounced off of the granite floor, slipping out of Greg's hands. Ariana created another gravity sphere to her left, sliding further across the ground, then creating one above her. She was pulled upward, onto her feet.

She ran toward the front door.

Greg cursed behind her. She felt a sudden vibration in her skull, felt the air crackling around her. She created another gravity sphere, this one to her right, and pulled herself violently to the side.

A bolt of electricity slammed into the door, missing her by mere inches.

Ariana felt her shoulder slam into a column, knocking the breath out of her. She pulled herself together, ducking behind the column, putting it between her and Greg.

"Well done," the butler congratulated. She heard his footsteps echoing as he walked toward her. "But playtime's over."

Ariana created a gravity shield around herself, then bolted out from behind the stone column, running toward the door – the entrance to Kalibar's suite. If she could just make it into the hallway...

Suddenly she tripped over something, falling onto her hands and knees on the unforgiving floor. She felt something pop in her left wrist, a terrible pain lancing up her forearm. She cried out, her left arm crumpling under her, and slammed the side of her head on the floor. She groaned, rolling onto her right side, clutching her throbbing wrist. It looked all wrong, bent at a crazy angle.

Then she realized what she'd tripped over.

Two Battle-Weavers, their faces staring lifelessly back at her, blood on the floor around them. She was lying in a pool of it, the dark red liquid seeping into her clothes. It was cold and wet, and slick against her skin.

Ariana felt her stomach churn, and she stifled the urge to throw up. She heard footsteps approaching, and looked up, seeing Greg some ten feet away, walking toward her slowly. The butler had a grim smile on his face.

Ariana rose from the ground, pushing herself up onto her knees with her good hand, then rising to her feet. She felt the room spin for a moment, feeling her grip on consciousness slipping. She backed away from Greg, resisting the urge to bolt toward the door again, knowing that he would expect such a move. He was clearly toying with her, the smile never leaving his face as he took another step toward her.

"Why are you doing this?" she demanded.

"Just following orders," he replied. The steak knife on the ground – some twenty feet away – flew upward, zipping into Greg's right hand. He cocked it back. "Nothing personal," he added apologetically.

Then he threw the knife right at her.

Ariana reacted instinctively, countless hours of practice kicking in. A powerful *pulling* sphere appeared in front of her and to the right. The knife entered the field, curving rightward mere feet from where Ariana stood. She poured as much magic into her magic stream as she could, the knife arcing around and reversing direction. Ariana cut off the magic stream, abolishing the gravity sphere. The knife flew away from her with incredible speed...and right at Greg.

It bounced harmlessly off of his gravity shield.

"Nice try," he said, the knife clattering on the floor to one side. Ariana's gravity shield vanished suddenly, and then she felt an overwhelming force pulling her to the ground. Her legs crumpled underneath her, and she screamed as she landed on her left wrist, agony shooting through her arm. The force continued, pushing her down onto her back. She tried to create her own gravity field to reverse Greg's, but it was no use...the man was simply too powerful.

He walked up to her, his shiny shoes clicking on the cool granite floor. He stood over her for a long moment, then dropped slowly to one knee, draping his forearm casually over his leg.

"A shame you weren't loyal to the Master," Greg murmured, glancing at her misshapen wrist, and then staring into her eyes. "He wants to speak with you." His pupils widened suddenly, his eyes unfocusing for a split second. Then they snapped back into focus.

He smiled warmly.

"Ariana," a deep voice bellowed from Greg's mouth. Ariana's heart skipped a beat; she knew that voice.

Xanos.

"No," she whimpered, feeling all hope leave her. She tried to get up, to crawl away, but she still couldn't move. "No!"

"What a fine Death Weaver you could have been," Xanos murmured, his voice sending chills down Ariana's spine. "You and Kyle both."

Ariana's eyes widened.

"Where's Kyle?" she demanded. "What did you do to him?"

"The same thing I must do to you," Xanos replied. The knife rose up from the floor again, flying into his hand. He didn't even look at it, his eyes never leaving hers. Ariana felt a crushing hopelessness come over her, even more powerful than the force pinning her to the floor. Her worst fears had been realized.

Kyle was dead.

She felt the force immobilizing her intensify, her arms flying out to her sides. She howled in pain, her left wrist pressing hard against the granite beneath her. Tears came to her eyes, pulled across the sides of her face by the gravity field. She gasped to take a breath in, her head beginning to swim.

Xanos knelt over her silently, the blade in his hand flashing in the dim light of the magical lanterns overhead. Then he brought the tip of the blade down to the center of her chest, under the rib cage.

And pushed.

Ariana tried to scream as the sharp point sliced through her clothes, digging into her skin, but only a pathetic mewling sound came out. She struggled to move, tried to scramble away, but it was hopeless. Xanos pressed harder, and the blade slid deeper into the skin, a sharp pain spreading through her chest as he did so. She glanced down, seeing a red circle expanding on her shirt around the knife. The tip dug deeper still, now completely embedded in her flesh.

She whimpered, unable to turn away, her eyes wide with terror.

Xanos paused for a moment, staring into her eyes wordlessly. Then he adjusted his grip on the knife's handle, and leaned into it.

Ariana felt a horrible pain shoot through her chest and up her left shoulder, and squeezed her eyes shut, opening her mouth to scream.

There was a thump, and then the sound of metal clattering on stone. The force pinning her to the ground vanished.

She paused, then opened her eyes.

Her shirt was slick and wet against her chest, the bloodstain large, but no longer growing. The pain in her chest was subsiding. She glanced about, and saw something round on the ground beside her, to her right. She frowned, reaching out to it, rolling it closer.

It was a *head*.

She cried out, leaping to her feet, staring down at the head. She realized then that there was something else on the ground...Greg's body, a few feet away, a blackened stump at its neck. The man had been decapitated, the stump of his neck charred black.

Ariana covered her mouth with her hand, then realized that her left wrist didn't hurt anymore. She stared at it; the bones were perfectly aligned, no longer twisted at a horrible angle. She squeezed the bones of her wrist with her right hand...no pain.

"What the..." she blurted out.

"My thought exactly," a raspy voice called out from behind.

237

Ariana whirled about, seeing an old man standing there, some ten feet from where she stood.

Old, she realized, was an understatement. The man was positively ancient, his back bent severely with age, his pale skin like crumpled parchment. Broken and rotting teeth jutted out from his desiccated gums. A large, pale scar ran across his forehead, with smaller scars scattered on his neck and arms. His simple clothes were torn and mud-caked, a foul odor emanating from them.

His face broke into a smile, making him appear even more revolting than he already was.

"Who're you?" Ariana stated, taking a step back. Her hand went involuntarily to her nose, and she stopped the movement just in time, breathing through her mouth instead. If the old wretch had noticed the motion, he didn't show it.

"I, he stated, rapping the butt of a long, wooden cane he held against the granite floor, "...am curious." Ariana took another step back, her eyes stinging slightly at the stench.

"I mean, what's your name?" she pressed. The old man shrugged.

"What does it matter?" he wheezed. Then he gestured at Greg's body lying on the ground beside her. "What matters is that this man lost his head...and that you are ignorant as to how."

Ariana glanced at the decapitated corpse on the ground, clutching her chest with both hands. Slippery wetness coated her palms.

"Who *are* you?" she repeated, taking another step backward. With a thought, a gravity shield appeared around her. The old man chuckled softly.

"I am," he stated, rapping his cane on the floor a second time, "...the greatest part of the whole."

"What is that supposed to mean?"

"My Chosen is dead," the old man replied, pointing one shriveled finger at Greg's body, "...because of you." Then he frowned slightly, the countless lines in his face deepening grotesquely. "Or rather, because of something *inside* of you."

"What?" Ariana asked. The old man raised one eyebrow, the scar on his forehead rippling with the motion.

"You don't know, eh?" he observed. He raised the butt of his cane at her, pointing it at her legs. "They're in your bones, little bird...I can feel them." He tapped his left temple with one yellowed, cracked fingernail.

"What are you talking about?" Ariana demanded. She thought about making a break for it then, of sprinting past this old man and bolting through the door. If she could just make it to the riser...

"The runes in your bones, little one," the old man clarified. He smiled grotesquely, his cataract-glazed eyes regarding her intensely. "I'd very much like to see them."

Ariana froze.

"Come, girl," he wheezed, swinging his cane around until it was pointing at the door to her bedroom. "Haven't got all day."

Ariana made up her mind, and bolted.

Except she didn't.

Her legs failed to move, her arms staying at her sides. In a panic, she tried to weave magic, to create a gravity sphere to one side, so that she could pull herself around the old man...but there was no magic to weave.

She had no magic at all.

She tried to move her head, but could not. She could only stare at the elderly man, stooped over his cane, a shock of short white hair sprouting from his liver-spotted skull. He began to walk toward her bedroom door, and she found herself doing the same, her limbs moving without her consent. She followed behind him, trying desperately to regain control over her body...but to no avail. He limped up to the door, pushing it open with the butt of his cane, then gesturing for her to walk in. Which, despite her best efforts, she did. Her body brought her to the edge of her bed, turned her about, and made her sit down on the edge.

"Do lie down," the old man ordered, hobbling up to the bedside. Ariana's body complied without her mind's consent, laying her down on her back in the middle of the bed. The old man sat on the edge of the bed beside her, regarding her with his sunken eyes. Ariana swallowed in a dry throat, her heart pounding in her chest.

"What are you doing to me?" she croaked, surprised that she could even speak. The rest of her body – from the neck down, other than her breathing – was effectively paralyzed.

"You, my dear," the old man replied, putting a desiccated hand on her left leg, "...are being protected by someone. A person I'd very much like to meet." He patted her leg, the sensation of his dry, cracked flesh making her skin crawl.

"I don't know what you're talking about," Ariana protested. The old man smiled.

"Oh, I know," he stated. Then his eyes unfocused, and he stared off into space for a second, his smile slowly disappearing. It only lasted a moment, and he turned his gaze to her soon afterward. "How interesting," he murmured.

"What?"

"It seems," the man answered, "...that another of my Chosen is about to be murdered." He sighed, taking his hand off of Ariana's leg and gripping his cane with both hands. "A shame...he was a good man."

"What are you talking about?"

"Your 'Dead Man,'" he replied. "I had him test the boy and the bodyguard. Someone just severed his communication stream to Xanos, and therefore to me. Which," he added, "...is what happened before all the other Chosen were killed." He sighed again, placing one hand back on her leg; if she could have shuddered, she would've. "You'll be happy to know it happened right as he was about to kill your friend."

Ariana's eyes widened, and she felt her heart skip a beat.

"Kyle?" she blurted out, daring to hope. "He's alive?"

"Oh yes," the old man answered. "For now. But I'm sorry to say that your bodyguard is not."

Ariana felt a lump rise in her throat, and she closed her eyes, feeling tears squeeze out from between her lids and run down her cheeks. She may never have quite warmed up to Darius, but he'd been a good man.

"It was not the runes in his bones," the old man continued, "...that saved Kyle. I had his drained as I am draining yours." Ariana opened her eyes, frowning at the man.

"What?"

"Oh yes, he was protected as you are," he replied. "A trip through the Void fixed that." He sighed. "I always suspected he was the focus of his protector, and that you..." he raised one gnarled finger and pointed it at her "...were just...a happy accident." He shifted his hand to her right leg, cupping her shin in the palm of his hand. "I left his runes alone, knowing that I could study yours while his protector was otherwise occupied."

"What runes?" she pressed.

"Someone opened you up, dear," he answered. "Likely while you were sleeping. Opened you up and carved wonderful runes in your bones, wards to protect you." He shook his head. "They must be amazingly sophisticated, to get past the defensive wards my Chosen have. Poor Greg."

"He was like...?"

"The 'Dead Man?'" he interjected. "Oh yes...but alive, you see. He's been working here for twenty years, you know. Excellent sources of reconnaissance, butlers. Access to everywhere, but practically invisible. And with his shard..." he put one finger on his own forehead, "...hidden under his skin, who would suspect?" He chuckled softly. "I have eyes everywhere, my little one."

"Who *are* you?" Ariana asked. "Are you...?

"Xanos?" the old man interrupted. "No. Xanos is a tool, one I use to escape my...limitations. But if you must know, my name," he added, "...is Sabin."

Ariana frowned, shaking her head mutely. The name meant nothing to her. Sabin shook his head, a smirk distorting the lines in his pale skin.

"It always amazes me how ignorant people are of the past," he mused. "Generation after generation, blindly moving forward, rarely looking back, having absolutely no idea of how the world came to be the way it is. Yet the past can be so instructive."

"What are you going to do to me?" Ariana demanded.

"I," Sabin replied, raising his palm from her right leg and bringing it to her left forearm, "...am draining your runes of their magic. No need to trigger them, after all...not that such a thing would worry me. When I'm done, I'm going to study them."

"And then?" Ariana pressed. She had a feeling she didn't want to know the answer, but *not* knowing was even worse.

"*I'm* not going to do anything," he answered. "My pawns are going to...convert a few in your government to my side, in a manner of speaking," he added. "After vacating a few positions, that is. Orik was the wrong person for the role...free will is such a messy thing." He released his palm from her left arm, tapping his forehead again, then lowering his hand to her right forearm. "Insubordination will not be an option this time...and when Xanos attacks, my new Chosen will save the day, winning the trust and admiration of the Empire."

"Why are you doing this?" she asked.

"Why, for the betterment of mankind," Sabin replied. Then he chuckled at Ariana's bewildered look. "Just because I'm *your* enemy doesn't mean I'm *the* enemy," he added. "You and your friends rebel against my cause – one that we actually share. We just differ on the means to the same end."

Ariana stared at Sabin silently.

"Of course you don't believe me," Sabin declared. "I've caused you pain, so you automatically hate me. But it's true; we both want an Empire built on the ideals of the Ancients...equality, knowledge, and justice. Left alone, your Empire would take countless generations to reach the sophistication of the first Empire...if it lasted that long. With my help, your people will surpass the Ancients in a matter of decades."

"We didn't ask for your help," Ariana retorted.

"I didn't ask for your permission," he countered. "You have no claim over this land," he added. "It was mine long before it was yours." He took his hand off of her right forearm, placing it on her forehead. "Your Empire would not exist if I had not willed it." He kept his hand on her forehead for a moment, then lifted it, placing both hands back on his cane. "But it hardly matters, my dear. Your runes are drained, so our conversation must come to an end."

Ariana grit her teeth, refusing to be silenced. She had one question left for this man, whoever he was.

"If you're not evil, then why was I kidnapped?" she asked. "Why were my parents killed?"

"What is 'evil?'" Sabin countered. "To cause others to suffer? To kill for the greater good?" He shook his head. "By that measure, Kalibar is as evil as I am." He put a hand on her cheek, patting it gently.

242

"Good and evil are a matter of perspective, my dear. Consider it a blessing that you'll never live long enough to understand that."

He lifted his hand from Ariana's cheek then, bringing it down to her right shin. He lowered his yellowed, dirt-caked index finger to below her knee, touching the skin there lightly. A searing pain coursed through her shin, the skin gaping open as if it had been cut with a blade. He drew his finger down her leg, her skin flaying open as he went, until a pearly whiteness appeared underneath the skin and underlying flesh.

Ariana screamed.

Sabin said nothing, prying the skin edges apart with his fingers, exposing the bone underneath. Ariana gasped at the agony shooting through her leg, every fiber of her being screaming to leap away, to escape that torture.

But she couldn't move.

Sabin stared down at her exposed shin bone, and Ariana followed his gaze unwillingly. Bright white bone lay there, countless tiny runes carved into the pearly surface. Her eyes widened, partly due to the pain, and to the shock at what Sabin had exposed.

"Marvelous," Sabin murmured. His cataract-glazed eyes peered at the patterns embedded into her bones, tracing them rapidly. He sat there for a long moment, hunched over her leg, staring silently. Then he glanced up at her.

"It seems your protector is more sophisticated than I had imagined," he stated, frowning slightly. "Far more so," he muttered. He sighed then, drawing his finger back over her wound. The edges closed under his touch, the skin knitting together as if it had never been cut. "But I am sorry to say," he added, "...that he is not sophisticated enough to save you."

Ariana stared silently at Sabin, her eyes glued to his finger as it moved to her other shin. The grotesque digit hovered over her skin, the nail yellowed and chipped. She stared at it, feeling suddenly lightheaded.

"Magic," Sabin continued, "...is a fickle thing. Its allegiance is to that which attracts it most powerfully." He paused then, his finger still hovering above her shin. She tried to squirm, but only her head could move. "And there is no greater attraction for magic than I," he declared.

Ariana swallowed past a wave of nausea, sweat trickling down her flanks.

"Your benefactor," Sabin stated, touching her leg with his finger, his dried skin sending chills down her spine, "...assumed that his magic would protect you. Now he is far away, and My pawns are set to strike," he added. "Divide..." He slid his finger downward, tracing a line down to her shin. The flesh parted easily, exposing the orange-yellow fat and rust-colored muscle below. "And conquer." Ariana moaned, feeling her head swim with the pain, squeezing her eyes shut and turning away from the horrid sight. Still, she felt his eyes upon her.

"Don't be afraid, little bird," Sabin murmured, his foul breath washing over her, making her gag. "It'll all be over soon."

Chapter 19

Kyle sat in his chair, his elbows propped on the round table before him, staring blankly at Marcus. Then his eyes widened, and he pointed at the old man.

"Wait, you're the one who gave Darius to Kalibar," Kyle exclaimed. "You're Kalibar's mentor!" Marcus laughed.

"I hardly *gave* Darius to anyone," he countered. "But as to the latter, you are absolutely correct." He broke out into a grin. "See? You *do* remember."

"Marcus," Kyle murmured, shaking his head. Kalibar *had* mentioned his mentor's name – on several occasions, in fact. He remembered clearly now; they'd been escaping from the Secula Magna, bound for Crescent Lake, when Kalibar had spoken of his former mentor. "Wait, I thought you..."

"Died?" Marcus interjected. "Yes, I admit I had to fake my own death. But as you can see, I'm very much alive."

"What happened?" Kyle pressed.

"Darius offered me a choice," Marcus answered. "I could either spend the few remaining days of my life at home, and die peacefully in my own bed, or I could go to Antara."

"Antara?"

"This island," Marcus replied, gesturing widely with both arms. "Built by Ampir, the man we both know as Darius." He chuckled. "It was hardly a difficult choice for me," he admitted. "I'd been struck

245

with a heart attack a day after Kalibar had last visited me, to ask me for a few guards. The heart attack should have killed me, but Darius wouldn't let that happen. He'd already revealed himself to me long before, so I knew his true nature. I didn't want to die, and he knew it. He offered to bring me here, to his home, to join the others."

"The others?"

"Darius is a...collector," Marcus explained. "Over the last few centuries, he's gathered some of the greatest minds of each generation, and brought them here...to live for eternity, never aging, never dying. In return for our immortality, he asks us to pursue our passions."

"Like what?"

"Whom have you met so far?" Marcus asked. "On the island, I mean."

"Um, a guy name Nalin...and Tek, I think." Then he frowned. "And a woman, she didn't talk at all..."

"Ah, Samb," Marcus replied. "She was a famous architect oh, three centuries ago or so. Darius had her design the downtown area, and even my house," he added. "Even as a mortal, she was famously...impersonal."

"And Nalin?"

"He was an engineer," Marcus informed. "He came here...maybe forty Doma years ago. Brilliant, creative, and a bit strange. If he'd been able to make magic, he would've made a heck of a Runic. He works with Tek – a Runic – to make hybrid devices."

"Huh?"

"Machines that combine magic with standard mechanics. Like a magic-powered engine, for example. He's been working on that ever since Darius gave him that book from Earth." Kyle's eyes widened.

"Wait, you know about Earth?" he pressed. Marcus shrugged.

"Only what Darius told us," he admitted. "He only found Earth maybe..." he paused then, frowning. "The conversion rate always trips me up," he admitted. "You see, for every year that passes on Doma, three years pass by here."

"Time goes faster here?"

"Correct," Marcus replied. "Darius can explain why far better than I," he admitted. "You should ask him about it sometime."

"I'll try," Kyle stated noncommittally.

246

"In any case, he only found Earth a short while ago. From what I hear, it's a fascinating place."

"It is," Kyle agreed. Marcus smiled.

"Yes, I forget you're from there originally," he stated. "In any case, there are about fifty of us living here on Antara, spending each day advancing the magical and physical sciences, building and sharing knowledge with each other."

"Just fifty?" Kyle asked. He'd only seen a small part of the city, but what he'd seen looked like it could house an entire, well, city. That did explain why the place seemed so deserted.

"Samb keeps busy," Marcus explained. "With a few new recruits every few decades, and no one leaving, eventually we'll need every last building."

"Why is Darius doing this?" Kyle pressed. "I mean, why does he need you guys to research stuff?" Marcus shrugged.

"To be honest, I don't know," he admitted. "Darius doesn't exactly speak his mind most of the time," he added with a rueful smirk. "In any case, I suspect that you're right...whatever ingenious inventions we've created, Darius already thought of millennia ago. After all, we still haven't eclipsed the technology of the Ancients...and Darius *started* with that technology." He shook his head slowly. "He showed me his old armor, the one he wore back in Ancient times. It was so far advanced of anything I'd ever seen, I couldn't begin to fathom it. I can't imagine what he's come up with in the last four thousand years or so."

"Wait, what?" Kyle asked. "I thought the Ancient Empire was destroyed *two* thousand years ago."

"True," Marcus agreed. "But Ampir created Antara less than a thousand years after that," he added. "And remember, for every year that passes on Doma..."

"Three passes here," Kyle finished. "Got it." Then he frowned. "You still call him Darius too," he realized.

"I met him as Darius," Marcus explained. "And lived with him for over nine years before he revealed his true nature. I have a hard time thinking of him as Ampir."

"Yeah," Kyle mumbled. It was difficult to reconcile the surly bodyguard with the heroic, but tragic, man in his dreams. Especially when

247

he remembered what Darius had done...standing idly by while Kalibar had been tortured. And allowing Rivin and Bartholos to die.

"What's wrong?" Marcus asked.

"Nothing," Kyle muttered.

"Something's on your mind," Marcus observed. "I can tell you, a terrible secret does far more damage untold...and you'll find that in telling it, it loses its power over you."

"Kalibar said the same thing about dreams," Kyle said, smiling despite himself. Marcus smirked.

"He had a good teacher."

"It's just..." Kyle began, then stopped, grasping for the right words. Then he sighed. "Did you hear about what happened to Kalibar?"

"How do you mean?"

"Well, when we were captured by the Dead Man, he...tortured Kalibar." He swallowed, willing the image of Kalibar's mutilated face from his mind. Marcus nodded.

"Yes, I know," he replied, his tone suddenly grave. "They took out his eyes."

"Yeah," Kyle mumbled. "And Darius watched the whole thing. He didn't do anything."

"Yes, I know," Marcus repeated. Then he gave out a long sigh. "A difficult choice, to let that happen...but the right one, I think."

"*What?*" Kyle blurted out. Marcus leaned back in his chair, crossing his arms over his chest. He said nothing for a long moment, staring at the tabletop. Then he looked Kyle in the eye.

"Kalibar was...stuck," Marcus stated. Then he shook his head. "He had a wife, long ago. He'd married her after becoming a Weaver, but before he'd met me. They had a child, and it died at birth."

Kyle nodded; he remembered the night Kalibar had told him, at the roadside camp. It seemed like forever ago.

"Kalibar's wife blamed him," Marcus continued, "...and became terribly depressed, as some women seem to do after giving birth. She killed herself soon after." He shook his head again. "I can only imagine the pain and guilt he felt after that." Marcus took a sip of his ambrosia. "I think he's been punishing himself ever since. Entering the military, his stint on the Council, his spectacular term as Grand Weaver...he took on as much responsibility as he could, and sacrificed

248

everything – his time, his freedom, his dreams – to prove that he could do it without letting anyone else down."

"You think he was making up for what happened?" Kyle asked. Marcus nodded.

"I don't think he ever let go of that guilt," he explained. "He never dared to remarry, or think about starting a family. When he retired, he'd already accomplished everything he'd set out to do...and, instead of enjoying his retirement, he decided to spend all of his time locked up in his mansion, rarely visiting his friends, bent on discovering the great mystery of how magic works."

"Another responsibility?"

"A distraction," Marcus corrected. "For all the years I knew him, Kalibar rarely displayed the one emotion I consider the most critical of all."

"What's that?"

"Joy," Marcus answered. "Tell me, have you ever seen Kalibar laugh so hard he couldn't breathe? Or tell jokes?"

"He's pretty serious," Kyle admitted.

"He's *boring*," Marcus corrected. "He wasn't always that way...in fact, he was quite the happy-go-lucky young man before...the tragedy. I myself implored him, after his term as Grand Weaver ended, to take a wife and settle down...to have children and set his guilt to rest." He sighed then. "When Darius told me about you, I immediately thought of Kalibar. You see, Darius's original plan was to have *me* act as your mentor."

"Wait, what?" Kyle blurted out. Marcus shrugged.

"I was the perfect choice, as far as Darius was concerned," he replied. "After all, I mentored Kalibar...and he'd known me for over a decade before he found you."

"So why Kalibar?" Kyle pressed. He felt quite uncomfortable with the idea that this man would have been his 'Kalibar'...that he might never have met his adoptive father if things had gone differently.

"Oh, it was all Darius's idea, really," Marcus confessed. "Apparently, I couldn't stop talking to him about Kalibar. I was proud of my protégé's accomplishments, of course." He took a sip from his ambrosia, then shrugged again. "I was also worried about him, and Darius must have picked up on that. A few weeks before my 'death,' he told me he had changed his mind, and was going to use Kalibar instead of me."

"Why?"

"Probably because he saw that you would have far more value to Kalibar," Marcus guessed. He smiled at Kyle's puzzled frown. "He knew that Kalibar would see you as the son he never got to raise...if he was put in the position of having to protect you. He spent his entire life making up for his failure to protect his first son, after all. It was Darius's genius to realize the inevitability of Kalibar's bond with you...and how that would lead to his salvation."

"What do you mean?"

"As I said, Kalibar was stuck. He couldn't move on after failing to save his son's life. That is, until he got to save yours...by sacrificing himself."

Kyle's eyes widened, and he felt a sudden chill run down his spine. An image of Kalibar laying there as the Dead Man's fingers gouged into his eyes came unbidden to his mind.

"Oh..." Kyle murmured. Marcus sighed.

"I rarely agree with Darius's methods," he admitted, scratching his temple with one hand. "But I can't deny their efficacy. It is easy to forget how truly ancient he is...and the wisdom that so long a life would yield. He plans everything, that one...*everything*. Plays us all like instruments, tuning us and forcing the sweetest of notes from us."

"But he crippled Kalibar," Kyle countered. "He didn't have to let it go that far," he added. Marcus smiled.

"You'll find Darius is not as heartless as you think," he countered. "Because of him, Kalibar went from a retirement filled with regret, stepping aside apathetically as an impostor vied for the throne, to discovering a reason to fight for his country...and his family." Marcus stood then, pushing his chair back and walking around the table to Kyle's side. The old man put a warm hand on Kyle's shoulder. "Can you imagine what he has in store for you?"

Marcus walked away then, his back to Kyle, moving across the large room toward the hallway Kyle had walked in from a short time ago. Kyle paused, unsure of what to do, then stood up, following Marcus into the hallway. The old man stopped suddenly halfway to the front door of the house, and Kyle stopped beside him.

250

"It's time for you to go," Marcus stated gently. "It was a pleasure meeting you." He gave one last smile. "Darius believes in you, Kyle," he added. "And so does Kalibar. You should too."

Kyle lowered his gaze, mumbling a "yes sir." Marcus pushed him gently but firmly toward the door.

"Tell Darius I said hello," he called after Kyle. "And tell him I said congratulations, would you?"

* * *

When Kyle opened the front door of Marcus's house and stepped out into the sun, Darius was waiting for him. The bodyguard had changed back into his characteristic golden armor, his huge sword strapped to his side. Kyle wondered how he'd gotten a hold of his armor after the Dead Man had confiscated it, then remembered who he was dealing with.

"Come on," Darius prompted, motioning for Kyle to follow him. They walked silently over the stone walkway leading back to the street ahead, sunlight glimmering off of Darius's armor as he moved. Kyle realized that his feelings about the man had changed since his talk with Marcus; he still resented what Darius had allowed to happen to Kalibar, but he no longer hated the man. Darius's intentions had been noble, but a lifetime of blindness was too extreme a price to pay for Kalibar's so-called salvation.

They continued down the street, the line of tall trees to their right now, the tall black fence with trees beyond to their left. Kyle began to worry that his continuing silence might make Darius think he was still mad, and the urge to break it soon became overwhelming.

"Marcus seems nice," Kyle offered. Darius said nothing, but turned his head ever-so-slightly Kyle's way. Kyle glanced at the man's expressionless face, then sighed. "I'm sorry," he mumbled. Darius still didn't respond. Kyle took a deep breath in, feeling rather annoyed that the man was making this so difficult for him. A normal person would have said *something*, after all. But he tried again. "Marcus..."

"I know," Darius interjected. Kyle frowned.

"I haven't even told..." he began.

"No need," Darius replied. Kyle grit his teeth.

251

"But can't I just tell…"

"No."

Kyle fought down a wave of frustration, kicking a loose pebble on the street.

"You suck sometimes," he muttered. Then, to his surprise, he felt a metallic arm drape around his shoulders. He turned to see Darius smiling at him.

"So do you," he countered. But he gave Kyle's shoulders a squeeze, then let go, lowering his arm to his side. Then he made a turn toward a small, nearly invisible dirt path to their right between the trees, and Kyle followed close behind. The path was too narrow for them to fit side-by side, and had short bushes lining either side. The path wound through a thick copse of trees, twisting this way and that, until it stopped, opening up abruptly to a large, rocky ledge. Darius stepped to one side, giving Kyle an unhindered view of what lie beyond.

Kyle's jaw dropped.

The rocky ledge was just that…a narrow outcropping that ended abruptly, dropping into a sheer cliff some ten feet from where it started. Beyond, there was endless blue sky…at least until he looked down. Hundreds of feet below, there was a mass of angry, churning gray clouds unlike any Kyle had ever seen. Bolts of lightning flashed in the depths of that roiling maelstrom, the clouds circling the cliffside in a narrow belt. Beyond, there was only blue sky and fluffy clouds…and a hint of darker blue miles below. Something that looked suspiciously like an ocean.

"Whoa…" Kyle blurted out, grabbing onto Darius's metal-clad arm. No matter how long he'd practiced flying with his gravity boots, he was still wary of heights. He turned to the bodyguard. "Wait, where are we? Are we in the *sky*?"

"Yep," Darius replied. Kyle shook his head, staring downward at the ocean below, barely able to believe his eyes.

"The entire *city* is floating?"

"Yep."

"Wow," Kyle breathed. Then he frowned. "What are those clouds there?" he asked, pointing to the dark, angry clouds surrounding the cliffside far below.

"It's complicated," Darius replied. He pointed to the border between the blue sky and the dark clouds. "This island – Antara – floats
above the surface of a planet far from Doma, on the other side of the
galaxy. The dark clouds are from that planet's atmosphere...mostly
substances you know as sulfuric acid, carbon dioxide, and nitrogen."

"Wait, but we're breathing oxygen," Kyle observed. Darius nodded.

"Beyond the dark clouds is Doma's atmosphere," he explained.
"This island exists in the other planet, but a continuously open
spacetime bridge supplies breathable air...and a view of Doma's ocean."

Kyle frowned, staring down at the roiling clouds, then at the blue
sky beyond.

"I don't get it," he admitted. Darius smirked.

"No one does at first," he replied. Then he dropped to one knee
on the rocky ground below, gesturing for Kyle to do the same. With
the tip of one gauntleted finger, Darius traced out the following, the
rock below turning a smoky black color as he went.

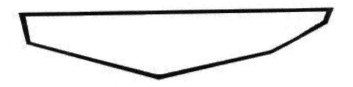

"That," he stated, is the island we're on now." Then he continued
to "draw," his finger leaving a dozen or so indentations in the rock.
"This..." he added...

"...is the planet's poisonous atmosphere, and the surface is a few miles below that." Then he drew another, arcing line around the island:

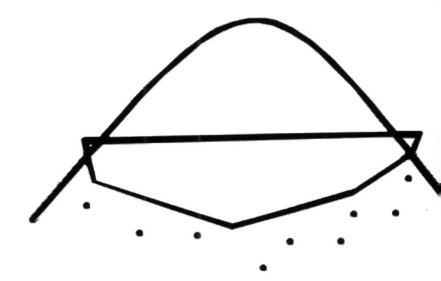

"This," he explained, "...is the shape of the spacetime dome connecting Doma and the other planet. As you can see, only Doma's atmosphere can get through to the city...and if you look out at the edge of the island like we are now..." He drew another two lines, representing their field of vision:

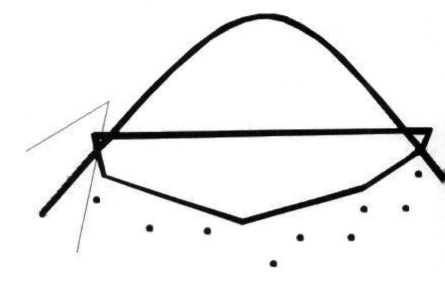

"...you can see the alien planet's atmosphere circling the island, and Doma beyond."

"Wow," Kyle replied, staring at the drawing on the ground, then at over the edge of the cliff. "That's pretty amazing." Then he frowned. "Wait, you're floating an entire *island* miles above an alien planet? Doesn't that take a lot of magic?" He had a hard enough time levitating *himself* for any extended period of time, after all...particularly after his visit to the Void.

"You could say that," Darius replied with a wry smile.

"Where does the magic come from?"

"From the milarite Core," Darius answered. Kyle frowned, vaguely remembering Darius having mentioned milarite before. "Remember when you were looking out of the windows earlier?"

"Oh, the green stuff," Kyle realized.

"Milarite is a mineral," Darius explained. "It's great at storing magic. The Core you saw was only a small column of the total. That column extends down into the island itself, and makes up most of the inside of the island."

"Wait, so the entire *island* stores magic?" Kyle asked. Darius nodded. "But it's like, ten miles long!" he exclaimed. A one-carat diamond could store enough magic to last Kyle for a full day's worth of training...an entire *island* of storage? It was inconceivable. "Who refills the Core?" he asked.

"Who else?"

"But Antara must use a ton of magic every minute," Kyle protested. "How could you possibly..."

"I make a lot of magic," Darius interjected. "And I'm more clever than you realize."

Kyle sighed, realizing that he wasn't going to get any more information out of Darius about that particular issue. He stared out over the edge of the cliff, at the rim of alien atmosphere below.

"Why not just float the island above Doma?" he asked. Darius stood up.

"Time," he replied. "For every three minutes that passes here, one minute passes by in Doma...a useful advantage." He gestured for Kyle to stand up. "And no one can find us here," he added. "As far as I know, I'm the only human being who knows how to teleport. And even if someone from Doma were to fly above the island, they wouldn't be able to see it...a gravity field warps light around Antara, making it invisible."

"But what if someone accidentally flew into it from above?" Kyle asked, pointing up at the sky. Darius smirked.

"They would die."

"Wait, what?"

"If half of your body were to experience time at three times the rate of the other half, what would happen?" Darius asked. Kyle frowned, thinking about it. Then he shrugged; it was too hard for him to visualize. "Image traveling between worlds," Darius continued. "Say you're going through headfirst. As your brain passes through the border between worlds, time is traveling three times as fast for one part of your brain compared to the other. Blood is moving three times as fast, the heart is pumping three times as fast compared to your brain."

"Okay," Kyle mumbled.

"Your brain cells can't communicate with each other," Darius continued. "Your blood vessels engorge with blood, because your heart is beating 270 times a minute instead of 90...the pressure in your vessels spikes, and they burst."

"That's bad," Kyle admitted.

"You have a seizure as your brain malfunctions," Darius continued. "The vessels in your face burst. And when your lungs pass through, part of them experiences three times the number of breaths as other parts...and they pop."

"I think I get it," Kyle stated, feeling suddenly queasy.

"Next," Darius continued, ignoring Kyle's comment, "...your heart passes through. Some chambers are beating three times faster than others, and your heart goes into an abnormal rhythm."

"And then you die," Kyle interjected, having heard quite enough at this point. Despite his parents both being doctors, he was still a bit squeamish.

"So I assumed," Darius murmured. Kyle frowned.

"Wait, what do you mean?"

Darius sighed, turning away from the cliff-side view and facing Kyle, his blue eyes unblinking despite the sudden breeze blowing through his hair. He stared at Kyle for a long moment.

"One person survived it," he clarified. Kyle continued to frown, but lowered his gaze, unnerved by Darius's piercing stare.

"Who, you?" he pressed. Darius shook his head.

"My son."

Kyle thought back to his dreams, those memories Ampir...or rather, Darius...had shared with him. He could still close his eyes and see the images in his mind as if it were a movie, each detail as crisp as if he were experiencing it firsthand. The large underground chamber with the stone dais in the center. The ceiling cracking under the weight of the Behemoth. His son standing on the dais, gazing upward as the air ripped open, forming a passage to another world...a portal that had been too small for Ampir to fit through.

Kyle could feel the panic gripping him, as it had gripped Ampir so long ago.

He pictured Ampir's son rising upward toward the shrinking portal, saw it close just as he made it through. Saw something small fall from where the portal had been, striking the dais and bouncing onto the stone floor below.

A toe.

Kyle frowned, opening his eyes. He lifted his gaze, seeing Darius staring back at him. He could still see that severed toe in his mind's eye.

It had been the boy's *big* toe.

Kyle felt goosebumps rise on his arms, felt his heart hammering in his chest. He stared at Darius's blue eyes, for the first time noticing how similar he and his long-lost son had looked. Darius's words came unbidden to Kyle's mind.

Blood vessels in your brain burst...your lungs collapse...

The big toe amputated.

"My dad," Kyle blurted out, feeling suddenly dizzy. His legs wobbled, then gave out, but Darius caught him before he fell, gently lowering him until he was sitting on the warm rock below. Kyle stared right through the bodyguard, feeling numb. His father had been found in the middle of the street as a boy, his face bruised and swollen, with a bleeding stump where his left big toe should have been. He'd had bleeding in his brain and both of his lungs had collapsed.

Darius said nothing, staring at Kyle.

It made perfect sense now. Ampir had been trying to tell him all along, through Kyle's dreams.

He shook his head. How could he not have seen this? It'd been right there, staring at him, waiting for him to see it all along.

Darius dropped to one knee in front of Kyle, his golden armor glittering in the sunlight, Kyle's distorted reflection rippling across that polished surface. Kyle gazed up into Darius's eyes, his mouth open. He realized he was hyperventilating, and tried to force himself to slow his breathing.

"I'm..." he blurted, stopping as Darius's gauntleted hand rested on his right shoulder.

"You're my grandson, Kyle."

* * *

"*What?*" Kyle blurted out. He stared at Darius, his jaw slack with disbelief. Darius said nothing, staring back at Kyle with his customary flat expression. Kyle just stood there, his mind racing. If he was Darius's grandson, then his father was Darius's son...but Darius had been

258

born over two thousand years ago. Kyle's father was what, forty-four? The timing was all wrong...it simply wasn't possible that Darius could be Kyle's great-great-grandfather, much less his grandfather. He said as much to Darius.

"That would be true," Darius replied calmly, "...if it weren't for the time rate difference between Earth and Doma."

"Wait, what do you mean?" Kyle asked.

"Remember that time travels at different rates depending on how fast you're moving compared to another planet," Darius explained. "Here on Antara, for every minute that passes on Doma, three pass here. So if you spent one year on Doma, three years would have passed here."

Kyle nodded; that much was simple enough, as long as he didn't think about it too hard.

"On Earth," Darius continued, "...for every minute that passes there, roughly 40 minutes pass on Doma."

"Wow," Kyle mumbled. "That's a lot." Then he frowned. "Wait, so how much time has passed on Earth since I left?"

"A few hours."

"That's *it?*" Kyle exclaimed. He felt a sudden elation, realizing that to his parents, he'd only been gone for a short time. While they would still be frantically looking for him, at least he hadn't been gone for weeks. Heck, he'd only have missed a day of school when he got back, if that. He couldn't remember what day of the week it'd been when he left, but if it'd been a Friday, he wouldn't have missed any school at all.

"That's it," Darius confirmed.

"So you're really my grandfather, then," Kyle mused. He stared at Darius, trying to find some resemblance there. He *did* look a bit like his dad, except his dad had hazel eyes, and lighter brown hair. In fact, now that Kyle realized it, the resemblance was hard to miss. How had he not noticed that before?

"Yep."

"I still can't believe it," Kyle admitted. It was hard enough to imagine that his dad was an alien from another planet, much less the son of an immortal being with god-like powers. It made sense, though; Kalibar had always maintained that Kyle produced more magic than

259

anyone in Doma, which would certainly be the case if he was the (nearly) direct descendant of an Ancient.

"What color were my runes?" Darius asked suddenly.

"Huh?"

"What color were the runes on my armor?" he clarified. "My black armor," he added. Kyle shrugged.

"Blue," he answered. "Why?" But Darius shook his head.

"They're not blue."

"What?" Kyle replied. "Of course they are," he added, rather defensively. He wasn't colorblind, after all; he'd been specifically checked for that at school. Darius hardly seemed convinced.

"Nope," he countered. Kyle crossed his arms over his chest.

"Well then what color are they?"

"They aren't," Darius answered. Kyle rolled his eyes.

"You're killing me," he grumbled.

"They aren't any color," Darius insisted. "My armor is completely black."

"Yeah, but its runes glow blue when..." Kyle began, but Darius cut him off with a gesture.

"Only to you...and me."

"Okay," Kyle grumbled, throwing his hands up in the air. "I give up. Why do they glow only for you and me?"

"Because of my gift," Darius explained. "Your people would call it a mutation. Most people can only sense magic...a subtle vibration in the mind. I can *see* magic."

"Okay..."

"And it's blue," Darius added. "I passed that gift on to you, Kyle."

Kyle frowned, staring at Darius for a long moment. Then he shook his head.

"But if I can *see* magic," he countered, "...then why did I have to have Kalibar teach me how to feel it in Crescent Lake?" Darius smirked.

"I was wondering if you'd ever pick up on that," he admitted. "You thought Kalibar's gravity shields were blue...and even told Kalibar that, but he told you they were clear. You never thought to question your teacher."

"Oh, *man!*" Kyle breathed. Darius was right...Kalibar *had* told Kyle that his shields were clear. Ampir's armor, the gravity shields, the faintest trails of blue light every time he wove magic...he'd thought nothing of them. And Darius had stood there, probably rolling his eyes while Kyle blundered about completely oblivious to his own abilities. "Oh *man*," Kyle repeated, slapping his forehead with his palm.

"You *should* be ashamed."

"Thanks," Kyle grumbled. Then he scratched his head. "So why me?"

"Why you what?"

"Why'd you bring *me* here?" Kyle pressed. "I mean, you could've brought your son – my dad – here and taught *him* magic." But Darius shook his head.

"My son will never be able to use magic," he countered. "If you don't have your Awakening...your first use of magic...in your teens, you lose the ability forever."

"Oh," Kyle mumbled. He vaguely remembered the Dead Man telling him that in the Arena, the first time he'd been kidnapped. "So why didn't you just go to Earth before my dad grew up?"

"I didn't *find* Earth until a few Earth weeks ago," Darius explained. "The ring I gave your father generated a signal...one that shot out in all directions, then teleported a certain distance, creating a burst of signals in all directions again. This happened over and over, until the signal eventually reached Doma...a process that took over two thousand years on Doma...and only about forty years on Earth."

"Wow," Kyle breathed. Then he stared at Darius, his eyebrows raised. "You waited *two thousand* years?" he asked in disbelief. Then he shook his head. "Didn't you get bored?" he added. Darius smirked.

"Actually, I gave up on ever receiving the signal after thirty years or so," he admitted. "I had receivers planted all over Doma, but never expected them to pick up anything. You can imagine my surprise when they did."

"So how did you find Earth?"

"It's complicated," Darius answered. "Maybe I'll show you sometime...in your dreams, while I still can."

"What do you mean?" Kyle asked with a frown.

261

"I can only send you my memories for a few more years," Darius explained. "Something about how the brain changes with age...I haven't figured out how to communicate that way with adults yet. Not without permanently damaging their own memories." Then he turned about suddenly, walking back the way they'd come. "Time to go back," he declared. "We've been gone too long already."

Kyle followed Darius through the narrow path back to the street beyond, winding his way through the lush vegetation. He felt a sudden pang of worry about his friends.

"Do you think everyone's okay?"

"I placed wards on your friends," Darius answered. "They'll be safe enough."

"Even from Xanos?"

"They're far more sophisticated than the Dead Man's shard," Darius replied. "Normally they send a distress signal if your friends are in danger, but the signals can't reach Antara."

"Why not?" Kyle pressed. "Couldn't you just teleport the signals here?"

"I could, Darius answered, not even turning his head. "But then I might give away the pattern for teleportation to my enemies...like Xanos."

"Ah, right." That would be bad. "So you can't teleport around Xanos?"

"Or around the Dead Man," Darius replied. "Or any of the Chosen."

"But wait," Kyle countered. "Didn't you teleport all those Death Weavers into orbit? The Dead Man saw that." Darius nodded.

"I cut his communication with Xanos right after I 'died.'"

"Oh." Then Kyle frowned. "How did you know how to do that?"

"I've been studying the Dead Man's shard."

"Oh."

"The Behemoth was controlled by a similar shard," Darius added. "I cut its communications too."

"So Xanos has no idea you're Ampir?"

"Nope," Darius confirmed. "And I want to keep it that way."

"But why?" Kyle asked. "Why don't you just reveal yourself and protect the Empire? You're so powerful, no one could possibly beat you...not even Xanos!"

"Maybe."

"What do you mean?" Kyle pressed. "We need your help!"

"When you get to be my age," Darius replied, "You'll realize that people do best when they're forced to help themselves."

Chapter 20

Kalibar woke with a start, the high-pitched wailing of the emergency alarm assaulting his ears. He bolted upright, his heart pounding in his chest.

A muffled *boom* echoed through the Tower, followed by distant screams.

Kalibar leaped out of bed, padding across his bedroom with his bare feet on the warm stone, reaching the door. He cracked it open, peering out.

The main suite was bathed in darkness.

He opened the door a bit wider, scanning the suite. The usual wards, once placed to help him blindly navigate the room, glowed a faint blue in the distance, but there were no other sources of magic visible.

No assassins hiding in the shadows, waiting to strike.

He turned back to the safe hidden in the wall of his bedroom, rapidly weaving the pattern to unlock it. The safe door swung open, and he grabbed his magic staff from it, and his old Battle-Weaver uniform. Black metallic vest over black shirt and pants, the golden triangle on the left breast, representing the pyramidal peak of the Great Tower. Magical armor, built by Erasmus himself, it had served him well through countless battles.

He pulled it on quickly, then walked back to the door, peering out again. Still clear. The sound of countless footsteps running down the hall outside of his suite was barely audible through the thick stone walls, followed by muted shouting.

He opened the door all the way, sprinting silently across the room. If they were under attack, he and Erasmus would almost certainly be the ultimate targets. That he was not surrounded by Battle-Weavers was a grave sign; activation of the emergency alarm should have brought a half-dozen to his suite in under a minute.

Ariana, he thought, feeling fear for his daughter grip him.

Kalibar made it across the large suite, reaching the front door. It was transparent, as always, and beyond he could see armored men rushing past, shouting loudly. There was another loud *boom*, accompanied by an almost blinding flash of light. Flashes of blue light – magic, Kalibar realized – flew from some of the men – his elite guards – toward an unseen opponent. One of the guards – wearing red armor instead of black – was barking commands to the others.

"Get in front of the Grand Weaver's door! Shields up, form a line, damn it!" He turned to Kalibar's door, slamming on it with one armored fist. Kalibar recognized the man immediately; it was the captain of his elite guards.

"Grand Weaver!" he shouted, pounding on the door again. "Come out! We need to bring you to safety!"

Kalibar hesitated, considering his options. If he went with his guards, he would gain their protection...but at the loss of the enormous number of wards protecting his suite.

The same wards they neutralized to get to Jax, he mused darkly.

He opened the door, and walked through into the hallway. The captain grabbed his left arm, pulling him away from a long column of elite guards filling the hallway beyond, their gravity shields forming an impenetrable barrier. They were, Kalibar knew, acting as human shields, allowing him and Erasmus to escape.

"What's going on?" Kalibar demanded. The captain shook his head, breaking into a run toward Erasmus's door further down the hall, pulling Kalibar with him.

"They came through the underground evacuation tunnels," the captain replied darkly. "Killed all the guards there, and somehow managed to open all of the doors." Kalibar saw the door to Erasmus's suite

265

burst open suddenly, saw two elite guards pulling a befuddled-looking Erasmus out into the hallway.

"Kalibar!" he shouted, trying to resist as the two guards forced him into a run down the hallway, toward the riser ahead. "Wait you fools, we're going the wrong way!"

"The evacuation route is compromised," Kalibar shouted back.

A *boom* echoed through the hallway, bits of dust falling from the ceiling far above. The floor shuddered under their feet.

Kalibar glanced back, saw the door to the evacuation route at the far end of the hallway, the column of guards standing ready. He stared at that door, seeing the blue tint of magic within it, a hint of the numerous defensive wards – and locks – he'd had added only a week ago.

Then the blue light faded...and disappeared.

Kalibar shouted a warning, activating his own gravity shields in an instant. The door burst open...but there was no one behind it.

Kalibar and Erasmus made it to the riser at last, the captain instantly activating it. Erasmus's two guards stood in front of the portly Runic, their shields forming a barrier protecting him. The riser began to descend slowly. They all stared down the hallway.

Something small and round rolled across the floor into the hallway from beyond the door, a small white sphere no bigger than an orange. It stopped at one of the guard's boots, then jumped into the air suddenly.

Kalibar's eyes widened.

Bright rays of blue light shot out from the column of guards, the walls, the doors. The light *pulled* into the levitating white sphere, vanishing inside of it. The guards' shields vanished one by one, the magic-powered lanterns on the walls winking out, leaving the hallway in complete darkness.

The riser descended, cutting off Kalibar's view of the hallway just as the screams started. Horrid, ripping sounds echoed through the hallway and down the riser shaft. Something small fell onto the riser from above, and Kalibar glanced down at it.

It was a finger.

Then Kalibar saw the blue light rise up from the floor of the riser, from the crystal on his staff, from his very body. Rays of it arced up toward the hallway above, toward that white sphere.

The riser began to pick up speed.

"My shields," the captain shouted, turning to stare at the two guards next to Erasmus. "I've got no magic!" The two guards turned to Kalibar, who realized that his own gravity shields had vanished. He tried to weave magic, but couldn't.

He had no magic at all!

The riser continued to pick up speed, shooting down the well-lit shaft, toward the lobby forty stories below. Kalibar grit his teeth, planning his escape route. If the guard had readied an armored carriage for them, they might have a chance to make it across the city. With a contingent of Battle-Weavers covering their escape...

Kalibar slid to the left, and caught himself right before his shoulder slammed into the wall of the riser shaft.

"What the..."

The riser dipped further to the side, falling even faster now, one edge scraping the wall of the shaft, a horrible screeching sound assaulting his ears as sparks flew from the impact. One of Erasmus's guards lost his balance, sliding down the riser and slamming into the shaft wall.

He flew upward into the air in a spray of red.

"Drop to the ground!" Kalibar shouted, following his own advice. The three remaining men did so immediately, spreading their arms and legs wide across the riser floor. Kalibar dug his fingertips into the shallow depressions in the riser's stone, straining to prevent himself from sliding down its angled surface. He felt panic grip him as he realized what had happened.

The riser had lost its magic. It was in free-fall!

Kalibar grit his teeth, closing his eyes and willing magic to form in his mind's eye, to weave the gravity pattern. But there was almost nothing there...only an empty void, one that he had never felt before.

So this is what it's like to live without magic, he thought.

He looked up at the men around him, lying spread-eagled on the floor, and realized that his suggestion had been futile. Even if they didn't slide into the walls zooming past them, they were still going to die when they struck the ground.

Kalibar closed his eyes, feeling despair overcome him. Without magic, there was no way to save Erasmus...or his staff.

267

His *staff.*

Kalibar turned to stare at the white crystal on the tip of his staff. Except it wasn't white, as it had been before he'd been cruelly blinded by the Dead Man.

It was the faintest of blues.

Kalibar burst into action, sucking what little magic remained out of the crystal. He dropped his staff, grabbing Erasmus with one arm, and the captain with his other. The staff rolled down the riser, shattering as it struck the wall.

"Grab the guards!" he shouted at the captain.

Then he activated his gravity boots.

Kalibar rose through the air above the falling riser, clutching Erasmus and the captain to his sides. He grit his teeth, willing more magic into his boots, but he had little magic left; streaming what remained to his boots was enormously difficult. Still he fought, knowing that if he gave up, they were all going to die.

He stared down the shaft, seeing the riser falling faster and faster.

And then it shattered.

A loud *boom* echoed through the riser shaft, and Kalibar yelled as pain lanced through his left ear. He felt his concentration waver, felt himself accelerating downward, toward the rapidly approaching floor of the shaft.

He *pulled* the last ounce of magic from his skull, groaning from the effort it took, and shoved it toward his gravity boots. Their descent slowed, but only slightly. And he had nothing left...no magic in his brain, no magic in his skull.

He stared down at Erasmus, then at the captain. He opened his left hand, letting go of the captain.

Then he slammed his left forearm into the wall.

Unbelievable pain shot up his arm as it splintered on the unforgiving stone, the limb flopping grotesquely in the air. He wanted to scream, but he bit it off, grinding his teeth and bringing his shattered forearm to his forehead.

He *pulled.*

Magic flowed into his mind, and he redirected it to his gravity boots, feeling them burst to life. At the same time, he wove magic, thrusting the pattern at the captain falling helplessly below, encapsulating him in a gravity sphere.

They were only fifty feet from the floor now, and still falling fast.

Kalibar pulled more magic from the exposed bones of his forearm, pumping the gravity boots with as much magic as he could. He gripped Erasmus tightly, feeling more of the portly man's weight as he decelerated. He heaved upward, letting the gravity boots' stabilization fields pull his friend to his side.

Thirty feet. Twenty. Still too fast.

He groaned, sucking the last bit of magic out of his bones, sending them to his boots in one final burst.

Then the ground rose to meet him, and he closed his eyes.

* * *

Kalibar felt his feet strike the ground, felt his legs buckle underneath him, his butt slamming into the cold stone below. He cried out, falling onto his back, the breath bursting from his lungs. His left forearm exploded with pain, and he howled, letting go of Erasmus and clutching his broken arm to his chest. He heard a loud snapping sound, and a scream.

Then there was silence.

Kalibar took a deep breath in, then opened his eyes.

He was surrounded by chunks of shattered stone, the remains of the riser having scattered across the stone floor underneath. Erasmus was lying on his back to Kalibar's left, rolling onto his side to try to push himself off of the floor. To Kalibar's right, the captain sat propped up against the side wall of the riser shaft, his jaw clenched in pain. Kalibar looked down, and saw that the captain's right leg had been broken below the knee, the red armor covering his shin bent at an impossible angle. The two guards laid on the ground beside the captain, appearing to be relatively unharmed.

Kalibar groaned, then sat up slowly, hugging his broken forearm to his belly. It complained bitterly with the movement, and he stifled a scream, pushing himself off of the ground with his good arm. Erasmus struggled to his feet as well, staring down at himself, then at Kalibar. He looked dazed.

269

"Damn," he mumbled. He glanced up the riser shaft, then down at the rubble at their feet, wiping sweat from his forehead. His hand was shaking.

"You okay?" Kalibar asked. Erasmus glanced up at him, then nodded.

"You?" he asked. Kalibar grimaced, cradling his broken forearm. Erasmus's eyes widened with horror. "My god," he blurted out. "Kalibar, your arm!"

"Yeah," Kalibar muttered. "I needed more magic," he explained. Erasmus frowned, staring at him blankly. Of course Erasmus wouldn't have seen the magic being sucked into that white sphere; he would only have sensed a sudden absence of magic in himself and the immediate surroundings. "That white sphere absorbed all of our magic," he explained.

"Well that explains why I couldn't weave anything," Erasmus grumbled. He stared at Kalibar's forearm, shaking his head slowly. "So you broke your own arm."

"Right."

"Of course," Erasmus grumbled.

"It would've taken too long for the magic to back-fill from my arm to my skull," Kalibar explained.

"You're a sick man, Kalibar."

"Saved your ass, didn't I?" Kalibar countered with a grin. Erasmus chuckled. Then they heard a groan; they turned around, seeing the captain still propped up against the wall, trying to rise to his good leg with little success. Erasmus rushed to the man's side, unstrapping the metal greaves from his broken shin, then pulling the exposed black pant leg upward. Underneath, blood-stained skin shone, a ragged cut running down his shin. The sharp end of his shin bone was poking through the wound.

"Leave me," the captain pleaded. "I'll just slow you down."

"Like hell," Erasmus retorted. He draped the captain's arm over one shoulder, then lifted him upward onto his good leg. The two guards rushed to the captain's sides, holding the man upright. The captain yelled out as his broken limb hung uselessly at a grotesque angle. Kalibar walked up to him, kneeling down to stare at the exposed bone. It was glowing a faint blue.

270

"I need your magic," he said to the captain, his tone apologetic. The captain nodded.

"Take it."

Kalibar lowered his forehead until it was inches from the limb, *pulling* the magic out of it, feeling it fill his mind. The magic quickly left his brain, sucked into the starved bones of his skull. Still he *pulled*, until he had drained the limb of everything it had. Then he stood.

"Come on old friend," Kalibar stated wearily, gesturing toward the hallway. They were hardly out of the woods yet; the lobby was only a short distance down the hall, but the enemy was still out there somewhere. With the riser out of commission, they would take a while to catch up, but Kalibar knew his lead would not last long.

The five men left the riser shaft, stepping up into the hallway leading to the lobby. They passed the painted carvings on either wall, of groups of enemy soldiers in black armor facing Ancient Runics and Weavers. They'd been carved by sculptors soon after the fall of the Empire, one of the few relics that had survived that age whole. Kalibar quickened his pace, ignoring the pain each footstep caused his left forearm. He realized that it hurt significantly less than before; he glanced down at his wound, and froze in his tracks.

The skin had nearly closed over his wound, a slight knob where the break had been.

"What's wrong?" Erasmus asked. Kalibar hesitated, then continued forward, shaking his head.

"Nothing," he muttered.

The hallway opened up into the main lobby of the Tower, a massive room with walls three stories high. Usually deserted at this hour, the lobby was filled with guards and Battle-Weavers; each door was covered by a few guards, the hallways leading to other risers walled off by Battle-Weaver gravity shields. On the ceiling, more guards stood, blocking the various hallways on the reverse-polarity section of the lobby. Three Battle-Weavers stood between Kalibar and the lobby; the Battle-Weavers instantly recognized Kalibar and Erasmus, saluting sharply. Kalibar pointed to the captain.

"This man needs medical attention," he declared. Erasmus turned to Kalibar.

"So do you," he countered. Kalibar shook his head, showing him his forearm. The skin had mended completely, the knob of bone nearly smoothed over. Erasmus's jaw dropped. "How in the hell...?"

"No idea," Kalibar interjected. "Not complaining though. Come on," he added. "We have a war to run." He turned to one of the Battle-Weavers. "You," he stated, pointing directly at the man. "Get me High Weaver Urson." As the head of the Battle-Weavers, Kalibar would need Urson to coordinate any large-scale counterattack. The Battle-Weaver nodded crisply.

"Yes, Grand Weaver."

Kalibar turned to one of the other guards. "I want the Tower evacuated *now*, he ordered. "The enemy came through the evacuation tunnels...they came from the 40th through the 42nd floors. They have a weapon I've never seen before," he added. "Our magic will be useless against it."

"Yes Grand Weaver," the guard stated, running to his superior officer to relay the order. Kalibar surveyed the lobby, collecting his thoughts.

"Now," he began – and then he heard shouting from above.

He glanced upward, at the upside-down lobby three stories above, and saw something small rolling across the ceiling-floor, passing through the legs of one of the guards and coming to a stop in the center of the ceiling.

A small white sphere.

"*Run!*" Kalibar shouted, grabbing Erasmus and bolting toward the double doors leading outside. He glanced upward, seeing the sphere dropping down from the reverse-floor above.

And then there was light.

Massive cords of blue light pulled away from the walls, the floors. Small rays were torn from each soldier on the ceiling, more rays pulling upward from each man around Kalibar. He saw a faint blue light rise from his own body, felt the magic draining from his mind. Still he ran, dragging Erasmus along with him, racing toward those double-doors.

Then he heard the screams.

"Duck!" he yelled, pulling Erasmus to the side, toward a granite table nearby. He dropped onto his back, sliding underneath the table and curling into a ball. Something slammed into the ground where they'd been only seconds ago.

A body.

More bodies fell onto the ground, guards and Battle-Weavers dropping from above, no longer held to the ceiling by the reverse-polarity gravity field. Tables and chairs fell onto the granite floor, shattering on impact. Water from the fountain on the ceiling above splashed onto the ground, forming a rapidly expanding pool. The ice-cold water rushed over Kalibar and Erasmus, soaking through their clothes instantly.

Kalibar could only watch as the bodies continued to fall, some striking the men rushing for cover. One guard slipped on the water, falling to the ground with a thump. A large statue from the ceiling above fell on his head, crushing it.

Then, mercifully, nothing more fell.

"Go!" Kalibar shouted, grabbing the edge of the table with both hands and pulling himself from underneath it, sliding through the chilly water. He rose to his feet, breaking into a run toward the double-doors a mere thirty feet away, Erasmus right behind him.

A high-pitched screeching sound tore at their eardrums from behind.

Kalibar glanced over his shoulder, spotting the white sphere levitating in the center of the lobby. Countless layers of rapidly rotating gravity fields surrounded the object. Except these weren't ordinary gravity fields; they had large holes punched through them. Each layer spun in a different direction than the other; at the outer edge was a much larger gravity field, glowing an intense blue.

Pulling *inward*.

Kalibar leaped toward the double-doors, grabbing hold of the polished doorknob with both hands. He felt the air pulling backward at him, sucking inward toward that white sphere, and tightened his grip. Erasmus grabbed the other doorknob, holding on for dear life. People and furniture slid backward through the water on the smooth granite floor, flying up into the air toward those madly rotating gravity fields. One of the wooden chairs was the first to strike the outermost layer.

It shattered.

Men screamed as they flew toward the deadly vacuum, dissolving into a horrid spray of blood and tissue as they struck the gravity fields. More furniture slid upward off of the ground, some already shattered by the fall from the ceiling; they were similarly destroyed.

Kalibar felt his legs rise from the ground, felt them being pulled toward that maelstrom, saw Erasmus's fingers slipping from the doorknob. Felt his own fingers, slick with sweat, sliding away from the smooth metal.

And then it stopped.

Kalibar fell onto his belly, the air bursting from his lungs. He heard a splash beside him, saw Erasmus lying in a shallow pool of water, groaning in pain. Kalibar grunted, rising to his knees, and turned around.

The white sphere hovered there, the remains of every man that had been in the lobby – over a hundred living beings – falling to a massive heap below. Kalibar stared in disbelief at the smooth white sphere, unable to believe that something so small could have done all this.

And then it happened again.

Blue light poured from the walls, the ceiling...even the heap of remains below, sucking inward toward the levitating sphere. The light from the heap was brightest of all, the now-exposed bone fragments relinquishing what remained of their magical stores. Kalibar felt his body go numb, and stayed there on his knees in the cold water. He knew he should get up, open the Tower doors and make a run for it.

But he could only stare.

An army of Battle-Weavers, a military comprising over a half-million soldiers, an Empire spanning countless miles...all of it could be defeated by something no larger than an orange.

Xanos, he realized with simple certainly, had already won.

He turned to Erasmus, who was shouting something at him, gesturing for him to get up, and smiled sadly.

"Goodbye old friend," he murmured.

And then the door burst open, throwing Erasmus to the ground. He slid in the water, coming to a stop on his side. Kalibar stared uncomprehendingly at Erasmus, then saw a boot step down before Erasmus's face, blocking Kalibar's view.

A golden boot.

A gauntleted hand reached down, grabbing Erasmus and lifting him to his feet. A moment later, Kalibar felt something grab the back of *his* shirt, lifting him bodily to his feet. He turned, and saw a pair of blue eyes staring down at him.

"Hey boss," Darius greeted, putting a gauntleted hand on Kalibar's shoulder. "Sorry I'm late."

Kalibar stared at Darius in disbelief, his jaw slack. Erasmus grabbed his other shoulder, pushing him toward the open door.

"Come on!" the Grand Runic urged, "...we have to get out of here before that thing goes off again!" Darius frowned, turning to look at the white sphere levitating above the floor. To Kalibar's eye, the blue light around the thing was starting to wane, the heap of bodies almost drained of their magic.

"What, that little thing?" the bodyguard asked.

He strode across the room toward the sphere, his boots splashing in the red-tinged water.

"Get away from it!" Kalibar shouted after him. "It's about to go off!" Darius ignored him, walking right up to the sphere and grabbing it in his gauntleted hand. He stared at it for a moment, then closed his fist, his fingers covering it completely.

Kalibar stared at the bodyguard in disbelief, watching as Darius's fist clenched, wisps of blue light glowing from the spaces between his fingers. Darius squeezed harder, his eyes narrowing slightly. The blue light between his fingers intensified.

Then it exploded.

A massive burst of magic shot outward from the sphere, slamming into Kalibar's mind and blinding his eyes. He cried out covering his eyes with one arm. The flash of light vanished as quickly as it had come, leaving the lobby in darkness. Faint starlight shone in through the windows, a few dim rays lighting on Darius's golden armor, sending scattered beams across the floor in random patterns.

Darius opened his hand, white dust pouring out of it.

"Darius!" Erasmus cried, running up to the bodyguard and giving him a bear hug. "You glorious bastard! How did you do that?" Darius shrugged, looking rather perturbed by Erasmus's unexpected affection.

275

"I squeezed real hard," he muttered. When Erasmus stared at him blankly, he smirked. "I wouldn't try it if I were you, though," he added. Kalibar frowned.

"I can't believe that grabbing it didn't trigger defensive runes," he stated. "Nearly all runic weapons have them."

"Lucky me," Darius grumbled. Then he gave a loud, high-pitched whistle, and someone extraordinarily familiar walked through the double-doors of the lobby. Kalibar's eyes widened, his heart skipping a beat.

"Kyle!" he exclaimed.

* * *

"Kalibar!" Kyle shouted, running up to the old man with his arms wide open. He jumped into Kalibar's arms, and Kalibar squeezed him tight for a long moment before lowering him to the ground. "My boy!" he exclaimed, looking Kyle over. Kyle gasped, staring at his adopted father with disbelief.

"Your eyes!" Kyle blurted out. Kalibar gave a weary smile.

"It's a long story," he replied. Kyle turned to look at Darius, who gave him the slightest of nods. He nodded back, grinning ear to ear, feeling an almost overwhelming sense of joy sweep over him. Darius had given Kalibar his eyes back! He turned back to Kalibar, then glanced at the lobby beyond, his smile fading.

"What happened here?" he asked. The lobby had been completely destroyed; it was flooded, for one, with a heap of reddish mush and fragments of stone and wood in the center. All of the furniture was gone, and the entire lobby was deserted save for Kalibar and Erasmus.

"Another long story," Kalibar said with a sigh. Then he shook his head at Kyle. "What happened to *you?*"

"Yeah, that's a *really* long story," Kyle answered, realizing that he hadn't come up with a cover story for what had happened to them. He couldn't very well tell Kalibar what had *actually* happened; he'd have to remember to talk to Darius about that later.

"They'll be time for stories later," Erasmus interjected sternly. "Unless you're forgetting about the enemies storming the Tower as we speak."

276

"Where are they?" Darius asked. Erasmus rolled his eyes.

"How would I know?" he countered. "Isn't that *your* job?" Darius raised an eyebrow, glancing at the heap of debris in the center of the lobby.

"Isn't that yours?" he shot back. Erasmus's eyes widened with indignation.

"How could..." he blurted out, slamming his mouth shut suddenly. He paused for a long moment, then pointed a finger at Darius. "There's something seriously wrong with you," he accused. "I ought to have you hanged!" But Darius wasn't even paying attention; the bodyguard's blue eyes were staring off into space, his expression suddenly unreadable.

"What?" Kalibar asked. Darius turned to face him, his voice tense. "Where's Ariana?"

"What?" Kalibar repeated. "She's...I think she's in her room sleeping," he guessed. Darius said nothing, bolting across the lobby toward one of the risers. Kyle ran after the bodyguard, his heart pounding in his chest, Kalibar and Erasmus following close behind. Kyle felt panic grip him; he'd never seen Darius so frantic before. He struggled to keep pace with the bodyguard, nearly slipping on the wet floor. Then he remembered his gravity boots, activating them and speeding a foot above the water, leaving a spray of it in his wake. Kalibar dodged the spray, somehow managing to keep pace with Darius and Kyle. Erasmus, however, soon fell behind, eventually collapsing against a wall. Kalibar hesitated, slowing his pace for a moment, but the Grand Runic waved him on.

"Go!" he shouted. "I'll coordinate the Battle-Weavers until you get back."

Kyle followed Darius across the hallway, toward the riser, but Kalibar motioned down another hallway.

"That riser is destroyed," he informed. "We can use this one."

They followed Kalibar's advice, eventually coming to a stop at a riser. Kalibar activated it, and they rose upward quickly, each floor a blur as they sped toward the 41st floor...to Kalibar's retirement suite, and Ariana's room.

The riser slowed, but Darius bolted from it before it had even stopped, leaping up onto the hallway floor. Kyle and Kalibar ran behind the bodyguard, struggling to keep up. Darius skid to a stop at Kalibar's door.

"I've got it," Kalibar shouted, rushing to Darius's side and pressing his hand on the door. It swung open, and Darius rushed in, sprinting toward Ariana's room. He slammed through her door with his armored shoulder, nearly taking it off of its hinges. Kyle rushed in behind the bodyguard, followed by a winded Kalibar.

Then they all stopped.

"Ariana?" Kalibar called out, walking up to Ariana's bed and kneeling before it. There, in the center of the bed, lay Ariana. She was covered from her belly down by soft white sheets, her arms tucked underneath. She was sleeping quietly, her face turned away from them. Kyle frowned, surprised that she hadn't been awakened by Darius's violent entrance. Kalibar grabbed Ariana's shoulder, shaking it gently but firmly.

"Ariana, wake up," he coaxed. When she didn't respond, Kalibar put a hand on her cheek, turning her face toward them.

Cold, dead eyes stared back at them.

Kalibar shouted, leaping backward from Ariana as if he'd been stung, and Kyle felt his entire body go numb. He stared at Ariana's pale face in disbelief.

"No," Kalibar whimpered, shaking his head and backing away. His back struck the wall, and he slumped slowly to his bottom, his legs giving out underneath him. "No, no..."

Kyle stared mutely into Ariana's unblinking eyes, already dried and glazed over. He felt lightheaded, as if his mind were rising upward from his body. He clenched and unclenched his fists, and though he could feel his hands, they didn't feel as if they belonged to him. He turned, seeing Kalibar stumble toward Ariana's bed. The old man threw the sheets off of her, then reached one arm under her shoulders, the other behind her knees. He lifted her gently from the bed, cradling her in his arms.

"My girl," he murmured, tears pouring down his cheeks. "My sweet little girl." He rocked her from side to side, cradling the back of her head with one hand. He closed his eyes, burying his face into her

278

shoulder. "I'm sorry," he whispered, a muffled sob escaping his lips. His shoulders shook then as he wept. "I'm so sorry, love."

Kyle stared at them silently, still unable to move, unable to even think. Or feel. He just felt numb. He knew he should be reacting like Kalibar, should be feeling *something*, but he just couldn't. He wondered if there was something wrong with him, wondered if the others would think he didn't care.

Then he felt a cool, metallic hand on his shoulder, saw Darius staring at him. The bodyguard's expression was unreadable.

"I'm sorry, Kyle," he murmured.

And then the dam broke.

A low wail escaped Kyle's lips, and he stumbled forward toward Ariana and Kalibar, landing on the bed just before his legs gave out. Kalibar wrapped one arm around Kyle's shoulders, holding him close, while Kyle stared at Ariana, her face still lovely despite the terrible paleness of her skin. Kalibar had already closed her eyes, for which Kyle was grateful.

Kyle realized he was crying, his body wracked by terrible sobs. He leaned in close to her, wrapping his arms around her slender shoulders and hugging her close. She was terribly cold; he had the sudden mad thought that if he warmed her up, she would come back to life.

"I'm sorry son," Kalibar whispered, rocking Kyle and Ariana gently. Kyle felt the old man's cheek press up against his own, felt the wetness of Kalibar's tears. "I failed her."

"No," Kyle mumbled, shaking his head. He let go of Ariana, wiping his own tears away with the back of his hand. He turned around on the bed, perched on its edge, and found Darius staring silently at Ariana's face, the gilded warrior as still as a statue.

Kyle felt the slightest spark of hope alight within his heart.

"Save her," he pleaded, standing up from the bed and walking over to Darius. He grabbed the man's armored bicep. "Save her," he insisted, his voice rising with desperation. Darius turned to stare at Kyle, his stony expression unchanged. He shook his head slightly. Kyle felt another sob burst from him, and he grabbed Darius's shoulders, shaking them back and forth. The bodyguard didn't budge.

"Save her!" Kyle shouted.

"I can't," Darius whispered.

"You *can!*" Kyle yelled. He shook Darius harder — to no effect — then balled his hands into fists, striking the bodyguard's chest-plate. "You *have* to!"

Darius said nothing, not even bothering to block Kyle's blows. Kyle slammed both fists into the man's armor, hitting the bodyguard as hard as he could. Then he stumbled backward, striking the edge of Ariana's bed with the backs of his knees, falling onto his butt on the edge of the bed. He pointed at Darius, his eyes filled with tears.

"This is *your* fault!" he accused, feeling rage build up within him. "You let this happen to her!"

"Kyle..." Darius began.

"No!" Kyle shouted. "You could have stopped this! She's dead because of *you!*"

"Kyle!" Kalibar shouted, laying Ariana on the bed and standing up to face his son.

"It's true," Kyle retorted, turning to face Kalibar. "He stood there and did nothing while you and everyone else got hurt! Just *ask* him," he added vehemently, turning back to face Darius. "You let everyone get hurt and die around you because you just don't *care*."

"*Kyle!*" Kalibar warned grabbing Kyle's shoulder with one hand. "I know you're grieving, but Darius is too," he stated. "Everyone grieves in their own way." Kyle hardly heard Kalibar, feeling his old resentment toward Darius building up within him. No, this time it was something more; he truly hated the man now.

But Darius said nothing, staring silently at Kyle for a long moment, then turning his gaze to Ariana's still form lying on the bed. The muscles of his jaw rippled, and he clenched his gauntleted fists once, and then again.

Then he strode up to Ariana's bed, slipping off his gauntlets and throwing them to the floor with a loud clang. He leaned over her, pushing Kalibar gently away, and placed one hand on her right shin, staring down at her pale face for what seemed like an eternity. Eventually, Kalibar put a hand on the bodyguard's shoulder, a concerned look on his face.

"Darius..." he began.

But Darius ignored Kalibar, gently pushing his employer's hand away. He shifted his hand to Ariana's left shin, then reached into the recesses of his armor with one hand, pulling something long and tapered out from within. Kyle recognized it instantly.

It was a green crystal.

Kyle heard Kalibar gasp, and the old man reached for Darius's hand, but the bodyguard batted Kalibar's hand away, rotating the crystal so that its pointed end faced downward.

"Darius, where did you get that?" Kalibar shouted. "Don't do it," he commanded, lunging for the crystal. Darius blocked Kalibar's arm in one fluid motion, nearly tipping the Grand Weaver over in the process. Kalibar leaped up from the bed, facing the bodyguard defiantly. "If you so much as touch that crystal to her head, Xanos will possess her, and we'll *all* be dead...is that what you want?"

Darius ignored Kalibar, lunging forward and slamming the green crystal into Ariana's forehead.

Kalibar shouted, leaping at Darius and grabbing the bodyguard's arm. Darius spun around with blinding speed, sending Kalibar flying into the bed by Ariana's feet. Then he returned to Ariana's side as if he'd never left it.

The crystal lowered itself slowly into Ariana's forehead, burrowing through her pale flesh. Then it stopped for a moment. Kyle heard a sickening crunching sound, and nearly gagged as the crystal suddenly sunk a few inches into her skull, then slid more slowly downward until it stopped, the broad base of the gem forming a vibrant green diamond-shape on her forehead. Darius reached down to press one finger on the butt of the crystal, and it sank a fraction of an inch lower, until it was beneath the level of her skin. Then he placed his hand over her forehead, closing his eyes. When he lifted his hand, the skin on her forehead had closed, appearing whole again.

"We're all doomed," Kalibar warned, rising up from the bed, his face pale. "Even if I had magic in me, I..."

"It's okay," Kyle interjected, breaking his gaze from Ariana's face. He walked up to Kalibar, clasping one of the old man's hands in his own. "He knows what he's doing," he added. Kyle's anger toward Darius had vanished, replaced by an immense sense of relief. But Kalibar pulled his hand away, shaking his head vehemently. He pointed one finger at Ariana.

"The minute she wakes up, everyone in this Tower is going to die."

"Kalibar," Darius stated suddenly, turning away from Ariana and toward the Grand Weaver. "It's all right."

"How?" Kalibar countered. "You don't know the first thing about..."

"Remember the being who gave you back your eyes?" Darius asked. Kalibar froze, then nodded. "After I killed the Dead Man, I kept his crystal," Darius explained. "Your...benefactor modified it."

"Wait, he visited you?" Kalibar blurted. Darius nodded.

"He's the reason we made it back here alive," he replied. Kalibar stared silently at Darius for a long moment, then turned to Kyle.

"Is that true?" he asked. Kyle nodded.

"It's true," he confirmed. "The Dead Man captured us, and uh, that guy showed up and killed him."

"Wait, *what*?" Kalibar asked, his expression incredulous. "You're talking about *the* Dead Man? He's alive?" Darius smirked.

"Not so much."

"He's the one who kidnapped us," Kyle explained. "He was brought back to, uh, life by Xanos, I think. He killed Master Banar and took us back to the Arena."

"Brought back to life?" Kalibar asked incredulously. He lowered his gaze, shaking his head. "How can we defeat an enemy who can raise the dead?"

"It gets worse," Kyle admitted. Kalibar's eyebrows raised.

"*Worse*? How?"

"The Dead Man was storing an army of Behemoths above the Arena," Kyle explained. Kalibar stared at Kyle for a long moment.

"Behemoths," Kalibar repeated.

"Behemoths," Darius confirmed.

Suddenly they heard a piercing scream, so agonizing that it set the hair on the back of Kyle's neck on end. All three men jumped, then spun around.

There, sitting bolt upright on the bed, was Ariana, her eyes wide with terror.

"Ariana!" Kyle exclaimed, bursting with joy. He ran to her and hugged her, squeezing her tight. But she pushed back against him, her arms incredibly strong, shoving him backward. He stumbled, slamming his back against the wall. Ariana stared at him for a moment, her

282

chest heaving, her eyes wide. Then she turned to Kalibar, scrambling backward in her bed.

"Ariana," Kalibar soothed, reaching for her. She shook her head, crawling backward until she met the headboard. Kalibar paused, then smiled at her kindly, stepping backward. "It's okay, sweetheart," he murmured. "You're safe."

Ariana sat there for a long moment, staring at Kalibar. Then she turned her head, glancing at Kyle – still up against the wall – and then Darius. Then she turned back to Kalibar, her shoulders relaxing.

"Kalibar," she stated with relief. She glanced at Kyle again. "Sorry Kyle," she said, smiling apologetically. "I thought..." Then she frowned. "Wait, what happened?"

"You were...hurt," Kalibar explained. "You're okay now. No one's going to harm you." Ariana lowered her gaze, apparently thinking this over for a moment. Then she shook her head.

"Something's wrong," she declared, glancing up at Kalibar. "I don't feel right."

"You've been through a lot," Kalibar said. Then he sighed. "Ariana..."

"No," Ariana interrupted, her eyes narrowing. "Something's *wrong*. She glanced up at Kyle with her lovely brown eyes, and quite suddenly broke out into a huge smile. "Kyle!" she exclaimed, leaping off of the bed and running toward him. He cringed, bracing himself against the wall right before Ariana crashed into him, giving him an enthusiastic hug. Too enthusiastic; he felt the air explode from his lungs, his ribs threatening to splinter under the incredible power of her embrace. He gasped for air, flailing his arms uselessly. Ariana leaned backward, frowning at him.

"What's wrong?" she asked. Kyle wheezed, his vision blackening. Ariana let go of him just before he passed out, stepping back from him with a concerned look on her face. He slid down the wall onto his butt, sucking air greedily into his tortured lungs.

"What's wrong?" Ariana repeated, bringing her hand up to her mouth. She knelt down, putting a cold hand on Kyle's cheek. "Kyle, what did I do?"

"Ariana," Darius interjected, kneeling down and putting a hand on her slender shoulder. "I need to tell you something."

"I'll do it," Kalibar interrupted, putting a hand on Darius's armored shoulder. Darius shook his head.

"This is my failure," he countered, his voice resolute. "I did this to her," he added. Kalibar stared back at the bodyguard for a long moment, then nodded silently.

"What are you talking about?" Ariana pressed, glancing suspiciously from Kalibar to Darius. "What's going on?"

"Ariana," Darius said, squeezing her shoulder gently. "Tell us what happened to you." Ariana frowned, then lowered her gaze, her eyes getting a faraway look. Then she shook her head.

"I...it's hard to remember," she admitted. Her eyes narrowed, and she bit her lip. "Something woke me up," she added. "In the middle of the night...I can't remember why."

"Go on," Darius encouraged.

"I remember Jenkins," she continued. Then she shook her head. "Or a butler." Then her eyes widened, and she looked up into Darius's eyes. "I think...I think I was attacked!" The memory seemed to startle Ariana, and she rested backward, sitting on her butt, gazing off into the distance.

"Who attacked you?" Darius pressed, his voice still uncharacteristically gentle. Ariana shook her head, looking confused.

"Someone in a blue shirt," she answered after a long moment. "He tried to kill me."

"Was it Jenkins?" Darius asked. Ariana frowned.

"I think so," she replied. "Yes, I think it was," she added more confidently. "But he had magic."

"Of course!" Kalibar interjected, slamming his fist into his palm. "The assassins...Xanos is putting crystals into our butlers!"

"What?" Ariana asked, turning to face Kalibar. Darius put one bare hand on her cheek, gently bringing her gaze back to his.

"Tell me what happened next."

"I...I think he stabbed me," Ariana replied, clutching her chest with both hands, her eyes widening. "Oh god, he stabbed me!" she exclaimed, her face contorting in terror. She slid backward on the floor, crawling until her back struck the wall behind her...until she was right next to Kyle. Darius frowned.

"Ariana, I need to know what happened next."

284

"What happened next?" Ariana repeated. She paused, then frowned. "What happened next..." Then she gasped, staring down at her left shin, peeling back her pants leg with both hands, exposing smooth, pale skin below. Darius glanced at her leg, then back at her, saying nothing.

"He cut me!" Ariana exclaimed, her eyes widening with terror. She glanced at Kyle, then Kalibar, then back to Darius, pointing at her leg. "Someone else...he cut me right here!"

"Who cut you?" Darius pressed, his voice still calm, almost hypnotically monotone. Ariana frowned.

"An old man," she answered.

"What did the old man look like?"

"He had bad breath," Ariana replied, wrinkling her nose. "And...he was *really* old," she added. "I think he told me his name."

"What was his name?" Darius pressed. Ariana frowned, her eyes narrowing. She sat there for a long moment, staring at the floor in front of her, then shook her head.

"I can't remember."

"What happened next?" Darius asked. Kyle caught Kalibar frowning, and knew the Grand Weaver was annoyed that Darius had switched topics so quickly. Kyle gave Kalibar a reassuring smile, hoping that the old man would trust the bodyguard enough not to interrupt. His hopes were realized; Kalibar pursed his lips, but remained silent.

"He said you'd died," Ariana answered, her eyes widening. "He said someone opened me up, and carved runes into my bones." She retracted her leg, grabbing it with her hands and staring at it intently. Then she looked up at Darius. "He said we should remember the past," she added. "Then something about...eyes...and..." She shook her head in frustration. "Why can't I remember?"

"Give it time," Darius murmured. "You're doing fine."

Ariana paused for a long moment, then sighed.

"I think he said something about me not understanding," she continued. Then she frowned, her eyes narrowing. "No, he said I wouldn't *live* long enough to understand." Then her eyes widened, and she grabbed her left wrist, staring at it. "He cut me!" she exclaimed, running her fingernail down her forearm. Despite her proclamation, the skin was perfectly intact. She frowned, looking at her other forearm, which was also intact.

"Darius," Kalibar warned, but Ariana stood up without warning, clutching Darius's armored biceps in her hands. The golden metal buckled under her grasp, her fingertips sinking into the metal itself. Ariana stared down at the crumpled metal, then let go, stepping backward.

"What's wrong with me?" she asked, gazing at her fingertips in disbelief.

"Ariana, sweetheart," Kalibar interjected, stepping toward her. But Darius barred his path with one arm, his eyes locked on Ariana.

"You died."

Ariana stared mutely at Darius for a long moment. Kyle stepped well clear of her, not wanting to risk her fury; if she could mangle Darius's armor, there was no telling what she could do to him.

"What?" she blurted out.

"You died," Darius repeated. His tone was almost cruel in its finality. Ariana shook her head.

"But I'm alive!" she retorted, looking down at herself. She stared back up at Kalibar, her eyes pleading. Kalibar sighed.

"It's true, honey."

"But I'm *alive*," Ariana insisted. Darius stepped up to her, grabbing her right hand and pressing it against her chest, pressing her back into the wall in the process. Ariana resisted at first, then relaxed.

"Feel your heartbeat," Darius commanded.

Ariana frowned, pausing for a long moment, her head lowered. Then her eyes widened.

"I can't," she whispered.

"I brought you back," Darius explained, letting go of Ariana's hand and stepping back from her.

"But how?" Ariana pressed, shaking her head. "That's impossible!"

"It isn't," Darius countered. He raised his hand up then, pressing two bare fingers against Ariana's forehead. He kept them there for a moment, then dropped his hand to his side. Ariana stared at him for a long moment, then brought her own hand up to her forehead, running her fingers across the smooth, pale skin there.

"I'm sorry," Darius murmured.

286

"What?" Ariana blurted out, her eyes narrowing. "What did you do to me?"

"It was the only way," Darius explained, his tone gentle.

"What did you *do* to me?" Ariana repeated. Kalibar grabbed Darius's shoulder.

"I don't have any magic," he warned, glancing at Ariana. Darius ignored the Grand Runic, his eyes locked on Ariana.

"I used the Dead Man's crystal," Darius replied. "It's inside you now."

Ariana stared at Darius for a long moment, her eyes as wide as saucers, her jaw slack. Then she stumbled backward until her back was against the wall, her mouth opening, then closing.

Then she screamed.

The sound was horrendous, the sheer agony and terror wrenching Kyle's heart. He backpedaled away from her, covering his ears with his palms, goosebumps rising on his arms. Kalibar backed away as well, with only Darius remaining where he was. Ariana took a deep breath in, then screamed again, clutching at her forehead with her hands, curling her fingers into claws. She went wild, raking her forehead, digging her fingernails into her own flesh. Darius lunged forward, grabbing her arms and pinning them to her sides, pressing her up against the wall.

"Calm down," he ordered.

But Ariana resisted, clenching her fists and pulling them upward. Her eyes were wild, her face twisted in rage. Darius didn't budge, his grip holding fast. Ariana pressed against the wall with her back, tiny cracks forming in the stone behind her.

"Ariana, *yield!*" Darius shouted. His voice slammed into Kyle's mind, shocking in the sheer power of it, and Kyle found himself backing away, and glanced at Kalibar, who had taken a step back as well.

Ariana froze, staring at Darius, her eyes still wide. But the madness slowly faded from them, and she unclenched her fists, lowering her gaze. She nodded mutely, and Darius released her, taking a step backward. She stood there for a long moment, then slumped slowly to the ground, propped up against the stone wall.

And then she cried.

Her pale, slender shoulders shook with each sob, and Kalibar immediately knelt beside her, putting his hand on one of them. Kyle hesitated, then moved toward her, putting a hand on her opposite shoulder. Darius took her chin in one hand, raising it up until her eyes met his. Despite her weeping, no tears fell from her eyes.

"We couldn't lose you," he stated. "Your family loves you."

Ariana continued to sob, holding a hand up to her forehead, the skin unblemished from her violence toward it earlier.

"He's *inside* of me," she moaned, squeezing her eyes shut and shaking her head. "I can't do this."

"He's dead," Darius countered. "His crystal is just a tool, Ariana. You're not the Dead Man, and you never will be."

"But it's *inside of me*," Ariana insisted. "I'm like him now!"

"It doesn't matter," Kalibar interjected. "We love you, Ariana."

"We all do," Kyle added, squeezing her shoulder. It was disturbingly cold, and the horrible truth was that it reminded him of the Dead Man. But he hid his momentary disgust, smiling at her. Ariana turned to face him, the barest hint of a smile appearing on her lips.

"I can't believe you're alive," she murmured, reached up and squeezing Kyle's hand. He howled, dropping to the floor, yanking his arm away. Her grip had nearly broken his hand! Ariana looked startled. "Oh Kyle, I'm so sorry...!"

"It's okay," Kyle mumbled, shaking his throbbing hand and bringing it to his lips. "Wow, you're strong," he added with a rueful grin. Ariana paused, then smiled faintly.

"Sorry," she repeated. "I'll be more gentle next time," she promised, slowly raising her hand up and patting Kyle on the cheek. Kyle tried not to cringe in anticipation of a bone-crushing slap to the face, but her touch was indeed gentle this time. He forced himself to relax under her icy touch. She turned to Kalibar.

"What now?" she asked.

"You're amazing," Kalibar replied, shaking his head in wonder. "How can you adjust so quickly?"

"I can't," she countered, lowering her hand from Kyle's face. She rose to her feet then, straightening out her pajamas. "I just need to get my mind off of it."

"I need to get downstairs," Kalibar stated. "Erasmus is handling our defenses, but he'll need my help."

"Wait, what's going on?" Ariana asked.

"The Tower is under attack," Kalibar explained, his tone grim. "And if we don't do something soon, we're going to lose."

Chapter 21

Kyle walked out of Ariana's bedroom, trailing behind Darius and Kalibar. Ariana walked at his side, her eyes on the floor. She looked terribly pale, her skin almost translucent. Her big brown eyes were startling against that whiteness, and lovelier than ever. Caught by a sudden, overwhelming fondness for her, he grabbed her hand in his own, and gave it a squeeze.

Ariana flinched, surprised out of her reverie, and glanced at Kyle. He smiled silently at her, giving her hand another squeeze as they followed Kalibar and Darius across the suite. She smiled back weakly, and squeezed his hand back – gently, thank goodness. She was clearly still shell-shocked by what had happened to her; Kyle couldn't imagine what it would feel like to know he had died, and that the Dead Man's crystal had been placed inside his brain. All things considered, Ariana was handling it pretty well.

"We need to get back to the lobby," Kalibar stated, leading them across the suite toward the front door. "Erasmus will need my help to organize our defenses."

"What's the situation?" Darius asked.

"I'm not sure," Kalibar answered. He opened the door, ushering Kyle and Ariana out into the hallway, then followed behind with Darius. "I woke to find guards in my hallway...I never saw who was attacking us, but they rolled out that...thing, that white sphere." He shook his head, his expression grim. "I've heard of crystals that can suck magic, but I've never seen anything like that sphere." Kyle glanced at Darius; the white sphere seemed awfully similar to the Void crystals the Dead Man had shown him earlier.

"Void spheres," he mumbled. Kalibar frowned, turning to him. "What?"

"Void spheres," Kyle stated, louder this time. "The Dead Man had a whole room filled with white crystals, he called it the Void. It sucked magic from me each time I went in to it. The white spheres are the same thing."

"Interesting," Kalibar murmured. "Void spheres," he muttered. "It's a good enough name." Kyle turned down the hallway toward the riser, then frowned...it wasn't there. The customary shield blocking the way to the riser shaft was missing too. He glanced at Kalibar, who shook his head.

"That one's out of commission," he stated grimly. "We'll use another one...there are four main risers that come to this level." They turned about, striding down the hallway in the other direction. Then Kyle stopped, pointing down the hallway.

"Uh, guys?" he stated. "Is that one out too?" For the riser at this end of the hallway was similarly missing. Darius stopped in his tracks, and Kalibar glanced at the bodyguard.

"It's probably my Battle-Weavers," he stated. But he stopped as well, standing beside Darius. Kyle felt a vibration in the air, saw the faint blue of a gravity shield appearing around Ariana. He began to weave his own shield. Then he felt himself fly backward, slamming into the ground, the impact knocking the wind out of him. He slid backward on the floor, then came to a stop, his ears ringing loudly. He gasped for breath, trying to get back on his feet, but his legs felt like jelly.

Then he heard a thump, and saw Kalibar landing on the ground beside him, grunting as he struck the floor. The Grand Weaver groaned, clutching his side.

Kyle looked down the hallway, and saw the riser lowering itself to their level, carrying three men in elite guard uniforms. The riser stopped, and the three men stepped out toward them, unsheathing their swords.

"Kyle," he heard Kalibar gasp. He turned, and saw Kalibar still clutching his side, gritting his teeth in pain. "...stream magic to me!"

Kyle complied, shooting a stream of magic toward Kalibar's forehead, realizing that he could see the faintest blue line where the stream flowed. Then he heard a shout, and broke off the stream, twisting his head to look down the hallway.

There Darius stood, his golden armor shimmering in the light of the magic lanterns on the walls, facing the three elite guards, his own sword still sheathed at his side. The guards stopped before him.

"Well, if it ain't Grand Weaver Kalibar," one of them stated, adjusting his grip on his sword. Darius said nothing, staring at the guards. The guard licked his lips. "As I remember it, you had me locked up what, 'bout ten years ago?" He shook his head disapprovingly. "Now, you shouldn't've done that," he scolded. Then he cocked his head to the side. "Looks like you met the magic-sucker," he observed. "This is gonna be too easy."

Darius shook his head, standing before the three guards, slowly unsheathing his huge sword. He smirked at the guards, lowering his sword to his side.

"For me," he growled. The guard who'd spoken earlier sneered at Darius.

"Step aside, little man," he drawled. "Before you get hurt."

Darius burst into action, moving almost too quickly for Kyle's eyes to follow. One second, he was standing before the mouthy guard, the next, he was crouching on one knee, his sword held to one side, the silver metal flashing in the light above.

Bright red liquid streamed down the edge of the blade, dripping onto the floor.

The guard tumbled to the ground, his head separating from his shoulders, his body falling forward and *thumping* on the granite below.

One of the other two guards lunged for Darius, swinging his sword at the bodyguard's head. Darius swung his sword upward with such force that it knocked the sword right out of the guard's hands, then spun in a full circle, swinging his sword in a tight arc over his right shoulder, chopping downward at the man's neck.

Darius's sword bounced away violently, throwing the bodyguard backward. He regained his balance rapidly, backpedaling a few steps.

A shimmering blue gravity shield surrounded the guard.

"Surprise," the man growled. "Time to die, fool."

"Kyle," Kalibar whispered harshly, grabbing Kyle's shoulder. "Magic, now!"

Kyle *pushed* magic toward Kalibar, struggling against the immense resistance of his skull, having been so recently depleted of magic by the Void. He poured as much magic as he could at the Grand Weaver, his head pounding with the effort. Kalibar closed his eyes for a moment, then opened them, turning to face Darius.

"Darius, now!" he shouted.

The guard's shields vanished.

Darius lunged forward, chopping downward with his sword, the blade slicing through the guard's left shoulder. The bodyguard continued forward, grabbing the man's left arm with one hand, yanking it hard. In one fluid motion, he ripped the arm from its socket, flinging it down the hallway toward Kyle, at the same time shoving his sword through the guard's back. The arm spun through the air, then landed between Kyle and Kalibar. Kyle scrambled away from the severed limb.

"Arm yourself," Darius shouted.

Kalibar grabbed the arm, twisting it around so that the exposed bone at the upper arm was facing his forehead. He brought his forehead within inches of the bones, and closed his eyes. Kyle could see faint traces of blue light streaming from the pearly white bone to Kalibar's head.

"Stop right there!" a voice shouted.

Everyone turned, and saw the last guard standing there, clutching Ariana in his arms, a wicked-looking knife at her throat.

"Don't move, or I'll slice her throat," the guard threatened, gripping the handle of his knife so hard his knuckles turned white. Ariana's eyes were wide, her body rigid. Kyle felt his heart leap into his throat.

"Don't!" he cried.

Darius stood there watching the guard for a moment, then slowly sheathed his sword. When he was done, he shrugged.

"Go ahead," he stated casually. "We never liked her anyway."

"What?" Ariana blurted out, glaring at the bodyguard. "Gee, thanks a lot," she grumbled.

Darius turned away from the guard and Ariana, and strolled down the hallway, stopping before Kalibar and pulling the old man to his feet.

"Stop it!" the guard yelled after them. "I swear I'll do it!"

"Good luck," Darius muttered, not bothering to turn around.

The guard tightened his grip on Ariana, his arm wrapped around her upper chest. She brought her hands up, wrapping her fingers around his arm.

And squeezed.

A loud snapping sound echoed off of the walls, and the guard howled, dropping like a rag doll. Ariana yanked on his arm – *hard* – and he flew forward through the air...right at Darius. The bodyguard stepped aside casually, watching as the guard slammed into the floor, his head bouncing off of the hard granite. The man slid to a stop, his arm twisted at an impossible angle, a large dent in his forehead. His eyes were open, but saw nothing.

Kyle stared at the dead guard, then at Ariana, feeling queasy.

"Never liked me, huh?" Ariana quipped, striding menacingly toward Darius. The bodyguard glanced at the fallen guard, then back at Ariana.

"You're growing on me," he admitted. Ariana shot him a look, then glanced down at the guard she'd killed. She stared at him for a long moment, looking suddenly shaken.

"I've never killed anyone before," she stated.

"You did what you had to do," Kalibar replied, putting a hand on her slender shoulder. She shook her head, her eyes never leaving the dead guard's face.

"It was too easy."

Kalibar said nothing, dropping his hand from her shoulder, then turning to Kyle, who was still on the floor. He walked up to Kyle, offering one hand.

"Come on, let's go," Kalibar urged, grasping Kyle's arm and pulling him to his feet. "Thanks for the help," he added, patting Kyle on the back.

"I didn't have much magic left," Kyle apologized.

"I didn't have any," Kalibar countered. Then he strode forward, toward the riser ahead. "Come on," he added, gesturing for all to follow. Gravity shields appeared around all four of them. "Now that we have magic, we might have a chance." He stopped suddenly, turning back to the three guards on the floor. "We should bring them with us," he stated, nodding at Darius. "We'll need to search them and identify them." He glanced down the hallway. "And we'll need more magic...I'll grab a few crystals from the safe in my room."

Kalibar left, leaving Kyle and Darius standing there in the hallway. Darius stared at the dead guards for a moment, then glanced at Ariana. She met his gaze, then nodded, stepping well clear of the man she'd just killed, and stopping before one of the other two. She paused for a long moment, then knelt, grabbing the man by the shoulder. She grimaced, hauling the man with unnerving ease onto her shoulder, and strode to the riser, setting him down there. Darius grabbed another guard, dragging him unceremoniously to the riser, and motioned for Ariana to retrieve the last guard...the one she'd killed.

"I can't," Ariana protested, shaking her head. Darius walked to her side, appearing – as usual – wholly unsympathetic.

"He's a dead man," the bodyguard retorted. "He can't hurt you anymore."

Ariana took a deep breath in, staring at the corpse, then nodding silently. She walked up to the guard, standing over him for a long moment, then kneeling down quickly. She closed her eyes, her mouth set in a tight grimace, then grabbed the man's armpits, lifting him up and draping him over her shoulder. She practically ran to the riser, depositing the guard next to the other two.

"Guys," Kalibar called out, stepping into the hallway, his arms filled to the brim with crystals. "Can you grab a few of these?" Kyle nodded, and he and Darius walked up to the Grand Weaver, each taking a few crystals and shoving them into their pockets. Kyle turned back to Ariana, who was standing on the riser as if frozen, staring at something that had rolled out of the dead guard's pocket.

A small white sphere.

"Ariana!" Kyle cried out.

"Get back!" Kalibar shouted. Kyle felt a hand grab the back of his shirt, felt himself being pulled backward from the riser. He resisted, trying desperately to get to Ariana, to pull her away from the deadly Void sphere. But Kalibar wouldn't let him. A large blue gravity field appeared behind them. He felt himself being pulled toward it, the air screaming past his ears, his clothes fluttering violently around him. He slid backward, away from Ariana, watching as the Void sphere rose upward from the center of the riser. Cords of blue light sucked inward from the walls, and upward from the riser below, and even from the center of Ariana's forehead, all converging on the sphere.

"Ariana!" Kyle screamed.

And then the riser dropped, and Ariana fell with it.

* * *

Ariana felt the floor dropping underneath her, felt the cauldron of magical power in the center of her mind's eye draining away. She tried to leap forward off of the riser, but her legs wobbled underneath her, and she fell to her knees on the platform below.

And then the platform fell out from underneath her.

She tried to cry out, but she could make no sound. She tried to move her limbs, but they were limp – and numb – as if they didn't even belong to her. All she could do was watch, catching a glimpse of the white sphere as it sped down the hallway toward her friends. The riser platform plunged faster and faster down the shaft, entering free-fall.

Then her vision faded, and there was darkness.

* * *

Kalibar watched the riser drop in horror, saw Ariana go limp right before she fell with it, the Void sphere sucking the magic out of her forehead crystal. He resisted the urge to run to her, knowing that there was no way to get past that terrible weapon without getting them all killed. He made the awful decision instantly, weaving a powerful gravity field behind them, then bringing it to life.

He felt himself falling as he was sucked violently backward by that gravity field, and streamed magic to his gravity boots, the stabilization runes embedded within righting him before his body struck the

296

ground. He tightened his grip on the back of Kyle's shirt, pulling his son with him. Darius slid backward on the floor beside Kalibar.

And there, floating forward from the riser shaft into the hallway toward them, was the Void sphere. A sunburst of blue light sucked inward from the walls, the floors, the doors...even the magical lamps hanging on the ceiling. The lights winked out one by one as the Void sphere passed, the magically locked doors swinging open slowly as they were purged of their power. Faint wisps of magic were sucked inward from Kalibar toward that powerful void, the ghastly creation draining him despite the forty feet he'd managed to put between them.

He wove magic, then pushed it outward...and watched as the pattern untangled before his eyes, getting sucked into the deadly sphere. He grit his teeth, knowing that the thing would have its fill soon, and would then unleash its devastation upon them. The only way to survive would be to get away from it for long enough, so that it could discharge, then re-enter its absorption cycle, allowing Darius to get close to it...and destroy it. But they would never survive its powerful vacuum if it discharged here.

He pushed himself harder, ignoring the faint trails of magic draining from his body toward the Void sphere, using what remained to fly down the hallway at breakneck speed. He cut his magic stream to the gravity field further down the hall as they approached it, pulling Kyle close to him, so that the boy would be held fast by the gravity boots' stabilization fields. He spotted Darius, still sliding down the slippery hallway, his momentum slowing. Kalibar concentrated, throwing magic outward toward the bodyguard, a gravity sphere to pull the man along.

The pattern untangled, pulled into the rapidly approaching sphere.

Kalibar's eyes widened in horror, and he tried again, but Darius was too far away now; being closer to the Void sphere, no magic could be cast to him. The thing was only thirty feet from the bodyguard now. Twenty feet.

And then it stopped.

Kalibar reacted in an instant, weaving automatically, his decades of training kicking in. A gravity sphere appeared around Darius, thrusting him backward violently away from the Void sphere, which levitated motionlessly in the middle of the hallway. The endless streams of magic it had pulled into itself had vanished.

A shimmering blue sphere appeared around the thing, expanding rapidly, followed by countless more. The inner spheres began to rotate.

Kalibar felt a powerful gust of wind slam into his back, threatening to pull him toward that lethal vacuum. He heard a high-pitched screaming sound, the air sucking violently into those expanding gravity fields. He braced himself, streaming as much power as he could into his boots, even then only barely managing to stop himself and Kyle from being pulled forward. He saw Darius sliding toward the Void sphere, granite tiles chipping and flying upward into the spinning void, cracks forming on the ceiling and walls. Chunks of stone flew inward from all directions, disintegrating as they slammed into the deadly sphere's gravity fields. Kalibar tried to weave magic, but there was little left in his mind. He felt the weight of the crystals he'd placed in his pockets, and *pulled* magic from them, weaving what little he could draw out in his mind's eye, knowing he had one last chance to save Darius before the bodyguard was torn apart. He thrust the magic outward.

The stone floor below Darius groaned, then ripped upward and backward, forming a steeper and steeper arch until it reached the ceiling high above, forming a curved makeshift wall that blocked off the hallway. Darius slid down the floor-turned-wall, leaping to his feet as he neared the bottom of the arch, then stopping before Kalibar. Kalibar dropped his magic stream to his gravity boots, his magic completely drained, and dropped to the ground. Darius turned to look at the wall behind him.

"Thanks," the bodyguard grumbled.

Kalibar nodded, staring at the wall he'd created. Even now, pieces of it were breaking off, the air screaming through the holes they left. More and more of the wall crumbled before them, and Kalibar knew it wouldn't be long before it collapsed altogether. He turned to Kyle.

"I need magic!" he shouted. Kyle nodded, closing his eyes. A faint beam of blue light shot outward from his forehead toward Kalibar. The Grand Weaver felt the power fill his mind, then dissipate as it redistributed into the bones of his skull. The beam coming from Kyle stopped, and Kyle shook his head.

298

"No more," he shouted back. Kalibar nodded, his heart sinking. He didn't have nearly enough power left to create another stone wall, and despite his legendary ability to generate magic, most of the magic he created would distribute itself into his depleted bones, leaving little to work with until he'd replenished them. He needed to find more magic.

The center of the makeshift wall collapsed suddenly, huge chunks of stone flying into the rapidly spinning gravity fields beyond, torn to smaller and smaller chunks that orbited frantically around the small white sphere. A blast of air struck Kalibar from behind, and he stumbled forward toward the hole in the wall. He felt Darius grip his arm, thrusting him backward, and then everything stopped.

The gusts of air slowed to a breeze, countless stone fragments orbiting the Void sphere falling to the floor with a dreadful clatter. Kalibar turned to Darius, who was already sprinting toward the giant hole in the wall.

"Now!" Kalibar cried.

Darius dove through the hole, tucking into a tight ball in mid-air, then flipping to land on his feet on the remains of the floor beyond. Cords of blue light streamed inward toward the Void sphere from the walls and floor as the sphere began to feed, the light much fainter than it had been before. Darius ran up to the sphere, grabbing it in one gauntleted fist.

The gilded bodyguard landed on the polished granite beyond, sinking to one knee, his fist tightening over the deadly sphere. Pulses of intense blue shone through the gaps in his fingers. Then there was a loud crack, and a massive burst of intense blue light shot outward in all directions, slamming into Kalibar's mind. He felt his brain instantly fill with magic, felt it thrumming momentarily with overwhelming power. Then the feeling faded, the magic redistributing into his starving bones.

Darius turned his hand over and opened his fingers, white dust falling in a stream to the floor.

"Woo!" Kyle exclaimed, leaping at Darius and giving him a bear hug. The boy turned to Kalibar, embracing him in turn. Then his face paled, and he turned to look down the hallway, and the missing riser beyond.

299

"We have to find Ariana!" he exclaimed.

A muffled *boom* rocked the hallway, the floor beneath them shuddering. Kalibar heard the sound of glass breaking in the distance, heard another explosion rock the Tower.

"We've got a problem," Darius warned. Kalibar followed the bodyguard's gaze, turning to see a doorway beside them, the door having been ripped from its hinges earlier. Beyond, Kalibar recognized his own retirement suite, the one they'd just come from. The huge glass windows on the far wall had shattered, the city of Stridon visible beyond. Kalibar's eyes widened, gooseflesh rising on his arms. He strode forward through the doorway and into his suite, ignoring the shards of glass crunching beneath his boots.

There, below the stars that twinkled serenely in the night sky, the city was on fire.

* * *

Kyle stared out of the huge, shattered window in Kalibar's suite, looking past the sharp, irregular pieces of broken glass. Beyond the tall fence surrounding the Secula Magna, the skyline of Stridon stood silhouetted against the night sky, the shadows of the buildings beyond limned with tongues of red light. A shroud of black smoke, even blacker than the sky above it, hovered above the rooftops miles away.

"No..." Kalibar whispered, his voice barely audible. The Grand Weaver stood at Kyle's side, shaking his head from side to side. Then he slammed his fist into the wall beside the window. "Damn it!" he swore. Kyle jumped, shocked at the rage in Kalibar's voice. The old man spun around, running a hand through his short white hair. He cursed again, this time under his breath, then turned to Darius. "Okay," he muttered, taking a deep breath in, then releasing it. "We need to identify and quantify the threat." He tapped his goatee with one finger, then strode toward one of the end tables next to the many couches in the suite. He placed one hand on the communication orb there.

"Who are you calling?" Kyle asked. Kalibar sighed.

"No one, apparently," he answered. "The entire communication system is down...I can't mobilize my Battle-Weavers from here." He turned to Darius. "We need to get back down to Erasmus," he stated.

300

"He has to have gathered some Battle-Weavers. We need to organize our defenses."

Kyle nodded, then glanced at Darius. The bodyguard was staring off into space.

"What's wrong?" Kyle asked. Darius turned his gaze to Kyle.

"He's right," he replied gruffly, turning back toward the front door. "Let's go." He began walking, and Kyle and Kalibar followed behind.

"We need to be cautious," Kalibar warned. "I don't have much magic left, and neither do you, Kyle," he added. "I doubt I have enough to repeat my previous performance if we meet another one of those Void spheres...or even if we meet up with any more of those prisoners."

"I can give you what I have," Kyle offered. Kalibar nodded, following Darius as the bodyguard opened the front door and stepped out into the ruined hallway.

"Please do."

Kyle obliged, streaming magic to Kalibar's forehead immediately. Despite having had no magic left to give just minutes ago, he'd already regenerated quite a bit. He also realized that he was streaming magic without even thinking about it; magic had become – in a matter of weeks – something automatic, a reflex. He marveled at the progress he'd made; he'd been spending so much time kicking himself for his failures that he'd ignored his accomplishments.

"Thank you," Kalibar said, nodding at Kyle. Then he raised an eyebrow. "You had a lot more magic than I did," he added. "How did you make so much so quickly?"

"I make more magic now," Kyle replied.

"Impressive," Kalibar murmured. The three stopped in the middle of the hallway then, and Kalibar turned to Darius.

"The nearest risers are out," he observed. "And we need to conserve magic. We'll have to take one of the emergency stairwells...but I want to stop by the 32nd floor first."

"Why?" Kyle asked. The 32nd floor was well known to him. It contained the Runic Archives, after all...the Secula Magna's vast collection of runic items and tomes regarding all things magic. It was where his ring had been kept each day for studying.

301

"Erasmus and I created something that might be of use," Kalibar explained. He smiled at Kyle then. "In fact, we used your idea to create it...your brilliant idea, I might add." Kyle frowned; he had no clue what Kalibar was talking about. "The sensory rune array," Kalibar continued. "To reverse-engineer magic patterns from nature."

"Oh, right." He'd almost forgotten about that. "It worked?"

"Oh yes," Kalibar replied. "And we used the concept to create a weapon...one that might just help us win this war." They walked down the hallway until they'd reached the door to the stairwell. Darius opened the door, ushering Kyle and Kalibar through.

"What kind of weapon?" Kyle asked.

"We had our naturalists bring us a killerpillar," Kalibar answered. Kyle's eyes widened. He remembered the little red insects from his trek to Crescent Lake; seemingly harmless, the little buggers would flash bright red if threatened, then kill anything near them. "They flung dreamweaver silk at the specimen to force it to sleep, then hauled it back for us. We set up the sensor array near it, then – using gravity fields from behind a protective wall – irritated it until it reacted."

"And you reverse-engineered its pattern?" Kyle pressed. Kalibar nodded, striding down the stairwell at a quick pace.

"We did...eventually. Erasmus did most of the work," he admitted. "He designed and created a prototype for a weapon using the killerpillar's unique ability."

"What's it do?" Kyle asked. Kalibar gave him a grim smile.

"Exactly what you might expect," he answered. "And if it works as well in the battlefield as it did in the lab, our enemy is in for a nasty surprise."

Chapter 22

Ariana groaned.

She was surrounded by blackness, and a silence so profound that it was overwhelming. She felt nothing, heard nothing, saw nothing. She could not move, because there was nothing for her to move. She had no limbs, no face, no eyes.

She groaned again, realizing that she was making no sound, that the sound was only in her mind. She tried to remember where she was, *when* she was, but all she could remember was her identity...everything else was gone. She had no past, no future. Even the present meant nothing.

Minutes passed, or maybe hours. Maybe days.

Then something appeared, not in her vision but in her mind. A subtle vibration. She latched on to the sensation, mostly because it *was* a sensation...something to distinguish itself from the eternity of nothingness. It grew, the vibration, becoming stronger. She felt it expand, felt her mind sharpen. Random sensations came to her, the smell of smoke, the sound of a bird chirping. Then bursts of color, a memory of her house in Mortown. Her parents' house.

The images came and went, replaced by countless of others, a rapid-fire chain of memories, random and senseless because of that randomness. She let the deluge assault her, having no other choice. She felt a burning sensation suddenly, far away from her. As it intensified, she realized that she could *move* the burning...that it was a part of her. She did so, bringing it closer to herself. The burning faded slowly, replaced by pins-and-needles, a sensation so powerful that it was agonizing. She cried out, and to her surprise, she *heard* the sound this time, echoing hollowly around her. It sounded strangely metallic and faraway, her voice, but it was *her* voice. She knew it now.

Slowly the pins and needles faded, replaced by the sensation of pressure. She realized that the burning sensation had become her left arm, and flexed it, feeling it rise upward. A sudden brightness — so unbelievably intense that it made her cry out again — seared through her mind, two bursts of light appearing before her. She raised her one arm to her face, the brightness fading slightly, and realized that she had eyes.

The brightness waned, became tolerable. Colors appeared in the distance, blurry at first, then sharpening. She blinked, feeling eyelids sliding over her eyes, marveling at the sensation. She'd felt it millions of times before, never paying attention to how strange and wonderful it was. She tried to move her eyes, but couldn't. She could only stare forward.

A long, wide tunnel extended above her, as far as she could see.

She felt more burning now, this time to her right, and knew that her right arm must be returning to her. She let it happen, having no other choice, feeling the sensation spread. The horrible pins-and-needles returned, pure torture that faded slowly, replaced by sharpness digging into her arms and legs.

She tried to move her eyes again, and found that she could.

Ariana lifted her head up slowly, the effort taking every bit of concentration that she had. She saw her body lying there, covered in chunks of stone of various sizes. A fine layer of gray dust coated her exposed skin. She lifted her head up further, spotted a deep gash in her left thigh.

Fear gripped her, panic rising in her breast.

She forced herself to look away, closing her eyes and resting her head back onto the ground. She felt an ache where the gash was, but it wasn't nearly as painful as she imagined it should be. She took a deep breath in, realizing with a start that it had been the first time she'd taken a breath since she'd awoken.

She held her breath, waiting.

304

Seconds passed, then minutes. No urge to breath came to her, no burning in her chest. No heartbeat pounding in her breast. She held her breath for what seemed like an eternity, yet nothing happened.

She exhaled, then opened her eyes again, lifting herself upward slowly until she was sitting on the hard stone below. She looked at the wound on her left thigh again, the sight of her exposed muscle and fat having less of an effect this time. She experimented, lifting her knee upward, and it moved easily, hunks of stone rolling off of it onto the ground. She tested her right leg, and lifted that knee as well.

Her right ankle was bent inward at a crazy angle, a sharp bone end jutting out of the side of it.

She jerked her head away from the sight, closing her eyes. A vision of an old man came to her, of her flesh parting under his fingertips. She shuddered, opening her eyes and ignoring her ruined ankle. It ached terribly, spasms of pain shooting up her leg.

Ariana leaned forward, twisting until she was laying on her stomach in the rubble, her legs behind her. She saw a hallway beyond the tunnel above her, and realized that she was in a riser shaft. How she'd gotten there, she had no idea...but it was clear that she'd fallen some distance. The pieces of stone around her were similar to the risers in the Tower, so she knew that she must be in the Great Tower.

She remembered Darius leaning over her, remembered herself screaming when they'd told her about...

Ariana reached up with one hand, pressing her fingertips against her forehead.

Then it came back to her...the realization of what Darius had done to her. Her guts twisted with dread, panic threatening to overwhelm her. Closing her eyes, she took a deep breath in, letting it out slowly. What had happened after that? She remembered walking out of Kalibar's suite...and then nothing afterward. She frowned, concentrating harder. Still nothing.

She sighed then, staring down the hallway ahead. She realized that she could hear voices beyond, could see people at the other end of the long hallway...men in black armor, the elite guards of the Great Tower. Ariana grit her teeth, reaching ahead with one hand and pulling herself forward over the rubble beneath her. Then she reached out with her other hand, crawling toward the raised lip of the hallway floor only a few feet away. She reached it, hauling herself up into the hallway. The vibration in the center of her forehead grow stronger, pulsing within her. The sensation was different than it had been in life, but it was obviously magic. Somehow, her magic had been taken from her, and even more inexplicably, it was returning.

She paused, lying flat on the floor, feeling the vibration turn into a rapid-fire pulsing, the pulsing growing into a roiling cauldron of power. She felt her limbs strengthen, her muscles nearly bursting with energy. She moved again, crawling down the hallway, the motions effortless now, as if she weighed nothing at all. Her power was returning, that horrifying strength that had crushed Darius's armor, and nearly broken Kyle's hand.

She felt a pang of guilt then, followed by an intense despair at what she'd become. Not quite human, not quite alive. A dead girl walking, the unwilling inheritor of the Dead Man's curse...the man she thought she'd finally freed herself from.

"Hey!" a voice shouted. Ariana looked up and saw one of the elite guards running down the hallway toward her, his gravity shields activated. He stopped before her, his eyes widening in recognition. "Ariana!" he cried, dropping to one knee beside her. "Are you alright?"

"My legs," she replied, grimacing slightly. "I think I fell." The guard looked down at her legs, then frowned.

"They don't look injured," he countered. "Which leg hurts?" Ariana stared at the man for a moment, wondering if he was daft. Then she rolled onto her side, glancing down at her legs. The smooth curve of her calves met her ankles without interruption, her right foot no longer deformed. She glanced at her left thigh, seeing nothing but a large tear in her pants, the underlying skin pale and smooth. She stared at it, hardly believing her eyes.

"Uh, miss?"

Ariana blinked, then turned to see the elite guard staring at her. She gave him the most convincing smile she could muster, then rose up from the ground in one fluid motion, forcing herself to move slowly. Still, the movement felt too quick. She could see the guard's surprise, and realized she would have to be more careful in the future if she wanted to keep her...condition...a secret.

"The right one," Ariana replied, nearly forgetting the guard's initial question. She pretended to gingerly test it. "It's sore, but not as bad as I thought."

"You can walk?"

"Yeah," Ariana replied. The guard turned about, leading her down the hallway toward the lobby beyond. She followed behind, her eyes widening as she entered the huge room. The place was in shambles, the floor littered with fragments of stone and wood, her boots splashing in at least an inch of red-tinged water covering the floor. There were people everywhere...elite guards, Battle-Weavers, and even white-cloaked Runics standing about. Near the center of the lobby, to one side of a huge pile of something red and mushy – garbage, it looked like – stood Erasmus, surrounded by countless guards. The portly Grand Runic was speaking with one of the guards, but stopped when Ariana and her escort drew near.

"Ariana!" Erasmus exclaimed, excusing himself and walking up to her. "Thank goodness you're okay," he added, looking her up and down. Then he frowned. "Wait, *are* you okay?" he asked. "You look terrible."

"Gee thanks," Ariana muttered. But she forced herself to smile – and found that she didn't have to try very hard. She was glad to see the foul-mouthed Grand Runic. "What's going on?"

"Ah, right," Erasmus muttered, "...you wouldn't know." Then he frowned. "Where's Kalibar and Kyle? They went to check up on you."

"Uh, I don't remember," Ariana admitted. "I fell on my way here and hit my head." Erasmus raised one bushy eyebrow.

"Did you ever see them?" he asked. Ariana nodded.

"Yeah, they came to get me, but I think we got separated."

"How so?" Erasmus pressed. Ariana shrugged. The Grand Runic frowned, running a hand through his impressive white beard. "Well, I've already sent Battle-Weavers to clear each level of the Tower. I'll have another team start from the top to make sure they're okay." Then he sighed. "Kalibar's going to be damn lucky if the Council never hears about him pulling that stunt," he added. "No offense, but running off to find you in the middle of a national security crisis was not his brightest move."

307

"Sorry," Ariana mumbled. Erasmus gave a tight smile, clapping Ariana on the shoulder.

"Don't be," he replied. "That's why we have two leaders, after all."

"Erasmus!" a voice called out. Ariana turned, looking past Erasmus, and saw Councilman Ibicus striding through the throngs of Battle-Weavers toward them, two of his own Battle-Weavers flanking him. The old Runic looked worried, his face pale and tired. "Thank goodness you're okay," he added. "What's going on?"

"Looks like Xanos sent those escaped prisoners to assassinate us," Erasmus replied grimly. "They came through the evacuation tunnels and took out our guards. We were lucky to escape with our lives."

"Unthinkable," Ibicus muttered. Then he glanced at Ariana, a look of surprise on his face. "Ariana," he added, frowning slightly at her. Ariana lowered her gaze, still self-conscious about her appearance. She hadn't looked in a mirror, but judging by the dreadful pallor of her limbs, she could only imagine how ghastly her face looked. It was as Erasmus had said...she looked terrible.

"Councilman Ibicus," she greeted shyly. Ibicus stared at her silently for a long moment, then turned back to Erasmus.

"Where's Kalibar?" he asked. Erasmus gestured down one of the many hallways radiating from the lobby.

"He went to coordinate the Battle-Weavers on the upper floors," he lied. "He'll be down later."

"Good," Ibicus stated. Then he frowned, glancing at the devastation littering the lobby. "What happened here?"

"The prisoners unleashed a new weapon in the lobby," Erasmus explained. "Some sort of small white sphere. It absorbed magic, then released it in a rather remarkable way...in any case, we've secured the lobby," he added. "I've set up a perimeter around the Tower. The gate is closed off, and Battle-Weavers are doing a sweep of each floor, starting from the ground up. They'll notify us when the Tower is cleared. Everyone knows to run if they encounter another one of these white spheres."

"Understood," Ibicus replied. "Convening the Council is of the utmost importance," he added. "Have we retrieved any of the others?" Then he held up his hand, shaking his head quickly. "Never mind...or rather, not here," he explained, glancing around the lobby. "We need someplace private to speak."

"Of course," Erasmus agreed, gesturing toward one of the hallways. "We can use one of the conference rooms."

Ibicus nodded, then gestured for the two Battle-Weavers accompanying him to follow along. Erasmus put a hand on Ariana's shoulder, pulling her along with them. They made their way out of the lobby and into the hallway, stopping at one of the many doors on either side. Erasmus opened it up, and they walked through into a small room with a rectangular table surrounded by chairs. Two small windows on the opposite wall gave a limited view of the campus outside. Ibicus turned to the Battle-Weavers, giving them a curt nod. They stayed outside the room, flanking the doorway. Ibicus shut the door, then sat down on the edge of the table. He glanced at Ariana.

"Why don't you wait outside, dear," he said, more of a statement than a question. But Erasmus shook his head.

"She can stay," he countered. Ibicus frowned, staring at Ariana disapprovingly.

"She's a security risk," he insisted. Erasmus snorted. Ibicus raised an eyebrow, turning to the Grand Runic. "I don't doubt that she's loyal," he clarified. "But I can only imagine what would happen if she were caught by the enemy," he added, glancing back at Ariana. "Who knows what secrets she would give up under the threat of torture?"

Ariana felt a chill run down her spine as she remembered that old man standing over her, his foul breath blowing in her face, his gnarled fingertip sliding down her leg...

"Cheery thought," Erasmus grumbled. "But I think she'd do better than you under those circumstances," he added wryly. Still, he turned to Ariana, his blue eyes apologetic. "Why don't you wait outside, Ariana." But Ibicus held up one hand.

"On second thought," the Elder Runic stated, "...we're not going to be discussing anything terribly detailed. Why don't you let her stay." Erasmus shrugged.

"So where were we?" he asked.

"The Councilmen," Ibicus answered. "It's imperative that we ensure their safety and return them to the Tower. We're vulnerable as long as the government is scattered like this."

309

"It was *your* idea to separate them," Erasmus countered. Ariana got the feeling that Erasmus didn't like Ibicus very much, for some reason. Ibicus raised an eyebrow.

"And if I hadn't suggested it, they'd likely all be dead right now."

"Right," Erasmus conceded, if grudgingly. "Well, we've sent contingents of Battle-Weavers to retrieve them. Each contingent only knows the location of one Councilman, for security purposes."

"Excellent," Ibicus replied. Then he turned to Ariana, frowning at her. She lowered her gaze, feeling exposed in the small room, with the bright lights illuminating her ghastly features. "Ariana, are you alright?" he asked. "You look pale."

"I'm fine," Ariana muttered, forcing herself to smile.

"You don't look fine," Ibicus countered, sliding down from the edge of the table and taking a step toward her. "What's wrong?" Ariana took a step backward, maintaining her distance from the Elder Runic.

"I didn't sleep well," she explained, trying to sound casual. Ibicus continued to frown, staring at her for a long moment. Erasmus glanced at Ariana, and — perhaps sensing her rising discomfort — stepped in between them.

"I hope," he interjected, "...to clear the Tower, secure it, and then convene the Council. We have to develop a strategy for finding the remaining prisoners...and more importantly, for dealing with these new weapons, these white spheres." He shook his head then, his expression grim. "We're not going to be able to protect the city if we don't figure out how to neutralize these things."

"I'm afraid it may be too late for that," Ibicus replied, his tone equally grim. Erasmus frowned.

"What do you mean?" he asked. Ibicus sighed, gesturing with one hand toward one of the windows on the far wall of the room.

"The city is being overrun as we speak."

"*What?*" Erasmus exclaimed. Ibicus raised an eyebrow.

"I thought you knew," he replied. "An army of Death Weavers crossed the city borders less than a half hour ago." He gestured toward the window again. "See for yourself."

Erasmus stared at Ibicus in disbelief, then strode toward the window, placing his palms on the wall on either side and staring out of it.

310

Ibicus followed behind the Grand Runic, looking over the shorter man's shoulder.

"I don't see anything," Erasmus retorted. Ibicus put a hand on Erasmus's shoulder.

"That," he replied, "...is because the enemy is behind you."

Ibicus reached his right hand into his pocket, pulling out something that flashed a dull silver. He rammed it into Erasmus's right side, and the Grand Runic howled in surprise and pain. Ibicus pulled his hand back, and jammed the object – a dagger! – into Erasmus's side again, then again. Blood welled up rapidly from the wounds, forming expanding circles on Erasmus's white shirt. Erasmus cried out, pulling away from Ibicus and stumbling toward the table, slumping over it. His blue eyes were wide with shock.

"*No!*" Ariana shouted, bolting forward. She wove magic, creating a gravity shield around Erasmus, then grabbed a chair with one hand, tossing it at Ibicus. A multi-layered gravity shield appeared around the Elder Runic, the chair bouncing harmlessly off of it. Ibicus smiled, turning to face her. His eyes glazed over suddenly, then refocused on her.

I'm certain I killed...

Ariana blinked, realizing the voice had been in her head. She faltered for a split second.

"Now now," Ibicus stated, walking toward her slowly. The gravity shield around Erasmus vanished suddenly. "I'm certain I killed you earlier, little bird."

Ariana froze, her eyes widening. A chill ran down her spine, her guts twisting in her belly. She backed up a step, staring at Ibicus mutely, shaking her head from side to side. Ibicus chuckled, taking a step toward her.

...protector is full of...

"I'm impressed," Ibicus continued. He raised one hand to the side, and Erasmus slid off of the table, falling with a loud thump on the ground. "Your protector is full of surprises, isn't he?" He took another step toward Ariana, the table at his side imploding suddenly, a ball of shattered wood falling to the floor. Ariana saw Erasmus lying on his

311

side on the ground, gasping for air. She glanced at Ibicus, then at Erasmus; she wanted desperately to run to the Grand Runic's side, but her legs wouldn't obey her. She was literally frozen with terror.

"You!" she managed to gasp. Ibicus smiled, taking yet another step toward her. He was only a few feet away now, his gravity shields bending the light ever-so-slightly around him.

"Ibicus was a fine choice, don't you think?" he stated, pointing to his own chest. "With Erasmus tragically murdered by an escaped prisoner, who else would ascend to be the next Grand Runic?"

"You killed Ibicus," Ariana gasped. "You're just another Dead Man!"

...not dead yet...

"Oh, the good Councilman's not dead yet," Ibicus countered. "Keeping him alive did take My...personal touch," he added with another grin. He stepped up to Ariana, his gravity shields shoving her backward into the wall. Then he leaned forward, crushing Ariana between his shields and the stone wall, squeezing the air out of her lungs. He stared at her, waiting.

Ariana stared at him defiantly, gathering magic in her mind, feeling her power increasing somehow, the cauldron roaring with magic. She wove, thrusting the pattern outward. She saw a brief flash in her mind's eye, a pattern of light, and then it vanished.

A gravity shield appeared around her, then dissipated.

Ibicus chuckled, peering at Ariana. He cocked his head to the side, looking her up and down. The pressure in her chest was so intense that she couldn't have taken a breath in even if she'd needed to.

"Interesting," he murmured. Then he stepped backward, releasing her. She stayed pressed against the wall, not even bothering to take a breath in. Ibicus frowned, lifting one arm up and pointing a finger at Ariana's chest. A burst of energy shot out from his finger toward her. She gasped, trying to dodge to the side, but she was too slow; the burst struck her...then stopped. She felt a strange sensation, that cauldron of power in her mind's eye weaving magic so quickly that she couldn't follow the patterns. A multitude of gravity shields erupted around her, shoving her away from the wall. The outermost layers struck Ibicus's shields, throwing the man backward. Ibicus recovered quickly, his eyes narrowing. He stared at her for a long moment.

...shields, what a...

"Twelve shields," he murmured, staring at her. "What a coincidence."

"Leave us alone!" Ariana cried, glancing at Erasmus. The man was still breathing, but his breaths were getting shallow, his face pale and sweaty. Ibicus said nothing, a ball of fire appearing before him, then shooting out toward her. It snuffed out almost instantly.

"What an *enormous* coincidence," he repeated, shaking his head slowly at Ariana. "That's the same defense I programmed into the Dead Man's shard." He stared at Ariana curiously. "He used it on you, didn't he?"

Ariana said nothing, sidestepping closer to Erasmus, her eyes on Ibicus. She knew she couldn't defeat the man, but if she could grab Erasmus and get away...

"Fascinating that I can't access your shard," Ibicus continued, watching her as she moved. "Your benefactor must have altered it." He shook his head then, marveling at Ariana. "I would very much like to meet him."

"What are you talking about?" Ariana retorted.

"You really don't know, do you?" Ibicus murmured. "It doesn't matter...he'll be forced to show himself eventually...or let the Empire be taken. Either way, I get what I want."

"Go to hell."

"I live there," Ibicus retorted. Then he sighed. "Now, I would love to keep you," he added, "...but unfortunately I have a plan to execute, and I can't have you getting in the way. As you can imagine, I created the Dead Man's shard with a few...vulnerabilities, in case he ever lost faith."

Ariana inched closer to Erasmus, now only six or so feet from the ailing Runic. She kept her eyes on Ibicus, weaving the gravity pattern. If she could pull Erasmus out into the hallway, she could alert the guards...

She nearly slapped her forehead. Of course!

"Guards!" she screamed, leaping for the door. She thrust out the gravity pattern, a sphere surrounding Erasmus. She pulled on it with her mind, lifting Erasmus from the floor and bringing him to the door.

"Oh, don't bother," Ibicus stated. Ariana spun around, facing the Elder Runic. "They're not really Battle-Weavers, dear...they're all Mine. And one will be coming in shortly to take the credit for Erasmus's death...and yours."

The gravity shields surrounding Ariana vanished one by one, until they were no more. She felt her crystal react, felt it weave magic insanely fast, more gravity shields appearing around her. A bolt of light crackled in the air between them, striking Ibicus's shields, which wavered, then vanished. But they reappeared quickly, and despite frenzied weaving from her crystal, its every pattern was countered instantly.

Ibicus smirked, reaching into his pocket and pulling out the same dagger he'd used on Erasmus. Ariana lunged to the side, but Ibicus moved just as quickly, barring her way with his shields and shoving her up against the wall. He pressed the tip of the dagger against the inner surface of his gravity shields, shoving it through one layer, then another. The tip inched closer and closer to Ariana's neck, moving through the shields as if they weren't even there. She squirmed, pressing her palms against Ibicus's shields and pushing hard. Ibicus didn't budge, but she felt the wall behind her creak, the marble cracking under the pressure. She pushed as hard as she could, hoping to break the wall behind her with her newfound strength, but it held.

"My my, aren't you strong," Ibicus murmured. "I look forward to seeing what upgrades were performed on your shard...after I pull it from your skull."

The dagger's blade sliced through each gravity field until the edge pressed up against the right side of Ariana's neck, pushing inward slowly, the skin denting under the pressure.

Then the door burst open.

Ariana saw a man in black robes dash into the room, saw Erasmus slide across the floor with remarkable speed toward him. The black-robed man leaped over Erasmus as he slid underneath, the Grand Runic continuing until he'd slid right out of the doorway. The door slammed behind him, and the black-robed man stood facing Ibicus, pointing a lone finger at the Councilman.

"Let her go."

Ariana's eyes widened in recognition; it was Master Owens! The gray-haired Weaver stood tall before Ibicus, facing the Councilman defiantly. Ibicus turned to face Owens, but did not release Ariana.

"Thank god you're here!" Ibicus exclaimed, nodding toward Ariana, his dagger still pressed against her neck. "She murdered Erasmus, she's a traitor!"

"Hardly," Master Owens replied, his voice cool. "I said let her go, Councilman," he warned. Ibicus shook his head.

"She's not Ariana anymore, Owens," Ibicus countered. "She's been killed...see how pale she is? Those bastards turned her into one of the Chosen."

Ariana's eyes widened, and she turned to Owens, trying to speak, to defend herself. But Ibicus's gravity shields held her fast to the wall, the force so powerful that she couldn't take a breath in to speak. She saw Master Owens stare at her for a long moment, saw his resolve wavering. She wanted to scream, but could only shake her head mutely. Ibicus's blade still pressed into the side of her neck, digging deeper into her flesh.

"Why didn't you have your guards help you detain her and get Erasmus to safety?" Owens asked, lowering his hand. "It took a lot of convincing to get them to let me in."

"Erasmus and I were having a meeting," Ibicus replied. "My Battle-Weavers were instructed not to allow anyone in."

"I see," Owens stated. He relaxed then, gesturing at Ariana. "Let me take her then," he added. "We'll need to interrogate her...she may have valuable information."

"It's too dangerous," Ibicus countered. "We need to kill her now before she conjures Xanos and kills us all."

"I'm a far better warrior than you are," Owens reasoned. "If a Runic with no combat experience can handle her, I shouldn't have any problems."

Ibicus said nothing, staring at Master Owens for a long moment. Owens glanced back at the door he'd entered from.

"About your guards," he continued, gesturing toward the door. "I've trained just about every Battle-Runic in the Empire, and I swear I've never seen them before." He shook his head then, turning back to

315

Ibicus. "They certainly could've used my training," he added. "I didn't have any trouble at all killing them when they refused to let me enter."

Ibicus stared at Master Owens for a long moment, his eyes narrowing. A half-dozen gravity shields appeared around Owens, warping the light around him.

"Fine then," Ibicus sighed. "Would you rather I burn this city to the ground than have Me lead you?"

"We lead ourselves," Owens countered coldly.

"You're like ignorant children," Ibicus muttered. "You worship the Ancients? In a generation, you could surpass them!"

"We *will* surpass them," Owens stated. "On our own terms, by ourselves."

"You'll fail," Ibicus countered. "Just like every other civilization since the Ancients failed. Man requires a hand to guide them, to steer them from self-destruction. To save them from themselves."

"Let her go," Owens growled, taking a step toward Ibicus. Suddenly, Owens' gravity shields vanished, and he was thrust backward against the wall...hard. The Weaver's head struck the wall with a sickening *thump*, and he fell immediately to the floor, his head bouncing off of the granite tile. Ariana tried to bolt from where she was pinned to the wall, scrambling with her arms and legs to free herself, but it was no use. She could only watch as Owens lay unmoving on the floor.

Ibicus turned back to her, and sighed.

"What a waste to kill you all," he lamented. Then he thrust his arm leftward, the dagger slicing across the front of Ariana's neck.

* * *

Ariana cried out as Ibicus attacked, feeling the cool, sharp edge of his dagger sink into her flesh. Pain lanced through her neck, the right side of her body going suddenly numb.

And then there was an explosion.

Millions of gray particles shot upward toward the ceiling over her head, arcing against the white marble of the ceiling, then falling like snowflakes all around her. The world tilted crazily, and she felt herself falling to the right, her shoulder slamming into the floor, then her head. She lay there, her temple on the cold floor, staring at the gray particles

316

as they rained down in front of her, forming a thin layer on the glossy granite.

And then there was a flash of gold.

Ariana blinked, seeing a golden boot step into her field of view. A gauntleted hand reached down, wrapping around her shoulders. She felt another arm scoop under her knees. And then she was rising upward off of the ground.

Eyes stared down at her, brilliant blue against golden skin.

Darius, she tried to whisper, but only a faint hissing sound came out. He stared at her silently.

She felt a sudden burning in her right leg, felt it come alive again, muscles twitching uncontrollably under her skin. The burning spread to her arm, her fingers feeling as though they were on fire. Her hand clenched into a fist, spasms running through her forearm, and then the feeling passed. She felt a slight tingling sensation in her neck, and panicked, reaching her fingers up to it, feeling only smooth skin there.

"Darius," she whispered again, but this time she heard her own voice calling out, saw the bodyguard's lips smile, though his eyes did not. There was something in his expression, something she had never seen there before.

"Hey kiddo," he murmured. His voice was soft, almost tender. It didn't seem right coming from the gruff bodyguard. Ariana stared at him for a long moment, then glanced down at where Ibicus had been standing seconds ago. Only a pile of gray dust remained, the tip of a long green crystal embedded in the center of it.

"What happened?" she asked, turning back to Darius.

"You're safe now," Darius murmured, wrapping his arms around her in gentle embrace. "I won't let them hurt you anymore."

317

Chapter 23

Kyle ran down the last flight of stairs, Kalibar right behind him. They were both huffing and puffing from the exertion, having descended forty stories, stopping only to retrieve Kalibar's weapon from the archives. Darius had taken the thing, a modified crossbow of sorts, and had been leading them down the stairs when he'd inexplicably sped up, leaving Kyle and Kalibar far behind. They'd both called after the bodyguard, who had, as usual, ignored them. Kyle nearly collapsed when they finally reached the bottom of the stairwell, leaning against the wall with one hand and gasping to catch his breath before Kalibar passed him, yanking the door open.

"Go," Kalibar urged, striding out into the hallway beyond. Kyle groaned, irritated that the old Weaver, a stickler for exercise, could have outrun him. He stumbled after the man, struggling to keep up. The stairway had taken them to a hallway leading to the main lobby of the Tower; directly across from them, Kyle saw two bodies lying on the floor. Kalibar ran to them, and Kyle realized immediately that they were Battle-Weavers...and that they were most certainly dead. He heard shouting from further down the hallway, and saw a group of guards and Battle-Weavers rushing away from them, toward the lobby. They were carrying someone, a man in white robes by the looks of it; drops of his blood marked their path.

"Erasmus!" Kalibar shouted, sprinting madly after the men. Kyle followed behind the old man. They reached the lobby, following the group of guards to the center of it. The guards lowered the white-robed man to the ground gently, and Kyle caught a glimpse of the man's face; it was indeed Erasmus, but he was clearly unconscious, and extraordinarily pale. His clothes were soaked in wet redness; Kyle could only assume it was blood.

The guards parted before Kalibar, allowing the Grand Weaver to reach Erasmus's side. Kalibar dropped to his knees beside his old friend, panic in his eyes.

"Erasmus!" he cried. Then he glanced up at one of the guards. "What's happened?" he demanded. "Is he alive?"

"Barely," one of the guards answered. Indeed, the Grand Runic was breathing, his chest rising and falling rapidly but shallowly. Kyle felt fear grip his innards; Erasmus was alive, but he wouldn't be for long.

"Get a doctor here, now!" Kalibar ordered, pointing directly at one of the guards. The man nodded, dashing off to complete his task. Then Kalibar turned to Kyle. "Give me your magic," he demanded, his voice stern. "All of you," he added, turning toward the Battle-Weavers scattered among the guards. Kyle complied, watching as lines of blue magic shot toward Kalibar from all directions. Kalibar himself turned to face Erasmus; the Grand Runic's robes split in the middle, the fabric tearing under Kalibar's power, exposing the flesh underneath. Kyle immediately spotted Erasmus's injuries; three stab wounds on the side of his chest, just below the right armpit.

Kalibar bent over Erasmus so that his ear was near his chest, then tapped Erasmus's right chest with two fingers. Then he moved to squat by Erasmus's feet, staring at Erasmus's chest as it rose and fell. He glanced upward at one of the guards nearby, pointing directly at the man.

"Get me a table long enough to hold a man," he ordered. Kalibar turned to another guard. "You, get me a small tube," he commanded. He turned to a third guard, asking for balm-tree sap. All three ran off, and less than a minute later, a table was brought in. Kalibar ordered Erasmus lifted onto the table, then asked one of the guards for a blade, and was handed a small knife. To Kyle's utter astonishment, Kalibar placed the blade on the side of Erasmus's chest over one of the puncture wounds, cutting into the flesh there to elongate the wound. Then he spread the skin edges apart with the fingers of his left hand, exposing the fat and muscle. Kalibar cut into the muscle between Erasmus's ribs, then reached into the incision with one finger, twisting his wrist and pressing hard. Kyle heard a sudden pop, followed by a hissing sound as air escaped from Erasmus's chest. The Grand Runic's color improved almost immediately, his flesh turning from dusky to pink, and he groaned, thrashing about on the table. Kalibar ordered the guards to hold Erasmus's arms and legs, while another pressed the man's pelvis to the table.

A guard handed Kalibar a small, long metallic tube, no greater in diameter than a man's thumb, and Kalibar slipped this into the incision he'd made. Kyle saw a blue, disc-shaped gravity field appear at the end of the tube, and air began whooshing out of the tube, followed by clumps of maroon clots. After a few moments, nothing more came out, and Kalibar took a jar of balm-tree sap, slathering it on the incision on either side of the tube. The skin began pulling together almost immediately, and Kalibar slathered the sap onto the base of the tube, holding it in place.

A man in a red uniform and black pants – the uniform of a field surgeon, Kyle knew – appeared, the crowd of guards parting for him. The man glanced at Kalibar, then at Erasmus, his eyebrows rising in surprise. Kalibar turned to the surgeon, his expression grave.

"He's been stabbed three times in the chest," he stated, pointing to the wounds. "The lung was collapsed; I released the pressure from air trapped around his lung and placed this chest tube."

"I see," the surgeon replied, regarding Kalibar's handiwork. "Well done, Grand Weaver," he added. Then he hesitated. "Where did you learn to do that?"

"I saw a few such surgeries performed in battle," Kalibar answered. "Though I never had the opportunity to perform one myself until now." The surgeon and the guards all stared at Kalibar – as did Kyle – amazed at the Grand Weaver's courage...and skill.

"We'll get him to the operating suite," the surgeon promised. Within moments, Erasmus was lifted from the table onto a levitating gurney, and whisked away.

Kalibar asked for a pot, creating a stream of water to splash on his hands, rinsing the blood from them. Kyle saw the crowd part suddenly,

320

and Ariana strode in, walking beside Master Owens. Kyle whooped with delight, running up to Ariana and wrapping his arms around her. He picked her up, twirling her about, and then put her down.

"You're alive!" he blurted out, his spirit soaring. Ariana gave him a subdued smile, and Kyle winced, realizing his poor choice of words. But Ariana put a cold hand on his shoulder, squeezing it gently.

"I'm okay," she corrected. Then Kalibar embraced her, holding her tightly for a moment and whispering something into her ear. He pushed her gently away then, turning to Master Owens. The man looked dazed, the hair on the back of his head matted with blood.

"What happened?" Kalibar asked. Owens gestured to Ariana, who brought one hand forward, opening her fingers to reveal a long, tapered green crystal.

"They turned Ibicus with this," she explained. "He tried to kill Erasmus and Owens."

"And Ariana," Owens interjected, rubbing the back of his head gingerly.

"Ibicus is dead?" Kalibar pressed. Ariana nodded. "Damn," Kalibar swore. "If he'd killed Erasmus, he'd have been next in line for Grand Runic...and no one would have been the wiser." He shook his head then, turning to stare down the hallway that Erasmus had been carried off to. "Hang in there, old friend," he murmured.

"Luckily your bodyguard reached us in time," Owens stated. "Ariana tells me he used this to kill Ibicus," he added, holding up a crossbow. It was Kalibar's weapon; a standard crossbow, except there was a metallic, rune-inscribed rod welded in where the bolts would have gone. Owens handed it to Kalibar.

"It killed a Chosen?" Kalibar asked. Owens nodded. Kalibar gave a weary smile. "That's the best news I've heard all day." He frowned then. "Where *is* Darius?"

"He left," Ariana answered, rubbing the side of her neck absently. When Kalibar lifted an eyebrow, she shrugged. "He said he needed to take care of something."

"Something more important than doing his job?" Kalibar retorted. "We've got a war out there," he added, gesturing toward the double doors of the lobby. He turned to one of the Battle-Weavers surrounding them. "You...I need High Weaver Urson here *now*. Stridon is under

321

attack; the Southwest Quarter is in flames. We need to identify the threat and issue a counterattack." The Battle-Weaver bowed, then vanished into the crowd.

"To be fair, Darius *did* save us," Owens stated gently. "And Erasmus, by extension. Your bodyguard has more than his fair share of faults," he added, "But bad judgment isn't one of them."

"Communication *is*," Kalibar countered. But he sighed, visibly deflating. "We'll do without him. In the meantime, we need a secure base of operations, and we need to establish lines of communication with our militia." He glanced down at the crossbow in his hands. "And we need to produce as many of these as possible."

"I'll get Erasmus's Runics on it," Owens promised.

"Thank you," Kalibar replied. He ran a hand through his hair, taking a deep breath in, then letting it out slowly. He looked older suddenly, almost haggard. "With Erasmus critically injured and the Council scattered, I *am* the government." He glanced about the lobby, at the dozens of men milling about. "If I fail," he stated, his voice almost too quiet to hear, "...the Empire will fall."

* * *

Kyle sighed, sitting down on one of the many chairs that had been brought to the lobby from other rooms in the Tower. The lobby had been rapidly converted into Kalibar's base of operations, and it hadn't taken long for High Weaver Urson to arrive with a few dozen more Battle-Weavers. Kyle had never seen Urson before, and had previously imagined him to be an old, grizzled man, but he was far from it. Young, perhaps in his late thirties, with long blond hair and green eyes, he was a striking figure in his black and silver suit of armor, a long black cloak spilling down from his shoulders. He walked and spoke with an almost cocky confidence, no doubt borne of his repeated successes on the battlefield. Urson and Kalibar had spoken for quite some time, but what they'd discussed was still a mystery to Kyle. Kyle was utterly exhausted, which was no surprise; he'd woken up yesterday morning in one of the Dead Man's carriages, and now it was after midnight. Not to mention that he'd spent a few hours on Antara, when only a third of that time had passed here on Doma. He'd had a heck of a day!

Kyle glanced to his right, where Ariana was sitting beside him. Despite everything that had happened to her, she didn't look tired in the least. She'd spent most of the last half-hour staring off into space, likely still processing everything that had happened to her. He couldn't imagine what it must feel like to be in her position. He wanted to talk to her about it, to understand what she was going through, but he was too scared that bringing it up would hurt her. Still, the silence between them was becoming increasingly unbearable, and eventually he had to break it.

"Hey," he said, tapping Ariana on the shoulder. She snapped out of her reverie, turning to look at him questioningly. Her big brown eyes were startlingly beautiful against her stark white skin; he suddenly felt bashful to look at her.

"Hi," she mumbled back, managing a weak smile.

"You okay?"

"No," Ariana admitted. "You?"

"I'm okay," he replied. "I'm just worried about you."

"I'll be okay," she said, staring down at her lap. "I just need time to think, that's all." She paused for a moment, then shook her head. "It's like this isn't real," she added. "Like this is just a dream, and any moment now I'm going to wake up."

"Yeah," Kyle agreed. He'd often felt the same way about his entire journey on Doma...that it had to be a dream. That any moment, he'd wake up on Earth, in his room, right where he'd been the night he'd been taken by Ampir. "I'm sorry," he added, giving her a sidelong glance.

"For what?"

"I don't know," Kyle answered. "For what happened to you, I guess."

"It's not your fault," she countered, putting a cold hand on his thigh. "It's not anyone's fault."

"Yeah," Kyle mumbled. He thought of Darius then, of how he'd spent so much time with the man on Antara, leisurely talking while Ariana had been attacked...and killed. If Darius had never taken Kyle to Antara, if he had been in the Tower when Ariana had been attacked, she might never have died. Darius had been wrong about his runes being able to beat Xanos, and Ariana had paid dearly for that mistake.

Her death *was* someone's fault.

"Don't worry," Ariana stated, patting Kyle on the thigh. He glanced at her, seeing her staring back at him. Her gaze was almost hypnotic, and it quelled his sudden anger at Darius. "I'll be okay, I think."

"I can't believe you're okay after that fall," Kyle said. And it was true; despite her amazing strength, her fall down forty stories of riser shaft should have killed her. Or – seeing as she was already dead – at least *maimed* her. Ariana shrugged.

"I'm not sure what happened," she admitted. Then she hesitated for a moment. "The man who...killed me, he said I had runes on my bones," she added. "After I fell down the riser shaft, I broke my leg, but it healed itself somehow. I think it was the runes."

"Huh?" Kyle asked. Then he spotted Kalibar stepping away from High Weaver Urson and walking toward them. The Grand Weaver looked utterly exhausted.

"I'll tell you about it later," Ariana promised, standing up as Kalibar walked up to them. Kyle stood as well. Kalibar stopped before them, gazing at Kyle with a critical eye. Kyle noticed that the Grand Weaver had strapped his modified crossbow – the weapon that had killed Ibicus – to his back.

"You need to get some sleep," Kalibar observed. He flagged down a guard, gesturing at Kyle. "Please escort Kyle to the temporary sleeping chambers," he stated. The many conference rooms and banquet halls on the first floor of the Tower had been converted into sleeping quarters and mess halls. The guard saluted Kalibar briskly, then gestured for Kyle to follow him. Kalibar turned to Ariana.

"You too," he stated. But Ariana shook her head.

"I'm not tired."

"Then at least watch over Kyle," Kalibar insisted, putting a hand on Ariana's slender shoulder. "I'll feel better with you there beside him." Ariana nodded, following Kyle and their chaperone out of the lobby and into one of the hallways. After a few turns, they arrived in a small room with two guards posted outside. Inside of the room, there were rows of cots lying on the floor, two rows of six. None of the cots were in use, so Kyle chose one farthest from the door. Ariana chose a cot beside him, and they both sat down, pulling off their shoes, then lying down.

"I wonder what's going on," Kyle murmured. He heard Ariana stir, saw her turn over in her cot to face him.

"The Southwest Quarter is under attack," she replied. "They think it's the rest of the escaped prisoners. They're setting buildings on fire." Kyle frowned.

"How do you know that?" he asked. She'd been sitting right next to him the whole time, after all.

"I heard them," she answered. He stared incredulously at her; they'd been a good fifty feet away from Kalibar and Urson when the two men had been talking, and the lobby had been extremely noisy. He hadn't been able to hear a thing. She frowned. "You couldn't hear them?"

"Not at all," Kyle confirmed. Ariana touched her earlobe with one finger absently, then lowered her hand.

"I guess my hearing is better now."

"What else did you hear?" Kyle pressed.

"There's more of those Void spheres," she answered. "The prisoners let them loose in the city. They've evacuated the area, but the spheres are coming this way."

"Now?" Kyle asked, suddenly nervous about going to sleep.

"Not for a while," Ariana clarified. "Urson's scouts say they're moving slowly, draining the city of magic."

"Great," Kyle grumbled. "Anything else?"

"Councilman Goran came back," Ariana replied. Kyle gave her a sour look; he hated the man, or at least the way he treated Kalibar. Ariana gave Kyle a sad smile. "It's okay," she added. "He can't bother Kalibar anymore."

"Why's that?"

"Kalibar claimed the Right of Dictatorship," Ariana explained. Kyle's eyes widened; he'd heard of the old law that allowed Kalibar and Erasmus to take complete control of the military away from the Council, from Erasmus during one of his typical tirades against Goran. If Kalibar had claimed the Right of Dictatorship, there was no way the pesky Councilman could get in his way anymore.

"Finally!" Kyle exclaimed. But Ariana didn't look pleased.

"It's not a good thing," she countered.

"Why?"

"It means they might execute him after his term," she whispered. Kyle felt a chill run through him, and he stared at Ariana for a long moment, hoping she was joking. But it was clear that she was dead serious. He rolled onto his back, staring up at the ceiling, feeling despair come over him. They couldn't execute Kalibar! He was the best Grand Weaver they'd ever had, after all...and their greatest war hero. The people of the Empire would never let the Council do something like that to him...would they?

"We've got six years," Ariana murmured. Kyle felt something cold grab his hand and squeeze it; he pulled away at first, then realized it was her hand.

"Sorry," he whispered. "I didn't realize..." But Ariana pulled her hand away. Kyle stretched his arm out, searching for her hand, and found her arm instead. He tried to pull it toward himself, but he might as well have been yanking on a statue. "Come on," he urged, yanking anyway. She paused, then yielded. He slid his hand down her arm, finding her hand, and squeezed it.

"You don't have to pretend to want to," she protested. But she didn't pull away. Kyle smiled, squeezing her hand again. She looked lovely in the darkness, and he was suddenly struck with an overwhelming affection for her.

"You're still beautiful," he countered, then felt a bolt of terror run through him. He'd never said anything like that to a girl before – he'd never had the guts to. But Ariana smiled, turning on her side to get closer to him. She stared at him for a long moment with those hypnotic eyes, and Kyle had the sudden insane urge to kiss her.

"Really?" she asked. "You think I'm beautiful?" Kyle nodded, emboldened by her smile, and squeezed her hand again.

"Really."

"Thanks," Ariana whispered back. She slid forward then, letting go of his hand and wrapping her arms about him, hugging him...hard. Kyle gasped, his ribs threatening to crack under her vise-like grip. Ariana pulled back, putting a hand to her mouth.

"Sorry!"

"Try again," he offered. She paused, then leaned in, hugging him gently. Her arms were cold, but he didn't mind. He hugged her back, savoring the moment. Eventually she pulled away.

326

"Thanks," she whispered. She stared at him for a moment — making him feel all sorts of strange and wonderful things — and then patted him on the shoulder. "You're tired," she observed. "You should get some sleep."

"Aren't you tired?" Kyle asked. Ariana shook her head.

"No," she answered. "I'm not tired at all." Then she looked worried. "I don't know if I need sleep anymore," she added. The thought seemed to bother her greatly, and she turned onto her back, covering her mouth with one hand, staring up at the ceiling.

"It's okay," Kyle said, giving her a wink. "I feel better with a brave Weaver watching over me." That got a smile out of her.

"I won't let anyone hurt my poor little tinkerer," she promised.

"Does that include you?" Kyle pressed, raising one eyebrow. Ariana smirked.

"No promises," she replied. "Now get some sleep."

Kyle complied, already feeling his eyelids getting heavy. He closed his eyes, visions of floating islands flashing in his mind's eye, of tiny fish blinking to and fro in a giant aquarium. It wasn't long before sleep claimed him, bringing a much-needed end to what had literally — and figuratively — been the longest day of his life.

Chapter 24

Dark clouds hover high above the ruins of Stridon, rain pouring down on the glowing embers of shattered buildings. The Behemoth towers over the wreckage, its diamond-shaped eye glowing a bright, sickly green in the darkness of the night. Its eye flashes, another beam of deadly light shooting outward toward a few untouched buildings nearby, burning through the stone with terrifying ease. The rain falls on the red-hot rubble, stream rising into the air around the Behemoth's massive legs.

Ampir stands on the slick roof of Stridon Penitentiary, watching the Behemoth as its beam fades, its domed head turning to find another target. The muscles in his broken shoulder spasm, and he grits his teeth, taking short, quick breaths.

Focus.

With a thought, he rises into the air above the roof, then accelerates forward. The city passes by underneath him, a seemingly endless landscape of destruction. Huge silver airships fly far above, just below the dark clouds. Smaller ships fly closer to the ground, pulses of green light firing from their turrets, destroying any buildings that still stand. Ampir spots a group of people running down the street away from one of the smaller ships. Survivors trying to flee the city.

They're hunting everyone down, he realizes. *And destroying every building.*

This isn't a war...it's an extermination.

Ampir veers off after the small airship hunting the fleeing civilians, picking up speed rapidly. He catches up with the ship easily, hanging back a hundred feet or so, then centering it within his visor's field of view. With a thought, he activates a few runes on the visor.

A large gravity shield appears directly below the airship, yanking it downward. It flies full-speed into the ground, shattering in a cloud of dust and debris, well clear of the fleeing citizens.

Ampir shoots past the wreckage, seeing more small airships flying over the city. He looks up, spotting dozens more of them coming out of one of the huge airships above, spilling out of docking bays on the huge airship's sides.

He ignores the smaller airships, activating another set of runes; he feels a vibration in his skull, the telltale sign of the invisibility field being activated around him. While useless against a Weaver, the field might fool the smaller airships; he flies upward toward the huge airship, accelerating quickly until he is only a few hundred feet below it. The smaller airships ignore him, diving toward the city, then leveling out a few dozen feet above the streets.

He faces the huge airship above, spotting the telltale blue gravity shield surrounding the ship's hull, covering it like a second skin. To anyone else, its shield would be nearly impenetrable.

Ampir flies up to the airship's right flank, stopping a foot away from its metallic hull. The runes on his right gauntlet glow bright blue; he punches his fist *through* the ship's gravity shield, his armor automatically nullifying its effects. He tears through the metallic hull, ripping a large hole in it with his good arm, then squeezes through to the ship's interior.

He finds himself standing in a long hallway.

The interior of the ship is bare-bones, with grated metal floors and ceilings, and walls made of thick white fabric pulled across thick metal beams...nothing at all like the sleek exterior. It was made quickly, and cheaply...evidence of the enemy's limited resources. Sabin had made the most of what little he'd had.

Ampir deactivates his invisibility field, then shoves his fist through the fabric wall in front of him, ripping a hole in it and stepping through. He finds himself in another long hallway. Two men are walking toward him, and freeze, their eyes widening as they spot him.

329

"Hi," Ampir greets.

He raises his right hand, a beam of white light bursting from it. The beam takes the men's heads clean off, burning a hole in the wall beyond. Both men slump to the floor lifelessly, nothing left of their heads but the blackened stumps of their necks.

Ampir walks up to another wall on the opposite side of the hallway, ripping through it and stepping through. This time he finds himself in a massive chamber dropping several stories down. Row after row of small airships are docked here...the same kind as the ones he'd seen hunting the civilians below earlier. He scans them quickly; he can destroy them all one-by-one, or...

He spots a bright blue glow on the opposite side of the huge chamber, coming from behind another white fabric wall.

Magic!

He activates his armor, flying above the grated metal floor, passing between rows of small airships, making his way toward the opposite end of the chamber. He reaches the fabric wall on the other end, ripping through it and stepping into the room beyond.

The room is twenty feet squared, the floors and walls similar to the hallways he'd just passed through. In the center of the room, however, is a truly massive crystal. Over ten feet high and half as wide, the uncut, unpolished crystal stands on a metallic base. Countless wires connect to that base, extending in all directions across the floor, some of them climbing the metal beams on the walls. The crystal glows a bright blue, evidence of the enormous amount of magic stored within. This must be the main power source for the massive ship, he realizes.

"Hey!"

Two black-robed Weavers step out from behind the crystal, gravity shields appearing around them. One of them points a staff at Ampir, a bolt of electricity shooting out from it and slamming into him. His armor deflects the attack effortlessly, automatically generating a counterattack. The Weaver's shields vanish, two gravity fields appearing around him...one from the waist up, the other from the waist down. The gravity fields pull in opposite directions violently.

The Weaver splits in half at the waist, his intestines spilling out onto the floor.

330

The other Weaver stumbles backward, staring at his comrade in horror.

"No," he begs, raising his arms up. "I..."

Ampir leaps toward the Weaver, slamming his gauntleted fist through the man's gravity shields and into his face. Bones crumple with the impact, the Weaver flying backward and slamming into one of the metallic support beams behind him. He falls to the floor, his limbs twitching once, then going still.

Ampir ignores the fallen Weavers, stepping over the wires on the floor and up to the massive crystal in the center of the room. He stares at its unpolished surface, realizing that it's a diamond. A single, massive diamond, larger than any he's ever seen. It could only have come from one of the legendary mines in the land far west of Stridon, across the ocean.

Orja.

He places a hand on the surface of the crystal, then leans in, pressing his forehead against the cool surface and *pulling.*

Sheer power gushes into his mind's eye, filling it instantly. He gasps, struggling to maintain his focus, redirecting the energy to his armor. Its systems come back online within seconds. Ventilation, gravity nullification, shielding, temperature controls, weapon systems, strength modulation...all awaken almost instantly in the wake of the ocean of magic coursing into him.

He stands there, his forehead slumped against the crystal's cool surface, draining its power until his armor and his mind are sated. Pushing himself away, he cocks his right fist back and slams it into the crystal. The giant diamond shatters in a burst of blue light, fragments of crystal scattering across the floor and falling between the holes in the metal grates. The lights in the room wink out almost instantly, plunging the ship into darkness.

A few seconds later, Ampir feels the floor start to tip to one side as the ship's gravity fields vanish, entering it into free-fall.

He flies upward into the air, ignoring the metal beams on the ceiling in his path. His fully-powered armor plows through the thick metal as if it were paper; he continues upward, bursting through one floor after another, until he suddenly he finds himself outside of it, seeing

331

thick, angry clouds above. Looking down, he sees the massive airship rotating slowly as it plummets toward the earth.

A minute later, it slams into the ground at terminal velocity, obliterating an entire city block below.

Ampir stares at the wreckage, then gazes across the Great River, at the other half of the city. Far in the distance, the Behemoth's giant head turns to face the fallen airship. Then its head tilts upward, its glowing eye focusing on *him*.

That's right, he mutters silently. *Come get me.*

He descends toward the city far below, accelerating forward at the same time, aiming for the Behemoth. Ahead, the Great River flows into the ocean, its black waters filled with debris. Down he soars, leveling out a few dozen feet above the ruins of the once-great city. The shore of the Great River passes rapidly beneath him, water spraying upward behind him with the violence of his passage. Miles ahead, the Behemoth's eye continues to track him.

Then it flashes.

With a thought, Ampir triggers his armor, feeling the fabric of spacetime bend around him, teleporting him thirty feet to the right. The Behemoth's deadly green beam shoots outward, passing through where he'd been only seconds ago. He ignores the beam, accelerating forward, now over halfway across the river. Activating his visor, he magnifies the image of the Behemoth, studying it quickly. Its domed head is covered in black metallic plates, not a shred of blue light leaking from it. Only one material could insulate against magic so completely...the same material that coated Ampir's armor...and Torum's uniform. A perfect insulator for magic...perfect for hiding the Behemoth's runes. There is no way for Ampir to know its capabilities...not without fighting it.

Very clever Sabin, Ampir muses.

Ampir activates runes on his visor, the colors shifting as it goes through the electromagnetic spectrum. No electromagnetic signals are coming to or from the giant machine...and no magic signals either. Which means the Behemoth isn't being controlled remotely. And artificial intelligence is too sophisticated even for Sabin. It has to be controlled by someone *inside* of it.

The Behemoth reorients on Ampir, its eye flashing a second time. Ampir bursts upward, the beam shooting outward toward him, missing him by only a few feet. The air around him ripples, superheated by the deadly ray, but with his armor fully charged, Ampir feels nothing.

He reaches the opposite shore of the river, flying over more ruins, only a quarter-mile from the monstrous war machine now. Though he cannot know its capabilities, Ampir feels no fear. His armor, even with the runes on his left arm crushed, is far more advanced than any other modern runic technology. With the ability to see magic since birth, Ampir has advanced beyond any other Weaver or Runic. His armor's exterior runes are merely a facade, randomly activating dozens of weak patterns when triggered, patterns that serve to confuse nearby enemies. The interior runes are effectively invisible...and incredibly complicated.

He slows as he reaches the Behemoth, stopping to hover in mid-air less than a hundred feet from its enormous green eye. Though the runes on its head are shielded, those within its eye are not. He studies them quickly.

The eye flashes.

Ampir doesn't move this time; the Behemoth's deadly beam shoots outward, engulfing him instantly. He feels his armor react, complex gravity fields appearing around him. The beam reflects off of Ampir, slamming into the Behemoth's head just above its eye...and deflects harmlessly off of its own gravity shields...just as he predicted. Ampir smirks; he'd expected more from Sabin.

Then Ampir's gravity shields vanish, nullified by a gravity field of the exact shape and opposite polarity created by the Behemoth. His armor reacts instantly, creating another, slightly different set of shields. These too vanish abruptly, the Behemoth automatically counterattacking...but more slowly than Ampir's armor. Another set of shields appears around Ampir, protecting him from the deadly beam. As huge as the Behemoth is, its runes are farther away from each other, making its response times more sluggish.

Again, as predicted.

At the same time, Ampir's armor senses the Behemoth's nearby gravity shields, nullifying them as well. The Behemoth's beam slams into its own head, the black metal glowing red-hot.

The ray of light stops abruptly, the eye going dark. The red-hot metal on its domed head fades to black, completely unharmed.

Ampir smirks, mildly impressed. Sabin had anticipated such a counterattack, and constructed his creation to be immune to its own weapon. Not that it matters; the exercise had simply been a test. If his armor alone can successfully overwhelm the Behemoth's defenses, then he has little to fear. All he has to do is strike; his armor will take care of the rest.

He circles around the Behemoth then, flying faster than its head can rotate. He moves in closer, facing the back of its head, seeing the blue gravity shield glowing around it...just like the airship earlier. He descends, his boots striking the metallic plate below, going right through the gravity shields. Bolts of electricity shoot outward from the plate, striking Ampir's shields. He ignores the assault, kneeling down. He raises his right fist into the air, then brings it down at the domed head.

The Behemoth's giant fingers come at Ampir from behind, closing around him and pulling him from its head before his fist can strike.

With a thought, Ampir bursts upward out of the Behemoth's grasp, flying clear of it. He looks down at the giant hand, spotting the huge white hemisphere embedded in its palm. Rays of brilliant blue light are flowing into it.

Ampir frowns, staring down at his left arm, realizing that the light is coming from *him*...from cracks in the black insulation where his arm had been crushed. He feels his armor's power draining rapidly, entire systems shutting down.

Shit!

A powerful force grabs Ampir, pulling him back toward the Behemoth's head. A shrill shrieking sound pierces his ears, a powerful gust of wind shooting past him as he slams into one of the metallic plates, sucked flat against its surface.

Then all sound stops.

Ampir feels a horrendous pain lance through his ears, and he cries out, tears streaming down his face. He tries to take a breath in, but can't...the air has been taken away. The Behemoth has created a complete vacuum around him, and managed to nullify all of his shields. If

Ampir's armor had been fully powered, such an attack would never have succeeded.

He gasps for air that doesn't exist, pain shooting through the left side of his chest, his left shoulder in agony.

Ampir closes his eyes, pushing past the pain. The Behemoth had to be controlled by someone...someone *inside* of it. The head was the most likely location, but the body was another possibility; if he gets it wrong, he will teleport into solid matter, and that will prove to be a fatal mistake.

He makes the decision instantly, draining magic from his armor and taking several strands at once, weaving them into a complex knot in the center of his mind's eye. He throws it at the Behemoth's head.

A blast of air heralds the arrival of the rift, the fabric of the universe ripping as a hole appears between Ampir and the Behemoth. He falls through the spacetime rift, landing on his left side on an unforgiving metal floor below.

He screams.

Footsteps approach, five cloaked men surrounding him, each protected by multilayered gravity shields. Their eyes are wide open, their mouths agape.

Ampir grits his teeth against the pain, his vision blurred with tears. He rolls onto his back, the movement sending another wave of pain through his left side. He finds himself in a large, spherical room, its translucent walls giving a panoramic view of the city ruins below. He is inside of the Behemoth's head, he realizes...he'd chosen correctly.

One of the Weavers points his hand at Ampir, a ball of pure white light growing at his palm. Ampir streams magic to his armor frantically, activating a few of its emptied runes.

The room around him *explodes*.

Ampir shields his eyes with his right arm, his armor protecting him from the sudden blast. The light fades, and he rolls onto his good side, pushing himself up from the floor slowly. He rises to his feet, looking around.

Remains of the Weavers litter the floor, blood staining the translucent walls.

He grimaces, clutching his left side, his breath coming in shallow gasps. Each breath feels like someone is stabbing him. Glancing around the large circular room, he sees the remains of numerous control panels scattered across the floor. Blue light leaks from holes in the floor, where wires conducting magic from the Behemoth's central power supply had been severed. He kneels down before one of these, lowering his forehead to it. His armor recharges rapidly, the Behemoth's power more than enough to fill its runes.

Then Ampir stands, staring through the magically translucent inner walls of the Behemoth's domed head, at the city beyond. Small airships fly over the city, the larger airships hovering far above. The city is in ruins...beyond hope. But there are many other major cities in the Empire that might not be...innocent people that don't deserve to die for the sins of their leaders. That don't deserve to die because of what *he's* done.

Ampir takes a deep breath in, ignoring the pain it causes his ribs. With a thought, he rises to his feet, staring at the translucent wall in front of him. The base of the Behemoth's diamond-shaped eye is visible on the inner wall of the chamber, glowing green against the black metal plates of its skull. It is as much a symbol as anything else, he knows. A message to the Empire from one of its greatest inventors.

Ampir walks up to the giant eye, staring at it.

It is time, he knows, for his penance. But when he is done, he will have his revenge.

Ampir stares at the diamond-shaped eye for a moment longer, then cocks his right fist back, its runes glowing bright blue.

* * *

"Wake up!"

Kyle's eyes snapped open, and he bolted upright, glancing about the dark room. It took him a moment to remember where he was; then he saw Ariana standing over him, shaking his shoulder. He groaned, rubbing his eyes tiredly. He must not have been asleep for very long, given how exhausted he felt.

"Come on," Ariana urged, shaking him harder. Kyle groaned again, then slowly rose to his feet. Ariana glanced at the door, then back at Kyle, her expression worried.

"What's wrong?" Kyle asked with a yawn.

"I'm...I don't know for sure," she answered. "I'm...hearing things."
Kyle frowned, straining his ears, but he heard nothing.

"Right now?" he pressed. "I don't hear anything."

"No, not with my ears," Ariana clarified. She reached a hand up to
her forehead, rubbing it gently. "I...think I heard it in my *mind.*"

"What are you hearing?"

"Just fragments of things," she replied. "Thoughts, I think. I felt
the same thing when Ibicus was near me. When he was being controlled by Sabin."

"Wait, who?" Kyle pressed.

"Sabin," Ariana repeated. Then her eyes widened. "*That* was his
name!" she gasped.

"Who?" Kyle repeated.

"The old guy that attacked me," Ariana explained. "He said his
name was Sabin. He spoke to me through Ibicus earlier."

"Wait, don't you mean Xanos?" Kyle asked. "Xanos controls the
Chosen," he added. But Ariana shook her head.

"I don't think so," she replied. "Not this time, anyway. It was definitely Sabin."

"Okay..." Kyle mumbled, rubbing his eyes again and stifling a yawn.

"The point is," Ariana explained, "...I think there's a Chosen
nearby...that's why I'm hearing these thoughts again."

"Wait, where?" Kyle asked, glancing about the room. Fear gripped
him. "Is it close?"

"I don't know," she admitted. "But we need to warn Kalibar. Come
on," she urged, pulling him up to the door. She grabbed the handle,
twisting it and pulling the door open. Bright light seared Kyle's eyes,
making them ache for a moment. He covered his eyes with his hands,
squinting against the glare, his eyes adjusting quickly. Ariana didn't so
much as blink, pulling Kyle into the hallway. The two guards standing
on either side of the door turned toward Ariana, glancing at her questioningly. She smiled sweetly at one of them.

"I need to speak with my father."

"Grand Weaver Kalibar is in the lobby with Councilman Goran,"
the guard informed, pointing down the hallway. Ariana nodded, pulling Kyle down the hallway with her. They passed a wall of Battle-
Weavers guarding the lobby, who parted to let them through. Kyle saw

337

Kalibar standing in the center of the lobby, talking with Goran. The Councilman did not look happy.

"...is forbidden by one of our most sacred laws," Goran was arguing, pointing one finger at Kalibar. "You don't have the authority to do this!"

"The *law* was intended to prevent traitorous generals from overthrowing the government," Kalibar shot back coldly. "There won't *be* an Empire if we don't hold Stridon."

"There are other cities in the Empire," Goran countered, lowering his finger. "Spero is only three days' ride from here. Instead of allowing the military into Stridon, we should have them escort us to Spero and fortify our position there."

"To what advantage?" Kalibar asked. "Stridon is the most heavily fortified city in the Empire. Spero offers us nothing."

"It offers us *time*," Goran retorted. "In case you didn't notice," he added acidly, gesturing at the lobby around them, "...the Council is fragmented, our Grand Runic is critically wounded, and the streets are filled with escaped prisoners. We barely have communication with your Grand Weavers, much less the military!"

"True," Kalibar acknowledged. Goran frowned, taken aback. Kalibar nodded, rubbing his chin. "It would give us time to organize, but it would also be risky. Xanos will expect that if we evacuated, it would be to the nearest major city. With their advanced weaponry, they could rip through any military escort we managed to coordinate, effectively removing the entire upper government of the Empire. Then, as with Ibicus, they could make puppets of any successors, and no one would be the wiser. Xanos would own the Empire."

"We could set a diversion, or go to an alternative city," Goran countered.

"It's an option," Kalibar agreed. "But if Stridon falls, it will be a blow against morale for the entire Empire." He gestured at the lobby around them. "This Tower is a symbol...when the first one fell two thousand years ago, the rest of the Empire crumbled, though many cities remained unscathed." He shook his head then. "We know that the Empire is an *idea*, Goran. To us, the buildings are just buildings. But to the people, this Tower *is* the Empire."

"And if we stay, and Stridon falls anyway?" Goran pressed. "Then we die, the Tower falls, and the Empire is lost anyway. At least if we evacuate, we have a *chance*."

"It's my decision," Kalibar countered. "The Right of Dictatorship gives me the authority. I've already ordered a legion to enter the city."

Kalibar spotted Ariana and Kyle walking toward them then, and held up one hand.

"Not now, Ariana."

Ariana hesitated, glancing back at Kyle.

"We really need to talk to you," Kyle told Kalibar, glancing at Goran apologetically. That did little to mollify the sour Councilman.

"We're having a meeting," he snapped at them, turning back to Kalibar. "We don't have time for your children, Kalibar."

"Kalibar..." Ariana stated earnestly, glancing at her adoptive father. Kalibar frowned, then gestured for Ariana to come closer. Goran rolled his eyes, throwing up his hands and turning away from them both.

"What is it, honey?" Kalibar asked. Ariana leaned in and whispered into Kalibar's ear. Kalibar stooped over to listen; she spoke for a long time, Kalibar saying nothing, his expression carefully controlled. Then she finished, and he stood up straight, turning back to Goran and putting a hand on the man's shoulder.

"We have a problem," he warned.

Then the lights went out.

Kyle gasped, crouching low instinctively, pulling Ariana down with him. A few dozen light orbs appeared high in the air around them, bathing the lobby in pale white glow.

Then there was a *boom*.

Kyle spun around to face the lobby doors, saw Battle-Weavers backing away from them. Another *boom* echoed powerfully through the massive lobby, the huge double-doors rattling on their hinges. One of the Battle-Weavers – High Weaver Urson – turned to the Weavers around Kalibar and Goran.

"Evacuate the Grand Weaver and Councilman Goran!" he shouted, waving them away from the lobby doors. The Weavers complied, pulling Kalibar and Goran backward. Kalibar resisted, turning to Urson.

"It's a Chosen!" he bellowed. "We need to evacuate everyone!"

"You first," Urson countered, pushing Kalibar back. "We'll delay them."

"What about Erasmus?" Kalibar pressed.

"We'll get him out," Urson promised. Kalibar nodded, letting himself be pulled back by his Battle-Weavers. Kyle felt hands on his shoulders, and was pulled back with Kalibar and Goran, Ariana at his side. Before Kyle knew it, they were surrounded by a ring of Battle-Weavers, a multi-layered blue hemisphere appearing around them all. They moved at a rapid but steady pace out of the lobby and into one of the hallways. Kyle glanced backward, seeing the lobby doors shudder again, another deep *boom* echoing through the room. Then he heard a horrible cracking sound, and the doors burst open. Rays of blue light arose from the Battle-Weavers standing closest to the doors, sucking outward into the night air. The Weavers scrambled backward, gravity shields appearing around them, then vanishing as quickly as they had formed. More blue light was sucked from them, and Kyle saw Urson levitating backward above the floor, beyond the range of the blue light, barking out orders.

And then the blue light vanished.

Kyle felt himself getting spun about, felt hands under his armpits, lifting him upward. He was carried forward, caught in a dense mob rushing down the hallway. Kyle heard screams coming from behind them, and the wind howling past their protective shield. The screams became higher-pitched, a horrible crunching sound echoing down the hallway. Kyle tried to turn around to see what was happening, but the arms holding him were like iron. The Battle-Weavers broke into an all-out run, pulling their charges toward the riser in the distance.

"Ariana!" Kyle yelled, realizing he couldn't see her. He felt the hands gripping him from behind squeeze him, and turned to see Ariana right behind him. Within moments, they reached the riser, along with Kalibar, Goran, and a few Battle-Weavers. Kyle turned around, staring down the hallway, at the lobby.

The floors were covered with blood.

Kyle felt his stomach churn, and he turned away, glancing at Ariana, who was still looking down the hallway. As the riser began to lift upward, her eyes widened, and she pointed forward.

"Watch out!" she cried.

340

Kyle turned back, saw a small white sphere flying through the air out of the lobby and into the hallway. Blue light sucked into it from every nearby surface. The magical lanterns bolted on the walls went dark as it passed.

"Fly, *now!*" Kalibar shouted.

The riser began to accelerate upward, but Kalibar was already flying upward even faster, rising off of the platform and into the air. Kyle activated his own gravity boots, wrapping an arm around Ariana's waist. She clung to him tightly, and he flew up into the air, the Battle-Weavers and Goran doing the same. Kyle saw the riser platform below him begin to glow blue, the light flowing out into the Void sphere.

"Go, go!" Kalibar urged.

Kyle saw Kalibar shoot upward even faster, and pushed magic into his own gravity boots. He blasted upward, Ariana gripping him so tightly that it was painful. He pushed through the discomfort, matching speeds with Kalibar and the Battle-Weavers. The riser – now some forty feet below – slowed its ascent, then stopped.

Then it fell.

Kyle turned his gaze upward, the riser shaft extending as far as he could see. Each floor of the Tower zipped by in a rapid blur, the magically powered lights on the circular walls glowing bright white. Kyle heard a loud *boom* from below, and looked downward, seeing the riser smash into the ground floor far below. Kyle felt a sudden burst of hope...the riser must have fallen on top of the Void sphere, after all. Surely the sphere couldn't have survived such an impact! But as he watched, the lights on the bottom of the shaft dimmed, then winked out, faint blue light pulling from the walls inward toward the center.

"It's following us!" Kyle yelled. Kalibar turned to Goran.

"We stop at the 40th floor," he shouted. Goran nodded, relaying the message to the Battle-Weavers. Kyle glanced downward again, watching as the lights in the riser shaft winked out floor by floor, the darkness moving upward toward them. Ariana looked down, then tightened her grip on Kyle, her powerful arms nearly crushing his ribs. He realized that she had no idea about the gravity boots' stabilization fields...she didn't realize that she barely needed to hang on to him at all.

"Easy," Kyle told her, trying to pry her arms from his chest. Ariana nodded, relaxing her grip. Then he felt something tapping his shoulder. It was Kalibar.

"Slow down!" he shouted, suddenly dropping below Kyle. Goran and the Battle-Weavers did the same, and Kyle cut back on his magic stream, rapidly decelerating. He glanced upward, seeing that they only had a half-dozen more floors to go before they reached the top. "Stop at the third from last," Kalibar ordered. Kyle eased back, slowing even further, trying to match Kalibar. The Grand Weaver slowed, then stopped at the third to last floor, shooting forward out of the riser and into the hallway, Goran and the Battle-Weavers following close behind. Kyle overshot a bit, stopping at the 41st floor.

"Kyle!" Ariana warned.

"I know!" he shot back, rapidly switching crystals, dropping downward through the shaft. Ariana shook her head, pinching his arm – hard.

"No, *look*!"

Kyle glanced down, realizing that the bottom half of the riser shaft had been left in darkness. And that no more lights were being shut off.

The hair on the back of his neck stood on end.

A high-pitched wail sounded throughout the wide shaft, and Kyle felt a blast of air tug at them, pulling them violently downward. He cried out, dropping rapidly, quickly passing below the 40th floor. The wailing sound intensified until it was a hideous screech, a torrent of wind sucking Kyle and Ariana downward. Kyle thrust magic at his boots, their descent slowing...but not stopping. He grit his teeth, shoving as much magic as he could at them, his mind struggling to keep up with the massive drain on his reserves. An hour or two of sleep had greatly replenished him, but he was nowhere near his full strength.

Their descent slowed, then stopped.

Kyle closed his eyes, the magic in his mind becoming more difficult to stream. He knew that he was running out – and no matter how hard he tried, they weren't moving upward against the powerful suction created by the Void sphere's gravity fields. He felt himself slipping downward, felt terror twist his guts as he realized that there was no way they were going to make it. He cried out, shoving as much magic as he could into the stream, giving everything he had left in one final burst.

342

Kyle shot upward through the shaft, rising upward against the powerful current, until the 40th floor came into view, with Kalibar standing at the edge of the riser shaft.

"Come on!" the old man shouted. Kyle felt a vibration, and then a blue sphere surrounded him and Ariana, and he was pulled upward and forward into the hallway past Kalibar. The sphere surrounding them vanished, a powerful wind ripping through Kyle hair, but it was nowhere near as strong as the current in the tunnel below. Kyle braced himself against the wall, pulling himself forward down the hallway. He could see Goran and the Battle-Weavers a few dozen feet ahead.

"Go, go!" Kalibar shouted, activating his own gravity boots and shooting down the hallway. Kyle followed suit, wrapping an arm around Ariana and lifting off of the ground, flying down the hallway after Kalibar. He picked up speed, catching up with the others in short order. Kyle felt Ariana tap his shoulder frantically, and he turned to glance at her.

"Kyle, slow-"

And then the wind stopped.

Kyle felt himself burst forward, careening toward the door at the end of the hallway. He heard Ariana yell out, felt her yank on his shoulders, twisting him around. He tried to slow down, but as he was facing the opposite direction, he sped up instead. He switched crystals again, and then he felt something strike the back of his head, and there was darkness.

* * *

Kyle groaned, feeling himself being pulled up from the floor. He opened his eyes, seeing a concerned-looking Kalibar standing before him. Strong arms had lifted him up from behind; he slid up onto his feet, tottering a bit at first, then catching his balance. He turned around, and saw Ariana standing there, her eyes filled with worry.

"You okay?" she asked. Kyle nodded sheepishly, rubbing the back of his head gingerly.

"Yeah," he replied. "What happened?"

"You were going to smash into the wall," she explained.

"She twisted you around so you hit her instead of the stone wall," Kalibar added. "You're lucky she did; I was looking in the opposite direction when the wind stopped." He gave Kyle an approving look. "I don't know how you managed to escape the Void sphere," he admitted. "I would never have had enough magic to do what you did."

"I thought I wasn't going to make it," Kyle confessed.

"But you did," Ariana interjected, putting a hand on his shoulder and giving him a relieved smile. "You saved my life."

Kalibar cleared his throat then, staring down the hallway toward the riser shaft in the distance.

"We should get moving," he stated, gesturing for Goran and the Battle-Weavers to follow him to the door at the end of the hallway. Kyle immediately recognized it as the door to the evacuation tunnels far below the Tower, having gone through it once before. He followed Kalibar, Ariana walking at his side.

"Thanks for saving me from the wall," he said, giving her a smile.

"I owed you," she replied. Kyle frowned, remembering his head striking something curiously soft before blacking out.

"Hey, you okay?" he asked. "Where did I hit you?"

"I'm fine," Ariana replied, her tone suddenly flat. He frowned, opening his mouth to repeat the question, but Ariana shot him a glare so venomous that his teeth clicked as his jaw snapped shut. Realizing that silence was almost certainly in his best interest, he said nothing more.

"Kalibar!" Goran shouted, pointing down the hallway. Kyle turned, seeing the lights in the riser shaft wink out on the far end of the hallway behind them. His heart leaped into his chest, and he turned toward the door, pulling Ariana with him. Kalibar made it to the door first, flinging it open and gesturing for everyone to go through, but one of the Battle-Weavers grabbed the door and ushered Kalibar through first. Kyle followed close behind, passing through to see the familiar spiral staircase leading to the evacuation tunnels beyond, descending into darkness far below. He and Ariana began running down the steps, taking them two at a time.

"Ariana, Kyle," Kalibar called out, gesturing for them to come back up the steps. Kyle frowned, but complied. The Grand Weaver pointed down the center of the spiral staircase, a long, narrow drop downward.

344

"We need to outrun that thing," Kalibar stated. "Do you need me to give you some magic?" he asked Kyle, who paused, then shook his head.

"I have some," he replied.

"Impressive," Kalibar stated. "Use your gravity boots, then." Then the old man vaulted over the railing with surprising ease, dropping downward. Goran followed suit, followed by the Battle-Weavers. Ariana grabbed onto Kyle, who gazed downward. The spiral staircase was pretty tight, the hole in the center narrow enough that a miscalculation could result in them slamming into the railing.

"Get on my back," Kyle told Ariana. She did so, wrapping her arms around his shoulders. He took a deep breath in, then activated his gravity boots, rising from the floor and over the railing. He maneuvered carefully to the center of the staircase, then dropped downward slowly. The walls from the staircase passed less than a foot from their shoulders as they dropped. He noticed a sudden flickering of light, and glanced upward, seeing blue light pulling from the walls and ceiling above.

The Void sphere!

Kyle fought down a wave of panic, steadily increasing his magic stream, accelerating downward quickly. The staircase zipped by faster and faster, a never-ending spiral into infinite blackness. He streamed even more magic to his boots, knowing that if the Void sphere managed to get within thirty or so feet from them, they'd be goners. And if it switched to its other mode...

He glanced downward, spotting Kalibar standing on the floor a few stories below. He shifted his magic stream, feeling his stomach flip as they rapidly decelerated. The floor rose up to meet him...and then stopped a few feet from his boots.

"Nice flying," Kalibar stated approvingly. "Let's go," he added, opening the door at the bottom of the stairwell and walking into the narrow, pitch-black tunnel beyond. Goran followed, and one of the Battle-Weavers gestured for Kyle and Ariana to follow behind Goran, the Weavers taking the rear. Kalibar created a light that floated above their heads, and they navigated through the tunnel as it twisted and turned through the earth. Kalibar set a quick pace, wanting to keep as much distance as possible between themselves and the Void sphere chasing them. Kyle glanced over his shoulder, peering beyond the Battle-Weavers, and saw only blackness beyond the short segment of illuminated tunnel.

The tunnel stopped suddenly, branching out on either side in a 3-way intersection. Kalibar turned left without hesitation, Goran following silently. Kyle trailed the Councilman, Ariana at his side. He felt her hand grasp his, and despite the dry coolness of her skin, he was grateful for her touch. They moved quickly down the hallway, eventually coming to a door.

"Interesting," Kalibar murmured, placing one palm on the door and cracking it open. Goran frowned.

"What?" he asked.

"This is a master-level door," Kalibar explained. "I had it installed by Jax himself after the assassination attempt against me."

"Why is it open?" Goran pressed.

"It has no magic," Kalibar answered, his tone grim. "And I'll give you one guess as to what removed that magic." He shoved the door open all the way, peering through. There was nothing but an empty hallway beyond.

"We don't have time for this," Goran warned. "That *thing* is behind us."

"And what's in front of us?" Kalibar countered. "We must be cautious." He gestured for the Battle-Weavers to take the lead, the three men walking through the doorway into the hallway. Kyle and Ariana followed Kalibar and Goran, until Kalibar halted abruptly, forcing Goran to stop behind him.

"What is it?" the Councilman asked Kalibar.

"Blood," Kalibar answered. Kyle peered beyond Goran and Kalibar, spotting a hint of red staining the smooth brick of the tunnel floor. As they moved forward, the blood appeared on the walls, spots of it even appearing on the ceiling some two feet above their heads. Kyle made a face as he stepped in a puddle of maroon clots, the fluid dripping down from his boots every time he took a step forward. It wasn't long before they found the source of the blood...two corpses lying motionless on the ground. They were naked save for their undergarments.

346

"Battle-Weavers," Kalibar observed, bending over one of the bodies and tracing a finger across a tattoo on one of the corpse's shoulders. "They died recently, probably within the hour."

"Who killed them?" Goran asked. "And why don't they have any clothes on?"

"I don't know," Kalibar admitted, straightening up.

"Ibicus had two men dressed as Battle-Weavers with him," Ariana interjected. "Before he attacked us."

"That explains it," Goran stated. "They're probably the Battle-Weavers you sent to search these tunnels earlier."

"They don't have any magic," Kyle observed. And it was true; not a shred of blue light emanated from their bodies. Kalibar nodded, his expression grim.

"A Void sphere must have drained them," he deduced. "But it didn't kill them...their bodies are too intact."

"Whatever killed them," Goran interjected, "...might still be down here." Kalibar scanned the tunnel.

"Perhaps," he replied. "We should be cautious."

There was a loud *bang* behind them, and Kyle flinched, ducking his head. He spun about, but all he saw was the door behind him...closed.

He'd left it open.

The door began to rattle violently, a low-pitched howl coming from behind it. Kyle backpedaled, following Ariana further down the hallway. He felt his heel strike something, and fell backward, landing hard on the stone floor below. Something wet seeped into the back of his shirt.

He rolled onto his side...and froze.

A corpse stared back at him!

Kyle scrambled to his feet, shuddering at the slick wetness dripping down his back, realizing that he'd tripped over one of the Battle-Weaver's corpses. He ran down the hallway after Kalibar and Goran, Ariana at his side. The howling sound behind them got louder and higher-pitched, until it was almost a scream. Kyle glanced backward, saw the door rip off of its hinges, flying backward into the hallway beyond. A sudden gust of wind tore at his hair and clothes, nearly yanking him off of his feet. He leaned forward against the wind, felt Ariana's arm around his waist, pulling him onward.

And then the wind stopped.

"Move, *now!*" he heard Kalibar shout.

Kalibar and Goran burst into all all-out sprint, and Kyle and Ariana followed suit, pumping their legs as fast as they could go. They weaved down the hallway, following its twists and turns, the brick-lined walls giving way to rough-hewn rock ahead. Kyle felt Ariana grip his arm.

"Kyle," she gasped.

He turned to her, realizing she was dropping behind. He pulled on her arm, but she continued to slow, stumbling forward and nearly slamming into the wall. Her eyelids fluttered, the skin of her forehead turning a faint blue.

"Come on!" Kyle urged, grabbing both of her arms and yanking her onto her feet. But she wobbled, falling back onto the ground. Then Kyle saw the blue light rising up from his own skin, saw it shoot down the tunnel the way they'd come. "Kalibar!" he shouted.

"Ivod!" Kalibar shouted back. "Pair mavu sill wes!"

Kyle swore under his breath, scooping Ariana up in his arms and lifting her from the floor. He followed behind Kalibar, struggling to keep up with the Grand Weaver. Brilliant blue light rose from his body, shooting in the opposite direction. The light floating above his head winked out, leaving them in utter darkness.

"Tet, mogo myki ohele!" Kalibar shouted.

Kyle grimaced, moving faster down the hallway toward Goran and the Battle-Weavers, who had created another light further down the hallway. Then Kyle stepped on something hard and uneven, and his ankle rolled. He cried out, dropping Ariana and tumbling to the ground.

"Rendi gomas raytar!" Kalibar shouted, stopping to extend a hand. Kyle grabbed it, pulling himself onto his feet – or rather, his good foot. His left ankle throbbed terribly, and putting even the slightest weight on it was agonizing. He limped forward, gritting his teeth against the pain. Kalibar gestured at Goran, who turned about and grabbed Kyle, wrapping one arm around his waist. Kalibar picked up Ariana, and they moved forward together, Kalibar – his entire body glowing blue – trailing behind. Kyle looked down, realizing he'd tripped on a pile of rocks laying on the floor. In fact, the rocks were scattered all about him. He frowned, then glanced upward, and saw a large hole in the ceiling above.

"Kalibar, look!" Kyle urged, pointing at the hole. Kalibar stared at Kyle in confusion, then followed Kyle's finger; the hole led to a dark chamber above, its features hidden in shadow. Kalibar dropped Ariana to the ground, then stopped the Battle-Weavers coming back up the tunnel toward them with one outstretched hand.

"Safinda waria nib nill," he ordered. The Battle-Weavers nodded, a large ball of burning *punk* appearing on the ground some ten feet from where they stood. Seconds later, the magic light above the Weavers' heads winked out, blue light shooting out of their bodies. "Vae sus!" Kalibar shouted, pointing upward. The hole was barely visible in the long shadows cast by the *punk*.

One of the Weavers ran up to the wall below the hole, bracing himself against the wall. Kalibar handed Ariana to one of the other Weavers, then climbed up the first Weaver's body, grabbing the ledge above and hauling himself upward with remarkable swiftness. Goran followed, trying to pull himself upward, but he was nowhere near as fit as Kalibar; the Grand Weaver extended a hand from above, pulling Goran upward through the hole. Kalibar gestured for Kyle to come next.

Kyle hobbled up to the Weaver's back, the other Weaver lifting Kyle up by the waist and propping Kyle on the first Weaver's shoulders. Kalibar and Goran grabbed Kyle by the wrists, hauling him up through the hole in the ceiling, then setting him down on the narrow ledge above.

"Thanks," Kyle mumbled. Then he remembered that his earring was out of magic; no one could understand him. He streamed what little magic he had left to it.

"Get Ariana, lift her up," Kalibar ordered. The Battle-Weavers lifted Ariana up, propping her against the wall. Kalibar and Goran reached down, gripping her under the armpits and hauling her upward. She flopped like a rag doll on the floor above. Kyle felt fear grip him; her eyes were open, but she was staring blankly off into space.

"Come on," Kalibar urged, gesturing for the Battle-Weavers to follow. The three men were outlined in blue light, the magic draining from them. One of the Weavers glanced down the hallway, his face

349

paling. Then he turned to Kalibar, saluting crisply, and ran down the hallway anyway. The other Weaver hesitated, then did the same, ignoring Kalibar's order and sprinting away.

"Damn it!" Kalibar cursed.

"What are they doing?" Goran demanded.

"Leading the Void sphere away from us," Kalibar replied grimly. He stood up then, turning away from the hole. "Come on," he ordered. "We can't let their sacrifice be in vain."

Kalibar picked up Ariana then, carrying her on his shoulder and slipping into the darkness ahead. Kyle squinted, his eyes slowly adjusting to the darkness, and realized that there was a faint outline of a rope ladder next to the wall ahead, a single rope with knots tied at regular intervals. Kalibar ran to it, scaling it carefully; within moments, he'd vanished into the perfect darkness above. Goran followed suit, and Kyle limped toward the ladder, waiting for the Councilman to start climbing before gripping the thick rope in his hands and pulling himself upward. He favored his bad ankle, using his arms to haul himself upward one knot at a time. For perhaps the first time in his life, he felt grateful for his slight build; that, and his hobby for climbing trees in his backyard. He'd been rather cruelly made fun of for both in school, but now all the jeers rang hollow.

Upward he went, his biceps burning with the effort. He ignored the pain, grabbing the rope with one hand above the next knot, then the other hand, gripping the rope between his thighs as he went. It wasn't long before he couldn't see anything at all; he climbed the rope blindly, trying to ignore the rising fear within him, the terror of what horrors might lurk in the darkness around him. He focused on the rope, just him and the rope, counting each knot as he ascended.

One, two, three...

He glanced down as he went, and was thankful that all he could see was darkness. Then he saw a flash of blue light below, which vanished as quickly as it had come. Even with the momentary illumination, there was no telling how high up they'd climbed, but he knew it was high enough that one wrong move would be fatal. If the Void sphere activated its gravity fields now, he would never be able to hang on.

...four, five, six...

He felt the rope vibrate once, then again, then felt hands grabbing his wrists and tugging him upward. He held fast to the rope, terrified of letting go, of falling into the void below.

"Let go," a voice hissed. He realized it was Goran's.

Kyle paused, then released one hand from the rope, feeling himself rising upward. He let go with the other hand, half-expecting to fall, but he did not. He felt his knees scrape against something hard, then felt his belly sliding on cool stone. He rolled over onto his back, sweat pouring from his forehead, stinging his eyes. He blinked against the darkness, then struggled to weave the light pattern. A white light flared up overhead, and dim as it was, he still had to squint until his eyes adjusted. They were in a narrow corridor, a ragged hole in the stone floor marking where they'd come from. The walls were made of gray stones mortared together, the ceiling some ten feet high. Kyle's magical light cast long shadows across the floor.

"Where are we?" Goran asked.

"No idea," Kalibar answered. "Kyle, I don't have any magic," he added, turning to Kyle. "Can you send your light forward?" Kyle nodded, casting his light forward, scanning the narrow corridor beyond. The hallway was some twenty feet long, a simple stone staircase at the end. Kalibar strode toward it, Ariana still draped over his shoulder, and gestured for Goran and Kyle to follow. Goran wrapped an arm around Kyle's waist, helping him hobble along behind Kalibar; still, he nearly tripped over a long metal pole laying on the ground, sending it rolling off to the side. They reached the staircase, Kyle hopping on his right leg from step to step. The stairs turned left, then left again, rising upward to meet a large metal door. Kalibar stopped before it, twisting the doorknob, but it didn't budge.

"Locked," Kalibar murmured. He shook his head in frustration. "I still can't weave any magic," he added. He turned to Kyle. "What do you have left?"

"Not much," Kyle admitted. Kalibar grunted, lowering Ariana from his shoulder. He sat her down on the landing before the door, propping her against the wall. Her head lolled to one side, her eyes still open, staring blankly ahead. Kyle frowned, peering closely at her; her forehead was glowing with the faintest of blue lights. He frowned, stepping backward, and realized that subtle rays were shooting from the walls and the floor – even the metal door – and were coalescing at Ariana's forehead.

Her eyelids fluttered.

"Kalibar," Kyle whispered, pointing at Ariana. "Look!"

Kalibar stared down at Ariana, then gasped, crouching beside her. He put a hand on her cheek, patting it gently but firmly. Ariana's eyes fluttered again, then opened, her pupils slowly converging on Kalibar.

"I think she needs magic," Kyle guessed.

"What are you talking about?" Goran asked. "What's wrong with her?"

"Kyle's right, she needs magic," Kalibar answered. Goran looked ready to ask another question, but Kalibar cut him off. "Go ahead Kyle," he urged.

Kyle nodded, closing his eyes and *pulling* magic into the center of his mind's eye. At first nothing happened, what little free magic he had still being streamed to his light. But he pulled harder, sensing the magic slowly building within the bones of his skull, so close yet so difficult to access. A thread appeared, and Kyle pushed it toward Ariana's forehead.

Ariana's eyes widened, and she gasped.

Ariana!" Kyle blurted out, shaking her slender shoulders. She turned her eyes toward him, but not her head. He grasped desperately for more magic, thrusting what little he could toward her. Ariana's leg jerked, then her arms, and she gasped again, turning her head to face Kyle.

"What..." she mumbled. Then she groaned, clenching her fists, then relaxing them. "Where am I?"

"You fell asleep," Kalibar answered, glancing at Goran, then turning back to Ariana. "We need you to do something for us." Ariana nodded, rising slowly to her feet. Kyle shoved the last bit of magic he had at her, then rose to stand at her side, putting all of his weight on his good ankle.

"What?" she asked.

"Can you open this door?" Kalibar asked, pointing to the heavy metal door. Ariana turned to it, then shrugged noncommittally.

"I'll try."

"Are you joking?" Goran asked incredulously. "That thing is made of solid metal," he added. Kalibar didn't respond, nodding at Ariana, who stepped up to the door, putting her delicate fingers on the metal knob. She pulled, but nothing happened. She glanced at Goran, then at Kalibar.

"It's okay," Kalibar encouraged. "Go ahead."

Ariana nodded, turning back to the door, her fingers curling around the knob, the muscles of her forearm tensing. The knob dented inward slightly under her grasp, the metal creaking under the strain. There was a sudden cracking sound, and the knob snapped, falling off the door and striking the stone landing with a loud clang. She ignored this, reaching her hand through the hole the knob had left, then pulling. The door creaked, the metal bending inward toward her. There was a snap, and the door swung inward, Ariana nearly falling backward down the stairs in the process. She managed to hang on, slamming her back into the wall to the side.

Goran stared at her, his jaw slack.

"Come on," Kalibar prompted, smirking at the Councilman. But instead of opening up into a hallway or room, there was a stone wall behind the door.

"Wait," Goran exclaimed. "What's a *wall* doing here?"

"Ariana, can you get us through this?" Kalibar asked. "We don't have any magic." Ariana stared at the wall skeptically. Then she turned about and ran down the stairs. A moment later, there was a loud clanging noise. Ariana returned shortly thereafter, a long metal pole in her hands. It was, Kyle realized, the metal bar he'd tripped on earlier. Everyone stepped back, giving Ariana plenty of room to work, and she slammed the butt of the pole into the stone, breaking off a small chunk of mortar. She struck again, then again, the ear-splitting racket forcing Kyle to cover his ears with his hands. Dust and pieces of rock flew all around her, forcing everyone else back down the stairwell. After a few minutes, the noise stopped, and Ariana's pale face peeked out from the stairway.

"Come on," she urged.

Kalibar and Goran ran up the stairs, followed by Kyle. A hole had been made in the wall, revealing a long corridor beyond. Kalibar squeezed through the hole, Goran and Kyle and Ariana following

353

close behind. Kalibar cast his light forward into the hallway ahead; the walls were stone again, but this time they were interrupted at regular intervals by long rows of vertical metal bars some seven feet high. Kalibar walked down the hallway slowly, gesturing for Goran to follow him. Ariana grabbed Kyle's hand, and he leaned on her, favoring his left ankle while following the two men. They passed one of the rows of metal bars, and Kyle peered beyond them, seeing several small, rectangular rooms.

"My god," Kalibar whispered, lowering his light to get a better look inside one of the rooms.

"What?" Goran asked, visibly tensing. Kalibar shook his head, turning away from the room.

"Of course," he mumbled, shaking his head slowly. "It's so obvious now."

"*What?*" Goran pressed. Kalibar turned to Goran, his brown eyes glittering in the dim light coming from above.

"This is how they broke out," Kalibar answered, gesturing at the barred rooms all around them. "They were right underneath us...literally...all this time!"

"Who?" Goran blurted, clearly exasperated.

"We're in the middle of the city," Kalibar explained. "...right above the evacuation tunnels, of all things." He shook his head, a rueful smile twisting his lips. "If we live through this, remind me to strangle our city planner."

"I'm about to strangle *you*," Goran muttered under his breath. But Kalibar ignored the comment, turning back to Kyle and Ariana.

"We need to keep moving," he stated, walking back to the hole they'd come through and inspecting it carefully. "If that Void sphere doesn't circle back and come for us, the escaped prisoners certainly will. And if they're smart, they'll search for us here."

"And *where* is *here?*" Goran nearly shouted. Kalibar said nothing, but pointed to a series of symbols carved in the stone above hole in the wall. Kyle couldn't read it, of course, but Goran's face immediately paled, his jaw dropping. Kyle frowned, turning to Ariana.

"What does it say?" he whispered.

"Stridon Penitentiary," she replied.

Chapter 25

The hallways of Stridon Penitentiary were long and somber, the walls and floors a dull gray under the light that Kyle levitated above their heads. According to Kalibar, they were in the sub-basement of the enormous building complex, an abandoned floor once used for now-banned experiments on prisoners waiting for the death penalty. Unlike on Earth, where responsible adults would never delve into the details of such things with children, Kalibar quite enthusiastically recalled the history of horrifying acts committed only a few decades before. The Ancients had not allowed human experimentation without consent, but it had taken a while for the new Empire to abandon its less savory habits. That being said, Kyle still recalled the prisoners who had died while Kalibar had his ring tested; apparently necessity outweighed other considerations when it came to the greater good.

In any case, the door to the abandoned floor had been long ago locked and mortared over, only a nondescript wall left in its place. The prisoners who'd escaped must have taken down the wall, dug a hole right down into the evacuation tunnels, and then made their way up to the Tower...all the while covering their escape route by recreating the wall. An ingenious plan, indeed.

The four of them continued down the hallway, Kyle putting more and more weight on his injured ankle as he went. It still hurt, but he was able to walk without assistance now. Eventually they made it to a dark, dusty staircase at the end of a long series of hallways, one that took them to the basement level. Not much different from the lower floor, this one held row upon row of barred cells stretching into the distance. Curiously, all of the magical lights on the walls and ceiling were out.

"They're all fed by massive magic storage crystals below-ground," Kalibar explained, leading the others down the hallway. "A network of crystals, actually. If one is drained, others are supposed to take over...the fact that *all* of the lights are out means that the entire network has been drained."

"Impossible," Goran retorted. "There's enough magic in those depots to last a year!"

"And yet..." Kalibar countered, gesturing at the darkness around them.

"Where are all the prisoners?" Kyle asked. Indeed, all of the cells they'd come across had been empty.

"Good question," Kalibar replied. "Only a few cell blocks were freed during the jailbreak last week...about eighty prisoners in all. This building alone holds six hundred, and the debtor's prison building holds two hundred."

"We've passed more than a few cell blocks," Goran observed, glancing about nervously. Kalibar nodded, frowning at one of the cells nearby. The bars had been bent to either side, forming an opening large enough for a man to squeeze through.

"We should be cautious," he advised. Then he turned to Kyle. "Kyle, lend me your magic, if you would."

"Wait, how did they bend the bars if all the magic got sucked out?" Kyle asked. He streamed magic toward Kalibar, giving the Grand Weaver what little he had left.

"The prisoners in this building were all Weavers and Runics," Kalibar explained. "The most dangerous criminals of all. The magic powering the prison's security systems was drained, but that doesn't mean the prisoners were."

"Great," Goran mumbled.

"Better give me your magic too," Kalibar told the Councilman. Goran did so; no matter what the man's opinion of Kalibar as Grand Weaver, there was no denying that Kalibar was the best equipped to defend them.

"There's no one alive on this floor," Ariana stated, walking at Kyle's side. Kalibar turned to her, a frown on his face.

"You can tell?"

"Yes," she affirmed. "I...uh, have really good hearing."

"And remarkable strength," Goran added, turning to Kalibar. "How is that, Kalibar?"

"A gift from the same man who gave me my eyes back," Kalibar answered, smiling at Ariana. "Impressive, eh?"

"Hardly," Goran retorted. "This all-powerful being gives you eyes and gives *her* super-strength, all the while doing nothing while the city burns?"

"I don't pretend to understand him," Kalibar admitted. Goran rolled his eyes, stalking off down the hallway. Kalibar sighed, walking behind the disgruntled Councilman, mumbling something under his breath. Kyle turned to Ariana, leaning toward her ear.

"What'd he say?" he whispered.

"He said he didn't understand why he'd betray the Empire again," Ariana replied with a shrug. Kyle stared at Ariana, then at Kalibar's back, his eyes widening. Wait, did Kalibar know about...? He felt his heart skip a beat. Had Darius told the Grand Weaver? No, it wasn't possible.

Wait, where *was* the bodyguard, anyway?

Kyle frowned, realizing that Darius had been gone for hours now. Where had the man been while they'd all been struggling for dear life? Or when Urson had faced those Void spheres? Kyle still remembered the screams of the dying, the blood spattering the lobby. For a man with seemingly unlimited power, Darius had done nothing to stop the wholesale carnage...which either meant that he had no idea it was happening, or that he let it happen anyway. Either way, it didn't bode well for any of them now.

"All the cell bars are broken here," Goran observed. Kyle realized the surly Councilman was right. Not one of the cells was occupied, and the bars were bent similarly to the first one they'd seen.

"Do you hear anything, Ariana?" Kalibar asked. Ariana paused, then shook her head.

"Nothing in here," she answered. "Nothing outside, either," she added. Goran frowned.

"You can hear *outside*?"

"Sort of," she replied. "It's hard to explain."

"Let's keep going," Kalibar interjected, pointing to a staircase ahead. "This should bring us up to the first floor, and into the city streets." He turned to Goran. "Urson said he would have his men evacuate Erasmus, but there's no telling whether or not they were successful." He paused at the foot of the staircase, taking a deep breath in and letting it out slowly. "My Battle-Weavers went out into the city to retrieve the surviving Council members. With the Tower under siege, they'll have no safe place to convene."

"And they'll go into the Tower unwittingly," Goran added grimly. "Which means we either go back to warn them, or we leave them to die."

"If we go back, we risk our own deaths," Kalibar countered.

"And then no one in the Empire will realize that Xanos can do to anyone what he did to Ibicus," Goran concluded. "If we die, Xanos will destroy the Empire outright, or create puppets out of any future elected leaders."

"And we can't exactly send a courier to tell them," Kalibar muttered. "No one would believe it from anyone but us." He shook his head, running a hand through his short white hair. "But I can't just let Erasmus – or the Council – die." He turned back to Goran, his tone firm. "I'll go back to the Tower, try to find some Battle-Weavers and fight. You take Kyle and Ariana...build up your magic reserves, then use your gravity boots to escape the city. Fly to Eastport."

"Eastport?" Goran asked. Kalibar nodded.

"As you said, evacuation will give us time," he reasoned. "The Tower is lost, for better or worse. Our only hope now is to make a stand elsewhere, and Spero is too obvious a choice."

"No," Goran countered.

"What?"

"I'm not going," Goran clarified.

"It's a suicide mission," Kalibar protested, but Goran cut him off.

"This has *always* been a losing battle, Kalibar," he stated. He crossed his arms in front of his chest. "We were always going to lose," he added firmly. "The only person who believed we had a chance was you, Kalibar...the entire Council thought you were crazy."

358

"Well thanks," Kalibar grumbled.

"That's why we nominated you," Goran continued. "Unanimously, remember? Half of us didn't like you, or agree with what you did in your first term as Grand Weaver, but we all knew that you were the best Battle-Weaver we'd ever seen. The most reckless and most daring, mind you, but also the most successful. You made a habit of winning handily despite impossible odds, and we needed your kind of crazy if we were to stand a chance."

"Well," Kalibar mumbled. For the first time since Kyle had met the man, he appeared to be at a loss for words. Goran smirked.

"Don't let it get to your head," he added. "I still think you're an imperialistic, morally suspect Populist." He sighed, uncrossing his arms. "The point is, we're all dead men, whether we stay or run. I've spent the last dozen mornings watching the sunrise, wondering if each would be my last...living in fear. I'd rather die fighting than die running."

"Okay," Kalibar decided. "Then we fight." He turned to Ariana.

"I'm not afraid of death anymore," Ariana stated. "But I *am* afraid of living in fear. I'm fighting."

"Kyle?" Kalibar asked. Kyle took a deep breath in, lowering his gaze to the floor. He wished he could be as steadfast as Ariana and Goran, but the truth was, he still wanted to live. He wanted to go home – back to Earth – and see his parents again. But he couldn't do that knowing he had abandoned his friends to die. Life with that kind of regret wouldn't be worth living.

"I'm in," he stated.

"All right then," Kalibar replied. "We stay and fight. But we need to be smart about it. The city is overrun with those Void spheres, and we know we don't stand a chance against them...so we need to avoid them."

"We could fly above the city," Goran offered, but Kalibar shook his head.

"Too risky," he countered. "Their magical vacuum will take us right out of the sky if they find us." He frowned then, stroking his goatee. "Those Void spheres seem to sense magic...I think that's why the last one followed the Battle-Weavers and not us. We'd already been drained, but the Battle-Weavers hadn't."

"But we *need* magic," Goran protested.

"We can disguise ourselves," Kalibar offered. All heads turned to him.

"Like hats and fake mustaches?" Goran asked snidely. Kalibar smirked.

"No, like dirt," he corrected. Goran frowned.

"How is dirt going to disguise us from those things?" he asked.

"Normally it wouldn't," Kalibar answered. "Every rock and clump of dirt in the city was saturated with magic...but with those Void spheres absorbing all of the magic around the city..."

"Ahhh, I see," Goran exclaimed. "That's brilliant, Kalibar!"

"What is?" Kyle asked.

"Almost everything in the world makes magic," Kalibar explained. "Normally, dirt and rocks – minerals in nature – are saturated with magic. So if you covered yourself in such dirt, excess magic produced by your mind would still leak out past it. But if the dirt were depleted of magic..."

"Then it would absorb any excess radiation, no matter how slight," Goran added. "We'd be effectively invisible, at least for a while."

"Ohhh," Kyle breathed. "But wait, aren't *we* depleted now? Our bones should do the same thing...absorb any excess magic."

"Until our skulls become saturated," Kalibar countered. "After that, magic has to travel through tissue to get to our spine...and tissue is terrible at holding on to magic. Leaking will occur."

"Got it," Kyle replied. "So we cover ourselves in dirt from outside, and then what?"

"Then we get information," Kalibar answered. "Find a Battle-Weaver, determine the status of the Council and Erasmus if we can, and travel back to the Tower if we can't."

"And if we encounter one of those Void spheres?" Goran asked.

"Well wait," Kyle interjected, struck with a sudden idea. "The dirt is like an insulator, right?" Kalibar nodded. "So it's like a sweater for heat...it keeps heat in, even if it's really cold."

"And?" Goran asked.

"Well won't the dirt stop the Void spheres from absorbing our magic?" Kyle asked. "Or at least slow it down?"

"By god," Kalibar breathed. "He's right!"

"I am?" Kyle asked.

"You *are*," Kalibar insisted, clapping Kyle on the shoulder and laughing joyously. "You clever, clever boy! It'll work...it's simple magicodynamics. It *has* to work."

"But wait," Goran countered. "These Void spheres create such a powerful magical vacuum, it'll suck the magic right out of the dirt."

"Yes, but much more slowly," Kalibar replied. "Just like a sweater in extreme cold. It could allow us to escape in time...with magic to spare." He nodded at Kyle, shaking his head in admiration. "Kyle, if we make it through this alive, you're going to become one hell of a Runic." Kyle gave him a weak smile, not at all sure that they would make it out alive.

"Let's go," Goran interjected, rapping his fist on the metal door in front of them. He turned to Ariana. "If you would..."

Ariana nodded, grabbing the door by its knob and repeating her earlier performance. This time she made quick work of it, clearly having gained confidence in her abilities. The door snapped open, and the four of them strode into yet another hallway. This one was as dark as the others, but at the end of it – a few hundred feet away – there was a large door. Kalibar and Goran strode toward it.

"I hear something," Ariana warned. The two men stopped, turning to stare at her. She paused for a long moment, cocking her head to one side. "It's like thunder," she clarified. Then she shook her head, putting a hand on one wall. "Wait...feel this."

Kyle put his own hand by Ariana's, and felt the wall vibrate ever-so-slightly under his fingertips.

"It's an earthquake," he exclaimed. Kalibar frowned, striding up to Ariana and putting his own hand on the wall. A few seconds later, Kyle felt another vibration.

*One, two, three...*he counted. *Four, five, six...*

He saw Kalibar's eyes close, his lips moving ever so slightly.

Twenty-one, twenty-two...

Another vibration.

"Earthquakes don't come at regular intervals," Kalibar murmured, stepping away from the wall. "Neither does thunder."

"Explosions?" Goran asked.

"Again, too regular," Kalibar replied.

"Then what?" Goran pressed. Kalibar shook his head.

"I don't know," he admitted. "Everyone stay quiet...Ariana, keep us informed if you hear anything unusual. The exit is straight ahead." Ariana nodded, and they resumed walking down the hallway toward the door beyond. The cells were deserted, as before, but the floor was stained in places with what looked like dried blood. Flies buzzed around a few motionless lumps laying on the floor further down the hallway.

"Prison guards," Ariana whispered. Kyle frowned; from here, he could barely make out the shapes. They eventually reached the bodies, and Kyle held his breath at the smell coming from them. He'd seen his fair share of dead bodies recently, the sight hardly triggering the fear and revulsion he'd had the first time. All he felt now was vague sadness, and a kind of morbid curiosity. He wondered if something was wrong with him, that he was so cavalier about the dead now.

"They haven't been dead long," Kalibar noted as he passed by. They continued forward, passing an intersection of hallways on either side. Kyle glanced down the left hallway, seeing more dark shapes lying on the floor. To the right, even more. The stench of blood was almost overwhelming, and he switched to breathing through his mouth. They kept moving, now only a hundred feet from the entrance.

"It stopped," Ariana murmured suddenly. Kalibar and Goran slowed down, glancing back at her. "The vibrations, I don't hear them anymore."

"Keep going," Kalibar murmured. Kyle glanced at Ariana, then swallowed in a dry throat, the hairs on his neck rising on end. The exit was only fifty feet away now, the floor ahead sticky with dried blood. The stuff sucked on their boots as they walked, the sound echoing through the hallways. They reached the exit at last, stopping before the door. All eyes turned to Kalibar.

"We go outside, and find depleted soil," he stated. "If we can't find any nearby, we'll have to drain it ourselves, then cover ourselves with it. Ariana, you're our lookout. If we're spotted, stay together unless I say otherwise."

They all nodded silently.

"Let's go," Kalibar said, opening the door.

* * *

Rain fell in heavy sheets across the stone steps leading up to Stridon Penitentiary, splattering into deep puddles on the road below. Lightning arced through the sky, followed moments later by the low rumble of thunder echoing through the city. Black smoke rose from the tops of the buildings in the distance, the wind carrying it at an angle through the sky, creating long fingers that reached over Stridon, as if poised to crush the city in its dark grasp.

Kyle stood just outside of the prison entrance, for the moment protected from the torrential downpour by the stone overhang above, supported by massive columns on either side. Ariana stood at his side, Kalibar and Goran ahead; the two men were peering out into the darkness. They spoke with each other for a moment, their words lost in the storm, then turned back to Kyle and Ariana.

"If we take the main road," Kalibar said, pointing to the wide road ahead, "...it'll be two miles to the Gate Shield. We should cut through the side streets."

"How are we going to get beyond the gate?" Goran asked. It was a good point, Kyle knew; the Secula Magna was surrounded by a magical fence that generated a massive domed gravity shield over the entire campus, preventing anyone from getting in unless they went through the front gate.

"The Gate Shield is down," Kalibar explained, pointing off into the distance. "We should have been able to see it from here if it were up." He gestured for them to follow him down the steps and into the street, his boots sinking ankle-deep in the water. Goran followed, as did Kyle and Ariana. It was only then that Kyle realized that Ariana was barefoot; ever since they'd revived her in her room, she'd been wearing a simple shirt and shorts, and nothing else. Her pale, delicate feet dipped into the chilly water, but she didn't seem to notice.

"Aren't you cold?" he asked. Ariana looked down, then shrugged.

"No," she replied. "I mean, I know the water's cold, but it doesn't bother me," she added, sloshing forward with the rest of them. They walked forward silently for a few minutes, then Kalibar took them left down a narrow side street. A bolt of lightning lit up the sky, followed by a rolling thunderclap. Unlike Ariana, he was freezing.

"Can we shield ourselves from the rain?" he asked Kalibar. Kalibar shook his head.

"We need to conserve magic," he replied. "Huddle together," he added. The four drew closer together, Kalibar and Goran in front, Ariana and Kyle behind, their shoulders touching. They were shielded from the wind a bit this way, but Ariana didn't provide any body warmth.

"Kyle's idea won't work in weather like this," Goran grumbled, glancing up at the thunderclouds above. "Even if we find depleted dirt, it'll wash off of us as soon as we put it on."

"Or we could just use a gravity field as an umbrella," Kyle countered. Goran frowned.

"Right," he muttered.

"Not that there's anyone around to attack us," Kalibar observed. Indeed, the streets were strangely barren; they hadn't encountered another person since they'd left the prison.

"Where is everyone?" Kyle asked.

"The main battle was at the Tower and the Southwest Quarter," Kalibar answered. "We're to the east of the Tower."

"Hey guys," Ariana called out from behind. Kyle turning, realizing that she'd dropped back, and was standing at the door of a building to their right. She pointed at the sign above the door...which of course, Kyle couldn't read.

"Good eye, Ariana!" Kalibar exclaimed, slogging through the flooding street toward her. Goran did the same, and Kyle followed behind. Ariana tried to open the door, but it was locked. Kalibar gave it a try, closing his eyes and bowing his head over it for a moment, then pushing it open easily. He stepped in, gesturing for the others to follow.

"What's going on?" Kyle asked as he stepped through the door. Goran frowned, turning to him.

"Didn't you see the sign?" he asked. Kyle blushed, shaking his head.

"He can't read," Kalibar explained, stepping forward into a large room with countless wooden shelves built into the walls. They held crystals of all shapes and sizes, some as small as a ping-pong ball, others larger than a watermelon. Their innumerable facets glittered faintly in the muted starlight. Kalibar conjured a small, faint light in the air above their heads, rays scattering in glorious colors and patterns across the wooden walls as they were refracted by the crystals.

"He's illiterate?" Goran asked incredulously.

"He can read and write," Kalibar clarified, "...but not our tongue." Goran harrumphed, clearly offended by Kyle's deficiencies. Kyle felt his cheeks burning, and he stared at one geode – a group of white-blue crystals – to distract himself. Then he frowned; the crystals were white, with a slight blue glow emanating from them.

"This one has magic!" he exclaimed, pointing to the geode.

"They all do," Kalibar replied with a weary smile. "This is a gem-stone shop, after all. The magic-sucking spheres must not have passed through this street. Everyone load up on as much magic as they can."

Kyle turned back to the geode, *pulling* on the magic therein, seeing rays of faint blue light rise up out of the white crystals and fly toward him. He felt the power burst into his mind, then slowly trickle away as it redistributed. He kept pulling, feeling his skull vibrate, then his neck. It was a subtle sensation – one that he had never noticed before – but he could definitely sense his bones filling with magic. He supposed that they'd always been filled to the brim, so he'd never noticed the slight vibration until its absence.

He soon depleted the crystal, or at least pulled as much as he could out, so that taking any more required more effort than it was worth. He turned to another geode, and pulled the magic out of it as well. After repeating the process on a few more gems, he felt like his entire body was humming.

"Everyone filled up?" Kalibar asked. He got three nods in return. "Let's move out," he stated, thrusting a few gems in his pockets. "Take a few for the road," he added. Kyle stuffed a few small geodes in his pockets, then followed Kalibar and Goran out of the shop and back into the street. The rain had slowed to a light drizzle, the wind dying down to a breeze. The sound of thunder was more distant now, the storm having passed on. A gravity shield appeared around Goran.

"I'm cold," he explained, rubbing his hands together briskly. Kali-bar created his own shield as well.

"I think it's safe to use our gravity boots," he stated, levitating a foot off of the ground. "Stay below the rooftops; any enemy lookouts

365

flying above will have a harder time seeing you that way." He flew upward then, rising a good twenty feet in the air, gesturing for the others to follow suit. Goran flew up next; Ariana turned to Kyle, climbing on his back. Despite her slim frame, she was still awfully heavy to carry around for very long...not that he was about to tell her that. Kyle created his own gravity shield, then activated his gravity boots, feeling her weight lessen to almost nothing as the boots' stabilization fields kicked in. He flew upward slowly, until he was level with Kalibar and Goran.

"Follow my lead," Kalibar ordered, accelerating forward. They flew down the street, the sides of the tall buildings zooming past on either side, water running over their gravity shields like rain on a windshield as they went. Kyle tensed up, concentrating on following Kalibar's path and speed as they curved around a bend in the road. They reached an intersection, and Kalibar made a chopping motion with his right hand, slowing down and turning suddenly to the right. Goran followed, and Kyle slowed down – somewhat abruptly, making Ariana hold on painfully tight – and turned as well, accelerating as he straightened out. They continued forward, weaving through the city streets, and after a few minutes, Kyle felt himself relaxing. It wasn't very hard to keep up with Kalibar and Goran once he got the hang of it.

Kalibar raised his right hand sharply, his fingers spread wide, and slowed down, Goran doing the same. Kyle slowed – smoothly this time – and watched as Kalibar descended, touching down on the wet street below. Kyle descended as well, then cut the magic stream to his boots altogether, landing on the street gently. He set Ariana down beside him, then watched as Kalibar walked to a black fence in the distance, some three stories tall. Kyle immediately recognized it as the magical fence surrounding the campus of the Secula Magna. The shimmering domed shield – the Gate Shield – that usually extended from the top of the fence was gone

"Ariana," Kalibar asked, "...do you sense anyone nearby?" Ariana frowned, then shook her head.

"No one nearby, but I hear something ahead, farther away."

"Good," Kalibar replied. He flew upward over the tall fence, landing gently on the other side, then gestured for the others to follow. They did so, landing on the well-manicured lawn beyond.

"This soil is depleted," Kalibar observed, kneeling on the lawn. He inactivated his gravity shield, then grabbed a hunk of grass and pulled it out of the ground, tossing it away. Then he grabbed a glob of wet dirt from the same hole, smearing it over himself. "Come on," he stated, gesturing for the others to follow suit. Soon they were all tearing at the grass, smearing cold, wet mud over themselves. After everything they'd been through in the last few weeks, getting messy was nothing alarming to Kalibar, Ariana, or Kyle. Goran, on the other hand, appeared thoroughly disgusted.

"Your Battle-Weavers won't recognize us if we meet them," he groused, flinging mud off of his fingers.

"Neither will the enemy," Kalibar countered, his gravity shield reappearing around him. "Shields up," he ordered. "Fly low to the ground, aim for the Tower. Go to ground if you spot a Void sphere." He flew up into the air, and Kyle flew up after him, Ariana clinging to his back. Kalibar kept them barely ten feet from the ground, the tall spire of the Great Tower still a few miles away. They picked up speed quickly, the slight drizzle pelting their gravity shields, leaving comet-tails of water in their wake. The Tower grew as they drew closer, towering over them, its pyramidal spire glittering in the starlight filtering through the clouds above. Kalibar slowed as they reached the cobblestone walkway surrounding the Tower, descending onto it. Goran and Kyle did the same, following Kalibar as he strode quickly toward the massive double-doors marking the entrance to the Tower. As they drew closer, Kyle noticed two shadowy figures standing on either side of the doors.

"Ariana?" Kalibar prompted.

"Battle-Weavers," she replied instantly. Kalibar nodded, walking toward the two men confidently, his gravity shield vanishing abruptly. The two men – they *were* Battle-Weavers, Kyle realized as they drew closer – shouted at Kalibar, gravity shields appearing around them. Kalibar stopped, raising one hand.

"I am Grand Weaver Kalibar," he shouted imperiously, wiping the mud off of his face with his free arm. "Councilman Goran is with me, as are my children," he added, gesturing to each as he spoke. The Battle-Weavers wavered, but did not lower their shields. Kalibar smiled. "Traven, isn't it?" he asked, pointing to one of the men. "Your father served with me in Kall." The Battle-Weaver's eyes widened, and he dropped his gravity shield, kneeling before Kalibar.

"My apologies, Grand Weaver," he blurted, "...we didn't recognize you." Kalibar gestured for the man to rise.

"You're a credit to your father," Kalibar countered, putting a hand on Traven's shoulder. "Where is Grand Runic Erasmus?"

"High Weaver Urson knows," Traven answered. "He didn't tell anyone else, in case we were interrogated."

"Urson's alive?" Kalibar exclaimed. Traven nodded.

"He's on the other side of the Tower."

"Is the area secure?"

"Yes Grand Weaver," Traven confirmed. "The military entered the city about an hour ago. They've neutralized most of the escaped prisoners. They're fighting off the Death Weavers and enemy soldiers in the Southwest Quarter as we speak."

"What about the Chosen?" Kalibar pressed.

"I think Master Owens took one out with that new weapon," Traven answered. "We haven't encountered any others since."

"Thank you," Kalibar stated. "We need to debrief with Urson. Traven bowed sharply, then opened the lobby doors, and Kalibar led the others through. The lobby was deserted, the room in shambles. Kalibar took them right through it, into a broad hallway beyond, one that led them to the other end of the massive Tower. After a few minutes, they reached a set of double doors at the end of the hallway, the two men guarding them reacting in the same way Traven had earlier. Kalibar somehow recognized these soldiers as well, greeting them by name, immediately defusing the situation. Kyle recalled Kalibar's advice to him way back when he'd first met Jenkins; despite having met the butler once or twice a few years ago, he had remembered the man's name, immediately earning Jenkin's respect and loyalty. Kalibar's insistence on knowing his subjects had paid off yet again.

"Urson's just beyond," Kalibar stated as the double-doors opened. The cool night air ruffled Kyle's hair as they walked through the doorway, the campus of the Secula Magna spread out before them. At least a dozen Battle-Weavers were standing just outside of the Tower, a tall man in silver and black armor standing among them, black cloak rippling in the wind. Kyle immediately recognized the man as High Weaver Urson.

"Urson!" Kalibar exclaimed, walking up to the man. Urson turned about, his green eyes narrowing for a split second, then relaxing. He broke out into a huge smile, walking up to Kalibar and embracing him, ignoring the mud covering the Grand Weaver. Kalibar chuckled, then held Urson at arm's length. "You're alive," he observed, looking the man over. Urson grinned.

"Better lucky than good," he replied. "Almost didn't recognize you," he added, gesturing at the dirt caking Kalibar's entire body.

"A bit of insulation," Kalibar explained. "Keeps those Void spheres from draining us," he added. Urson frowned.

"You'll have to explain how that works."

"Kyle will," Kalibar replied. "He's the one that figured it out. Where's Erasmus?"

"In a random residence in the Northeast Quarter," Urson answered. "Guarded by a dozen of my best men."

"Is he...?"

"Alive and well," Urson reassured. "I'm keeping him there until I can confirm that the city is secure."

"What's our status?"

"The Tower is secure," Urson replied. "The fighting is mostly limited to the Southwest Quarter. A full legion entered the city about an hour ago. Most of the enemy soldiers and Weavers have been killed. A few of those Void spheres are still roaming the city, and we've evacuated the areas around them." He shook his head. "Containing them is going to be a problem."

"What about the Chosen?" Kalibar pressed. "There were...reports of one near the Tower right before it was attacked."

"Dead now," Urson answered. "After you were evacuated, that Void sphere decimated most of my men in the Tower. We managed to escape, then regroup with Master Owens and a few Runics. They had that new weapon with them..."

"The killerpillar gun," Kalibar interjected.

"...and they managed to kill the Chosen with it," Urson continued. "We haven't encountered any more Chosen since."

369

"Why hasn't Xanos sent more Chosen?" Kalibar wondered aloud. He turned away from Urson, gazing out beyond the gently rolling grassy hills of the campus, to the shadowy cityscape surrounding them. "They're his most powerful weapon. It doesn't make any sense."

Kyle frowned, following Kalibar's gaze. Black smoke lingered in the air above the tall buildings several miles away, mixing with the angry thunderclouds above. Brief flashes of lightning pulsed from cloud to cloud, faint rumblings echoing through the cool air. He felt a cold hand grasp his left arm, and turned to see Ariana staring up at the sky, her eyes wide with terror.

"Kyle...!" she screamed.

And then the heavens opened up above them.

Chapter 26

Massive thunderclouds loomed over Stridon, their black underbellies flashing as jagged bolts of lightning lit up the night sky, crackling thunderclaps rattling the windows of the buildings far below. Light from the countless unseen stars beyond lined the very tops of the clouds with the faintest silver, a stark contrast with the black tempest that roiled underneath. The thunderclouds blanketed the sky, dwarfing the city below, as if mocking the petty constructs of Man.

A faint light grew within that dark underbelly, widening and brightening until it shone like the sun. The thunderclouds tore open, a giant ray of light bursting through, cutting a swath through the gloom. The ray descended onto the buildings of the Southwest Quarter, bathing them in a huge golden spotlight. The stone walls flashed, their windows glittering brilliantly, like diamonds in the sun. The air above the rooftops rippled, the golden-brown walls turning a pinkish hue, which deepened into a dull red. The redness spread from the rooftops down, until the top halves of each were glowing in the dazzling spotlight.

And then the stone sank into itself, the rooftops turning to mush, molten rock dripping down the sides of the buildings. The spotlight intensified, every building in its path melting like so many burning candles, black smoke rising upward into the night sky.

A powerful wind tore at Kyle flinging chunks of dried mud from his clothes. He braced himself, feeling Ariana's powerful fingers digging into his arm.

371

"My god!" Kalibar cried.

The beam of light vanished, the dark clouds rushing inward to fill the void it had created, the four city blocks below glowing red-hot against the blackness of the night. Countless jagged bolts of lightning pulsed within the thunderclouds where the beam had been only moments before, the clouds darkening until they were almost pitch black.

A faint white light shone through the darkness.

"Run!" Ariana screamed, yanking Kyle backward by his arm. Kyle cried out, pain shooting through his shoulder, and stumbled backward, falling onto the ground. Ariana let go of his arm, and he clutched it to his side, scrambling to his feet, his eyes on the single faint light piercing through the clouds above. It grew brighter, then sharper, turning from a dull glow to a brilliant white beacon.

The clouds parted suddenly, a massive domed head piercing through, a single white diamond-shaped eye staring down at them.

"Run!" Ariana screamed again.

Kyle tried to turn and run, but his body refused to obey. His legs gave out underneath him, and he landed on his butt on the grass below. His eyes were riveted on that brilliant eye hundreds of feet above, that domed head more massive than any he could have imagined. Enormous fists punched through the clouds, each wrought of black, shimmering metal.

This was a Behemoth, but not the one he'd been attacked by earlier. This was twice the size, its eye white, not green. Tiny white lights ran down the length of its limbs, like stars glittering in the night sky. Its legs, each twenty stories tall, descended through the clouds. Down it fell, until its enormous feet smashed into the buildings below, miles from where Kyle stood. The buildings crumbled as if made of sand, the Behemoth crashing through them silently, its feet slamming into the ground.

Kyle saw Kalibar cover his ears, saw Urson doing the same. Gravity shields appeared around them.

A deafening *boom* blasted Kyle backward, knocking him onto his back on the wet grass, the air blasting from his lungs. Pain shot through his ears, and all he could hear was a loud, high-pitched ringing sound. He covered his ears too late, crying out in pain, barely able to hear his own voice. Ariana appeared in front of him, grabbing him under his armpits and lifting him to his feet. The ground shuddered underneath them.

The ringing in Kyle's ears faded, his hearing gradually returning.

"Get them out of here!" he heard Kalibar shout. "The city is lost, run for your lives!"

"But the Empire!" Goran protested.

"I can't save the Empire," Kalibar shot back. "But I *can* save my family!"

The Behemoth stood among the ruins of the buildings it had demolished, flaps on the front of its shoulders lifting upward, revealing dark chambers underneath. Dozens of tiny white lights shot outward from those chambers, arcing through the night sky like shooting stars, spreading outward across the campus as they fell. One of the lights arced toward Kyle and Kalibar, landing on the grass a hundred feet away, then bouncing toward them until it came to a rolling stop a few dozen feet away.

"*No,*" he heard Kalibar breathe.

The white object lifted up into the air until it was at eye-level, a white sphere floating in the cool night air. Kyle stared at it, then looked down at his arms, seeing blue light escaping through the gaps in the mud covering him, shooting forward toward the levitating sphere.

"Fly, *now!*" Kalibar shouted, grabbing Kyle.

Kyle felt Kalibar's arms tighten around him, felt a powerful force pull him to Kalibar's side. They shot up into the air, twisting around and flying away from the white sphere, the ground dropping underneath them with dizzying speed.

"Ariana!" Kyle cried, searching the ground frantically for her.

"Goran has her," Kalibar shouted back. Kyle searched the sky, spotting Goran flying a dozen feet to their left, Ariana clinging to his back. The Behemoth stood there in the distance, one leg lifting upward and forward, then slowly descending onto a few buildings below, demolishing them. There was a muffled *boom* a few moments later. Despite himself, a part of Kyle's brain began to count.

One, two, three...

The Behemoth's other leg lifted upward, demolishing a few buildings as it swung forward.

...ten, eleven, twelve...

The leg lowered to the ground, debris flying up into the air around it as it crushed everything in its path.

...twenty-one, twenty-two...

Another muffled *boom* echoed through the air.

"It's coming after us!" Kyle heard Urson shout. The High Weaver was flying a dozen feet below them, pointing to the Void sphere speeding toward them. Kyle wasn't too worried....it was moving far too slowly to catch up with them. His eyes swept the landscape, searching for other spheres. There were dozens of them, moving across the campus toward the Tower in a slow crawl, none of them moving as quickly or purposefully as the one chasing them.

Kyle looked forward, saw the Behemoth's lone eye turn to look directly at them. A chill ran down his spine.

"It's using the spheres' movement to track us!" Kyle realized. He saw Kalibar glance back at the Behemoth, felt them accelerate forward with gut-wrenching force, arcing tightly to the right. The white sphere fell farther behind, far too distant to absorb their magic, but the Behemoth's diamond-shaped eye tracked them unerringly, growing even brighter as Kyle watched, until it flashed once.

"Kalibar, dodge!" he shouted.

Kalibar shot upward and to the left so quickly that Kyle felt the blood drain from his head, his vision blackening. He grit his teeth, desperately trying to hold on to consciousness, feeling his whole body go numb. An impossibly bright light burst into life below them, hot air rushing up and around them, searing Kyle's lungs. Kyle coughed uncontrollably, his eyes watering with the heat. He heard Kalibar coughing, knew that the only thing preventing them both from burning alive was Kalibar's shield.

The impossibly hot air rose up around them, following them as Kalibar shot almost straight upward, a huge expanse of the lawn below bursting into flames, the grass blackening and curling instantly. Despite the gravity shield, Kyle felt the temperature rising, sweat pouring from his roasting skin. Sweat dripped from his forehead and into his eyes, making them smart even more.

Water!

Kyle wove magic in his mind, creating a stream of water at his feet. He felt hot air rush in, burning his skin, heating the dried mud on his clothes until it was unbearably hot. But it was quickly followed by a blast of cold air that swirled around him. The cool air felt incredible, and Kyle continued his water stream as they flew ever upward, until he was so cold he was shivering.

"Nice work," Kalibar shouted, leveling off and shooting forward. They were hundreds of feet above the massive campus of the Secula Magna now, the dormitories like miniature toys below. The intense spotlight below them faded, the superheated earth below the vaporized grass still glowing red-hot from the Behemoth's beam. To Kyle's relief, he spotted Goran and Ariana flying above them, Urson and his Battle-Weavers to their left. The Void sphere that had been tracking them earlier was nowhere to be found.

"I think we lost it," Kyle observed.

"We need to lose *that*," Kalibar countered, gesturing back at the Behemoth. Kyle twisted his head around, spotting the gigantic war machine as it stepped forward onto the three-story fence surrounding the Secula Magna, the black metal crumpling under its incredible weight. The lawn beyond buckled, the foot sinking deep into the soil as it touched down, creating a massive crevice there. As Kyle watched, the Behemoth's eye flashed once.

"Watch out!" Kyle shouted.

Kalibar dipped downward and to the left, making Kyle's stomach flip-flop. Kyle kept his eyes glued to the Behemoth, watching as its lone eye pulsed one more time.

And then it turned blue.

A tidal wave of blue light rose upward from the earth around the Behemoth, traveling upward instantly to be sucked into its eye. Light burst forth from the buildings around the machine, all condensing into blindingly bright rays that were pulled into that massive eye. Kyle looked down at his arm, saw the gaps in the mud caking his clothes start to glow blue, rays of light shooting toward the Behemoth's head. He saw Kalibar's shield waver, felt gravity take hold of them, pulling them into free fall.

"Give me your magic!" Kalibar shouted, shooting forward in stuttering bursts, then losing control of his gravity boots. Kyle responded immediately, streaming magic toward Kalibar's forehead, which – with extraordinary good fortune – happened to be wiped clean of mud.

375

Kyle felt Kalibar gain control of their fall, slowing their descent while picking up speed forward, gaining distance from the Behemoth. Kyle saw Goran and Urson far ahead of them, trails of faint blue light shooting backward from their mud-caked bodies.

"Get to ground!" Kalibar shouted at them, descending at a steeper pace, clearly struggling to maintain control of his boots. Kyle grit his teeth, his magic continuing to drain.

"I'm running out," Kyle warned.

Kalibar veered toward the ground, decelerating rapidly and touching down behind a small hill. A patch of grass before him tore free of the earth below, and Kalibar crouched down, creating a small waterfall to wet the dirt. He grabbed handfuls of mud and rubbed them on himself.

"Replace your mud," he instructed. Kyle did so, covering himself with fresh mud. The blue light seeping from his body faded, the fresh mud insulating him from the Behemoth's terrible eye. Goran, Ariana, and Urson dropped through the air to land next to them, and Kalibar instructed them to cover themselves as well.

"We need to get out of here!" Goran exclaimed. Kalibar stared at the Behemoth grimly, then shook his head.

"There's no point," he countered. "Xanos will find us wherever we go."

"So what then?" Goran shot back. "We lay down and die?"

"No," Kalibar answered, studying the Behemoth. "We fight."

"*What?*" Goran exclaimed. "You just said we'd already lost!"

Kalibar said nothing, studying the Behemoth and the countless Void spheres dotting the landscape for a moment longer. Then he turned to Urson.

"The Void spheres sense magic," he stated. "You should be invisible to them if you're insulated enough. If the Behemoth uses the spheres to help track us, that should make it harder for it to track you."

"What are you talking about?" Goran pressed.

"I'm going to fight that thing," Kalibar replied. When Goran opened his mouth to protest, Kalibar held up one hand. "I'm going to use the Void spheres against it."

"What's your plan?" Urson asked. Kalibar turned to the High Weaver.

"The Void spheres are attracted to magic," he explained. "If I fly near them, they'll sense my magic and come after me...which means I can lead them to *that*," he added, pointing at the Behemoth.

"You'll never make it," Urson protested. "Those spheres will drain you."

"Not if I insulate myself," Kalibar countered. "I can leave a part of me exposed so they'll sense me, but drain me slower." Urson shook his head.

"That's a suicide mission," he stated. "We need you to organize the evacuation. I'll go instead."

"Guys!" Ariana interjected, pointing toward the Behemoth. Everyone turned, seeing the giant killing machine in the distance. Its diamond-shaped eye facing the Southwest Quarter. The eye flashed, a beam of white light shooting outward and striking another set of buildings, reducing them to molten stone.

"We need to act *now*," Kalibar stated. "Urson, I make more magic than you do," he reasoned. "I have a better chance of making it."

"But wait," Goran interjected, "...doesn't *he* make more magic than you?" he stated, pointing at Kyle.

Kyle blinked, staring at Goran, then turning to Kalibar. It was true, he realized; he made significantly more magic than Kalibar. If anyone had a chance at leading the Void spheres to the Behemoth, it was him.

"Not an option," Kalibar stated.

"Why not?" Goran pressed. "He has a better chance of succeeding than you do."

"It's too dangerous," Kalibar insisted. "I won't risk my son's life over my own."

"So you'll risk the entire Empire instead?" Goran pressed. Kyle hesitated, then cleared his throat.

"He's right," he spoke up, turning to Kalibar. Kalibar frowned.

"Kyle..."

"I'll do it," Kyle interrupted. Kalibar shook his head.

"I won't let you."

"Ampir saved his family instead of the Ancient Empire," Kyle reminded him. "And millions of people died."

"Yes, but..."

"If I don't do this," Kyle continued, "...then I'll be just as guilty as he was." He stood up straight then, taking a deep breath, then letting it out. "And if you stop me, then you will be too."

Kalibar stared at Kyle silently, his jaw dropping. Then his mouth clicked shut, and he sighed, his shoulders slumping.

"You're right," he replied at last. Then he turned to Goran and Urson. "We should give Kyle our magic," he stated, reaching into his pockets and pulling out the gemstones he'd gotten from the gem shop earlier. Some were still glowing faint blue, protected by the mud on Kalibar's clothes. "Take these," he added, handing them to Kyle. "Drain them of their magic."

"Ok," Kyle agreed. He felt magic flow from Urson and Goran into his mind's eye; it wasn't much, but it was something. He placed the gemstones in his pockets, then reached down, scooping up more handfuls of mud and smearing it on his body, making sure he was covered completely, save for a small section of his forehead. He hesitated, then covered that too while Ariana helped cover his back.

"You'll need to expose part of yourself," Kalibar reminded him. "Otherwise the Void spheres won't follow you."

"They will if I use these," Kyle countered, pulling out one of the gemstones. Kalibar glanced at the gemstone, then chuckled, shaking his head.

"Good idea," he conceded. He reached in to give Kyle a hug, then stopped himself, clearly not wanting to mess up Kyle's mud. "You're going to make one hell of a Runic," he murmured.

"I'll go with you," a voice stated. Kyle turned to see Ariana standing there, her hands on her hips. She faced Kalibar defiantly. "I can sense that thing's thoughts," she explained. "I'll be able to anticipate its next moves and protect Kyle."

"Ariana..."

"I'm going," Ariana interrupted, her tone final. "Kyle needs me." She walked up beside Kyle. "Come on," she urged.

"Cover yourself with mud first," Kyle stated. Ariana nodded, doing so with remarkable quickness...far faster than a mere mortal could have. Then she climbed on Kyle's back. Kalibar sighed.

"Good luck," he stated. He took a deep breath in, then let it out. "I love you both," he added. His lower lip quivered slightly, and he turned away, facing Urson and clearing his throat. "Urson, I need you to create a diversion."

"Tell me what to do," Urson replied.

"After Kyle gets airborne, get the Behemoth's attention and hold it for as long as you can," Kalibar commanded. "Gather as many Battle Weavers as possible to mount an attack." Urson frowned.

"An attack?"

"You'll know when to strike," Kalibar replied. Urson hesitated, then bowed.

"Yes your Excellency."

Kalibar turned back to Kyle, swallowing visibly. Then he nodded. "Go."

Kyle streamed magic to his gravity boots, flying upward, the wind tearing at his clothes. The boots' stabilization runes kicked in, pulling Ariana to his back and minimizing her weight. He accelerated forward, aiming for a cluster of Void spheres in the distance.

"Hold on," he called out.

Accelerating quickly, he zoomed a dozen feet over the ground, reaching into his pocket and pulling out a gemstone. He held it in his palm, then flew within a few feet of one of the Void spheres, watching as blue light streaked outward from the gemstone. He passed the sphere, aiming for the next one. Ariana gave him a squeeze.

"It's following us!" she confirmed.

Kyle zoomed past a second sphere, then a third, then cut to the left toward another cluster of Void spheres in the distance.

"Slow down," Ariana urged, giving him another squeeze. "They're falling behind!"

Kyle complied, glancing at the gemstone in his hand. The blue light streaming from it was fading fast; he thought about dropping it, but then realized that it might make the Void spheres follow it instead of him. He placed it in an empty pocket, retrieving another gemstone. Bright blue light emanated from it.

He flew forward over more Void spheres, until at least a few dozen were trailing behind him. He found that he could tell how far away they were based on how bright the light streaming from the gemstone was. At a distance of about forty feet, the spheres still followed him, but they drained the gemstone at a relatively slow pace compared to when they were closer. Still, with so many following him, the gemstone was being drained quickly. He replaced it with another.

"That's the last of them," Ariana yelled as they zoomed over yet another Void sphere. "Watch out," she warned. "The Behemoth sees you!"

Kyle glanced at the Behemoth, perhaps a half-mile in the distance. The monstrosity's eye was looking right at him!

"He's going to attack," Ariana warned, giving him a squeeze. "Dodge to your left," she added hurriedly. "He's going to sweep to our right!"

The Behemoth's eye flashed.

"Hold on!" Kyle cried.

He cut to the left, feeling the G-forces pull the blood from his head, his vision blackening. An impossibly bright beam of pure energy shot outward from the Behemoth's eye, cutting across the night sky. It missed Kyle by a few dozen feet, sweeping rightward...just as Ariana had predicted. Still, the heat of the passing beam was so intense that it burned Kyle's skin; he grit his teeth against the pain, focusing on maintaining his magic streams.

"It's going to attack again," Ariana warned, clutching him tightly. "Stay the course," she added.

"What?" Kyle shouted back.

"Go straight!"

Kyle swallowed, glancing at the gemstone in his hand. Its light was fading...he replaced it with another. He was already halfway through his supply...he needed to reach the Behemoth, and quickly.

The Behemoth's eye flashed again.

Kyle took a deep breath in, resisting the urge to dodge out of the way, aiming straight for the Behemoth. Another deadly beam shot outward from its eye...to Kyle's left. It swept leftward, no doubt anticipating that he was going to dodge that way again. He let his breath out, not realizing that he'd been holding it. They were only a few hundred feet from the Behemoth now.

"I'm going to circle around it," Kyle shouted. It'd be safer to lead the Void spheres to the back of its domed head, where its deadly beam couldn't reach them.

"Watch out!" Ariana cried. "It's going to create some sort of gravity pulse!"

Then the air around the Behemoth's head *exploded*.

The Behemoth's eye turned away from them, its head rotating slowly. Dozens of small lights flew across the sky toward the Behemoth; Kyle blinked, realizing that the lights were coming from black-cloaked figures flying high above the campus.

Battle-Weavers!

The Battle-Weavers swooped around the Behemoth, keeping their distance from the deadly machine. Flashes of light shot from the Weavers, slamming into the Behemoth's metallic armor. Or rather, into the blue gravity shields surrounding its body like a second skin.

"Change crystals!" Ariana called out. Kyle glanced at the gemstone in his hand, realizing it was fading quickly. He grabbed another, then aimed to the left of the Behemoth's head, blasting past it. He slowed abruptly, cutting to the right, circling around its head. He felt Ariana's arms tighten around him, felt her slip down to his waist.

"Hold on!" he cried.

He continued to decelerate, stopping ten feet from the back of the Behemoth's dome-shaped head. The huge, black metal plates covering it stood before him.

"Kyle!" Ariana warned, pointing at the dozens of Void spheres flying right toward them.

Kyle grimaced, realizing that the Void spheres still hadn't absorbed enough magic to switch to their other phase. If he didn't give them more magic – and soon – his plan wouldn't work. The Behemoth was perfectly insulated, giving off no magical energy. It wouldn't activate the Void spheres by itself.

He reached into his pockets, pulling out the rest of the gemstones, holding them outward.

Cords of blue light shot outward from the gemstones, converging on the rapidly approaching Void spheres. He resisted the urge to retreat, knowing that they'd have to be as close as possible to the Behemoth's head when they activated.

Come on...

The Void spheres zoomed up to him, dozens of them surrounding him. Blue light shot outward from the gemstones, making them shine like a miniature sun.

Suddenly the rays of light began to wink out.

Kyle felt his heart leap into his throat, and he reacted instantly, pulling a cord of magic into his mind's eye, redirecting it into his boots.

"Hang on!" he shouted.

He burst away from the Behemoth's head, the air screaming past his ears, his gut dropping sickeningly with the sudden acceleration. He glanced back, seeing the Void spheres congregating around the Behemoth, hovering motionlessly behind its head.

Then they activated.

Layers of spinning gravity fields appeared around each Void sphere, a sudden gust of wind pulling Kyle back toward them. Kyle grit his teeth, focusing on his mind's eye, pulling more magic into it and streaming it to his boots. He accelerated, but much more slowly now, barely moving forward. The combined vacuums of the Void spheres were too powerful.

"Kyle!" Ariana warned, her voice rising in alarm. He realized that they'd stopped moving forward...and were starting to slide backward toward the Void spheres. He streamed even more magic to his boots, realizing that it was getting significantly harder to do so; he was running out of magic. They stopped sliding backward...but barely.

Suddenly he heard a loud screeching sound coming from behind them, and glanced back. A large metal plate from the back of the Behemoth's domed head was being pried off by the Void spheres' devastating power, exposing green crystal underneath. As Kyle watched, the plate tore off completely...and more plates began to peel off of the gargantuan machine. But he hardly had time to celebrate...they were being pulled backward again.

"Kyle!" Ariana shouted.

"I'm running out!" Kyle yelled, struggling to stream more magic to his boots. But he'd nearly run out of magic, his skull bones holding on to the magic they had greedily. They slid backward toward the Void spheres, accelerating at an alarming rate. They were only forty feet away now, and the distance between them was rapidly shrinking.

"Fragel zin morf!" Ariana cried.

Kyle blinked, then realized that the magic in his earring was depleted. Not that it mattered...even if he had understood Ariana, there was nothing he could do. They accelerated backward toward the Void spheres helplessly, now only a dozen feet from the nearest rotating gravity field.

Shit!

Kyle struggled, *tearing* magic from the bones in his skull, but he had nothing left. He closed his eyes, clutching Ariana's hands in his own, waiting for the end.

Suddenly he felt Ariana's hand slip from his, felt her slide her hand across his forehead, flinging the mud from it. Magic burst into his mind's eye, filling it with bright cords of light. He grasped at them desperately, shoving them into his boots. They stopped sliding backward abruptly...but even with the magic coursing into him, he still didn't have enough to gain any distance from the Void spheres' deadly gravity fields.

Then, without warning, the Void spheres' gravity fields vanished!

Kyle burst away from the Behemoth's head, careening through the air at incredible speed. The blood drained from his head, stars floating at the periphery of his vision. He cried out, feeling Ariana's arms slipping from his waist. He slowed down, trying to grab her arms, but he was too late...she fell from his back, plummeting toward the ground!

"Ariana!" he screamed.

Suddenly, a dark shape flew underneath Kyle, colliding with Ariana...and plucking her out of the air! It was Kalibar, he realized.

"Go!" Kalibar shouted, gesturing for Kyle to fly away from the Void spheres. Indeed, blue rays were already starting to converge on the dozens of spheres. Bright rays shot outward from the crystalline flesh exposed on the Behemoth's domed head where the metallic plates had been pulled off. Kyle glanced down, realizing that rays were also coming from *him*...the mud on his body had dried and cracked, much of it having been pulled off by the Void spheres' powerful vacuum. Magic was leaking from those cracks and draining into the Void spheres.

Kyle complied, bursting away from the spheres and following Kalibar as the old man flew toward the campus ahead. They descended steadily, until Kalibar landed on the ground a few hundred feet from the Behemoth. Kyle landed beside the Grand Weaver, turning to look at Ariana. She was slumped lifelessly in Kalibar's arms, her eyes open but unseeing. Kyle remembered the burst of magic he'd gotten right before he'd fallen into the Void spheres' clutches...Ariana must have given him her own magic, depleting herself completely. She'd sacrificed herself to save him.

"You okay?" Kalibar asked. Kyle nodded. "Good work," Kalibar added, gazing at the Behemoth in the distance. The Void spheres were still clustered around the back of its head...at the exposed crystal there. Thick rays of bright blue light were being sucked into the dozens of Void spheres, the Behemoth's magic rapidly draining.

"Look!" Kyle exclaimed. "It's working!"

"We should back away," Kalibar stated, turning around and striding quickly away from the Behemoth. Kyle followed suit.

"What now?" he asked.

"I'm almost out of magic," Kalibar replied. "Do you have any more of those gemstones?"

"No, I'm all out."

Kyle glanced back at the Behemoth. Suddenly the rays of magic sucking out of the Behemoth vanished...and the Void spheres activated. Rapidly rotating layers of gravity fields appeared around the dozens of spheres. Luckily he and Kalibar were far enough away to not be pulled in. Still, he followed Kalibar as the Grand Weaver continued to retreat, not wanting to risk another near-death experience. He looked back, seeing more metallic plates peeling off of the Behemoth's head, hunks of green crystal beneath breaking off and flying into the Void spheres' gravity fields.

The Behemoth leaned forward, pulling its head away from the spheres. Their combined gravity fields were no match for the Behemoth's enormous weight; the distance between them was sufficient enough that no more plates were being peeled off now.

Then the Behemoth's eye flashed.

"Watch out!" Kalibar cried, breaking into a run, clutching Ariana tightly to his chest.

A huge spherical gravity field appeared around the Behemoth, and the Void spheres shot outward in all directions. The shockwave struck

Kyle and Kalibar, nearly throwing them from their feet. Kalibar skid to a stop.

"Damn!" he swore. "We need to corral the Void spheres again...but we don't have enough magic."

Suddenly Kyle saw dark shapes in the sky around the Behemoth...the Battle-Weavers! They swooped in behind the Behemoth's domed head, hurling fiery missiles at the Behemoth. Explosion after explosion struck the Behemoth's vulnerable spot where the plates had been removed, hunks of crystal falling from the wound. Just as quickly, the Battle-Weavers dispersed, flying far away from the massive thing...and toward the scattered Void spheres.

"Look!" Kyle exclaimed.

The Battle-Weavers flew over the Void spheres much as Kalibar had, forcing the spheres to follow them. The Weavers then circled back toward the Behemoth, the Void spheres trailing close behind. Other Battle-Weavers continued their assault on the Behemoth, striking it in the back of the head in wave after wave of attacks. More chunks of green crystal fell from the Behemoth's head.

"It's working!" Kyle declared.

Suddenly the Behemoth's eye flashed, and a deadly ray shot outward at the Battle-Weavers attacking it. The Behemoth's domed head rotated rapidly, the beam sweeping across the night sky. Kyle watched in horror as a few Battle-Weavers burst into flames instantly; their burning corpses fell from the sky, landing on the charred grass below.

At the same time, the Battle-Weavers leading the Void spheres toward the Behemoth reached the deadly monstrosity, flying up toward the back of its head like Kalibar had done earlier. Rays of blue streamed from the Battle-Weavers as the Void spheres drained their magic; a few of the Weavers fell from the sky, their magic completely drained. They plummeted downward, slamming into the ground at the Behemoth's feet with lethal force. More and more Battle-Weavers fell from the sky, the remaining Weavers herding the Void spheres up to the gaping wound on the Behemoth's head. Massive cords of bright blue magic streamed from the Behemoth's exposed crystalline innards, pouring into the dozens of Void spheres.

Then the blue rays pulling into the spheres vanished.

"Damn it, they're too close!" Kalibar swore.

The remaining Battle-Weavers burst away from the Behemoth...just as the Void spheres activated. Spinning gravity fields appeared around the dozens of spheres, pulling the Battle-Weavers back toward them. Only a few Battle-Weavers managed to escape in time; the rest were sucked into the deadly gravity fields, disintegrating in a spray of blood and mangled flesh.

"Damn it!" Kalibar cursed.

More plates on the Behemoth's head were pulled off, hunks of green crystal ripping out of monstrosity, turning to dust as they struck the spinning gravity fields.

The Behemoth's eye flashed.

Another massive gravity field appeared around the monstrous machine, shoving the Void spheres away from itself. But this time, the effect was weaker; most of the Void spheres were only pushed a short distance away. These levitated up toward the Behemoth's exposed crystalline flesh again, attracted to the magic it exuded. Massive amounts of magic coursed from the Behemoth, absorbed by the Void spheres. The Behemoth's head turned, no doubt in an attempt to use its deadly eye to shoot them out of the sky. But the Void spheres circled with it, clustering at the back of its head. It generated another massive gravity field, attempting to push the Void spheres back. But this was even weaker than the last, and the Void spheres quickly returned, draining even more magic. The blue rays emanating from the Behemoth were noticeably paler now.

Then they vanished.

The Void spheres activated again, and this time the Behemoth could do nothing to stop them. More and more plates were ripped from its domed skull, exposing huge expanses of green crystal beneath. Hunks of crystal flew out of the wound and into the spinning gravity fields in a continuous stream. The Behemoth stepped away from the Void spheres, the spheres' gravity fields again no match for its immense weight. It spun around slowly, turning its head to face the Void spheres. Its eye flashed, a deadly beam destroying a few of the spheres.

But the remaining Void spheres returned to sucking the magic from the Behemoth, flying to the back of its head and draining it even further. It took another step away from its attackers, its huge foot slamming into the ground, creating a deep indentation there. Jagged bolts of electricity burst outward from the Behemoth's domed head, striking the Void spheres and shoving them away. But the spheres simply flew back, unfazed by the Behemoth's assault. The rays of magic streaming from the war machine were fading fast...the Behemoth was running out.

Its eye flickered...and went dark. It stood there motionlessly, a massive shadow against the night sky.

Then, very slowly, it began to tip forward.

"Get back!" Kalibar ordered. The Behemoth was falling forward...right toward them.

"Get on my back!" Kalibar cried, turning his back to Kyle. Kyle hopped on. "Stream magic to me," Kalibar added, flying upward and to the side, away from the falling giant. Kyle tried, but he had no magic left.

"I'm out," he shouted back.

Kalibar flew away from the Behemoth as it continued to fall face-first toward them. Its domed head loomed over them, descending rapidly. But instead of speeding up, Kalibar began to slow down!

"Kalibar!" Kyle warned. They were right in the path of the falling Behemoth...and still slowing down. He closed his eyes, gritting his teeth and *pulling* desperately for magic. He could feel some within the bones of his skull, but they resisted him, holding on to their power greedily.

The Behemoth loomed over them, blotting out the sky.

Kyle *tore* the magic from his skull, a sharp pain lancing through his skull as he did so. He threw the magic outward at Kalibar, a wave of nausea coming over him. Bile welled up in the back of his throat, and he swallowed it down, gagging on the bitter fluid.

Kalibar shot forward, just as the Behemoth's head reached them. It barely missed them, slamming into the ground. The earth crumpled under its enormous weight, a shockwave of dust and debris flying outward in all directions from the impact. The shockwave struck Kalibar and Kyle, tossing them from the Behemoth. Kyle felt himself tear free from Kalibar, the world spinning madly around him. Then he slammed into the ground, the air exploding from his lungs. He tumbled across the grass, coming to a stop on his belly.

He lay there, gasping for air, his ears ringing. Turning his head to the side, he saw the Behemoth's massive head a hundred feet away, obscured by a huge cloud of dust. He felt something grab his arm, and turned to see Kalibar there, Ariana lying a few feet to the side of the Grand Weaver. Kalibar's mouth was moving, but no sound came out.

Kyle grunted, pushing himself off of the ground, spitting dirt out of his mouth. He looked back at the cloud of dust kicked up by the Behemoth, at the shadowy outline of its head beyond.

A huge, diamond-shaped white glow appeared through the dust.

Kyle stumbled backward, his eyes widening. He felt Kalibar grab him by the arm again gesturing for him to run. The Grand Weaver scooped up Ariana, breaking into a run away from the Behemoth. Kyle ran behind him, looking over his shoulder, seeing the cloud of dust starting to dissipate. The Behemoth's giant eye stared back at them, flashing once, then again.

Faint rays of blue pulled from Kyle and Kalibar, from the very ground itself, converging on the Behemoth's eye.

Kyle ran faster, pumping his legs as hard as he could, trying to keep up with Kalibar. He heard a creaking sound, then felt the ground tremble. He looked back over his shoulder.

The Behemoth's head was rising, its eye glowing brighter now. One massive hand slammed into the ground, sending another shockwave outward. The Behemoth pushed itself up onto its hands and knees, rising slowly above the cloud of dust.

"This way!" he heard Kalibar shout. The Grand Weaver angled to the left, toward a group of people in the distance. It was Goran and Urson, he realized...and a few of the surviving Battle-Weavers. Kyle and Kalibar skid to a halt before the group, and Kalibar handed Ariana to Goran. Behind them, the Behemoth rose to its feet, the blue rays entering its eye vanishing. It looked down at the Void spheres lay scattered at its feet.

Then its eye flashed.

A beam of white light shot outward from its eye, striking the Void spheres in front of it. The Behemoth's head turned slowly, its deadly beam searing the ground in a broad circle, annihilating the Void spheres all around it. When the beam finally vanished, all that remained was molten rock and dirt forming a glowing red circle on the ground.

"Sa devon en morf?" Kalibar asked. Everyone shook their heads. "Kam!" Kalibar swore.

"Orpus eng flazi," Kalibar urged.

"Pas mor," Urson countered grimly, looking over Kalibar's shoulder. Kyle turned around, and saw the Behemoth standing before them, staring right at them.

Then its eye flashed.

Chapter 27

"Does anyone have magic?" Kalibar asked as he handed Ariana off to Goran. Urson and Goran both shook their heads. "Damn!" he swore. "We need to retreat." They'd seriously damaged the Behemoth; if they could get more magic, they might be able to finish it off. But Goran shook his head, staring at something over Kalibar's shoulder.

"Too late," the Councilman muttered.

Kalibar turned around, seeing the Behemoth standing there, its lone, diamond-shaped eye staring down at them. Decades of training kicked in, automatically *pulling* for a strand of magic to weave. Except there was no magic...the Behemoth had drained it all.

The Behemoth's eye flashed.

Kyle backpedaled, bumping into Kalibar and throwing his arms in front of his face. Kalibar wrapped his arms around Kyle, turning away from the Behemoth and holding him close. He closed his eyes, waiting for the end.

I'm sorry son.

A flash of light seared his eyes, even through his closed lids, and he held Kyle tighter.

I did the best I could.

A blast of superheated air slammed into him, tossing him backward and to the side at incredible speed. He felt himself flying through the air, Kyle still clutched in his arms, hot air searing his lungs.

And then he realized that there were arms encircling his waist, felt himself slowing down. His feet touched down on the ground gently, the air cool once again.

Kalibar opened his eyes, looking down at himself. He was utterly unharmed...and so was Kyle. A few dozen feet before him, a massive glowing red circle had been seared into the ground...right where he'd been standing moments ago. Goran and Urson were on the other side of that glowing circle, having barely escaped the Behemoth's deadly beam.

"Go, now!" he heard a familiar voice yell from behind. The arms around him let go, and he turned around, seeing none other than Master Owens standing there.

"What..." Kalibar began...and then he saw them.

Dozens of men in white robes zoomed through the air toward the Behemoth, each holding a weapon in their hands...something that looked like a crossbow. The men – Runics, Kalibar realized – spread out, surrounding the massive machine.

"Fire!" Owens shouted.

Beams of bright blue light shot outward from the crossbows, slamming into the Behemoth's domed head. The black metal plates protecting its innards turned to dust under the assault, exposing the green crystal underneath. The Runics circled around the Behemoth, fired another volley. Dozens of blue beams ate into the crystalline flesh, gouging huge holes in the Behemoth's head.

The Behemoth took a step backward, its eye flashing.

The Runics scattered just as a beam of white light shot out from the Behemoth's eye, cutting across the night sky. The Behemoth's head turned, the beam sweeping to intercept a few Runics, immolating them. The remaining Runics circled back toward the Behemoth, firing their weapons again. The deadly blue rays slammed into the Behemoth's head, blasting huge holes in its domed skull. Hunks of its huge white eye disintegrated, leaving blackened craters in their place.

The Behemoth's eye flickered.

Volley after volley of the Runics' attacks struck the Behemoth, eating into its head and body. Hunks of green crystal fell in a steady stream from it, along with a massive chunk from the side of its head.

The Behemoth stumbled, then toppled over, falling as if in slow-motion. Still the Runics attacked, ripping into the falling machine even as it slammed into the ground.

The earth quaked, a deafening *boom* echoing through the night air.

The Behemoth's eye flickered, then went dark.

Kalibar stared at the fallen monstrosity, barely allowing himself to believe what he was seeing. He felt Kyle squirming in his arms, and let go, watching as his son turned to gaze upon the Behemoth. Kyle blurted out something unintelligible, pointing excitedly. Kalibar didn't need to be able to understand his words to know what he was saying.

"We did it," he murmured, watching as the Runics hovered over the Behemoth, blasting away at its armored back.

"Yes we did," Master Owens agreed, putting a hand on Kalibar's shoulder. "But we couldn't have done it without you."

"You mean we couldn't have done it without Kyle," Kalibar corrected. Owens smiled.

"Without *both* of you."

Kalibar watched as the Behemoth gradually disintegrated, then frowned.

"Hold up," he stated. "Stop the Runics. We need to preserve as much of that thing as possible."

"Hmm?" Owens replied.

"That thing has advanced runic technology," Kalibar explained. "It may prove invaluable in fighting Xanos in the future."

Owens nodded, sending two magical flares high up into the sky. The Runics stopped almost immediately, flying toward them and landing beside them.

"We did it!" he heard Kyle exclaim. Kalibar turned to the boy, taken aback. Despite the fact that Kalibar himself still had no usable magic, Kyle had already managed to power his earring. The boy had enormous power...and he was only at a fraction of his full potential.

"We did," Kalibar agreed, putting an arm around the boy's shoulders. "Thanks to you," he added. "You saved us, Kyle...and the Empire." Kalibar hugged his son, then held him at arms' length. "You were right to question me," he added. "I would have doomed the Empire trying to protect you and Ariana."

"Thanks for letting me try," Kyle replied. Kalibar smiled, shaking his head.

"You're going to be a hell of a Runic, you know that?" he said. Kyle shrugged, modest as usual. But Kalibar noticed that he was holding himself differently, more confidently. Something had changed about him...ever since he'd returned from being captured again by the Dead Man.

"He certainly is," Master Owens declared, beaming at Kyle. "Very impressive, Kyle," he added. "Master Banar would have been proud of you."

"Thanks Master Owens," Kyle replied. Then he turned to Goran, who was still holding Ariana. "I'm going to wake Ariana up," Kyle stated. But before he could walk over to her, Kalibar heard shouting behind them, and turned to see his Runics backing away, their killerpillar weapons raised. He looked beyond his Runics, seeing an old man limping toward them. The man looked ancient, his spine bent in a near-hunchback, his pale, wrinkled skin covered in a thin beige robe. He carried a cane, leaning on it heavily as he made his way slowly toward them.

"Who is that?" Kalibar asked Owens. The Weaver shook his head.

"I don't know," he answered. "Stay here."

Owens strode toward the old man, gravity shields appearing around the Weaver.

"Stop," he ordered. "Identify yourself." The Runics aimed their killerpillar crossbows at the old man, who stopped, craning his neck to gaze upon Owens. His dry lips parted into a hideous smile, exposing rotted stumps of what used to be teeth. He let go of his cane, which stayed upright, and clapped his hands slowly.

"Well done," he declared, ignoring Owens and facing Kalibar. "I'm impressed."

"Who are you?" Kalibar demanded. The old man sighed, resting both hands back on his cane.

"That," he answered, "...is complicated."

"Identify yourself," Owens commanded, "...or suffer the consequences."

The old man raised one eyebrow, regarding Owens with a critical eye.

393

"Now now," he stated, "...show some respect for your elders, Owens." Master Owens frowned.

"How..."

"Do I know your name?" the wretch interjected. He smirked. "You'll find there is little I don't know," he continued. "Or maybe you won't. It all depends on you," he added, pointing one gnarled finger at Kalibar.

"Are you with Xanos?" Owens pressed. The old man sighed.

"Always asking the wrong questions," he lamented. "You should pay more attention."

"What do you mean?" Kalibar interjected. "What depends on me?"

"Your fate," the old man answered.

Kalibar stared at him, the strategic part of his mind automatically assessing the situation. Despite numerous deadly weapons aimed directly at him, the old man had no gravity shields protecting him. Indeed, there was only a faint glow of magic around the man. Which meant that he was a Weaver or Runic, but not extraordinarily gifted in magic production. Yet he showed absolutely no fear, despite facing some of the most gifted Weavers in the world.

Which means he's a fool, Kalibar concluded. *Or very, very dangerous.*

"Can you elaborate?" he asked.

"My Empire is at the brink of a revolution," the wretch declared. Goran's eyes widened at that.

"*Your* Empire?"

"You will lead the way to a level of progress unprecedented in human history, Kalibar," the old man continued, ignoring the Councilman. "This is my gift to you. This will be your great legacy...what countless future generations will remember you for."

"You're Xanos," Kalibar deduced. The old man chuckled.

"Which Xanos?" he asked. "The 'god' worshiped by mindless religious fanatics? No. Any leader would recognize that as propaganda." He smirked. "Useful propaganda, mind you."

"So Xanos isn't real?" Kalibar pressed.

"You weren't listening," the old man chided. "Xanos the god is an illusion. Xanos itself is very real."

"I don't understand."

394

"You don't need to," the wretch replied. "As I said, you will lead the revolution." He smiled grotesquely. "I want it to be you," he added. "You're a man of great principle, Kalibar...in fact, you remind me of myself when I was your age."

"And if I refuse?" Kalibar pressed. The old man sighed, then reached into a pocket in his tattered cloak, retrieving a long, tapered green crystal. Kalibar's breath caught in his throat.

"You'll do it anyway," the old man replied.

Kalibar froze, staring at the crystal, at its glittering facets. Imagined it sinking through his skull, piercing his brain.

"Wrong answer," Kalibar stated. "Kill him."

The Runics fired their killerpillar weapons at the old man. Or rather, beams of bright blue light shot from each weapon — and from each Runic, and from Owens — toward the old man's body. Owens' gravity shields vanished instantly.

The old man stood there unharmed, shaking his head.

"Clever," he murmured. "Reverse-engineering the killerpillar's abilities. Tell me...how did you do it?"

Kalibar stared at the old man, swallowing in a dry throat. There was no magic radiating from any of the Runics anymore, or from Owens. None at all. And yet the faint blue glow around the old man hadn't brightened.

"How are you doing this?" Kalibar asked, taking a step back. The old man raised an eyebrow at him.

"How did you get your eyes back?" he countered. "Who killed so many of my Chosen?" When Kalibar didn't respond, the old man gestured at Ariana. "Who created that little masterpiece?"

Kalibar took another step back, glancing at Ariana.

"Tell you what," the wretch continued. "I'll make you a deal. You tell me who did all these wonderful things, and I won't kill your children."

"You wouldn't," Kalibar retorted, stepping between Kyle and the old man. The old man rolled his eyes, gesturing at the devastation around him...and the burning Southwest Quarter in the distance.

"Really?"

"Don't do this," Kalibar urged.

"You know my terms," the old man shot back. "Give me a name."

"I don't know who..."

"Well that's a shame," the wretch interrupted. He raised the butt of his cane at Ariana. "I'll take her first."

"No!"

A gravity sphere appeared around Ariana, shoving Goran backward onto the ground. She levitated in mid-air in the center of the sphere, still unconscious.

"As I recall," the old man murmured, "...this little bird doesn't like fire." He gave a crooked smile. "I do think she should be awake for this, don't you?"

"Wait!" Kalibar pleaded. "I think I know who it is!" The old man cocked his head to one side.

"I'm listening."

Kalibar took a deep breath in, letting it out slowly.

"I believe the man who helped me," he stated, "...who helped Ariana," he added. "...is Ampir."

Kalibar felt Kyle tense up behind him, heard the boy gasp. The old man glanced at the boy, then back at Kalibar, his expression unchanged.

Then he lowered his cane.

"Ampir," he murmured.

"Yes," Kalibar replied. "I think..." he began to add, but the old man raised one hand to stop him. A chuckle escaped his lips, sounding more like a death rattle than anything else.

"Ampir," he repeated, chuckling again. He shook his head. "*The* Ampir, I presume."

"Yes."

"I do believe," the old man stated, "...that you are correct." He gave a horrid smirk. "In fact, I believe I met him recently." He shook his head again. "Always was remarkably clever, that one. I knew I recognized him from somewhere."

Kalibar glanced at Owens, who shrugged. The old man raised an eyebrow.

"You don't know, do you?" he mused. "The gods take strange forms when they walk among us, eh? I suppose I'm no different."

"What do you mean?" Kalibar asked.

396

"Never mind," the old man replied. "Well then," he continued, lowering his gaze to the ground and tapping the butt of his cane on the ground. "This changes things a bit, I think."

"My children..." Kalibar began.

"Yes, yes," the old man muttered, waving one hand dismissively. The gravity sphere around Ariana vanished, dropping her to the ground with a dull *thump*. He paused, then turned away from Kalibar, facing the fallen Behemoth. A massive translucent blue dome appeared around it.

Then it *exploded*.

No sound escaped the dome, the Behemoth vanishing in a dark green haze. After a moment, the dome vanished, leaving nothing but a massive hill of thick dust in its place.

The old man stared at what remained of the Behemoth for a moment, then rose up from the ground, levitating a few feet above it.

"Wait," Kalibar blurted out, taking a step forward. "What are you going to do?"

The old man turned in mid-air to face Kalibar, flashing another grotesque smile.

"Our business here will have to wait," he answered. "Apparently I have an old friend to deal with first." He pointed his cane at Kalibar. "I'll finish with you later." He lowered his cane, the corner of his lips curling into a smirk. "Your victory here is impressive, Kalibar. Enjoy it while you can."

With that, the old man shot up into the sky, a loud *boom* echoing through the night air. He vanished into the darkness, and within moments there was silence.

Kalibar stared up at the sky, his mouth agape.

"Well then," he heard Owens say. He glanced at the Battle-Weaver, then turned to check up on Kyle, who looked dazed.

"You okay?" Kalibar asked. Kyle nodded mutely. Kalibar turned to Ariana, walking up to her and scooping her up in his arms. Then he glanced at Kyle. "Do you have any magic?"

"Yeah," Kyle answered. Kalibar shook his head, marveling at his son's growing abilities. He had no magic yet himself. Kyle walked up to Ariana without having to be asked, streaming magic to her. Her eyes opened almost immediately, and she stiffened in Kalibar's arms, looking up at him, then at Kyle.

"Where am I?" she asked. Then she gazed outward at the remains of the Void Behemoth, and at the Runics gathered all around them. "What happened?"

"It's over," Kalibar answered, giving her a weary smile. He set her down on her feet. Owens walked up to her, wrapping an arm around her slender shoulders.

"We're safe now," he said, giving her a squeeze. Kalibar turned to stare at the remains of the Behemoth, then at the Southwest Quarter, entire city blocks still smoldering from the Behemoth's deadly attack.

"Not all of us," he muttered. "We need to organize a rescue effort for the portions of the city that were attacked." He turned to Urson. "I want you to return to the Tower, organize scouting parties to do a fly-over of the city. Look for any remaining enemies, search for survivors. Coordinate with our troops on the ground."

"Yes sire," Urson replied. He rounded up the few surviving Battle-Weavers, and they flew up into the sky, making their way toward the Tower.

"Councilman," Kalibar stated, facing Goran. "We've won this battle, but it's going to take a lot of work to recover from it...especially the Southwest Quarter. I'm going to have the military help with the repairs and rescue efforts."

"Wait," Goran retorted. "Bringing the military into the city was bad enough...but keeping them here? That's a clear violation of..."

"Relax," Kalibar interrupted. "I'm decommissioning one contingent. They'll lay down their weapons, and the remainder of the legion will leave the city. I need military engineers and lots of hands if I'm going to rebuild this city."

"Whose contingent are you decommissioning?" Goran asked, stiffening slightly. Kalibar chuckled.

"Not yours," he replied. "But I do believe Ibicus's replacement on the Council would be more than happy to lend his troops – and his bankroll – to the effort."

"Indeed," Goran agreed, visibly relaxing.

"In the meantime," Kalibar continued, turning away from the remains of the Behemoth and beginning a slow walk toward the Great

Tower in the distance, "...we need to reconvene the Council, and prepare a strategy for how to approach the public about everything that's happened."

"Agreed," Goran replied. "But how are we going to explain all of this..." he added, gesturing toward the Behemoth and the Southwest Quarter beyond, "...without causing a panic?"

"Leave that to me," Kalibar stated. "In the meantime, I would appreciate it if you'd return to the Tower and oversee the return of the Council. Arrange for a meeting in the War room in an hour or so."

"Yes, Grand Weaver," Goran replied, saluting Kalibar sharply. He paused, then reached out to Kalibar with his right hand. Kalibar grasped it, and they shook once. Goran smiled, the expression looking decidedly odd on the dour man's face. "You're a good man, Kalibar," he stated. Kalibar smiled.

"As are you," he replied. He let go of Goran's hand then. "I would count you among my friends," he added. Goran raised one eyebrow.

"Don't expect me to agree with you very often."

"I look forward to our future disagreements," Kalibar said with a grin. Goran nodded, then stepped backward, rising up into the air. A moment later, the Councilman was shooting through the sky toward the Tower. Kalibar watched him go, then turned back to stare at the massive pile of dust in the distance. He paused, then lowered himself down to the ground, sitting on the scarred, blackened lawn. He ran a hand through his short white hair, then shook his head slowly, a chuckle escaping his lips. Then his shoulders began to shake, laughter erupting from him.

"We made it," Ariana exclaimed, lowering herself to the ground next to Kalibar and putting one slender arm around his shoulders. Kyle sat down on Kalibar's other side, leaning on his shoulder. Kalibar wrapped his arm around each of his children, holding them close.

"I'm proud of you guys," he stated, giving them a squeeze. Moisture blurred his eyes, and he blinked back tears. Pride filled his heart...pride in his brave, wonderful children.

"Thanks," he heard Kyle mumble.

"I love you two, you know that?"

Kyle and Ariana smiled, giving Kalibar a squeeze. Kalibar was thankful that Ariana didn't squeeze him too hard.

"We love you too, dad," Ariana replied.

"Ditto," Kyle agreed.

Kalibar sat there with his children, staring off into the starry sky, the dark clouds high above already starting to dissipate. A warm breeze blew through his hair, and he closed his eyes, feeling Kyle's warmth and Ariana's cool embrace. He smiled, feeling as if a great weight had been lifted from his shoulders.

He'd done everything he could to protect his children...and his people. Risked his career *and* his life...and the lives of his children. And in the end, against impossible odds, with their world seeming to crumble all around him, they'd managed to succeed.

At long last, they were finally safe!

Chapter 28

Kyle walked down the pink and gray cobblestone path, his gravity boots clicking on the sun-warmed stone below, Ariana at his side. The path was one of many winding its way through the campus of the Secula Magna — and just happened to be on the opposite side of the campus from where the Behemoth had been only a day ago. Just as conveniently, the Southwest Quarter of the city was hidden by the rolling hills of the outer campus, and by the stately Great Tower less than a mile from where they walked. From here, they couldn't hear the sounds of metal on metal, the shouts of workers laboring to rebuild the devastated portions of the city. Though several city blocks had been destroyed, the vast majority of their occupants had been mysteriously evacuated before the Behemoth had struck. All stated that they'd simply found themselves in their homes one moment, then found themselves outside of the city the next. It was a miracle, they claimed...and Kyle knew that was closer to the truth than they'd ever realize. Not just that an immortal Ancient had almost certainly teleported them to safety, but that he'd chosen to help them at all.

Kyle sighed, enjoying the feeling of the sun's warmth on his face, a soft breeze running its cool fingers through his hair. There was no one else around the immediate area; in fact, they hadn't seen anyone but the campus gardeners, busily working to reseed the burnt sections of the lawn, and that had been ten minutes or so ago. He glanced at

Ariana, walking quietly at his side, her hand in his. There was something extraordinarily serene about this moment, hand-in-hand with Ariana, the sound of birds chirping from the scattered trees close by. The half-hour they'd spent in the sun had warmed Ariana's skin significantly; her hand felt almost normal in his, only slightly cool to the touch. He stared at her, marveling at her pale beauty; slender and tomboyish, she was not possessed of the impressive proportions Kyle had found so utterly fascinating in Desiree, his onetime crush on Earth, but in this moment she was impossibly lovely to him anyway. Her eyes were on the cobblestone path before them, but her mind was clearly miles away.

"You okay?" Kyle asked, squeezing her hand. She jerked her head up, staring into his eyes. Then she smiled.

"Yeah," she answered. "Well, no," she added, lowering her gaze again. "I'm still trying to get used to not sleeping."

"Oh," Kyle replied. He didn't know what else to say; Ariana hadn't had a minute of sleep since she'd been revived, and not for lack of trying. It seemed that her need for sleep had been lost. She'd spent most of last night pacing back and forth in room, waiting to feel tired. For some reason, not needing sleep had been more alarming to her than her enormous strength, or her ability to sense nearby Chosen. Kyle couldn't imagine what it would be like not to sleep...to have each day come and go in one unbroken stream, with never a break in-between.

"Darius came to visit last night," Ariana stated, lifting her gaze upward toward the sun and closing her eyes. Her alabaster skin was nearly blindingly bright with reflected sunlight.

"Oh yeah?" Kyle asked. "What did you guys talk about?" Ariana opened her eyes, lowering her gaze and shrugging.

"Not much," she admitted. "He asked how I was doing, then stayed with me for a few hours. We didn't talk much, but it was nice to have someone there. I thought I was going to go crazy before he came, not being able to sleep."

"He *is* a nice guy," Kyle agreed. "Sometimes." Ariana smiled.

"Sometimes," she agreed. "I wonder what's going on inside his head," she added. Kyle shrugged, suddenly wishing that he could tell her about Darius, about who the bodyguard *really* was. It was terrible

402

to have a secret he couldn't tell anyone, but it was even more painful to keep one from her. After all, she had no problem confiding in him. It didn't seem fair to not be able to return the favor...to have someone he could share *everything* with.

You know, a girlfriend.

"What are *you* thinking?" Ariana asked. Kyle blushed, and he turned his face away quickly, staring at the Tower to their left. He felt her nudge him gently with her shoulder. "Come on," she insisted. "You can tell me."

"Nothing," he mumbled.

"Liar," Ariana retorted playfully. She squeezed his hand gently but firmly. "Tell me what you were thinking just then."

"I dunno," Kyle mumbled, not knowing what else to say. Ariana raised an eyebrow.

"Was it about me?" she asked. Kyle felt his cheeks flush, and Ariana laughed. "It *was!*" she exclaimed, clearly delighted by his chagrin. As lovely as she was, Ariana clearly had been well-schooled in the art of torturing boys. It was, Kyle's father had noted long ago, all part of a massive conspiracy to keep men preoccupied and hopelessly confused, so that women would maintain their rightful role as the dominant sex.

"Tell me," Ariana continued, clearly fascinated by his growing terror. She stopped walking then, turning his shoulders with her hands, so that he had no choice but to face her. He didn't even bother trying to resist, knowing that she had more than enough strength to force him if she wanted to. She smiled then, gazing at him with those big almond-shaped eyes. "Please?"

"Uh, I was just thinking," Kyle stammered, taking one step back, his mind turning to mush. "It's nice walking with you."

"How nice?" Ariana pressed, a strange smile on her lips. Kyle shrugged.

"Really nice, I guess." Ariana's eyebrows rose.

"You *guess?*" she exclaimed. Kyle froze, staring at her like a deer caught in the headlights of an oncoming tractor trailer. But she only laughed. "It's really nice to be with you too," she admitted. Then she turned quiet again, staring down at her shoes.

"What's wrong?" he asked.

"Oh nothing," she replied, then shook her head. "I was just wondering if you had..." She paused then, biting her lip rather fetchingly.

"Had what?"

"A...girlfriend back home," she answered. "You know, back on Urth."

"No!" Kyle exclaimed, shaking his head vigorously. Then he realized he'd shouted it out far too loudly, and he cleared his throat nervously. "No, I've never, uh...nope," he mumbled, wondering if it was possible to die from embarrassment. To his surprise, Ariana looked relieved.

"Good," she replied. Then she cocked her head to one side, staring at him curiously. "Never?" she pressed.

"I'm, uh," Kyle began, and then he gave up, shrugging helplessly. "Nope," he admitted.

"But you're so kind," she exclaimed, putting a hand on his shoulder. To his alarm, she seemed, well, alarmed by his admission.

"I'm shy."

"That's true," Ariana agreed, for some reason seeming quite relieved by that answer. They resumed their walk forward on the cobblestone path. A flying insect of some sort buzzed around Kyle's head, and her hand shot out disturbingly fast, moving so quickly he could barely register the motion. The insect buzzed no more. "If you ever go back to Urth, you should just try talking to them, like you did with me in the Arena," she counseled. "Just be yourself, and you'll have a girlfriend in no time."

"I don't want one," Kyle blurted out, causing Ariana to stop in her tracks. She gave him a funny look, then her eyes widened, and she put her hand to her mouth. "Wait, no!" he cried. "I mean, I do, but not on Earth." Then his cheeks flushed furiously, and he had the sudden urge to disappear. But Ariana seemed to relax a bit.

"You want a girlfriend here?" she asked, staring at him with those hypnotic eyes. He winced, realizing he'd trapped himself.

"Uh, yeah," he mumbled, breaking her gaze and staring down at his gravity boots. He briefly...but seriously...entertained activating those boots, and flying as far away from this conversation as he could.

404

"Anyone in particular?" Ariana pressed, leaning in a bit. Kyle shrugged, looking at anything but her. He tried to gather his thoughts, to no avail.

"I dunno," was all he could manage.

"You *are* shy," Ariana proclaimed. But her tone was hardly judgmental. She smiled, leaning in close, then kissing him on the cheek. Her hair smelled faintly of flowers, her lips cool but soft. She pulled away, and Kyle put a hand to his cheek, his skin there tingling pleasantly. "It's okay," she added, patting him on the shoulder. Then she removed her hand, her expression becoming serious. She stiffened slightly, lowering her eyes, then staring back into his. "Would you ever want a girlfriend that couldn't sleep?"

Kyle stared at her, his jaw slack. Then he realized she was waiting for an answer. Despite every bone in his body screaming for him to keep his mouth shut, he didn't. The word just came out.

"Definitely."

Ariana broke into a smile, leaning in and giving him a big hug. Too big, in fact; Kyle gasped as the air was crushed from his lungs, his arms flailing helplessly as spots began to appear in his vision. Ariana let go of him, and he nearly dropped to the ground, managing to hold himself up by putting his hands on his knees. He gasped for air.

"Sorry!" Ariana blurted out, clearly mortified. Kyle stood up, a pained smile on his face.

"No problem," he squeaked, holding his bruised ribs with one hand.

"Even if she could break your ribs?" Ariana asked with grin. Kyle paused, then shrugged.

"I guess."

"You *guess?*" she shot back, putting one arm around his shoulders. He flinched reflexively, but her touch was gentle this time. She walked forward then, bringing Kyle with her. "Well I'll try not to," she conceded.

"Gee, thanks," he replied.

"You'd better not get me mad then," Ariana warned. "For your own good."

"I'll keep that in mind."

Ariana laughed, brushing her long brown hair back, the wind rustling her tresses. Then she gave him a slight squeeze. "Thanks," she said, leaning her head on his shoulder. Soft hair tickled his neck, the smell of flowers intoxicating him.

"For what?"

"For being you," she replied. Kyle raised an eyebrow.

"What, a wimpy Runic?" he pressed. She laughed.

"You're *my* wimpy Runic," she countered.

"I *did* cripple the Behemoth, you know," Kyle stated. "While you were taking a nap." Ariana rolled her eyes.

"Uh huh."

"Thanks for saving me, by the way," Kyle added, giving her a squeeze. She smiled at him.

"That," she replied, "...is what girlfriends are for."

* * *

After their walk, Kyle and Ariana returned to the Tower. They'd both wanted to travel outside of the campus to watch the – quite literal – army of engineers and Runics as they rebuilt the city, but Kalibar had forbid them from passing the repaired gate surrounding the Secula Magna. Master Owens had suspended Ariana's lessons, and Kyle had not yet been given a replacement for the late Master Banar, so each of them ended up with a lot of time on their hands, and little to do with it. So they mostly hung around while everyone else in the Tower buzzed about busily, observing the organized chaos around them.

Neither of them had seen much of Kalibar – or Erasmus, who had apparently made a remarkably quick recovery from his near-fatal wounds – since the Behemoth had been defeated. Kalibar had his hands full in restoring order to the city, having already delivered a speech to the public in Stridon Square. Kyle hadn't been able to witness the speech, but it had apparently gone well enough. Other than a short-lived riot in the Southwest Quarter (followed by rampant looting), the city had maintained order throughout. The massive influx of decommissioned military types might have had something to do with it; even without runic weapons, the trained soldiers were a formidable deterrent to crime.

406

After the speech, Kalibar and Erasmus had been pulled into a series of meetings with the Council, with short breaks in between. All that Kyle knew was that some of the meetings had been about the two men using the Right of Dictatorship. Kyle had feared that the Council would try to prosecute Kalibar and Erasmus for invoking the Right, and there was no doubt that some of the Council members wanted to. But to his relief, Kalibar had proven awfully popular with the citizens of Stridon after heroically leading the attack against the Void Behemoth, not to mention helping to invent the weapons that had finished off the thing. And Goran himself had moved to exonerate Kalibar and Erasmus, much to Kyle's surprise. As a result, the Council had formally endorsed the Right of Dictatorship, safeguarding the Grand Runic and Grand Weaver from future prosecution.

Eventually, Kalibar and Erasmus managed to escape their evening of meetings to join Kyle and Ariana for dinner. Everyone met in Kalibar's old retirement suite, joined by Darius, all of them starving after a long day's work. When a rather ruddy-cheeked Jenkins arrived to take their orders, he got a boisterous welcome indeed.

"Jenkins!" Kalibar cried as the butler arrived. "You look well," he added. And that he did; whereas previously his color had been pale and his eyes sunken, Jenkins now appeared his usual vigorous self.

"A bout of pneumonia," the butler explained, bowing at his charges. Kalibar smiled.

"Glad you're feeling better," he stated. "We'll all be having the roast duck," he added, "...for old time's sake."

"And some wine," Erasmus piped in. "Lots of it," he added with a grin. Kyle still couldn't believe how well the Grand Runic looked; he suspected the portly man's miraculous recovery was more than a matter of luck...not that Darius would ever admit to it.

"Of course, sires," Jenkins replied, turning about at once and leaving the suite. He soon arrived with plate after plate of steaming duck, the smell so delectable that Kyle's mouth watered almost painfully with the smell of it. This was followed almost immediately by glasses of red wine for each of them, along with several extra bottles for good measure. Kyle took a tiny sip from his, then made a face, passing his glass to Darius, who took a much larger gulp. Erasmus frowned at his glass, shooting Jenkins a suspicious look.

"Are you sure you didn't poison this?" he asked the butler, raising one eyebrow. Ariana glared at the Grand Runic.

"It was an honest mistake," she complained, giving Jenkins an apologetic look. They'd interrogated the poor man rather vigorously after Ariana had implicated him in her assassination attempt. They'd exonerated Jenkins only after they'd identified Greg's body in Kalibar's suite.

"Still, I'd better have someone expendable test it first," Erasmus stated, turning to Darius. "Here, take a sip, would you?" When Darius refused to be baited, Erasmus chuckled. "Shirking your responsibilities again, eh?" he needled. "Where *were* you all that time...you know, when Kalibar actually *needed* his bodyguard?"

"Can't imagine why anyone would want to kill you," Darius replied, biting into a steaming piece of duck. Kyle bit into his own, practically drooling over its deliciousness. Ariana nibbled on hers, then pushed her plate toward Darius, who was more than happy to take it off of her hands. Erasmus snorted.

"At least the Council back-stabbed me *literally* for once," he countered. "But seriously, where were you?"

"You want to know?" Darius asked. Erasmus nodded, as did everyone else. Indeed, Kyle himself was curious as to what the bodyguard had been doing while they'd been running for their lives, nearly dying on more than one occasion. "I had to take care of something," Darius answered.

"Something more important than your job?" Erasmus retorted. Darius nodded serenely, finishing his own duck and starting in on Ariana's. Erasmus frowned. "Like what?"

"I had to go to the bathroom," Darius explained.

Erasmus stared at him.

"A bowel movement," Darius added, "...if you must know." When Erasmus continued to stare at him in disbelief, Darius stopped eating for a moment, looking up at the man. "You ever try to take a dump in full plate mail?" he asked.

"A bowel movement?" Kalibar piped in incredulously. Erasmus rolled his eyes.

"I'm *eating* here," he complained, gesturing at his steaming plate of delicious goodies. Darius shrugged, a hint of a smirk on his lips.

"It was diarrhea," he explained.

"Come on now!" Erasmus exclaimed, throwing his fork onto his plate with a clatter.

"There was blood," Darius added.

"Oh for cripe's sake," Erasmus spat, pushing his plate away. It slid to the center of the table, nearly upending Ariana's glass of wine. Darius snatched the glass before it tipped over, then generously offered to take it off of her hands. Moments later, it was empty.

"Don't drink the water from the lake around the Arena," Darius counseled. Kalibar chuckled, and then they all laughed, even Darius. They all finished their duck, and within moments Jenkins had removed all evidence of their gluttony, replacing their plates with bowls of what appeared to be ice cream. It was, Kyle soon discovered, the creamiest, most delicious ice cream he'd ever tasted. And it left him with a profound contented feeling that he'd never quite experienced before, as if all the stress of the last few days had simply melted away. He turned to Kalibar to ask him what it was made of.

"Sweetroot," Kalibar replied with a wink. "Among other things. Highly concentrated," he added. And Kyle supposed it must be true; he couldn't imagine being possessed of any desire for violence or even anger under its decidedly delightful effect. The others soon finished their ice cream, except Ariana, who apparently had no need or desire for eating. They all sat back in their chairs contentedly while Jenkins cleared the table, except for Erasmus, who asked – with uncharacteristic politeness, no doubt on account of the ice cream – for more wine. Eventually, even his prodigious appetites were sated, and they all sat about the table, trading war stories and jokes, laughing and enjoying each other's company. Under the influence of wine and sweetroot, Erasmus even gave Darius a hug (much to the bodyguard's discomfort), thanking him tearfully for saving his life – and then promptly asked for more wine, in hopes of erasing the memory of ever having done so.

Eventually midnight came and went, and full bellies making for sleepy heads, they all turned in. Kyle said goodnight to them all, even managing to sneak a quick smooch from Ariana, and then made his way happily to his bed. With his mind free from worry and his belly delightfully full, his eyelids soon became heavy, and he fell fast asleep.

409

Chapter 29

The following day, everyone in the Tower got ready for the dedication ceremony in the newly repaired Tower lobby. Kalibar and Erasmus had ordered the Empire's finest sculptors to create two painted statues, one of a Battle-Weaver standing tall against an unseen enemy, his staff held valiantly before him. The other was of Runic, clad in his traditional white robes, holding a killerpillar weapon. The statue of the Battle-Weaver was placed on a majestic solid-gold pedestal in the center of the lobby, while that of the Runic was placed on a similar pedestal high above, in the center of the reverse-gravity lobby. All of the Battle-Weavers had been invited to the lobby, while the Runics stood on the ceiling high above.

"We are here today," Kalibar declared, standing behind a podium erected in front of the Battle-Weaver statue, facing the crowd, "...to preserve the memory of those who gave their lives for the Empire, and for its people." He gestured at the statues. "I owe my life to them," he added, "...and to you that stand before me today, as does every citizen of Stridon."

There was hearty applause at that, which slowly died away when Kalibar raised his hand up for silence.

"Two thousand years ago, our ancestors, who had created an Empire based on the ideals of freedom, the advancement of knowledge, and equality among men, had that Empire taken from them. Cities

410

were destroyed, the Tower fell. All seemed lost." He paused for a moment, staring out at the crowd, his jaw set firm.

"But their enemies," he stated, "...and ours, failed to understand that the Empire is not made of buildings. It is not a thing of stone and mortar. Freedom does not lie in any city. It exists in the hearts and minds of the people. And, so long as we endure, so long as the *idea* of a people united by a common dream, of a better future for our children, and of the freedom of every man to choose his *own* destiny, for better or for worse, survives...this Empire will not fall."

"I dedicate these statues in memory of those who died to preserve these freedoms. Their sacrifice is not in vain. Our enemy is strong, and is possessed of the ability to subvert our fellow man, to create puppets of good and just men, like the late Councilman Ibicus. Our enemy seeks to take what is most precious to us: our free will. Do not be fooled by their claim to create a better world in this way, that they might create an Empire more advanced than that of the Ancients. For we all know that the Empire is not about magic, nor the technology it provides. It is made of the very ideals that our enemy wishes to take from us, a sacrifice of our self-determination for an empty promise of security."

Kalibar's eyes hardened, and he scanned the crowd, gripping his podium with one hand.

"Is there any man here who would give up their freedom?"

The crowd roared, a resounding "*No!*" echoing through the lobby.

"I will give up my life," Kalibar declared, slamming his fist into the podium, "...to defend *your* right to be the captains of your own lives. I will die, as did those we commemorate, before I allow this Empire, this great nation and all it stands for, to perish." His voice softened then.

"I will give *my* life," he stated, "...for you, who have taken an oath to do the same. For those who have lost their lives saving mine. Every breath I take is a testament to their bravery. I will remember them. *We* will remember them. And we will endure."

* * *

411

After the dedication ceremony, Kalibar and Erasmus returned to their respective duties, leaving Kyle and Ariana to themselves. They chose, as they had yesterday, to spend the time with each other, going on another walk through the campus. The great engine of the Secula Magna had been restored, crowds of white and black-clad students rushing to and fro to their various classes, the terror of two days ago having already been replaced by the comforting routines of everyday life. Ariana was to resume her studies with Master Owens tomorrow, and a Runic instructor for Kyle had apparently been selected. Rather alarmingly, Erasmus had pulled Kyle aside to inform him that he was to present his idea on sensory rune arrays to the top Runic scholars in the Secula Magna, including a demonstration of Erasmus and Kalibar's functioning prototype. Kyle had enough trouble presenting a book report in front of fifteen classmates; the idea of speaking before the some of the finest minds in the Empire was the stuff nightmares were made of. But Erasmus had left no other option available.

Kyle sighed, dreading every passing minute as he walked with Ariana. She smiled, squeezing his hand gently. She already knew what was on his mind, and despite her insistence that he would do fine, he hardly believed her. Then he felt a hand on his shoulder, and he turned to the side, seeing a very familiar man walking beside him.

"Darius!" he exclaimed. The bodyguard, decked out as always in his shimmering golden armor, smirked at Kyle and Ariana.

"Can I tear you from your girlfriend for a minute?" he asked. Kyle blushed, and he glanced at Ariana, who would've blushed if she could have. He was, for a moment, jealous of her lack of blood. But she nodded, letting go of Kyle's hand and turning about while Kyle and Darius continued forward. She waved to him, and he waved back, feeling a mixture of embarrassment and infatuation. He turned to Darius, who was in mid eye-roll.

"Hey," Kyle mumbled. Darius said nothing until Ariana had disappeared far in the distance, no doubt in consideration of her remarkable hearing.

"You want to go home?" he asked.

"To Antara?"

"*Your* home," Darius corrected, staring at Kyle with his intense blue eyes. Kyle felt his jaw drop open, and snapped it shut with a click.

"You mean..." he began, then stopped. Darius nodded. Kyle turned his head away from the bodyguard, coming to a stop on the cobblestone path. He suddenly had the urge to sit down. "When?" he asked.

"Tomorrow."

Kyle said nothing, feeling a strange numbness come over him. The thought of going home – of seeing his mom and dad, and his best friend Ben – should have filled him with joy, but instead he felt a sort of dread come over him. He thought of Ariana, of her kissing him, and suddenly had no desire to leave.

"It'll only be for a day or two," Darius added, undoubtedly sensing Kyle's trepidation.

"So you'll bring me here again?" he pressed. Darius nodded. Kyle frowned. "Wait a second...how many days will go by here if I go back to Earth?"

"Forty or so days here for every day on Earth," Darius answered. Kyle's eyes widened.

"*Forty?*" he exclaimed. "So if I go home for a week..."

"Close to a year," Darius replied.

"Oh, *man...*" Kyle breathed, feeling despair come over him. "I don't want to be gone for a year," he added miserably. There was no telling what could happen if he were gone that long. Ariana would miss him terribly, not to mention Kalibar.

"We'll make it half a day then," Darius proposed, putting a heavy hand on Kyle's shoulder. "Twenty days on Doma." Kyle smiled with relief.

"A half-day at most," he agreed. "You promise?"

"I promise."

Darius resumed walking forward, and Kyle joined him, feeling a remarkable weight lift off of his shoulders. He realized that he'd been worried sick about whether or not he'd ever get to see his parents again. He turned to Darius, staring at the taciturn bodyguard for a long moment, a smile on his lips.

"Thanks," he said, leaning to the side and resting his head on Darius's gold-plated shoulder. To his surprise, Darius did not pull away.

"You're welcome."

"You know," Kyle continued, "...you're a terrible grandfather."

"Oh really?"

413

"Well, first of all, you're supposed to give me presents all the time, and candy, and let me do whatever I want." Darius raised one eyebrow.

"Your other grandparents do that?"

"Yup," Kyle confirmed. Darius shook his head.

"That explains a lot," he grumbled. Kyle frowned, lifting his head off of Darius's shoulder.

"Hey, what's *that* supposed to mean?"

"Never mind," Darius replied. "Now, about your parents..."

"Yeah?"

"Tell them nothing."

"Okay," Kyle agreed.

"Come on," Darius said, stopping and turning about on the path, back toward the Tower far in the distance. Kyle turned with him, and they resumed walking. "Finish your presentation."

"Thanks for reminding me," Kyle sighed. He'd almost forgotten about his upcoming presentation. Butterflies flitted about in his belly.

"It's a good idea," Darius opined.

"I'm sure you already came up with it a long time ago," Kyle countered.

"Nope," Darius replied. "Never needed it. I can see patterns."

"Oh, right," Kyle mumbled.

"Ideas," Darius stated, gazing at the Great Tower in the distance, its pyramidal peak shimmering in the sunlight like a giant diamond, "...change the world." He turned back to Kyle. "But only if you act on them."

"Why didn't *you* just destroy the Void Behemoth?" Kyle asked. The question had been bothering him ever since they'd won the battle against the massive machine. "Heck, why don't you just rule the Empire yourself?"

"I tried something like that once," Darius admitted. "Somewhere far away from here. It didn't turn out well."

"What happened?"

"People are all too eager to be led," Darius replied. "I was a god to them, and they grew to rely on me instead of on themselves." He shook his head then. "The best god for Man is a god that forces them to do without him."

"But you helped save the Southwest Quarter," Kyle countered.

"From another god."

"Right," Kyle mumbled. "But what about all the Battle-Weavers and Runics that died? Why didn't you save them?" he pressed. "You could've killed the Void Behemoth without even blinking!"

"True," Darius agreed. Kyle waited for him to say something more, but he didn't.

"So why didn't you?"

Darius remained silent, and Kyle sighed, knowing what that meant...the dour bodyguard wasn't going to answer. He kicked a stone on the pathway, watching it roll into the grass.

"You're a jerk sometimes, you know that?" he said. Darius smirked.

"Sometimes?"

"Ninety-nine percent of the time," Kyle corrected. He kicked another stone, then sighed again. "I wonder who Xanos is," he mumbled. He frowned then, recalling what Ariana had told him back at the makeshift bedroom in the Tower a few nights ago. "Ariana said something about the Chosen being controlled by someone other than Xanos."

"Who?"

Kyle scratched his head, struggling to remember their conversation. Then he snapped his fingers.

"She said it was an old man," he recalled. "I think it was the same guy we met in the Arena, and after the Void Behemoth died," he added tentatively. "She said his name was Sabin."

Darius stopped suddenly, staring off into space. Kyle stopped as well.

"What?" Kyle asked.

"Go back to the Tower," Darius ordered, stepping away from Kyle suddenly.

"Why?" Kyle asked. "What is it?"

"I'll tell you later," Darius replied tersely. "Go on, prepare your presentation."

"Where are *you* going?" Kyle pressed.

"Back to Antara," Darius replied. Then he put a hand on Kyle's shoulder. "Say goodbye to Ariana and Kalibar tonight. Let them know you're going home, and nothing more."

"Okay..."

And then Darius was gone.

Chapter 30

Kyle stared up at his bedroom ceiling, at the crystal chandelier in the center, its facets no longer glittering in the near-complete darkness. Then he sighed, rolling over onto his side, his head sinking into the plush pillow so that he could barely see over it. Despite the late hour – it was almost midnight – he couldn't sleep. The day had gone well, he supposed; his presentation to the Runics had gone almost *too* well. He'd stammered his way through the first part of his speech, which would have been humiliating if the gathered Runics – mostly old men in white robes, none of whom had battled the Behemoth – hadn't been so kind and patient. Their kindness wasn't exactly surprising given the fact that they all knew what he'd done to save the Empire...and that the killerpillar weapon had been created as a direct result of his idea.

After he'd gotten more comfortable, Kyle had managed to explain his original idea well enough. Of course, the Runics been a bit skeptical until Erasmus unveiled the prototype sensory rune array, and showed them that it actually worked. When Kalibar unveiled the killerpillar gun, demonstrating on an unfortunate animal, the Runics had been absolutely astounded.

By the end of the presentation, the gathered Runics – over thirty of them – had glorified his simple idea, claiming it was the greatest piece of magic theory they'd ever heard of. He'd been called all sorts of names – and not the kind he'd become accustomed to at school back on Earth. He hardly thought of himself as a genius; his idea had been awfully simple, almost to the point of being obvious.

Still, he couldn't help but feel flattered at all the praise he'd received. His idea to use magic-depleted mud to insulate himself from Void spheres had also been met with enthusiasm. Even now, Runic engineers were busy constructing crystalline armor that used magic to generate a powerful light deep within its recesses – where no one would ever see it – any time it filled with the slightest bit of magic. This used up the magic, keeping the armor effectively depleted, providing constant insulation.

Kyle smiled when he thought of how happy the Runics had been, and how proud of him Kalibar had seemed. While he'd once been depressed about his failure to succeed as a Weaver, he knew now that he was destined to become a Runic. Flying around and blowing things up just didn't hold the same allure it had before; it wasn't nearly as exciting as the idea of building fantastic magical items of enormous power. Or even, he thought, his own armor, like Ampir's.

Like his grandfather's.

Kyle sighed again, rolling onto his back once more, staring at that chandelier some ten feet above his head. He was still trying to process the fact that Darius was his grandfather...and that he was Ampir, marked by history as a traitor that had doomed the Ancients, yet in reality a silent, unsung hero. It hardly seemed fair that the man should slip away into the shadows, with hardly anyone knowing that he'd saved those people in the Southwest Quarter. But then again, he'd let so many Battle-Weavers die...not to mention Ariana. How would people react if they *did* know about him? Maybe it was for the best that Darius had made it quite clear that Kyle was to tell no one about him.

Except, of course, to let them know that Kyle was going home.

Kyle sighed a third time, absently picking at his lip. He'd told Kalibar after dinner. The Grand Weaver hadn't been too surprised that Ampir had been the one to bring Kyle to this world in the first place, having already figured it out for himself. His surrogate father had not taken the news of Kyle's leaving well at first – not until Kyle had insisted that he'd return within a few weeks. Then he'd been happy for Kyle, that he could see his real family again. Of course, Kyle had insisted that Kalibar *was* part of his real family, after which the Grand

417

Weaver had given him a hug, even getting a bit teary-eyed. It had been a difficult conversation, but good.

Ariana, however, had been a bit tougher.

At first she'd been terrified that he was going to leave for good, to never return. Kyle insisted, as he had with Kalibar, that this was not the case. Then she'd insisted on coming with him. He'd had a much harder time with that request; if Darius had been around, Kyle would have demanded that she be allowed to come with him. But the bodyguard had still not returned from whatever it was he was doing, and so Kyle had to say no. She'd been mad at first, but recovered quickly, saying her goodbyes and hugging him for a long time. Then she'd given him a kiss – on the lips! – and promised him there'd be another waiting for him when he returned.

Kyle pressed his fingers to his lips, remembering that kiss, and sighed a completely different kind of sigh. He was suddenly less enthused about going back to Earth tomorrow, eager to spend more time with Ariana. But only slightly less enthused; he was still practically giddy at the idea that he'd be seeing his parents soon. He smiled, imagining walking up to the front door of his house, of ringing the doorbell. Of his mom answering the door, then rushing to hug him and smother him with kisses. Of his dad picking him up from school and giving him a big bear hug, tears in his eyes. The thought made him have to wipe some of his owns tears away with the back of his hand.

He stared up at chandelier above him, thinking of how Ariana and Kalibar would feel while he was gone. He'd be back – Darius had promised, after all – and he would be ready for whatever adventure awaited him then. Not that he was looking forward to any more action; no, he'd had quite enough of that in the last week or so. When he thought of everything that had happened to him since he'd arrived on Doma, it was mind-boggling. He tried to think back at the boy he'd been then, when he'd woken up in that strange forest, and felt like an entirely different person now. He'd experienced more in the last few weeks than most people experienced in a lifetime, narrowly avoiding death time after time, all in an effort to save himself...and the people he loved.

The experience had made him a little braver, a bit more confident, and had made him appreciate life – his own and those of his friends

– more than he ever had on Earth. He vowed not to take a moment of his life for granted now, knowing that it could end tomorrow, and that the moments he spent with his friends were the most precious of his life. He knew now that Darius had been right back on Antara...if he didn't fight back, his loved ones could be taken away from him. And they *would* have been taken away had he not risked his life to save them.

And that, he supposed, may have been Darius's plan all along.

Suddenly, there was a gust of wind, followed by a loud thump. Kyle bolted upright in his bed, staring off into the darkness, seeing a shadowy figure at the other end of the room. It moved toward him, and he cried out, frantically creating a gravity shield around himself. The shield blew back his bedsheets, shoving them across the room. The mattress caved inward under the curved surface of the spherical shield.

The dark figure reached the edge of Kyle's bed, and leaned over it, putting two black-clad hands on the footboard. A beam of starlight from the window reflected off of a silvery visor. The gravity shield around Kyle vanished suddenly, and Kyle fell onto the mattress with a thump.

"Get up," a gruff voice commanded. "It's time."

Epilogue

The old man hobbled down the long underground tunnel, the butt of his wooden cane clanging on the metal platform below with each step he took. The platform extended far into the distance, surrounded by a tubular tunnel made entirely of large white crystals. Each crystal was over seven feet long, with a broad hexagonal base that tapered to a razor-sharp tip pointing toward the center of the tunnel. The metal platform levitated a few feet above the crystals below, suspended by an unseen force.

The old man smiled to himself, countless wrinkles on his face deepening as he did so. His face was ancient, his features ruined by time. He gazed forward with cataract-glazed eyes, continuing down the shaft at a glacial pace.

A shaft he'd been walking through for miles.

He hardly minded the walk, no matter the hours he'd spent taking it. The automatic nature of this body's shambling gate, the repetitive *clang, clang* of his cane on the metal below, freed the better part of his mind for more important matters.

He vaguely recalled being mortal, engaging his body with some mindless task to allow his mind to wander free. A mind freed from its overbearing consciousness proved fertile soil for ideas to grow forth from, after all. And how many wondrous ideas had come to him during such walks, during his mortal life and far beyond! He would hardly be here today, walking in the midst of his own creation, had he not so exercised his brain.

After what seemed like an eternity, he finally made it to the end of the metal platform. The tunnel continued forward ahead, but was much narrower, the crystals forming a channel barely large enough to fit a human head through. There was no way forward.

The old man glanced upward at one of the crystals above his head, focusing on what lay beyond its glittering facets. There, embedded in the broad root of the crystal, he could barely make out a shadowy form. A long-dead corpse forever encapsulated in its crystalline grave.

An unwilling Chosen.

He turned his eyes forward again, at the narrow channel beyond. There were Chosen in every one of the countless crystals – his Void crystals – lining the shaft he'd been walking through. A brain entombed in every crystal, each connected to one another in one massive network.

The old man smiled, staring into the narrow tunnel beyond. No man could have gone further, nor even a Chosen. And no one ever had...except for him.

With a thought, the Void crystals around him flashed, then stopped their faint glowing. The old man rose up from the metal platform, levitating a foot above the grated steel, his cane dropping onto it with a clang. He closed his eyes, raising his arms out to his sides.

Then his head tore off, rising above his neck.

It flew forward down the narrower tunnel, barely clearing the countless razor-sharp tips of the Void crystals. It accelerated forward, rapidly picking up speed. The tunnel curved downward, traveling deeper into the earth as he went. Faster he went, Void crystals zipping past him in a dizzying blur.

Then the narrow shaft opened up into a massive cavern, a Void chamber so large that it defied explanation. The walls, the ceiling, the floors were all made of glowing white Void crystals. Massive Void crystals hung like stalactites from the ceiling, some well over a hundred feet long, their facets shimmering dully in the faint light cast by their smaller brothers.

The old man's head slowed, descending into that chamber. Down it went, his head rotating through the air, until his eyes faced the center of the chamber. A single, translucent rod-shaped crystal hung from the ceiling there, so long that it reached the floor. It was nearly fifty feet in diameter, this crystal. On the floor, encircling the base of the massive central crystal, grew a corona of green crystals some twenty feet tall.

The source of his Chosens' shards.

His head descended further downward, toward a headless body levitating directly below it. His head fused with the body's neck, leaving a thin, jagged white line between the two. Within seconds, he was once again whole.

The old man smiled, staring down at his new body's hands. They appeared much younger than those of his other body, the skin smooth and supple. He remembered being young once, long ago. Such a gift, youth. A gift only appreciated once it was lost.

He sighed, gazing forward toward the center of the massive cavern, at the huge cylindrical crystal extending from the floor to the ceiling. He peered through its translucent surface; despite its girth, he could see a faint shadow in the center of it, something suspended deep inside.

The old man levitated forward toward the giant crystal, until his nose was nearly touching its slick surface. From here, he could see what was suspended inside of it. An emaciated body, its arms and legs mere bones covered in a thin veneer of flesh, its ribs jutting out from its sunken chest. Rope-like sinews ran up its neck, and its mouth was eternally open in an agonizing scream.

The old man stared at the pathetic figure trapped in its crystalline tomb, even as it stared back at him. Every Void crystal had a body encased within, an undead mind in various states of awareness.

But this one, this one was different.

The old man ran his fingers down the smooth surface of the crystal, marveling not for the first time at how remarkably well preserved the body inside appeared. He stared at its head, noting the faint blurriness around it, a halo of imperfect crystal encircling it. There was perfection in that imperfection, he knew; for that faint blurriness was due to millions upon millions of microscopic metal wires, countless fibers extending from deep within the corpse's brain. These spread outward through the entirety of the crystalline tomb, connecting every single

422

brain in every single Void crystal to that brain. And by extension, every Void crystal in the miles upon miles of Void channels that had led him here.

Millions of minds, all subjugated to this one being, an enormous nervous system of the greatest consciousness that had ever lived, the most powerful intellect ever constructed.

The old man sighed, turning away from the crystal and its entombed occupant. He closed his eyes then, picturing a man in black armor, a man he'd recognized earlier without realizing from where. Or more importantly, when.

Ampir.

The implications were paradigm-changing, of course. There was no doubt that the man protecting the second Empire was the same man who had abandoned the first.

He should have suspected the bodyguard earlier.

The old man chuckled, turning back to face the massive crystal in the center of the chamber, at its shriveled captive deep within.

"You haven't changed a bit, Ampir," he murmured.

He placed his palm on the crystal's surface again, staring at the undead being within. Ampir had not aged at all, through some miracle of preservation. The body suspended before the old man had not been so lucky. It had nearly run out of time before achieving immortality, had decayed long past a normal mortal's ability to survive. But in a testament to its will, and its genius, it *had* survived.

And now there was no body it could not possess, no mind it could not subvert to its own use. Not with the power carried by the enormous Void crystal that surrounded it, a construction long ago steeped in legend. The crystal was the machine that the devout called God, a tool deserving of such worship.

But if there was ever a god, it was not the machine. It was the man *within* the machine.

The man within Xanos.

30170237R00241

Made in the USA
Middletown, DE
23 December 2018